THE TREES ARE DYING

THE TREES ARE DYING

BY
ED SURMA

© 2020 by Edmund W. Surma

All rights reserved. This book or any portion thereof may not be reproduced or used in any manner whatsoever without the express written permission of the publisher except for the use of brief quotations in a book review.

ISBN: 9798565519532 (paperback)

Chapter 1

SUMMER

Bespeckled birds looked down upon a blanket of warm, comforting green. Sunlight glimmered from the leaves as they rustled in the south wind, joining with wren, finch, and oriole in composing the symphony of the forest. Life. Aliveness. The vibrant essence of the planet that this land reflected.

Beneath the forest canopy lurked a different mood. Subtle, subdued—yet terrible in its power.

The maples first expressed the dysfunction, being the most delicate, the most fragile. A yellow leaf, a shriveled limb, a crack along the trunk zigzagging like wooden lightning. Next were the stately chestnuts, paltry in the production of their tasty kernels, they too displaying a sadness in their drooping leaves and peeling bark. As time unfolded, ash, beech, even the mighty oak displayed signs of the malignant force. Details prominent to a shrewd eye, concealed to distracted vision. More powerful than sight was feeling, slithering through the woods like a leprous breeze. Beneath the canopy of green, atop the carpet of last year's fallen leaves, a brooding, a dread, an anemic undertone to the apparent vigor. Every tree, deciduous or coniferous, sapling or mighty patriarch, radiated the same dense sorrow. Not openly, trees being too stoic to announce their feelings however serious the plight. Yet in intuitive openness their hidden messages could be perceived. And perceived those messages were.

They could have been mistaken for children, The Twelve who tramped among birch and fir like a row of ducklings without a mother. Their statures aligned with the appearance of youngsters; their countenances radiated the smooth freshness of youth. Their apparel would have brought a smile to the most serious adult's face had humans the capacity to perceive them, their costuming seeming part of a juvenile game. Their behavior showed no sign of immaturity. No frolics, no giggles, no imaginative adventures among the forms and shadows that surrounded them. Instead they brooded—brooded like the forest as they too succumbed to the dark spell. They marched, faces toward the ground, watching only the path and their small feet as they clop-clopped forward. On occasion the surrounding beauty piqued their interest, when sunlight pierced the leafy canopy, illuminating bursts of brilliant green and subtle browns spattered with wildflowers large and small. The muted spaces held their own attractions: colorful mushrooms poking from the detritus, boulders dappled with multicolored mosses. Crisscrossing streaks of color sliced the canopy as thrush and jay soared by. Yet none of The Twelve could relish the beauty, could escape the suffocating feeling that surrounded them. Each ruminated upon His words, a proclamation that darkened their souls as much as the rising Sun illuminated the land. Each of The Twelve recalled His radiant countenance, His unearthly beauty, His deadly utterance, trying to argue past His proclamation in their rumination, trying to thrust His words from their minds. Instead His words echoed through their minds like a boulder tumbling down the walls of a canyon. Nothing else filled their thoughts, nothing else lay upon their heavy hearts but those words, words that their furtive glances through the forest confirmed.

"We must have breakdown before we have breakthrough."

What did they expect from Him? Each of The Twelve, in his or her own way, felt the changes unfolding about them, their sensitivities being what they were. Did they expect Him to deny it? He would never hide the Truth. Did they expect Him to heal it, make it go away? His is the way of Peace. The way of Love. How could He have allowed this to happen? Did He not have the power to change it? Was He punishing the worlds?

Yet when He spoke, He did not speak with malice. There was no bitterness. His voice, His face, His entire being radiated calm. His eyes glowed with Love. Perhaps He wished He could have said something else, at least dampened the reverberations that He knew His words would convey. Yet as always, He spoke Truth. He hid nothing. And so they left, unwilling to believe even though they knew they must.

"Do we approach a stop?" She of Red asked, as much a request as an inquiry. Those that tramped before and behind her looked forward to those who held the lead. He of Brown turned to She of Yellow as they passed under a sprawling sycamore. Wordless, they reviewed where now they were, what distance lay ahead, at what moment the Sun would settle below the horizon. Decision made, He of Brown lifted his right arm. The Twelve dispersed across the soft forest floor, forming a perfect circle—four aligned to the Directions, the others spread equally around the perimeter, perfect symmetry beneath the foliage above. For a few moments, breaths fluttered, each of The Twelve winded from the distance travelled. As breath calmed, feelings did not. Flutters of distress replaced flutters of breath. They forced smiles upon their faces, desperate to broadcast hope, desperate to mask the fear lurking within their bowels. Glances meant to reassure were exchanged, eye contact made then quickly broken lest any hidden emotion escape. With no answers to offer, The Twelve sought refuge in their practices.

She of Black removed shoes and stockings, caressing bare loam with bare toes, ejecting her angst into the Earth. He of Brown and He of Yellow rose together, precisely contorting their bodies into various postures, seeking energy from within and without. Likewise, the others took up their personal rituals of solace and assurance, grasping for That Which Is Beyond in his or her own way, seeking the Greater, the More Powerful. Nothing filled their emptiness. Each returned to the circle, facing the center, waiting for another to break the spell, waiting for another to uplift the mood, waiting for another to somehow make the nightmare go away.

He of Red sought first to uplift. "I affirm this moment in perfection! I affirm the perfection of all! True be my words!" The slightest smiles appeared on the faces of The Twelve. Muffled sighs and palpable relief flowed around the circle. A woody groan sounded in the distance as if one tree were grating another in a gale, though the wind was but a puff.

She of Black beamed a smile at her companions.

"I declare the truth of my words. No power there is greater than the power of Love, and Love now rules. Love breathes about us. Love breathes within us. All is Love, and Love is all! It is so!" The surrounding forest darkened, as if a cloud were passing before the Sun.

He of White rose. Palms upward, eyes upward, he expressed his declaration.

"With the rise of my voice, I open myself to the One Above All, in knowledge of Your ever-presence, Your all-encompassing Love, extending forth to we who serve You in all perfection and holiness. Upon us, upon Your creation, I affirm You bestow Your blessings and healing light."

The Twelve applauded. Icy wind rustled through the leaves like a predator on the hunt, bringing unexpected shivers to the circle. Covert glances escaped under the rustling sycamore leaves, uncertainty tugging at the assuredness that seconds ago seemed so apparent. Deep breaths into hearts, into abdomens, finding center. They were above fear. They spoke Truth—certainly they did—and Truth would prevail. They attained stillness, stillness crying loud for relief, waiting for another to rise, for another to declare the superiority that each clung to. She of Brown came to her feet.

"I proclaim—"

Every bird, every insect ceased its sound. From the East, from the West, from every direction about them, slowly toward the circle of The Twelve came a throbbing, a throbbing muffled by the tangle of roots and loam yet present, distinct, and approaching. Each of The Twelve came slowly to stand, faces announcing their alarm, hearts pumping to a rhythm of dread. Earth voiced Her displeasure.

She Beyond Color lifted hands to shoulders, not prayer, not supplication, a gesture to calm her companions as subterranean tremors raced toward their circle, closer, closer. No calm was attained. Eyes turned to the land at their feet—anticipating eyes, questioning eyes, frightened eyes—wondering if Earth would swallow them, wondering if some Otherworldly force would burst out and destroy them all. The trees commenced a subtle quiver; vibrations met twelve pairs of feet in ominous caress. Sparrow and thrush evacuated their perches. Leaves shook, branches tremored, trunks swayed. The stable Earth convulsed. Yelps, groans, screams escaped the lips of The Twelve. Wrenching shudders barraged through body, through heart and soul, through every concept and feeling within the group that cowered at the power of Earth. Then, silence. Birds settled to their perches, beaks still. Bee and beetle peered forth from their shelters. Only anxious rasps of breath affronted the ears of The Twelve. A glance down, a glance sideways, a glance toward each other. They realized they still lived. They realized sweat-drenched brow and armpit. They realized that fear, terror had overcome them, no matter their denial. They thought themselves beyond the weaknesses of the mortal kind. Cheeks burned crimson as they grasped how quickly indeed they capitulated to the terrors of the vulgar emotions. Eyes turned again toward the ground; they did not wish to see their own weakness reflected in their companions. No movement conveyed The Twelve until the first oriole sounded.

"Let us go." He of Black was known for keen logic, if not depth of feeling. All wished for something comforting, something to inject strength and certainty into their rattled consciousnesses. No words of solace came forth; no inspiration rained upon them. Wish as they might, no affirmation, no aphorism, no spell arose that would illuminate the circumstances they faced. He of Black was right. Move on and hope that an answer would come. Move on and not face each other, not have to admit their shortcomings. They gathered their cloaks, draping themselves as if to shut out the surroundings as the atmosphere of despair locked about them.

Being the first to speak, He of Black claimed the position of leadership. He reconnoitered the surroundings and though finding no clue as to which direction to take, he signaled all to follow. Their first steps fell timid upon the ground, as if treading upon the land would awaken the tremors again. When assured that the soil was firm beneath their feet, they kept an even pace, as much to show courage as to conserve strength. Neither nervous haste nor timid advancement, a methodical step, step, step brought The Twelve through the undergrowth: carpets of fern in the damp places, brambles and vinca where sunlight penetrated the canopy. The moroseness did not seem so dense; yet as they walked, their pace slowed, their steps became heavy. For the slightest glance right or left captured the signs about them.

A stand of birch caught the gaze of He and She of Yellow.

A glade bathed in sun, gentle grasses carpeting the floor—eight trunks stood as if the patch had been cleared for their advantage. Without need for study, the Two of Yellow noticed the usually white bark now a sickly, foul brown. The two did not speak, for there was no need. All felt the despair flaring from each leaf tip.

She of Brown turned toward the silver maples. The spots upon the leaves—a deep sapphire that made one think of twilight sky, moon-illuminated ocean—would have been pretty had they belonged there. Yet the beauty of each blotch belied its essence of sickness and pain, a cancerous pox upon the green-gray foliage. Some leaves valiantly held themselves open, stretching forth to absorb the life-giving Sun, while others curled upon themselves, shriveling, drying, descending through the death process.

Despair touched The Twelve as it touched every wooden inhabitant of the forest. Dogwoods hung forlorn, limbs drooping toward the ground like overburdened beasts, sagging peripheries to otherwise sunny meadows. Stately sycamores shed their bark in great swaths. The footfalls of The Twelve slowed like the pendulum of an expiring clock, the tap, tap, tap of shoe upon Earth slower, slower until they halted, aimless, without purpose or direction, scattered among the trees. Elm, beech, poplar, evergreen showed their despondency through discolor and slump. Even the mighty oaks, the royalty of the forest, glowed less in the sunlight. His words echoed through their awareness, and amid cringes both inward and obvious, they capitulated to His wisdom. His prophecy was reality. They could no longer camouflage their fear. They could no longer deny what eyes and heart told them. Though each looked at the forest in his or her own way, all were forced to admit that He, as always, was right. Rightness that tore through them like venomous teeth, burning, searing, forcing from them an admission that all dear to them was at stake, threatened, at the edge of a precipice about to be bowled over. Like a tide rising up to drown them, the realization came to each exactly, precisely.

"The trees are dying."

Long silence reigned among The Twelve. Did the Earth still quake, or did each stand on buttery legs, strength and hope drained? Thoughts turned to the unthinkable. Plague of fear arose from dark recesses of the mind to tear at the fabric of their reality. Their world hung together as delicate as the blossoms on a springtime cherry tree, needing only the slightest quiver to bring everything raining down. One such quiver they had just felt. They feared to raise a voice, as if the slightest sound would invoke the wrath of Earth again. They feared the images that coursed through their minds, images of finality. Was all to be destroyed?

"From where we gaze…"

The faint voice of She of White betrayed the anxiety within her, yet her utterance brought forth a hint of hope as subtle as the forest murmurs around them. Here a warbler expressed its song; there a dragonfly buzzed near an unseen pond. The leaves rustled, admitting sparkles of sunlight into the darkness. Amid the despair sparkles of life.

"And…" He of Brown drawled out, expressing the wish of all for an answer.

"From where we gaze, our eyes find only pain. Darkness." She of White stood in contemplation, eyes gazing off into nothingness. Then she roared like a threatened beast, slapping hands to hips. "Problem, problem, problem! Not but problem do we see. How do we rise? How see we the Truth ever present?"

He Beyond Color understood yet could not find the strength to agree. "See you not the blight? How strength fades in every corner about us? Feel you not how they suffer? Such is beyond denying!"

"As the Bright One said," She of Red reminded them. "Have you memory of that? Did you not stand before Him, as I did, and hear his words?" She of Red glared. "To Him we went for help! To Him we supplicated, seeking blessing, seeking guidance, seeking the power to heal. He bestowed upon us what? What? This He affirmed! Affirmed! Not once did He make gesture to help! Maybe," she added with faltering voice, "maybe He has not the power. Maybe this overcomes even Him." Tears welled in her eyes. He of Brown extended a hand to console her.

"We stand in the problem," He of Black observed, "perhaps because we are *part* of the problem." He rubbed his chin, waved off the gasps of his companions. "This it could be! Part of the problem. Why else could we not see the way out? What comes, what happens—we are within it."

"Not so!" both She of Black and He of Yellow retorted. "For all we have done," He of Yellow continued, "for all we do, say you that we are part of the problem?" Cold anger directed straight at He of Black filled his eyes. A ripple of disharmony penetrated The Twelve, as palpable as the prior earthquake, if not as physical. He of Black would not be subdued. "Then see you differently?" He of Black's nostrils flared in defiance. "Bestow upon us your wisdom!"

"Enough," He of Brown insisted, rising again. "Does this talk find us solution? What claims can we make? Know we what is happening? And if know we do, what solace does that give? As He said, breakdown. Then breakthrough. We must find solution. Solution!"

Silence hung like the canopy of leaves above them. With a shake of his head, He of Yellow blew out his anger. He of Black nodded but turned away. No reparations came between the two. The others itched with tension.

"Our vibration wanes," She Beyond Color concluded. "There lies our solution. Raise our vibration. Ascend to higher levels." Her eyes scanned the morose gathering. "Join me. Let us rise above."

Nods acknowledged the words spoken. Slowly, as if the air draped thickness about them, The Twelve took their places. Each found a spot among the dying trees, forming once again a perfect circle. They needed no signal to begin. Eyes closed, breaths calmed, they tuned into the stillness within, to the Source of Being that they knew flowed through them. The sounds of the forest, the percolations of a distant stream were no distraction, instead injecting more of the life force into the meditative circle, providing connection to creature, to tree, to Earth. Their stillness complete, only the slow rise and fall of their chests signified that these were twelve animate beings. Shadows lengthened as The Twelve focused, seeking that place that was both within and beyond. Not one stirred. Two of Black, of Brown, of Yellow, of Red, of White, and Beyond Color formed a vessel longing for fulfillment from some greater power, some greater intelligence. They sat. They sat as the Sun traveled its course. They sat as the forest creatures followed their cravings. They sat as the breeze whispered through the leaves above. They sat until exhaustion beyond the physical overcame them, until tears flowed from twelve pairs of eyes.

"We have failed."

All turned to She of Black. Rage flared; resentment reared like an aroused stallion. Eleven small bodies twisted toward their vocal companion, seething. Yet before any could spew their aggression, emotions dispersed. None could deny her words. The

Twelve could do nothing. The Twelve had no solution. It was as He said. *Breakdown*. Heads hung. Shoulders drooped. A few mouths moved without sound, as if the words had been snatched from their tongues and stuffed in the darkness of the Earth. Each searched for something to hang their devastated identities upon. Each longed for a way of service as annihilation took place. Perhaps they could ease some of the pain. Perhaps they could save some piece of each world. But each knew the truth in his or her heart. Breakdown. Breakdown of everything they loved. Breakdown of that which they hated. Inevitable breakdown. The realization overwhelmed them.

He of Black wretched as if the awareness were seeking to eject itself from his body. She of Yellow wailed, immediately joined by both He and She of Brown. He of Red picked up a fallen limb and beat it against the trunk of a red oak, smacking it until his hands burned in vibration. Swift wings beat the air as bird and insect sped away. Undergrowth rustled as those upon the ground took exit. Even the trees swayed as if desiring to pull up root and abandon the outburst. Shriek and shout, flail and thrash—such fury had never before flowed from The Twelve. Finally, spent, disheveled, and ashamed, The Twelve fell to forest floor as one. Rasping breath, muffled sobs oozed along the soil like a slimy invertebrate as The Twelve wallowed in their despair. They frighted to look upon each other, embarrassed at the displays of weakness that erupted with the dropping of their personae. Yet the release accomplished much. No longer did the demons of anxiety stalk their thoughts. No longer did their egos prod them into sham. Now they lay open and accepting upon the black loam of the forest floor. Eyes dried. Noses cleared. Breath calmed. Voices returned.

She of Brown was first to raise hers.

"All cannot be destroyed. Such is not possible. Realignment. Realignment is what we experience."

"Realignment to what?" He of Black queried. "The blight we see—is that realignment? The trees are dying. The Earth quakes. Such are the harbingers of what is to come."

"'The trees are dying' is not what He spoke," She of Brown continued. "He spoke of breakdown. Did He prophesy destruction of all?"

"Her words sound of Truth," He Beyond Color responded. "He spoke thus: 'We must have breakdown before we have breakthrough.' Did He speak of doom? We are part of the problem!" Before another could object, He Beyond Color continued. "It is we who make this a problem! It is we who see change—yes, even death—and judge such to be the destruction of all. Realignment. Some things must pass, yet much will come forth anew. Realignment, that be it."

Flares of hope shone until He of Black asserted his views.

"Look about. See the despair. Call this realignment? The trees are *dying*!"

He of Black was answered with silence. Each of The Twelve grasped for hope yet knew all they could clutch was despair. She of Brown sighed in exasperation.

"We went to Him for answers and got none. Would there be someone to guide us, to tell us what to do? Just tell us what to do!"

"What say you?" He of White's question came not from lack of hearing. She of Brown rolled from back to side, propping herself up with an elbow.

"Guidance! Tell us what to do! If He be not the one, then—" She ceased her speech at He of White's gesture.

"How utterly stupid! Utterly stupid! Of us!" He of White continued. His slander was in no way an admission of fault, as if acknowledging an error made The Twelve even more superior. "Guidance! Advice! One who knows and such knowledge disperses! *That* is the answer!"

Recognition dawned as radiant as the sunrise. One by one The Twelve grasped He of White's words. They *had been* stupid not to think of it. Trudging through the forest, meandering about in disappointment, when they could have gone to where answers could be found. Smiles returned to their faces. Assuredness, certainty replaced their despondency. The Two Beyond Color stood, dusting the forest detritus from their clothing. The others likewise rose.

"Have we the time?" She of Yellow inquired.

He of Black stepped around a stately sycamore, gazing through the foliage canopy to determine the location of the Sun. "Time we have!"

"Are we prepared?" He of Red asked in mocking fashion, knowing that all of The Twelve itched to burst forward. Their laughter, as loud as their previous moans, was their affirmation.

He of Red located the moss upon the trees, studied the shadows, gained his bearings. With a nod to all, He of Red turned southeast, waited for his companions to fall in. She of White stepped behind him; He of Brown aligned behind her. She of Yellow, He of White, She of Brown—each took a place in line that offered balance, power. No thoughts of superiority entered their placement. When She of Black took the final spot in the line, He of Red raised an arm in victorious salute.

"To The Oracle!" Shouts of acclamation propelled them forward. The Twelve engaged their capacities again.

Feet fell lightly; emotions soared in spite of the surrounding blight. The Twelve marched through stretching shadow and approaching chill, hope fueling their limbs like fresh peat upon a home fire, overcoming any spattering of desperation that entered their thoughts. The Oracle. Few approached The Oracle, as just being in the presence of the telluric power of such an entity weighed upon heart and soul. Fewer still grasped the utterances that proceeded from The Cave. Sometimes directions as clear as the glowing Sun on a summer day, mostly riddles wrapped in obscurity cloaked in darkness. Yet to The Oracle they must go. Who but The Oracle would reveal what they could not see, guide them through their confusion, provide direction, affirm their actions? The thoughts of their destination stirred The Twelve like wind trapped in a corner. Each withdrew to silent speculation regarding the proclamations they would receive. Riddles? Who would solve them? Fantasy commingled with desire; each envisioned riddles that he or she would resolve to the amazement and admirations of the others. The one who solved the problem, the one who saved the worlds. Yet each knew only through cooperation, through joined efforts would they resolve the heavy burden that surrounded them. Cooperation. In silent communication all agreed that The Twelve would work together, bonds reaffirmed, affection stirring in their hearts. When He of Red signaled a halt, their hearts ascended even higher.

Ahead the trees thinned. Evening sunlight shone upon the culmination of their quest. The Hill. Rising from the meadow, The Hill glowed ruddy in evening light, the rocks like a warm hearth beckoning homeward. The Twelve felt that warmth course through their psyches, through their awareness, calling, beckoning. In spite of the distance they had traveled, they ran to where the ground began its ascent. Yet quickly as they rejoiced, just as quickly did subtle fatigue grasp them. They had spent the day trudging on road, scrambling through wood, wrangling the avalanche of emotion that had fallen upon them. But the tiredness they now felt did not come from the exertion of muscle. The way was not overly steep; though rock and rubble lay about, they did not have to weave through tree trunk and bramble. They left the melancholy of the trees behind them. Still, each lift of foot demanded more from their diminutive bodies; each step drained more from their enlivened spirits. No words remarked upon this impediment, none of The Twelve wishing to shatter the enthusiasm that had gripped them so shortly ago. On they climbed, as if nothing stood in their way, as if nothing dragged upon their diminutive bodies. Their destination lay before them; they would not stop, would not succumb to the sweat that stung their eyes, to the cramps that gnawed their limbs like vermin too long without supper. They fastened eyes to the ground below them, tracking each rock, each pebble that passed beneath their feet, willing themselves onward, upward, forcing step after step until the piercing agony of a shriek shuddered them to a halt.

    He of Red clutched a leaden gray boulder as he sucked air into his lungs. Sweat flowed from his forehead, soaked through his shirt like a personal tsunami. He flung off his cloak as he slumped upon the boulder, grasping his sides, trying to squeeze away the stitches of pain that knifed into his viscera. He of Red chose to lead The Twelve; He of Red confronted the impediment most directly. All circled him. She of White knelt to his left, She Beyond Color to his right, laying their hands on his shoulders, connecting to Energy beyond the visible, directing such Energy to their exhausted companion. He of Red closed his eyes, accepted, renewed his strength under the capability of his healers. When his breath returned, his attendants withdrew, The Twelve circling as best they could upon The Hill.

"Strong" was the single word He of Red could gasp.

"The force also reaches us," concurred He of Black. The Twelve stared up The Hill, toward the forest, to the sky above, as if explanation was to be found in the physical. He Beyond Color breathed deep and extended his arms to his sides. The others did the same, joining hands, closing eyes, coming together in a circle of Power that they hoped would overcome this new nemesis. The Twelve aligned to the Four Directions, to Father Sky and Mother Earth, invoking the primal Powers to support them. Their supplication made, The Twelve silenced all thought, entered stillness, becoming conduits of those Forces greater than themselves. A warmth descended upon each—a tingling rose through their feet, energies subtle, invisible, powerful. The energies joined at their hearts, emanated through the arms, their hands, uniting the companions within a scintillating vortex that effloresced within the center of the circle then burst upon them. Black, Brown, Red, Yellow, White, Beyond Color quivered in elation, glowed with the Powers, absorbing, radiating, resplendent upon the hillside. They dropped hands and opened eyes, smiling, assured. Once again He of Red took the lead. Once again the others fell in line behind him. A simultaneous deep breath and twelve pairs of feet lifted in synchronization, stepped forward as one. As one they advanced, eyes fixed upon the locus where their answers would be found. As one the unseen barricade welled up before them, surrounding, adhering, restraining. Unwilling to surrender, they marched forward, step after painful step, inching up the hillside as if walking in the kind of mud that would suck the boots right off one's feet. Little ground passed beneath them before they halted again, all bearing the marks of exertion. He of Red squatted; She of White kicked a stone downhill. Silence reigned for many moments.

17

"There will be no stopping." All eyes turned toward He of White. "We face resistance. Resistance shall have no meaning. There will be no stopping."

"Do you not see him?" She of Brown snapped. "Do your eyes not perceive the state of He of Red? Think you he can go on?"

"It is not for He of Red to suffer alone," He of Black asserted. "We. *We*. We make our way to The Oracle. Together we overcome whatever lies before us. We are twelve; we are The Twelve! Our strategy is this: He of Red walks last. I take the lead until fatigue overcomes me. Then the next of us moves to the fore. One at a time, we lead though what opposes us. Is this plan agreeable?"

Through his speech was hardly inspiring, the others nodded in assent. He of Black stepped forward. The others lined behind him. All dripped sweat, felt the parch of exhaustion in their mouths. Yet forward they went, until He of Black quivered in fatigue. Pause, let another take the lead, forward again in pain and exhaustion. Vision blurred, memory clouded. Another break, another stepping forward, another agonizing tramp toward their goal. The Sun pressed toward the horizon. Once more they fell to their knees, sucking the atmosphere into their lungs, as another bravely chose the fore. Their legs bowed like trees in the wind, their chests ached, they took one more step, one more, one more. Finally, near collapse, twelve little pairs of feet stepped upon their goal. Three-quarters of the way up The Hill, the ledge stood firm and flat. The place where bodies could stand, sit if they dared. The place where those seeking knowledge present and future faced The Cave.

Flaunting tufts of grass, gnarled crusty juniper nearly concealed the entrance among gray rock. Here and there a patch of leafy plants grew, plants that could provide colorful blooms in springtime, but often did not. The low Sun shone at the backs of The Twelve, directly into The Cave, yet no illumination penetrated the entrance, some barrier forbidding light to penetrate. The darkness sent a shudder through The Twelve, face to face with this portal to The Underworld. The warnings echoed through their thoughts. No one approached The Oracle lightly, not even The Bright Ones. No one came without proper respect. This Power would sweep away the flippant and the feeble. As one they drew a deep breath, reassured themselves. They were not just anyone. They came with good purpose and knew The Oracle would respond. They would receive the answers they craved.

"And then we must return." He of Black interjected at a whisper. The others looked about, grasping the new dilemma that confronted them. Few moments of daylight remained. In times of certainty, darkness would not deter The Twelve; their awareness would guide them safely through the deepest night. Now, bedraggled, befuddled, at desperation's end, traveling in daylight was task enough. Now they faced a return in the night. The blight of the forest, the unseen force, their own exhaustion, hunger, thirst. A shudder passed through The Twelve as their other choice spewed a much greater fear upon them. They stood before The Cave. Ground terrible in its power, ground almost forbidden. A gaping crack in the fabric of the land. A gateway to something that strained their power of comprehension, let alone their stamina to abide its presence. Furtive glances passed from one set of eyes to another. She Beyond Color drew in a breath, as if to offer encouraging words, but her mouth snapped shut. Within the inky blackness of The Cave, something stirred. Something felt, not seen. Felt as in a sudden jolt, a desire to cower, a desire to flee. The Oracle had awoken.

The Twelve aligned across the rocky ledge, their shadows dancing upon the hillside, ominous attendants to the specter before them. None could describe the sound that emanated from The Cave, the indication of The Underworld manifesting within The Twelve's reality. They had no need to announce themselves; the stirrings within their consciousness told them they were sensed, recognized. Varied songs rode the air from below, the birds' evening chorus. Again the sound emanated from The Cave; the birds retreated to silence. The sky turned from blue to indigo to violet; the first stars flickered above the hilltop. A pressure surrounded the attending pilgrims, pressing, stiffening, rooting them into their places. Each of The Twelve strained to see, though they knew their attempts were in vain. No one truly saw The Oracle. No one could place the voice; no one could identify the gender, if gender was a concept appropriate. Features could not be discerned within the swallowing blackness of The Cave. Only eyes were seen by those who stood where The Twelve stood now. Eyes of some color, or none, indescribable.

Shivers rippled through The Twelve as icicles of unseen cold clutched them. Somehow the sky darkened further, as if night were growing ever deeper at the approach of what the seekers had awoken. Breath quickened, fingers twitched as The Twelve recalled the terrible power that had come to be before them. Once before they had stood in this place, when through guidance unknown they came together, naming themselves The Twelve, grasping the reality that personal pursuits, egotistical desires rooted in the vision of the immediate had become the philosophy of the human world. Their purpose amorphous then, they beseeched The Oracle for guidance, for a glimpse of the future paradise they vowed to bring about for the physical

Earth, which they had convinced themselves Earth desperately longed for. The Twelve had appointed themselves the bringers of Peace and Love to that world and lacked only the means and methods, the how of accomplishing their selfless task. The Oracle had responded in riddle, riddle so deep that they had failed to find meaning, addressing their adopted land through subterfuge and the mystic. Yet they had told themselves their actions had been proper; the results led them to one conclusion, a conclusion they had felt before they ever approached The Hill, before they ever ascended to the ledge. They, The Twelve, were Righteousness. They, The Twelve, were Truth. One day all would become clear to them and their true position would be known. In the meantime they would spread that message of Peace and Love, invisibly crossing the veil that separated their world from the physical Earth. Never making themselves known, they seeded ideas in the minds of the few, knowing that the seeds planted would blossom into sweeping fields of happiness, prosperity, health, harmony. And they watched as the inhabitants of that world—even those whose lives they touched—grew more and more unhappy, succumbed more and more to hatred and polarity. And so they turned to Him, He of The Bright Ones, the embodiment of Love and Peace, seeking both advice and approval. He proclaimed their work worthless. He affirmed that the Earth they sought to serve tumbled toward self-destruction. In desperation they turned to the Voice of The Underworld.

As The Oracle manifested from the depths, His words poured through their thoughts, filled their hearts like a sickening medicinal syrup. *"We must have breakdown before we have breakthrough."* A syrup that gagged the twelve companions, that made them scramble willy-nilly for any alternative. The Oracle saw all. The Oracle pierced heart and mind and brought forth secrets hidden. The Oracle dwelled beyond space and time; neither proved a boundary to its penetrating powers. Surely The Oracle would see clearly through the confusion. The Twelve straightened in courage, knowing that at this important time, they would be acknowledged. The Oracle would affirm their actions, would see the desired results and confirm that they had done their part in bringing the positive. If Peace and Love did not reign, it was through no fault of theirs. If Despair arose, they could not be held accountable; they were The Twelve—righteous, truthful, blessed. This Despair threatened annihilation, yet they, The Twelve, would overcome, would tame, would annihilate that Despair. They stood before The Oracle awaiting their acknowledgement, the recognition of their altruistic efforts, awaiting the guidance, the answers they needed so that they could succeed.

Within The Cave two pinpricks of light appeared, enlarging, brightening, becoming the opalescent disks of those unfathomable eyes. Words came forth, simple words that stabbed like a rusted knife, penetrating slowly, each syllable inching deeper into flesh and consciousness.

"To this place The Twelve have come again. Their presence sullies the rocks they stand upon."

Twelve mouths fell open in unison. Tears welled in some eyes; anger burned in others. Confidence collapsed. Courage evaporated. Taxing exhaustion dulled body and mind, more forceful than the plodding march, more forceful than His foreboding proclamation, more forceful than the Despair that filled the land about them. Defeat, humiliation flooded each supplicant before The Cave. And still worse came upon them. The ephemeral connection of heart and mind that bound The

Twelve, that connection that empowered and enlivened them, that connection evaporated. Chill blades of aloneness pierced each before the dark presence. Breaths, faces, heartbeats broadcast their astonished fear. For so long they existed in harmony, acting, thinking together. Now each stood without buttress against the world. Their imaginings, their selfhood as saviors, spreading goodness, evaporated beneath the crushing gaze. Twelve individuals, standing together but so alone, unique yet so common. The Oracle stripped them of all accoutrements.

He Beyond Color swallowed, summoned forth his courage. With one step forward, he bowed toward The Cave, his cloak drooping about his body.

"The Twelve greet you in honor and respect. We come as bearers of light and spirit, seeking the wisdom of the great—"

"Silence."

The Twelve shuddered, as if the Earth had quaked again. Gasps, even whimpers, escaped the once confident Twelve. Standing there brought a terror primal, a realization of ends worse than death. He Beyond Color staggered back to his companions, She of Brown offering a steadying hand. He of White raised a hand as if to make an address, then let his hand flop to his side. He of Brown and She of Red stepped backward, unconscious of their movement, conscious of the force emanating from The Cave. The Twelve lowered their heads, as if their eyes beheld blazing radiance instead of the depth of blackness. From that blackness The Oracle spoke again.

"You are known. Into you I see further than you have ever dared gaze."

As if they had not shuddered enough in The Oracle's presence, the supplicants now shivered in the nakedness of their souls, stripped of all pretense, all conception, all certainty of who they were and what they represented. The Oracle continued its relentless dissection.

"Through toil and strife, The Twelve approach. The Twelve who serve so many, who do so much again seek the way in which to proceed. This is The Twelve that stand here, is it not?"

Glances flitted about like frenzied insects amid The Oracle's circuitous utterances. The Oracle knew them better than they themselves, then asked who they were. Riddles?

He Beyond Color swallowed, looking for direction from his companions since other communications failed. Should he speak again? She of Black lifted her eyes toward The Cave, assertion rising within her. Steely eyes within the darkness riveted upon her; the sight would have felled her but for He of Brown's steadying hand. More glances exchanged, The Twelve remained silent. Within The Cave the voice retained an unemotional cadence that carried more power than a scream.

"Speak now, you of The Twelve, regarding your approach. The path upward to stand before me. With ease did your power propel you to my presence?" A gutty rumble emanated from The Cave, throbbing through the rock ledge like a rogue wave disrupting a calm sea. One by one realization came to The Twelve. Laughter. The Oracle laughed. At them. A sound that brought no like response from The Twelve. She of Red, He of Yellow became nauseous. The Browns, the Whites burned in anger. From the common kind The Twelve would ignore derision, laughing back at the ignorant in their self-assurance. From The Oracle…

"To me you come to seek answers. Shall it be I who answer this question for you?" Heads bowed, The Twelve sensed those silver-gray eyes sweep over them, bringing a flush to their faces that none understood.

"To you I question anew. Where are the powerful Twelve? To me they have approached before. Crowing in their strength. Where now are those Twelve?" Again The Oracle's laughter pierced them, longer, deeper. All gagged at the sound. She of White sunk to her knees; He of Yellow joined her upon the ground as The Oracle's laughter peeled forth from The Cave, echoing down the slope with such force that the trees of the forest quivered. One at a time, two at a time, The Twelve succumbed to the power, all kneeling before the terrifying specter.

"And now lost are your tongues. Where went the power of The Twelve?"

Though night had fallen, a darkness more oppressive enveloped The Twelve. Always The Twelve perceived hope within themselves. Always they perceived hope surrounding them, in the Earth, in the Sky, in the trees and creatures. Always they perceived hope in The Bright Ones, and in That Which Is Beyond. Now hope lay crushed under the palpable Despair that enveloped their land, that enveloped all the lands. No hope. No hope at all. Darkness.

He of White opened his mouth, closed it without a word. She of Red could not produce an utterance. None could raise their eyes to The Cave.

"In darkness your vision is swallowed. When eyes finally penetrate, you find naught but black. Like a thirsty beast darkness drinks you dry."

Rage, frustration, terror overwhelmed She Beyond Color. "Help us! Blight! Despair! By what means do we stop it? By what means to we stand against it? You know answers! Answers!"

"From me you seek the answer that you wish. You ask not to grasp what you see; you ask to manifest before you the vision you desire. Have you knowledge of what unfolds? Do The

Twelve decide the fate of all? Are The Twelve so exalted that their way is the way that must be?"

Red rage and red shame tinted She Beyond Color's cheeks. If she had had strength to stand, she would have rushed The Cave, grasped the entity within and throttled it, choked the life out of it. If such could be done.

"If without knowledge you speak, then keep yourself in silence. My voice is that which drew you here. Attend to it."

In spite of their fear, their shame, The Twelve leaned their ears toward The Oracle.

"I ask once more. What force so hindered your approach?

Still upon their knees, The Twelve searched their thoughts, looked to each other, furrowing brow, shaking head. She Beyond Color, chastised as she was, made it her duty to answer.

"The Twelve know not," She Beyond Color acknowledged.

A new sound emanated from The Cave. Longer than a grunt, deeper than a hum, an unexpected emotion. Satisfaction.

"Shortcomings are admitted by The Twelve. At last."

Tears sprouted from some; anger sprouted in others.

"The Twelve approached. They wondered. 'What negative presses us so? From what place does it come? Earth? Sky?' So The Twelve wondered. So The Twelve searched without. Never, never did The Twelve look within."

Furtive glances passed among the kneeling bodies. What weakness did The Oracle sense within them?

"So proud you come forth. Can you affirm that your pride produces good?"

He of Brown shouted in answer, "Our deeds serve well! We bring Peace and Love!"

Again the rumbling laugh of The Oracle brought silence.

"Answer me this, you of The Twelve. Are you inclusive?"

He of White rose to the challenge, physically and emotionally.

"You know nothing! Look upon us! Two of White, male and female, Two of Red, male and female, Black, Yellow—"

"And those many who are inferior to you?"

He of White did not know if he had stumbled or been pushed but found himself again on his knees. None of The Twelve dared look at each other, nor dared raise their eyes to The Cave.

"Now see you your truth?"

Anger burned within all. All craved to lash out at the amorphous consciousness that spoke from The Cave. They knew such was impossible, and not merely because what addressed them possessed no corporeal form. The words of The Oracle pressed against them, pressed every inch of their bodies, every aspect of their souls, like the force they encountered upon their approach. Their looks of fright were replaced with the grimaces and glowers of pain, of agony digging deeper and deeper through the layers of their self-righteousness. Cringing, gasping, groaning, writhing, The Twelve groveled before the unworldly presence within The Cave until a spark of recognition flickered, until they came to see themselves unmasked, naked. For so long they had judged themselves as a benevolent light, fulfilling a task of spreading good, righting evil. Now each knew that buried under that rosy chivalry lay the aspects none dared admit, the vomit and feces of their beings. A totality that contained Despair along with Hope, Darkness along with Light, Evil along with Good. The Oracle had penetrated them, and The Twelve, individual and collective, had to face what had been revealed. There was no escape from the power erupting from The Cave. The Twelve could rationalize no more. The Twelve could deny no more. The grating, guttural laugh sounded again.

"Open now are your eyes. Open now are hearts and minds. The denial you carry be the force that impeded your ascent. For that denial it is that blinds you from the heights, that constrains you from the depths. To be True, to be of Power, one must see all."

She of Yellow jumped to her feet, screaming through tear-streaked cheeks.

"We work to help! We work to bring good! You now accuse us—"

"Of helping not at all." She of Yellow quivered but returned the stare of those translucent eyes. "Actions taken from blindness bear no good results in finality. Such actions bring only their own destruction."

The breath disappeared from all of them, sucked completely from their lungs, as if a tempest surrounded them. What anger they had, what opposition they mounted against the words from The Cave vanished, destroyed by the piercing vision and wisdom of The Oracle. Silent tears fell from the eyes of all.

"Hear now as prophecy I speak." The Twelve surrendered to the voice within The Cave. All bowed and brought their attention to The Oracle.

"There will be breakdown before there is breakthrough."

The echoes of Him who first spoke such words reverberated through the awareness of The Twelve. Now The Oracle confirmed His utterance. Nods of submission greeted The Oracle's words.

"There is no other way."

Not a word of challenge from The Twelve.

"Already the signs are seen by you."

At least one let a whimper escape.

"Now, attend to these words."

The Oracle paused to let each of The Twelve gather themselves.

"What is to happen is not for you to judge. Across The Worlds a Blight walks, a Blight deeper than the signs before your eyes. The trees, silent dwellers that they are, they announce the despair but are only harbingers of what shall unfold. In this foundation where we now stand, you see its spread, you sense its malignancy. You see its manifestation upon that which you call Earth. Yet know many, many beyond the trees suffer. The Blight visible portends the Blight invisible. Upon The Worlds *this* opposes *that*, facing each other as two inflamed animals blind to anything but enemy in front, numb to anything but selfish burn in the gut, all shackled to being right, none committed to being correct. No *all* remains, only *one* or *other*. Some seek to escape it, as if they can turn their backs upon the very air they breathe. Some believe that they are immune, as if what happens within The Worlds can happen only to another. All act against the flow while believing the flow they are. See you?"

The Twelve nodded in obedience, if not enlightenment.

"Connection cannot be lost, but what form does connection take? Even in blood and fire, connection is there, a Web from one end to the other. If one strand is enflamed, do not all strands burn eventually? Do not look upon other; there is no other. Do not attach to self; self is nothing but a point in the Web. See not this or that. See not one or the other. Wherever you see right, accept the possibility of wrong. Wherever you see wrong, accept the possibility of right."

"Wait!" She of Red screamed. "Wait!"

The Oracle embraced patient silence.

"There *is* right and wrong! One hurts another—that's

wrong! One, many hurt the trees, the creatures, the Earth—that's wrong! That you cannot deny!"

"I will console you. There is right; there is wrong. The answer is not found in opposition. It is within. Truly within. Beneath the chintzy thoughts, beneath the petty emotions. Many are those who know this; do not The Twelve understand? The Avatars of that which you call Earth speak of it, but most use those words only for further separation. The answer is found within. The place of Peace, of Love is within. Look there without fear. Look past the darkness within and come to the Light. Then, look at other, no matter how fearsome, loathsome, or despicable other might be. Within other you will find also that Light. If that you can do, truly, you will serve."

The Twelve bowed as one. The eyes of The Oracle came upon them, penetrating beyond their flesh.

"Speak."

All looked about. Finally She of Brown raised her voice.

"What do we? The trees are dying! The creatures! The Earth! The Worlds! All suffer! Can we not help in this moment?"

The Oracle passed its eyes from one to another, slowly but not maliciously. All felt the power, power unlike earlier, power that somehow soothed. Power that empowered.

"You question well. I will give you the solution. Are you prepared?"

All Twelve straightened, adjusted their legs, tried their best to ready themselves for the revelation of The Oracle.

"Surrender."

It took a moment for the words to take root. Mouths gaped at the absurdity of The Oracle's directive.

"Never!" screamed He of Black. "We will never give up!"

Before any could further the outburst, the laughter of The

Oracle rolled over them. Eyes averted. Heads lowered. Then a wave flowed gently from The Cave, a calming touch that brought all to attention, to openness.

"Confusion grows from words prejudged. Do what must be done. You may need extend a hand to the loathsome. You made need extend a fist to the comely. Perform what is required whether or not you find enjoyment in such action. Exactly, precisely, without judgement, without avoidance. That is surrender."

He of Black nodded at the wisdom of The Oracle.

"Sights will be seen that appear cruel. Indeed, pain will pour forth without regard to object. Such cannot be avoided, and such will be good when all is accomplished. Remember such. You see not the end, only the means. Let not passion guide you. Look within. Feel the connections that surround you. Sadness will come; you cannot avoid it. Yet sadness may be tempered by understanding."

"But is there nothing, nothing we can do? Do we surrender to watch everything die?" She of White embodied the passion, the anxiety of them all.

"There are Those greater than you. Seek Their guidance. As stated, look within. Seek that guidance. Open to possibility. Renounce all outcome. Yours is not to determine the end. As seen now, the course is set. Many changes arise. Cleansing is here. Not all is death when new is born, yet before the new may come, the old must be banished. We must have breakdown before we have breakthrough. But…"

The Oracle became hushed. The Twelve hung on the pregnant silence, waiting, waiting for what would be birthed from the blackness of The Cave.

"The slightest act of kindness might change the world."

The pearly eyes faded into the blackness of The Cave.

For unimagined time The Twelve sat cross-legged facing The Cave. Their bodies itched, burned, ached, yet none could move, none could break the spell. Finally they noticed a warmth, a brightness they could not explain. The Sun now shone upon them from above The Hill. Stiff, exhausted, they gained their feet, helped each other achieve balance, and commenced their journey home.

Chapter 2

AUTUMN

Monday through Friday the avenue hummed with activity, city dwellers walking, biking, driving to their employment, commuters passing through. Saturday brought only more bustle. Venues of commerce beckoned with their various wares as one person after another entered then exited, some with treasures purchased, others frowning from unfulfilled wishes or sneering at the pretense of the shopkeepers. Aromas of various foods from various parts of the globe wafted from various eateries making ready for the luncheon crowds. Sidewalks clattered with the constant tap of footwear worn by the mass of people flitting from one destination to another, some stopping at the open-air newsstand to glance at the day's happening, if not buy a paper copy. Cars, trucks, motorcycles, buses, taxis lurched forward or squealed to a halt, honking like a gaggle of geese on parade. The comings and goings of human and machine could have been mistaken for chaos, even catastrophe. For the city dwellers, the activity confirmed their satisfaction of living in a prime location.

Clumps of litter festered in gutter and cranny like refugees huddling against a storm. Both the litter and the microbes that festered upon it went unseen by those who crowded the sidewalks, and the scents of the garbage, the gasoline and diesel fumes expelling from the passing vehicles brought no thought of the effects upon the pedestrians or their surroundings. The excitement of city living outweighed any of the perils that density engendered. Even the vagrants, cramming into undisturbed corners where they could beg coins and enjoy cheap alcohol, were merely another of the distractions that this sardine-can lifestyle brought. City life was worth it: employment, entertainment, culture, comfort. If one wanted quiet, if one wanted calm, one could find an establishment that offered escape for a reasonable price. If one searched hard enough, one could even find a tree.

The park occupied a few dozen acres, Nature's island in the midst of the big-ticket real estate. If one stood in the very center, one could breathe almost fresh air, could hear a bird sing over the din of the traffic. The Saturday morning park denizens differed from the weekday crowd, people interested in exercise and sunshine instead of catching a bag lunch away from office or retail outlet. A place where the body could run or jog while inhaling less of the city's noxious atmosphere. That was his reason for walking the few blocks to the black wrought iron gates, gates hung from brick columns on either side of the paved path, an unnatural but stately entrance to Nature's alcove. To him, this boundary acknowledged a place of exercise, not escape. He loved the city, loved the crowds, loved the sights and the sounds and smells of urban living. It was just that the city streets were a bit too crowded for a workout. Especially on Saturday.

He arrived at the left-side gate, grasping the ivy-covered brick to begin his stretch routine. Lengthen the calves, extend the hamstrings. Lean against the column, grab the ankle, stretch the quads. A few jogs in place to get the blood pumping. His workout qualified as a fast walk, enough to bring sweat to his brow and armpits but not something athletic. The perfect pace, he told himself when the Sun glowed like it did on this autumn day. Fast enough for exercise, slow enough to check out the women scattered about the park, exercising to trim their figures or just enjoying the sunshine, stretched out on the grass, barefoot, skirts hefted up, enjoying the solar glow upon their legs. He sighted down the paved path, a touch aroused in anticipation of the sights expected, plotting his route for optimum inspection of the ladies. Ladies. A memory brought a smile. Last Saturday and the Saturday before. Ahead of him on the trail. What a luscious body! She stuck in his mind like some cutesy song he couldn't get rid of. In the intervening days, his thoughts came back again and again to the sight of her flowing hair, her supple figure. She did not wear exercise clothes: dressed like some warrior princess of old, boots well up her calves, skirt barely reaching her thighs, a stringy back that showed a good amount of flesh when the breeze flipped her long hair aside. It was the boots that turned him on the most. Then there was that something in her hair. At first he thought headphones, but when he saw her the second time, he knew that wasn't right. Did she have leaves on her head? Okay, she was strange, so what? From behind she looked just fine. He grinned at the thought. Twice he saw her, twice he stepped up his pace to intercept her, find some reason to speak, and neither time did he succeed. She didn't run, didn't jog, but as fast as he walked, she was always in front of him. Could today be his day?

He turned into the park, legs, arms pumping, scooting past the rusting bike rack and filthy drinking fountain. The first segment of his route traveled down the little dip where foliage grew dense and muggers could hide, then climbed to the first meadow. Success—young ladies lounging in the sun, on the back bench or spread on the grass. The redhead looked particularly enticing, lying on her stomach reading a book, long, shapely legs bent at the knees, wagging back and forth above her. Check her out on the return trip, he concluded, find a way to talk to her. The path followed a righthand bend, passed the big tree with the funny peeling bark, then swerved left at the big clump of bushes that flowered in the spring. Heat encased his legs, and a heart more accustomed to sedate office life throbbed in his chest, but he paced on in the name of fitness. Up a slight rise, curve around another clump of bushes. Glance forward. Spot her.

If he had known colors better, he would have called her dress emerald green. As short as always, exposed thighs inserted into knee-high boots, dark green, crinkling as she strode down the path. Smooth white flesh glowed through the lacing across her back. She floated ahead of him, motion smooth and elegant. This time he would not fail. Step up his gait, catch up to her, see if her face, her tits matched what he saw from behind. His stomach tightened; they approached an intersection, carousel to the left, fountain to the right. He had to make sure he didn't lose her. A little bend took her momentarily out of sight, firmed his resolve. Catch her at the crossroads. Should he play dumb? Ask her where the paths go? Who knows where it would go from there? Arms flailing, breath bellowing, he burst toward his rendezvous.

A quick glance confirmed his location: two benches on the left with a plaque dedicating the site to some dead person. Ahead, the goldfish pond, downhill so he could gain ground. Would she stop and watch the fish? He sighted her again, his athletic shoes slapping the pavement, sweat sprouting, heart thumping. She kept the same lyric pace, never in a hurry, never exerting herself, always remaining in front of him. He wondered about his knees but threw the thought away. He began to run. Thank God he had spent a hundred and ninety bucks on athletic shoes. His heart pounded like a steam locomotive in a Wild West movie. Downhill toward the pond—his advantage; he would catch her. Stinging sweat dribbled into his eyes. Damn, why hadn't he worn a headband? She turned, looked toward the sparkling water, the teeming orange and white fish, the lily pads. Great! She would stop! He'd catch her! No! Just a glance and she was on her way again, up the hill opposite the pond.

Screw the burning calves; screw the burning lungs. *Move!* The pursuit became a quest, a Holy Grail crusade for this elusive epitome of beauty. Sucking air through thin-stretched lips, he upped his pace again. As if cued by his determination, she peeked over her left shoulder, flicking her flaxen hair aside, an instant of eye contact that enflamed his resolve. Sweat soaked his pricey athletic shirt, and still he gained no ground on the woman stepping calmly ahead of him. Focused on her attractive body, receiving another glance his way, all that mattered was her. Eyes did not note foliage denser with each step, arching overhead, shutting out the Sun but for here and there pinpricks of light glistening upon the ground. Eyes did not note manicured terrain giving way to ragged undergrowth. Eyes did not note concrete sidewalk giving way to dirt path barely packed by travel. He noticed none of this, only the escalating thump of his heart and the sight of her. Sounds of humankind turned into songs of birds, rustles of creatures along forest floor. She disappeared around a bend. He gasped, stumbled, pumped his legs even harder, leaned into the curve and attained the straightaway. She was gone.

"Son of a bitch!" Three wobbly steps and a flailing hand grabbed the overhead limb of a huge oak. Doubling over, other hand clutching his aching side—how in *hell* did she get away? Rough bark scraped his skin as he plunked against the tree. He wretched, panicked. Heart attack? Cheeks aglow, sweat seeping from every pore, he slumped to the ground, using the tree as a back rest. Enough energy remained to stomp his left foot on the ground. He sagged against the tree, fuming, wincing as cramps gnawed through his legs like hungry termites. Screw it. Get up, stretch out, head back. He sucked another breath, gave himself a shove toward vertical, thumped back against his wooden support. Another moment and his stomach calmed as suddenly as it had rebelled; his heart resumed its normal beat. He marveled at his quick recovery and scanned his surroundings. How far he had gone? How far it was back to the gate? Three years of walking this park, never saw this part before. The plants presented a tangle of leaf and stem; they needed to get a lawnmower in here. Some nature place they let grow wild? Where did the asphalt go? The path? A movement tweaked the corner of his eye. Before he could utter an obscenity, she walked down the path to stand directly in front of him, shining the full beauty of her face at him, porcelain white with a blush of pink on the cheeks, eyes that matched the brilliant green of her dress. He blinked, swallowed, blinked again, forgetting his fatigue and his confusion. Her lips curled into a mere hint of a smile. He popped to his feet.

"Hello." He started casual, would make his next move based on her response.

"Hello," she replied, her voice tender, sweet, yet projecting strength beneath the tones. Her smile widened, her teeth straight and white as the keys of a piano. He took her smile as encouragement.

"This park has a lot of pretty things, but I never saw a goddess before." In his thoughts he patted himself on the back. Goddess. Great line for her. He craved her reply.

"I thank you, but you have yet to discover me."

Her smile he could not fathom, and what in the hell did her answer mean? She turned, took a few steps toward the foliage, her back toward him. Was she laughing at his silly attempt to impress her? He had chased this lady through the park like some infatuated schoolboy. She knew it; she had looked back at him, twice. But she had played some kind of game with him, somehow staying ahead of him the whole time, teasing him the whole way down the path. She had to be laughing now. Yes, she was really, really good looking. Beautiful. Goddess? A great description! And yeah, she had decorated her hair with greenery. Sprigs of something that looked real, like she had plucked some plants right there in the park and made them into some kind of crown. Goddess should have been the perfect compliment for a chick like her. Had it worked? His thoughts sprang forward. Was she some kind of tree hugger, some weird chick that lived on tofu and granola? Is that the kind of chick he wanted to lay?

"You are right in part."

Her lilting voice startled him out of his reverie. What did she just say?

"Uh, what?" He could have smacked himself—what a stupid response. She turned toward him but did not approach. The look on her face revealed nothing.

"I do not eat those foods. I do hug trees." She turned again toward the woods; he remained cemented in place. Too weird, too weird for him. The way she dressed, the way she eluded him. Did she just read his mind? He had run into a few weird women before, like the coworker of Charlie's girlfriend they had said was a perfect match. What a dipshit! Now he was in the park with this crazy bitch. Sure, she was beautiful, but maybe her beauty wasn't worth it. A scene flashed before him—buddies around the poker table, he talking about the weird chick with the leaves on her head. They would all get a good laugh at that, but first he had to dump her. Get out of here. He looked around to get his bearings and realized had no idea where he stood. Then she aimed those brilliant green eyes at him, eyes that absorbed him like a hummingbird sipping nectar. She took a step toward him, another, never breaking her gaze, coming close enough that he sensed her delicate perfume, like flowers maybe, maybe honey, something that smelled real good. Two steps from his sweat-covered body, she stopped. His trepidation vanished.

"Come."

Delicate fingers clasped his palm, softness beyond what he could have conceived of in the touch of women. His hand encircled hers, succumbing to her delicate touch. From beneath that dainty texture came a power, a strength, something unseen, radiance emanating from her being, penetrating his dull humanness. His feelings moved beyond desire, beyond lust, as he encountered an unknown emotion that combined courtly romance, admiration, and reverence, something he had never felt for any woman, not even his mother or the third-grade teacher he had had a crush on. Her feet made no sound as she walked—more like glided—along the dirt path. How could he not have caught someone who walked so delicately? He glanced down to make sure she *was* walking, felt a gentle tug on his arm. The trees grew close against the path; she led him to the right border, where she placed a gentle touch on the trunk of one of the forest sentinels. No tree hugging, no throwing her arms around the trunk, just a caress of the gnarled bark. A few paces later she stepped toward the left, again making a gesture to a tree. When she reached out for the third one, his observation came forth.

"Looks like that guy is ready for fall."

Her grip compressed about his fingers. When she spoke, he heard melancholy.

"Why say you that?"

He took a breath, seeking to enliven her with cleverness.

"The leaves are all brown. They're falling off. When the leaves fall, it's fall." He desired a giggle for his poor joke. Instead, silence. They had walked a few steps more when he heard her breath rasp into her lungs.

"Autumn does not touch them. The trees are dying."

The sound of sorrow in her velvety voice drew his gaze

41

toward her. A few moments ago, his response would have been a silent "Oh brother." Or something more vulgar. Now he wanted to know. The same white skin, the same blushed cheeks, yet something about the eyes, something he hadn't notice before. She looked forward as if focused upon something distant. Discomfort crept over him, but not from aversion to her. That gaze, that stare saw something deep and terrible. He wanted to see what those eyes were seeing, know what thoughts were stirring behind them. Some touch of pain smoldered in his heart.

"You don't think about trees dying. They live a long time, you know." He cringed; it seemed all semblance of intelligence disappeared in her presence. She voiced no reply, but her fingers tightened about his hand. A grip that unleashed a stampede of thoughts. A few minutes ago, all he wanted was to rip off that skimpy dress and lanky boots and dive into her. Luscious! Now what was she? What difference did the trees make to her? Why did she talk so strange? And where were they anyhow? Her wispy steps gained weight, slowed as their conversation took its mortal turn. Ahead the Sun shone on a wild meadow—not the manicured lawn of a park but rather clumps of clover with a lone honeybee attending, hodgepodges of differently colored grass, some weedy-looking things with little yellow flowers. On the other side of the clearing, the path pierced the darkness of denser woods. Were they so deep into the park that nobody took care of this place? And how big was this park anyhow? He thought he covered it from end to end every weekend. He looked ahead for signs of civilization—a bench, a water fountain, a lamppost. All he saw was another path cutting across the meadow, intersecting the one they traveled. Which one led back to the clogged streets of the city?

"You thirst. You hunger. We shall enjoy a repast."

The chill ran straight up his spine. They were in the middle of woods. No snack bar, no food truck, no wagon vendors with their ice cream and cold sodas. What repast? They reached the meadow. On the left was a tree. Were those apples? Were they going to eat apples right off the tree? He drifted toward a laden branch.

"Those are not fruits that you wish to consume."

"They're apples, aren't they?" At her glance his hand snapped back to his side. "Sorry. My produce comes from the grocery store.

"Closely observe from what the fruit dangles." Apples shone red in the sunshine; broken branches, withered leaves, a rank smell surrounded the glistening fruit. He backed toward her.

"Some kind of poison or something?" He stopped at her side.

"That is something you might say. Let us sit and enjoy what we have."

Reaching the sunny patch of grass, she sat daintily, tucking her legs to one side beneath her, placing a soft leather bag in her lap. His chest tightened. How long had they walked together? No way she could have hidden that bag in her skimpy outfit. He tried to mask his disbelief; whether he did or not, she took no notice. His knees crackled from the exercise; it took two grunts for him to reach his seat. Before he could inquire, she produced a small loaf of bread and a corked bottle from the bag. She brought no knife, instead breaking off chunks of bread with her fingers, one for each of them. His stomach growled. It had to be past lunchtime. He lifted the fluffy brown bread toward his mouth and stopped. Eyes closed, she whispered some chant, the sound of which brought chills of beauty, rapture. When she ended, she directed her eyes straight at him. He wobbled, woozy, dreamy, entranced with her milk-white hand as she touched his lips with her piece of bread. He took a bite, chewed slowly, felt the urge to offer her his piece in return. She uncorked the bottle, held it to his mouth, poured a gentle sip of the finest red wine he had ever tasted. Without thinking, he wrapped his hand around the bottle, touched it to her lips, gazed on the pucker as she sipped her portion. Ritual complete, she leaned the bottle against her thigh. He blinked, waggled his head, absently chewed his morsel. The meal continued in silence until both bread and wine were gone. She replaced the empty bottle in the leather bag, leaned back, stretched out in the warm autumn sun. Her body was a perfect proportion of lean and curve. She noticed his attention, dipped her head so that her flaxen hair part covered her face. At her smile he breathed deep, head spinning—and not from the effects of the wine. She brushed her hair aside. Once again her emerald eyes pierced him.

"Many are the questions you are contemplating." He straightened as if to speak; a delicate wave of her hand silenced him. She turned toward the woods, not ignoring him, as if trying to catch sight of something. Without facing him, she spoke. "Many are the questions that run through my mind." He knew she was not patronizing him. "You see the blight upon the forest?" He nodded, not wishing to break her soliloquy. "More there is than the browning of leaves, the cracking of limbs. You see merely the fringe. The blight visible portends the blight invisible." Her mouth turned to a frown, a pained frown, as if she had spotted some torment that touched her directly. "Is there to be nothing but blood and fire?" A tear trickled down her cheek. Judgment flashed in his mind: crazy chick crying over—over what? Dead trees? Judgement dissolved into lustful attraction; she looked so vulnerable that he wanted her right then, right there on that grassy meadow. Before arousal could take hold, lust dissolved, transforming into a different desire, the desire to know, the desire to see what she saw, however obtuse that may have been Who was she? Where did she come from? What in the hell was she doing to him?

"Don't trees die all the time?"

She turned to him. His stomach hollowed as thought vanished. Sadness overwhelming, sickening. The sky blackened, the land blackened as if a suffocating blanket squeezed the visible from his eyes. Breath became challenging; a nauseous blast of vertigo caused his stomach to wrench. Sheer terror arose in his heart. All disappeared. He existed alone, lost, teetering between death and insanity. A crush of force like a suffocating snake enclosed him. Though silence reigned, his ears felt a crush of decibels. Though light was nil, his eyes burned in fluorescence. He opened his mouth to scream, scream as he never had. No sound came forth. He felt himself vanishing, succumbing to annihilation, dying in agony. Then, She was there. No lustful conquest, no weird tree hugger, Her eyes, Her porcelain skin, Her flaxen hair all glowing, radiating light both visible and invisible, light overpowering, filling the darkness, filling his consciousness, overcoming his thoughts, his feelings, his existence, blasting him as surely as the fear had just done a moment ago. An eternity in a new agony. Then all was normal. There She was, in the meadow, staring at him. Not staring. Her gaze clutched him, grabbed him heart and soul, split him open as he realized it was Her filling him with the same dread, the same agony that She beheld but never uttered. His mouth moved before he realized he was speaking.

"What can we do?"

Her arm stretched, hand gentle against his cheek. Her soft smile returned. She pointed. His eyes followed Her index finger.

"See you the path that brought us here?"

She accepted his nod as the answer. Her dainty arm traced the route to the intersection.

"There paths meet at a crossroads. Which route is ours?"

The word "home" sprang to his mind; he chose a less challenging answer. "How about there?" He indicated with a point.

Her expression did not change. "There lies the easy path that leads only to destruction. Many are they who travel that path, though they know it not."

He felt no recoil at Her cryptic statements. He sensed Her desire for exploration of—of what? Intrigue goaded him on.

"That one?" He signaled with a nod of his head.

"There the path is strenuous, the path of understanding. Few are they who travel that path, and fewer grasp the purpose."

"But it's better than destruction" he quipped. A smile peeked through Her lips.

"A good perception."

"I guess it's that one." He marked his choice with only his gaze. Her smile broadened.

"Fewer still follow that path. That is the path of regeneration. That is the path you will walk with me."

He rubbed his chin. "I'd think everyone would want that."

Her hand alighted on his shoulder. "Few are willing to relinquish who they are, even to make room for something greater."

Without thought his hand reached for his shoulder, came to rest on the hand She had laid there.

"Why is that path about regeneration?"

"One can only know by choosing that path." Her look rippled through him—excitement, fear, adventure, dread. Without words he stood, then offered his hand to Her as She took to Her feet. She kept his hand in clasp as once again he detected the warmth beneath the softness, the light that brightened Her milk-white skin. They reached the crossroads. They stepped boldly upon the chosen path as the woods once again swallowed them. Steps weaved left and right as She touched one, then another of the trees, coddling his hand each time, awakening his consciousness to the surroundings. Some trees passed from summer glory to autumn mellow, leaves losing their green hues to embrace fiery reds and yellows. Others tumbled to the blackness of death. His gaze lengthened beyond the edges of the path; his sensitivity aroused, the signs of blight were obvious. Crumpling deciduous trees with leaves fallen, coniferous trees like browning pyramids. As his eyes sighted a particular stand of trees, dry and dilapidated, a chill cascaded down to the soles of his feet. From within the certainty rose that he was no longer strolling in a circumscribed park. Another chill rattled him, potent enough to warrant a glance from Her; yet desire overcame any trepidation that may have hindered the journey. He would proceed. He looked to Her, Her beauty still apparent though Her look was pained. Her lips pulsed in silent communication.

"What are you saying to them?" He was curious about Her words, but most of all he wanted to hear Her voice. He wanted the assurance of Her company. The chill within would not vanish. He knew he was approaching something formidable and would not return unaltered.

"I speak not to them. I pray."

"You mean like 'Our Father, who art in Heaven'?"

"In a way." He felt Her eyes upon him. "Great are the words of tradition, words sanctified by the heartfelt expressions of the many, words given by The Bright Ones who manifest upon this plane. Great too are the words spontaneous, words that come from that place within."

Her words made no sense, yet Her thoughtfulness touched him. He only wished he could agree with Her, but he felt Her actions were to no avail. He had given up on prayer long ago, and he felt that no prayer would help these woods.

"You're praying for the trees to get better?"

"I pray for all who live upon this land. In part I pray for myself."

"For yourself?" He admired Her candor; She was no selfish hypocrite who pretended to serve others. An inappropriate thought snuck in. If you find out a girl's religion, you find, you find, something. His mind searched for the conclusion of the aphorism, then remembered. In the bar at happy hour. Dave. Something about which sexual position would satisfy the girl. He broke his reverie, noticed She gazed toward him. He wondered if She spotted his blush.

"I mean, I guess, yeah, that's a good thing. What do you want—I mean, what do you pray for, for you?"

Her eyes returned forward; She stepped left to pat another dying tree.

"Too many turn to prayer for asking. Is not the lifting of one's thoughts a form of prayer? The connection to That Which Is Beyond? The act of prayer brings peace. Acceptance. Understanding. When seeing distress, one feels distress. Prayer passes one through the distress, even though the heinous remains."

"You mean just saying the words makes you happy?" He felt silly the moment he responded. He wondered if Her eyes rolled.

"I mean remembering who we are and what lies within. It is we who have the power over ourselves; it is we who connect to Beyond."

He wasn't sure what She was talking about but somehow

connected with Her words. All the things that pissed him off. Work, the government, the asshole in the apartment below him, the people at the grocery store. He could go on and on. Say a prayer?

"You grasp what I mean. I encourage you to try it."

He took no notice of Her penetrating his thoughts. "You mean, say the 'Our Father' and see if I feel better?"

He felt a pause in Her step even though She continued forward.

"There is much power in those words. The sanctified prayers of the ages do remarkable good. Yet there are other methods. Have you ever spoken words of your own?"

"You mean, made something up?"

"I mean speak your inspiration."

Now it was his step that paused. Inspiration? No one used that word with him. Debug a thousand-line computer program in a week? Yes. Inspiration? No. What in the world could inspire him? All that crap that he was supposed to pray about? That stuff sucked! Words tumbled through his mind; words that popped up as the images of his life cascaded through his thoughts, a jumble of words that straightened out, formed lines for reciting. Inspiration! Words sailed from his mouth like butterflies upon the wind.

"I feel so nice and blissy
I will not be so pissy
No matter who screws with me.
I'll escape to serenity."

The giggle that escaped Her mouth was condescending, but when Her fingers interlaced with his, the gesture redeemed Her and then some. Delight returned to Her morose eyes.

"I commend your heartfelt prayer."

He wanted to believe that was a compliment. "Heartfelt?"

At the squeeze of Her hand, a warmth flowed up his arm and throughout his body, settling in his chest.

"Your heart," She continued. "Your words speak true to your feelings. There is power when such is spoken."

"Power?" He liked the thread of this conversation. She raised his hand to Her lips and kissed it.

"There is great power in the prayers of the ages. There is great power in the prayers of the heart. I would that you make yourself more powerful still." She continued walking forward but shimmied a few inches closer to him. He noticed.

"How do I do that?" he asked, as much to please himself as to please Her.

"Escape."

She had to feel the twitch as his glance shot toward Her.

"Escape? Escape what?"

"Escape nothing. Remove that word from your consciousness." She sensed his confusion, pausing to allow his attention to focus.

"Unless you are in a building afire, escape is the mark of weakness. You are not of that type. Escape not to serenity. Escape not to bliss. You are of power. Stand in your power and meet what confronts you. From that serenity arises."

They walked on in silence, weaving one edge of the path to the other, where She could place a soft hand upon the dying trees. He offered no resistance, absorbed in contemplation of the words She had spoken. "You are of power." Never had someone said something like that to him. His throat scratched; his eyes moistened. He brought Her hand to his mouth and kissed it. Not chivalric, not sensual, but with gratitude, humbly acquiescing to Her wisdom. Thoughts swarmed through his mind, yet no words would form, no acknowledgment of Her insight until almost childish yearning produced his utterance.

"I wish someone had told me that a long time ago."

She raised their clasped hands to caress his cheek. Her gesture was almost motherly, filled him with confidence, with strength. He guided their hands between them; She glided closer so that their arms touched as they walked.

"Too, too many live in weakness. Assured there is something better somewhere else, and their task is to get there while they pay no attention to the ground they stand upon. A better world when they change, when they heal, when they die. What a world we would live in if everyone quit treating this world as something to escape!"

Many slow steps were taken, but his mind churned at the speed of light; his body burst with sensation, the strange feeling in his chest roiling, tumbling. He might have thought he was having a heart attack had he not felt so good. He unclasped Her hand, stepped even closer and wrapped his arm around Her waist. She returned the gesture. He felt Her smile more than saw it, and when he led them to the left, to place their hands upon a once stately sycamore rotting from the inside, Her glow penetrated him on every level. They walked on soundless, grieving over the surroundings yet empowered in each other's embrace, empowered through their own hearts. Their pace slowed as the path rose ahead of them. When they topped the rise, the sight overcame him like a visual tidal wave. Below stretched a wide valley of sparse forest in which every tree was dying or dead. The sight penetrated his heart, his gut; the rending feeling crushed out any thoughts of city, of apartment, of home. In this awesome blight, who was he? What was it that his life had to offer? Where did it lead? What was the point? A soft shake against his waist brought him to present; he spied something nestled amid the dying trees. Farmhouse? No, the shape wasn't right for a dwelling; it looked more like a small chapel. Old, weather-beaten, a place that had not been tended for a while. He didn't notice that they had stopped. She squeezed him to Her side, then stepped away.

"What in hell is this place?"

Her smile would have been coquettish under other circumstances. "I do not trifle when I say that I do not know. This vision is for you. As far as I can, I will proceed with you, but I can offer no explanation. I can only offer questions. Are you willing?"

Images of the day cascaded through his thoughts. Wake up, pee, scramble a couple eggs, make toast. Check email, a quick read of the news website, lace up his workout shoes. Go to the park. Find Her…and…regeneration. Puffs of breeze rattled the dried leaves before them, a hollow sound like naked bones rasping against each other. He focused on the dilapidated structure. If he were to go in there, what? What would change? What would his life be like? And…

"Can I?"

Their eyes met. Her smile was silent but called Her words back to his consciousness. "You are of power." He smiled back, nodded, extended his hand toward Her. She clasped it but did not step forward.

"Speak not. What you see, what you do requires no words."

He nodded. She squeezed his hand. They approached the rustic structure.

The path was easy and smooth, as if apologetic for the surrounding desolation. Not a bird sang; not a rodent or reptile scurried through the grass. The occasional breeze continued to pester the dead leaves for the only break in the silence. The Sun shone upon the land, but no radiance reflected back. The old building attracted him even as details confirmed the abandonment of the place. Parts of the soffit hung loose. The molding of the left side of the gable hung cracked from the main structure. One tiny window fronted the place, near the peak of the roof, dust-caked and opaque. He eyed strange markings on the door, a message written large in some unknown alphabet. Greeting or warning? Dread and curiosity battled within his gut: get the hell out of there or go see what's inside. With a squeeze of his hand, She signaled him to stop.

"As I spoke, words are not necessary. You are of power. Remember."

She released his hand, stood upon tiptoes, kissed his cheek. The gesture startled him, drew his attention to Her. Was it the desolation that made Her eyes glow so bright? Or feelings for him? She backed away, never breaking Her gaze. A gust of wind flipped a lock of Her hair toward him. Two more steps back. Her skirt rippled, dead leaves rattled, some breaking free, blowing toward him as the wind reached his face, firm, pressing. He blinked, quivered, stared upon Her, saw hair leaping, clothes rippling. Howling wind pressed him like so many thrusting hands. He staggered, braced in resistance, succumbed to the gale that propelled him toward the dilapidated structure. Fear increased with every blast that cut through him. He tried to reach for Her through the gale. Clothing, hair whipped about, She crossed Her hands over Her chest and bowed. The tempest staggered him backward. He slammed into the door, paralyzed. Without sound, the door gave way behind him. A final blast of wind shoved him inside. The door slammed.

The only sounds emanated from him: gasping breath,

pounding heart. In total darkness he groped for the door, wondered if it would open, panic strangling him, pleading with his feet to run. Escape. No hand found the door. Escape. Arms flailing, he found no wall, no substance where but moments ago he had been forced into the structure. Escape! Quivering, tears flowing, breath choking, he opened his mouth to scream. No sound came. Escape? "Remove that word from your consciousness." Would he do as She said? A ragged breath filled his lungs yet brought calm. Fear. Dread. The hollow in his stomach. The weakness in his legs. No. "You are of power." He would not run. He would stand in his power. What did his life have to offer? What had he; what would he become? Curiosity overtook his ill feelings. More than curiosity. Again Her voice sounded in his mind. "Regeneration." Regeneration. He would not escape. He would meet his fate. He turned.

Had She not warned him against speech, he would have uttered the most vulgar expletive of surprise he could have mustered.

Cavernous darkness stretched before him, dizzying darkness, immense and black, sliced by tiny shafts of light from windows high above, pitiful illumination that did nothing but make tricks upon his eyes. He sensed walls, roof, structure, massive and robust, stretching many, many paces away from where he stood. He wished for Her presence, the feeling of strength that pulsed below Her delicate touch. Would She appear? No, She would not. "This vision is for you to follow." For him, only him. His eyes searched—for a feature, for a clue, an indication of why he was at this place. He stepped in a hovel; now he stood in a—a what? A cathedral? A cathedral of his own making, cavernous and empty? Yet as his eyes adjusted to the heavy darkness, he noticed something at a distance he could not judge. The apparition called him, beckoned him to approach. He turned his eyes toward his feet, toward the unseen floor beneath him, wondering what obstacles might lie between him and that hazy destination. He took a step, his running shoe soft against something firm, solid. Smooth stone. Another step, then another as he tried to discern what awaited him ahead. He paused, tilted his head. Sounds, like streams splashing through a forest, on both his left and right side. Indoors? An odor reached his nose, a sweet metallic smell that touched his consciousness without identification. He continued forward, the distant image clarifying in the muted light. A raised area with candles flickering at the corners, their dancing light illuminating the vision like some religious scene from his childhood. He squinted. An altar? Cathedral, altar—what vision had he conjured? As he pondered the sights, he realized sounds upon his ears. Muffled sounds, moans, weeping, quiet mourning within the gloom. He swallowed, firming his resolve against the chills along his spine. More steps, the view clarified. A rock dais, candles at each corner, surrounding sculpted rock, maybe as high as his waist. An altar. Had to be. With each step the sounds of mourning, the sounds of the streams grew louder. He was almost upon his destination when from behind a shaft of light, a brilliant beam penetrated the gloom, illuminating what lay before him, melting his legs like a flame to wax. Upon the dais was a coffin.

Terror clasped his throat like a disembodied icy hand. Gasping, he begged his feet to turn from the sight. Run, asshole, run, get out of here, get out of the woods, get out of the park, get home and stay there, forget She ever existed. His body disobeyed. Enough time for his mind to engage. Heart jackhammering in his chest, eyes fixed on the sight before him, he clenched his teeth, fought the urge to flee. Ascend the dais. See what lies in that ornate stone coffin. Again his frightened self arose. No, no, get out, get the hell out of there. His internal quarrel peaked when new sounds joined the pounding of his heart and the dirge surrounding him. Howling. As if a chorus of beasts were joining the mourners, adding their inhuman voices to the lamentation. He felt their presence in the darkness, surrounding him with their barbarous keening. Warning him? Testing him? Trying to stop him? He sucked in his breath, gave his quaking body a conscious shake. He would not be stopped. A vision for him. Regeneration. One step, a second, a third and he stood before the dais of exquisitely laid rock, thigh high, joints so tight that no mortar was needed. Three stairs carved into the rock invited his ascent.

Sweat trickled about his neck. He swallowed through painful dry mouth. His left foot lifted, extended, planted on the first stair. The beam of light, piercing the darkness from behind, diminished as if the Sun had passed behind a cloud. The candle flames shrank, leaving only murky twilight. Next foot, next step, the sounds of the mourners dwindled. Third step, the stone platform, light extinguished, sounds ceased. Darkness. Chill. Silence more sinister than the previous lament. One step forward, another, he stood at the base of the coffin. The candles reclaimed a bit of intensity. His eyes widened. A gasp escaped him. This was no coiffed, adorned cadaver giving the illusion that death was merely a long nap. The linen draping the body lay rumpled, stained. A hand near him, dirty or bloody. One step forward, another, enough light to view the draped corpse. The linen under that creepy hand, at the waist of the body, bore a wretched-smelling stain. Blood. He leaned over; there on the other side, another hand, almost blue in the light. Or almost blue in death? Lying atop slumped linen soaked with water. Why such treatment of the body? This person had died a ghastly death, pierced through with some wound that still oozed vital fluids. No embalmer, no mortician had tried to hide this, allowing full display of the horror of passing. Why? Who was this? The face remained in shadow. A step forward, he reach where the chest would be, where the light failed to illuminate. Another step forward, he reached the head of the coffin. Still no light shone upon this soul. He waited. The sounds of mourning, human and animal, intensified; he paid no attention. He stood solid as the rock sarcophagus, waiting, waiting. Cries of anguish, howls, as if these unseen banshees surrounded him. He did not move. The lamentation reached a crescendo. Candles flared. Light burst through the distant window. The scene erupted in stinging brilliance that snapped his hands to his face in protection. He squinted through pained eyes, having to look, having to see, having to know.

He saw himself lying in the coffin.

No cry of horror burst from his mouth. Pain, fear fell away. The mourners fell silent as he leaned toward that face, studying it as if seeing it for the first time: the high cheekbones that women found attractive, the slightly crooked nose that he had broken when he fell off the swing set at eight years old. The mousy brown hair, the pointed chin hovering just above the Adam's apple. As the connection between him standing and him lying below snuck into his consciousness, the logical analysis continued. This face had not died a violent death. No sunken flesh, no bluing of the lips, no pallor of death. How could a face look so peaceful upon a body so maimed? Like a seed poking through freshly turned loam, a different thought emerged. His eyes scanned the body. He could not explain his conclusion but knew with certainty. This body was alive. The him within the sarcophagus was alive. Alive, damnit, alive! Maimed, wounded, perhaps at the gates of death, but alive. The him standing there knew it.

He bent, bringing his ear as close to the face as he dared. Breath, slowly entering, slowly leaving the nostrils? He gazed across the torso. A subtle rise and fall of the chest? His hand extended to where the heartbeat would declare itself, then paused. The cacophony in the darkness resumed, swelled, pealing through the darkness as if the heralds of death were closing in to pluck the him that lay in the coffin, the him that stood beside it. A violent shake rattled him; he clutched the stone to keep from falling. The whole morning of strangeness. Her, the woods, the chapel that morphed into a Gothic cathedral. Was it all some strange metaphor for death as he lay dying somewhere? Was his body sprawled by the drinking fountain, by the lake, somewhere in the park? Dead of a heart attack? Maybe the police, the EMS were there right now, covering him with a sheet until the coroner could fetch the body. Another tremor shook him. Regeneration. Was that like when you died and came back as somebody else? Really, was he dead? He gagged. Cold sweat burst from his body, weakening him even more. He was dead. That was it. Didn't they say that your life flashed by when you died? It didn't happen. Instead here he was in some strange hallucination. Some trick his brain played as the cells began their journey to decomposition. Well, if that was so, then here he was. Too late to change anything. From nowhere, immense calm arrived. He straightened, straining to see what crept through the blackness surrounding him. He spied no detail, no motion, yet his ears registered the rising volume. He would have cursed them all away had he not remembered Her words: "Speak not." His eyes returned to the face in the coffin. Alive. Alive but dying— he in the coffin, he standing there. The connection reached completion. Realization knifed through his consciousness. More than the darkness, more than the dirge roaring about him, the blossoming thought frightened him. Terrified him. There was no escape from that thought. No escape. Now was the time to stand in his power and meet what confronted him. To answer the question of all existence.

If this was his death, what had been his life?

Had he lived at all?

What shitty excuse for living was his life. What shitty excuse for living was he. He. Who was "he"? The man standing there or the man lying in the coffin? Neither? Both? As if moved by someone else, his hand reached forward, came to rest on the chest of the body in the coffin.

Now, for certain. A heartbeat. With each throb, each thump emanating from that mangled body, something erupted into he that stood there, tore into his body, his soul. His gut blazed with pain, ripped from one side to the other, torment beyond the physical cutting him like he was an empty piñata. Every failing, every shortcoming in his life, every foul deed he had perpetrated, from stealing cookies in kindergarten to lying to that chick to get her in bed; every vice and sin rose to his awareness like tongues of flame erupting from the fire in his viscera. The shame of his life crushed him. The tears, the sobs exploded from him as he out mourned the spectral mourners surrounding him. He wretched, slobbered, dripped sweat from every pore. Then a million needles pricked every surface of his body, as if his flesh were being picked apart by an infinite swarm of perverse vermin. He quaked, one hand clutched to chest, one hand upon the body before him, writhing in the pain of a life wasted. Beside him, above him, around him, spine-chilling sounds penetrated his ears, choking him, crushing him, beating him like ethereal hammers. Images avalanched upon him until he could stand no more.

"Stop!"

Silence.

He sucked a breath, another, bracing himself over the coffin, staring at the angelic calm face that lay there.

"I failed."

Soft warmth filled the atmosphere.

"Son of a bitch, I failed!"

Mellow, soothing light filled the hall.

"I didn't know"

His eyes cleared of the tears he had shed. He focused on the wounded man that lay before him—wounded, not dead, laid in a stone coffin in cavernous darkness.

"Can I try again?"

The wounded man who had his face, who carried his wounds.

"I'll do better."

The wounded man who now opened his eyes.

And smiled.

And clasped the hand of the man standing there. Warm, reassuring.

The pain, the guilt, the anguish, the shame dissipated like morning fog in the sun. Not forgiven, not denied, but accepted. Life remained to be lived. How would he live it? The same? The answer came with certainty. He stood erect. With one last look at he who lay within the container of death, he who stood there nodded his head in agreement.

He who lay there became faint, indistinct, until only empty stone remained. The coffin became filmy, transparent, then evaporated into nothing. The dais, the candles—all disappeared. He looked around. He stood in a ramshackle little building with a small window above an old door. A few steps and he opened that door, without resistance, viewing woodlands with the hint of autumn in the air. Across the meadow She waited.

He felt more than saw Her eyes as She looked at him, looked through him, appraising his thoughts, his feelings, his soul. A smile broke upon Her face, radiant, beautiful, knowing. With sure steps he approached until they were but inches apart. Arms reached toward each other, grasped. Their lips met in a kiss of unbridled passion and purity. He stepped back to face Her; their hands clasped.

"I thought I was going to die."

Her look turned coquettish.

"You are now more alive than ever you have been."

He grinned at Her mysterious compliment, then darkness crept across his face.

"Maybe." Her eyebrows raised. "What I saw in there. What I saw *in me*. It ain't good. Ain't good." Something between anger and grief welled up. Her touch drew him back to the present.

"None there are who are perfect."

"Yeah, but—"

"None there are who are perfect. Do not compare yourself to the heroes of your world's fantasies. Those heroes are for naught but escape or control. Succumb to neither. If perfection were required, none would walk the face of this land. Suffering does not correct the fault. Correction comes only through action. Look forward. Redemption lies in front, not behind."

She pulled him close so their bodies met with the slightest touch, a touch that would have been sensual but now filled him with a different kind of warmth. Their eyes met again, and in those eyes he found everything he so desperately sought: acceptance, forgiveness, empowerment, love.

"The pain you feel is the pain that all carry. Unlike others, you now know. This knowledge is power. As you look about your world, as you see the decay around you, you know that you are no better. And so you will come from compassion. There are times when strength is needed. There are times when the sword is required. If even behind that lies compassion, the correct action is performed."

"I can't save the world."

She kissed his cheek.

"There are none that can. Events are set in motion, flames pass through the Web of Creation, and destruction comes to manifestation."

"Then what's the point?"

Again Her hands squeezed his.

"Enough there is that can be saved."

"How?"

Her eyes glowed, a shining green light that enflamed his heart.

"Be gentle. If a magnificent deed is called for, you will answer, yet it is in the little that hope is manifested.

He blinked; there was something wrong with his eyes. Her image became blurred, fuzzy. Was he crying? He blinked again. His eyes felt fine.

"Remember to tread with ease. There is enough unrest in the world, enough contention. Do not feed the polarity. Tread with ease."

Her hands seemed to melt in his grip.

"You feel that great deeds are required. Perhaps, perhaps. But the slightest act of kindness might change the world."

Her face approached, or did it? Was that wisp of touch on his lips Her kiss? He blinked. He blinked again.

He stood between pillars of ivy-covered brick, between wrought iron gates opened wide. The sights, the sounds, the smells of the city welcomed him.

Chapter 3

WINTER

B lue and purple, an occasional flash of green, the colors of labradorite, her favorite crystal, perfectly blended to embellish her toenails. She hoped the jam of people bustling along the sidewalk noticed as the Sun shone at the perfect angle to highlight her decorated feet. Luckily her pedicurist had found the perfect application of colors. Luckily the weather was so warm that she could wear sandals in the alleged dead of winter. Luckily she hadn't put away her airy summer clothes. Her bodice and flared skirt, perfectly black against her pale skin, furthered her personal mystique. She sidestepped an overweight mother pushing a stroller, whispered a quick prayer for the baby who fussed in her head-to-toe fleece, overdressed for the temperature, if not the calendar. Hand forming a blessing mudra, she knew her connection to the Universal Energies would serve the infant, even if the mother was a nitwit. She veered to the left, slowed to examine the wares in the window of her favorite shop on that block. Eclectic and unusual fashions for plus-sized women that suited her taste and anatomy. One of the clerks waved from behind a rack of frilled and beaded skirts. She returned the wave but decided window shopping was enough for this day. She walked on.

She had really wanted to flaunt the wedge snow boots she had bought a week ago—black to match her new pullover maxi dress and the leather jacket she purchased last year—but so much preferred bright Sun and warm breezes to snow and cold. Her black tourmaline and silver pendant caught the sun's rays, and the stares of the passersby filled her with a satisfying giggle. She thrust her ample bosom forward to highlight her glowing jewelry. Jewelry! Up a block, turn left, and bingo! The New Age shop. Maybe a good day for new accoutrements. Her feet found the route, her eyes spotted the wooden sign, her steps slowed. Maybe go in, but certainly scout for any interesting wares in the window. The first display, new books, arranged on stands and risers with crystals and greenery accenting the presentation. One book especially garnered her attention, a "delicious discussion of chakras and sexuality." Maybe she should finish reading one of the four books currently on her nightstand before buying another. Besides, she had other plans for today; tomorrow was Sunday, the perfect day to lounge among the crystals and incense of the store. Thoughts of the book's contents brought a brief excitement. Then she huffed, brought to reality as if someone had dropped a dead fish between her rotund breasts. There had to be a man around who appreciated a Rubenesque woman with so much knowledge of the occult. A man who wasn't hung up on weight, a man who knew those girls in the beer commercials didn't drink the beer and had silicon breasts. She distracted herself with the rest of the display. Those crystal wind chimes looked really good; she might want one for her balcony, but would anyone really hang crystals outside where the birds could poop on them? The Tibetan bowls, the stones carved and polished into the shapes of hearts and animals. Maybe. She really needed to clean her bathroom, promised herself she would, and wanted to look into that online course on the Akashic records and planetary prosperity. She was just about to go, and then she looked up.

Perhaps his energy had crept into her awareness subconsciously. Perhaps her spirit guides had directed her eyes upward. The impetus did not matter; what mattered was that she did look up, and he was there. Standing above the Tibetan bowls, holding a tarot deck and nice quartz fire point, approaching the cash register. And his head turned, turned toward the sidewalk where she stood, turned toward her. The high cheekbones, the funny crooked nose, the mop of mousy brown hair that needed a trim. She experienced a flutter unexpected, a caressing shiver through her body, an electric warmth that sparkled like her labradorite toes. For an instant their eyes met. Connection established, a certainty. He turned toward the back of the shop, disappearing into the reflections of the street that danced across the plate glass window. She remembered to exhale, schemed her next move. Maybe go in, hang out at the counter, check out the jewelry, wait for him to approach. He had to recognize the unmistakable zap of energy that passed between them. A mosquito snapped her out of her reverie, its tiny proboscis like a wanton dagger in her arm. A mosquito in the middle of winter. She sighed. It had to be a sign. Maybe he was new at this stuff, not aware enough to sense the subtle flow between them. She turned down the street toward her apartment. Just another exercise in frustration. Yet as she walked through the honking horns, the burring sounds of car and truck, the exhaust fumes, her thoughts returned to him. Maybe they would end up friends. And if they started as friends, maybe something more.

She could always turn around and hope he was there. She looked into her arm, into the drug store bag tucked in the crook of her elbow. Three tubes of eyeliner, a box of caramel candy, and a box of tampons, not the goods to be holding when meeting a sexy man. No, her intuition told her he would be gone by now. Yet she trusted what she felt. Connection. It happened. They would meet again. She paused, then forged ahead, both to her apartment and to her new strategy. Maybe he *was* a regular customer. Then the owner would know him. *She* never missed an attractive man. Tomorrow. Ask her tomorrow. And if he's not a regular, they will meet some other way. She knew it. She sighed and looked about. Above the bobbing heads of people on the sidewalk, she spotted the entrance to her building. Good. Go home, do a nice calming meditation, then consult her tarot decks. See what the future might hold for her. And him.

The climb up the two flights of stairs left her winded. She

paused, promised she would get herself in better shape as she unlocked the door to the welcoming space of her apartment. The quartz cluster in the living room window caught the sunlight, shimmering her apartment into an aura of celestial light. She unstrapped her sandals at the door, flicking them directly from her feet to the shoe shelf in the foyer, keeping to her rule of never wearing shoes within her domicile. Her overstuffed black purse took its place next to the door. Once she had her sundries put away and had dropped the bag in the recycling bin, she plopped onto her overstuffed sofa, flexed her toes in relief from the long walk of the shopping expedition. She eyed her seven tarot decks, which lay on the coffee table, selecting a traditional deck formulated by one of the famous Hermetic orders of the nineteenth century. She didn't remember putting the deck there; last night she had used it in her bedroom. This had to be an omen; her intuition agreed. Pull a card now, guidance for her upcoming meditation. She removed the deck from its box, cradled it in her hands to make the heartfelt connection to its oracular power. Seven repetitions of the Four-Fold Breath cleared her mind to receive a true answer. Free of intruding thoughts, she shuffled the cards, asking for a sign, a direction for how to proceed, how to connect with that handsome man. Certain that her answer awaited, she drew a card and held it in front of her face. She opened her eyes to gaze upon the answer. The Blasted Tower.

She smacked the deck upon the table and headed for her meditation space. The Blasted Tower. Ruin. Failure. She'd never see him again. But before she reached that corner of the room dedicated to spirituality, her powers of rationalization instituted her rescue. The Blasted Tower. Sudden change. Disruption of old ways. Of course! The old ways disrupted. Her rut of nonromance, of rejection would end. She would meet him. He would like her. They would get together. Maybe. No, it had to happen. It had to. Comforted, she entered her sacred space, reaching for the mahogany box from under her altar. She eyed the varieties of incense, then stuck a stick of white sage in the incense holder. Open her psychic powers, her intuition, so she could truly divine how to make the connection with him. She flicked the lighter, applied the flame to the white sage, then fanned the tentacles of smoke to her heart, to her head, through her straight black hair, purifying, setting the stage for spiritual inquiry. The supporting cushions of her meditation chair welcomed her, invited her to a connection with her silent inner being. The pillows were cool upon her back, but after a couple wiggles, her relaxation would not come. She reached under her bodice and unclasped her wireless satin front-closing bra. In a well-practiced move, she slipped the straps down each arm and extracted her undergarment, freeing herself without having to disrobe. The brush of the satin against her nipples made her think of him again. She remembered the tarot card; she affirmed that the old ways would be broken. She organized her transformation checklist in her mind. See her Reiki practitioner, get her chakras rebalanced, have an acupuncture session, do a cleansing fast. Break the old ways, open up to the change. With a deep breath, she uttered her invocation.

"By the Light Above, the Unending Flow of Love Energy, the Infinite Forces of Planet and Stars, the Angelic and Archangelic Forces, I open to and accept All Good, All Love, All Peace and Presence within me. Spirits, attend me! Grace me with your Infinite Presence and Wisdom! I await you! So Mote It Be!"

Attention back upon her breath, she sunk her body into the comfort of her chair as the calming in-and-out rhythm quieted her thoughts. Her eyelids drifted shut as her eyeballs turned toward the center of her forehead. Her fingers curled into a meditative mudra while her feet settled into the welcoming softness of her prayer rug. Floating through her mind came the image of the Blasted Tower. With a cleansing breath, she let the image drift by, knowing she would soon ponder that mystery but now was the time for stillness. She returned her breathing to regularity, the flow of air into her lungs, out from her lungs, in, out, in, out—smooth, soft rhythm. Her shoulders melted into the soft cushion; her thighs, her calves softened. Little whispers invaded her bliss, happy whispers about wonderful changes to come. A deep cleansing breath. She acknowledged those whispers, relishing the positive transitions to come. She knew it; the card affirmed it. No maybe about it. Her concentration strengthened, her mind cleared of residue wanted and unwanted. Quiet focus, calm breathing, in and out, in and out. A feeling warmed her heart like a sunflower unfurling toward the dawn light. Relationship. Partnership. Companionship. Delicious sex. The smile on her stoic face betrayed her loss of concentration, and she allowed that smile to remain. A new life. She knew it. She felt it. No maybe about it. And strange enough she felt supported in that affirmation, energy on one side, energy on the other, like sitting between two warm ovens baking deliciously fragrant bread, like sitting between two loving grandparents. She tried to return to her purpose and realized that perhaps her purpose had been obtained. These feelings could mean but one thing—that her wishes, her desires were acknowledged by the Spirit world. Blessings rained upon her. Her prayers were answered. It was time to leave her sacred space. Have a cup of chamomile tea, take up her tarot deck, give herself a reading, perhaps the Celtic cross, a good, thorough reading to lead her to her anticipated bliss. A deep breath spread her chest, filled her belly. She could recall no meditation like this one, where energies glowed so palpable beside her. She hoped the feelings would last when her eyes opened. She hoped they would last forever. One more deep breath, then one more, drinking in the exquisite feelings that surrounded her. She wiggled her toes. She stretched her arms. She opened her eyes.

Her altar stood where it always had, the northeast corner of her apartment, her lucky direction. The stick of incense still smoldered. The various crystals, feathers, figurines, pebbles rested comfortably in their places. On her left stood a diminutive female with a strange pale of red about her. On her right, an equally compact male with skin a subtle yellow. The female laid her hand upon her shoulder. The male raised his hand in a gesture of greeting.

"Hello."

She fainted.

The woman behind the counter pretended to organize the gaudy jewelry in the display case, but he knew her eyes were on him. He was accustomed to knowing things without physical acknowledgement. Been happening ever since…not that he minded the knowing, or the gaze of the woman running the store. While she was as old as his mother, he was sure, her long, wavy gray hair and smooth white complexion had a certain appeal. Perhaps because he stood surrounded by objects of the "occult," he could not restrain his thoughts: is this what She would look like when She got older? If She ever got older. That he doubted. The quiet energy of quartz turned his thoughts to his hands, to what he held as he stood with the fluffy music playing in the background. This crystal, it was kind of cool, speckled red embers frozen in quartz like tiny fish frozen in ice. He shot another glance toward the window. The strange lady in black was gone. He had had only a quick view of her, but she stuck in his mind. Her eyes, something alluring, even pretty about her eyes. But her? Too short, too fat *her*? He blinked; the lady at the counter snapped her head toward the counter. He chuckled over the situation. What if his buddies were to see him in here? Was he really going to by this stuff? Buying this stuff, checking out that chubby chick that dressed like someone at a funeral. Yet he felt a subtle vibration in his left hand, felt the crystal gaining heat in his grasp. What did the little card say on the display? "For moving forward, enhancing the ability to take action." He could put it in a window and let it glow in the sun. He could put it about his bed. Would that move him forward? Where was he now? He still worked his job, in fact just got a promotion. Had worked his way up the corporate ladder. But he had sure changed the way he spent his spare time. Volunteering to support the IT of two Nature-oriented charities. Meditation. Getting up at zero dark thirty every morning to sit in a kitchen chair and breathe. Yes, it calmed him down, and stuff came to him, thoughts, messages. Like "find this crystal." Again, his eyes wandered to the window. Come to this place and see this lady… he couldn't be attracted to *her*, could he? His type of woman had long legs, sometime so skinny that her breasts were smaller than eggs. Scrambled eggs. The last time he had gone to the bar…yeah, the last time, that ditz who thought IT was some kind of birth control. No, he didn't miss the frustration of the bar scene, and the poker nights lost their appeal when he began sensing how each deal would play out, knowing when to hold and when to fold. He laughed, startling the store clerk, thinking some old singer had made money with a song like that. His thoughts returned to his merchandise.

Tarot cards? What fat ladies with too much makeup used to sucker money out of women desperately looking for a boyfriend. He stopped midthought, looked over his shoulder toward the front window. That was the kind of woman he expected to see in this place. Overweight, dressed like a blingy mortician, probably some kind of witch. All she needed was a pointy black hat. He turned back to the shelf in front of him, yet her face stayed in his mind. Something about that face. Had he seen her before? Met her somewhere? He shook his head, focused on a display of dainty, scantily clad girls, some patting unicorns and dragons, all with wings. The bright yellow sign decorated with plastic flowers declared the population of the shelves for the totally clueless. Fairies. Yet no matter how much he gazed upon these little resin sex bombs, her face returned to his consciousness. His kind of woman? Tall, overly skinny, long-legged. Not her. But…her eyes *were* pretty. The top of her breasts peeked out of her bodice, enticing. She might even know a few things about the stuff he was fumbling around with right now. Could they be friends? He reached for a pack of incense. White sage. Incense and a long wooden holder to catch the ashes. He laughed out loud, drawing a startled, maybe reproachful look from the lady at the counter. What next, a crystal ball? The laugh melted his apprehension as he remembered why he was there in the first place. Time to learn, time to understand. Regeneration. He had thought about seeing a psychiatrist as soon as he left the park that day. But he knew that what had happened to him was not a hallucination. He knew he had not experienced a "psychotic break." Which might have been more comforting. He tried four books on UFOs, thinking maybe he had been captured by some alien who had played some strange game with him. Pretty crazy stuff, but not as crazy as what he had gone through. And none of the aliens acted like Her. Or looked like Her. What happened to him was real. *She* was real. And so he had things to do, things to learn. Why that led him to this shop he did not know. But to here he was led.

He stepped toward the front of the store with the deliberateness of a sloth, more and more thoughts bombarding his consciousness. His friends, the ones who still talked to him, kept telling him he was getting weird. So what? He wanted a different life. He wanted to learn what was happening to him. He wanted to learn what was happening to his world. He wanted to do something with his life besides spend all week in an office making money only to throw it away every weekend. He wished She would come again, guide him, lead him along. But for a whisper to come to this weird froufrou shop, he had neither seen nor heard Her again.

When he arrived at the counter, the proprietress smiled as he placed his purchases before her. As her slender fingers clasped the cards, there was no mistake that she was measuring him with her eyes, looking for some clue as to the reason for his appearance.

"Some of the greatest names in the Hermetic tradition influenced this deck. For over a hundred years, this deck has guided those who have appreciated it. A classic." Head tilted forward, she sort of looked upward with her blue-gray eyes, gauging his response. Her lilting voice had no effect on him.

"Hmm…" he responded, glancing once more toward the window. "I don't know too much about this. She told me—" He clamped up at her nod. Did she just think he was pleasing his girlfriend or something, or did she know who "She" was? No, she couldn't know. Could she? Or did she know who the woman in the window was? He thought a moment. Did it matter? He smiled in return.

"Just something I don't get."

Her eyebrows raised.

"These things are just for fortune-telling, right? I mean, how can they help you? I mean, how does anyone use them for, you know, for—" He waved his hand in a circle as if trying to stir the perfect words into his awareness.

"For spiritual growth?" she offered.

Her eyes betrayed amusement but no judgement, like a schoolmarm awaiting the recognition of emerging intelligence.

"Yeah, for that."

Her eyes lingered upon him a bit before she turned to the cash register, scanning the bar code on the tarot deck, on the incense, keying in the price of the crystal and incense holder, then peeling off the price stickers with pink manicured nails. The crystal she wrapped in tissue, then placed his goods in a store-branded paper bag. She added a little flyer advertising sales and psychic readings. As she handed him the bag, their eyes met again, her hand clutching the bag as he grasped it.

"Come back and tell me."

He knew not whether to smile, wink, or moan. A come on? A spell cast upon him? Or just a pledge asked from her new customer? At his nod of acquiescence, she released the purchase to his possession. He approached the door to depart. There stood a tall, beautiful Black woman fumbling with the old-fashioned knob. In an act more expedient than gentlemanly, he opened the door and let her through. His eyes followed as she darted in, panting, as if she had run from wherever to get there. He could not help assessing her as a possible partner, but still his thoughts turned to the woman he had encountered before. He slowly pushed the door closed and stepped into the street, which was pulsing with the regular Saturday bustle, but could not help but here the lady's nervous babble.

"Do you have books about those, those, what are those little things called? Fairies? Leprechauns? You know, little people?"

A laugh approached his lips as he heard the bolt click in place, but then again, what was he doing in that store? He sees a Goddess, that lady sees fairies Was that any crazier than what he went through, what he experienced, what ripped down to the very center of his soul and left him an unknown seeking to find a new self to replace the one he thought he knew so well? He weaved through the pedestrians, his bag crushed and clutched so no one would take notice of where he shopped. Movement brought a sense of relief, a sense of life. It would be a good day to go to the park, get some steps in before lunch. He shifted the bag to his other hand. He would go tomorrow. Today he would take a look at this stuff. He didn't need the exercise as his jaunts now happened three or four times a week. He had given up alcohol, was eating more vegetables; his waistline showed it. Still, a swing through the trees. Was he turning into an exercise junkie? Or were his visits to the park simply a longing to see Her again?

The three flights of stairs to his apartment were enough exercise for now. Once he was through the door, he prepped for his sojourn into the metaphysical: bag on the plexiglass coffee table, bottle of water from the fridge, plop on the futon sofa. He unwrapped the tissue paper from the crystal, held it at arm's length toward the living room window. Great place for it; he'd put it there in a minute. He peeled the cellophane from the incense box. Kind of pungent. He had expected something sweeter. He stuck a stick in the holder, took the lighter from the beaded box on the coffee table, and applied the fire to the tip of the stick. The wisp of smoke curling toward the ceiling brought a chuckle. The only thing he used that lighter for was to light his marijuana pipe. No more. And where had he gotten that box? That's right, some chick he had dated who wanted to get married the second week they were together. He reached for the tarot deck. After peeling that cover of cellophane, he found a little booklet in the box. Good! Instructions. Descriptions. Explanations. He thumbed through the deck. Lovers. The Devil. Wands, Swords, not exactly a poker deck. What did all this have to do with— what did that lady call it—spiritual growth? Maybe in confusion, maybe in desire, the image of Her appeared in his consciousness. Would She answer if he—he what? Called to Her? Prayed to Her? He sat the cards on the table, reaching for the booklet. Yep, fortune telling. That's all it was about; lay the cards this way or that way. What had he bought these for? He flipped the booklet to the coffee table, watched it skid across the plexiglass. He slapped the arm of his sofa. Three months ago, his entire life had overturned like a dumpster flipped above a garbage truck. Now what? Fortune-telling? He had given up a lot; now what? When was something going to happen? Would She come back? Would he reach, what did that one book call it, "eternal bliss?" His eyes returned to the coffee table, to the face-down cards and the rest of his wares. He blinked, reached toward the table, stopped, blinked again. Those dumbass fortune-telling cards. He had just put them down, one big thick stack of laminated cardboard with red and yellow and black and white pictures on them. One thick stack piled on top of another. Now, inches from his fingertips, lay seventy cards in a perfect fan spread, precisely spaced, waiting for him. His breath rasped like a sticky drawer. Had She done this? Someone else? Something else? The questions gave way to a desire—no, a command. His hand inched forward, hovered over the spread, floating back and forth as if guided by a force not his own, and locked on a card, toward the right edge of the spread, fingernails scraping the edge from the plexiglass. He turned the card in his fingers as slowly as a moth emerging from a cocoon and inched it toward his line of sight.

The illustration showed waves of distress rocking the stones of some castle. As flames belched from the windows, lightning slammed into the structure, knocking two unfortunate guys into a fall. Or had they jumped? The Blasted Tower. What the hell did this mean? More than curiosity compelled him to search the booklet.

She rammed the key into the lock, burst into her flat, her new collection of literature falling like a psychic avalanche upon the kitchen table. She placed both hands on the back of a faux leather dining chair, sucked in a great breath, arcing her back in tense exhaustion, straightened, bent forward, lengthening the spine. Again, again, again she stretched until her wind, her nerve returned. She backtracked up the hall, plopped a hand on the door frame, stared into her office. Just like she had left it. Manila folders on her desk, four more stacks of them lined neatly on the floor. The tax returns of five clients waiting for her analytical brain to ferret out deductions, exemptions, anything to recoup a few dollars. Work she needed to finish. Work that had forced her to give up her weekend. She returned to the dining table like a timid kitten. Work. Too much work. That had to be it.

Looking at the table, wondering why she had bought all this. Just too much work, so much work that she had hallucinated. It couldn't be real, it couldn't, but in her heart it was more real than the linoleum beneath her bare feet. Work. Folder after folder of receipts, deposits, statements, 1099s, W-2s waiting to be entered into the software. But, but…

With a nervous deep breath, she tiptoed once more to her office, as if sneaking up on something. Everything was the same as she had left it. Her clients' folders. Her stack of color-coded plastic clips. Her calculator. Her computer. Though the computer now displayed a seductive screen saver, incredible beach, crystal blue water, plenty of nightlife above the shoreline, where she would go once tax season was complete. And there, on the printer table, a book lay open.

The sight of the book tightened her, made her pull shaky elbows to her side, made her lock her knees. She had bought that book nine years ago, her senior year in college, required reading for her Special Topics in Economics class. And she kept it, even though everything in it was wrong. Wrong! Economic predictions that the world would end years ago! Okay, it was good to study when predictions went wrong. And she did study it. She should have tossed it when she graduated. With a deep breath, she leaned against the door frame, wanting to slam the door shut and pretend it had never happened, pretend it would all go away. But imagination doesn't take a book from a shelf. She shuddered as the scene unfolded again in her mind. Look up from the computer and two elves, fairies, whatever were standing there. Black, like her! African American elves! Something Disney could have invented to be politically correct. Two of them, lecturing her on economics. Whatever they were—elves, fairies, dwarves, leprechauns—they weren't hallucinations.

Hallucinations didn't touch you. Hallucinations didn't read from a book and set it on the printer table. Hallucinations didn't come up with messages like theirs. Even if they did disappear into thin air when they were done.

A sigh like a falling leaf, a flip of her hair from her forehead, she returned to the kitchen. A cup of tea. A cup of tea and a peek at the books. She took down her favorite mug, dropped in a lemon herb tea bag, and filled the cup from the instant hot water tap. At a glimmer of light, she jerked, froze, relaxed. Just the Sun on her trophy shelf. High school volleyball state champions two years in a row. Second place, then third place, then national champions in college. She should have stuck with sports. Hard work, but lots of fun and lots of girls to meet. By now she would have a good relationship. And no money. Take the safe route. Get a finance degree, get an MBA, get a CPA license and you're making more money that you can count. While fellow graduates were counting beans in some fluorescent light cubicle, she had already created her own practice. In three years, no doubt her second goal would be attained: an office, a staff of six managing the books for clients great and small. Now, these little freaks show up and…does it all get thrown away? She stroked her long black locks, popped off the tieback and let her hair fall about her shoulders. Images of manila folders and calculations danced through her mind as she sat down. No, she resolved. Work could wait. She could spare a few minutes for a cup of tea, for a glance at these books. She blew across the top of the mug and took a sip. Relaxing lemon herb tea. Relaxing, just like the meditation class she took. Relax. Do the five-minute breathing exercise at your desk. Open your eyes and you are refreshed. Open your eyes and you are ready to dive into whatever work is at hand. Open your eyes and there are two little freaks telling you the world is going into the shit can. And preaching the economic theory to prove it. Price mechanisms. Exponential reserve index. Jevon's Paradox. And wrong predictions of forty-some years ago somehow turning out to be right.

Another sip of tea, mug to the table, her fingers wandered to her purchases. Three books she would never have time to read and a deck of cards. She touched the card deck like she would touch a hot roll from the oven. She still couldn't fathom why she had bought it. With a sigh she pulled one of the books toward her, flipped it over to read again the description on the back cover. One look at the author's picture and she was sure he spent a lot of time with fairies. A *lot* of time. She plopped the book on the table, wondered why gay men vexed her when she was as homosexual as they were. It wasn't like they were after the women *she* was interested in. Next one. Written in 1911. Maybe people believed in fairies back then. Third one. Written in the 1600s. Now that was a strange purchase. She returned her attention to the first book. Gay or not, this guy might know something.

Two cups of tea, four hours, digging through one book, then another, underlining, marking pages with the color-coded plastic clips that were supposed to be a business expense deduction. The tea caught up with her, so she rose, went to the bathroom, cutting a glance toward her office to make sure that everything that belonged there was there. And anything that didn't belong there was not there. As she dropped her slacks and positioned herself on the toilet seat, a chill quivered her spine. Her eyes darted about the bath. The bohemian shower curtain, matching window dressing—nobody peeking from behind them. With two cups of tea waiting to be released, she couldn't do a thorough search. She guessed that her visitors wouldn't be interested in urine. She finished in the bathroom, made herself a sandwich, sliced an apple, and wondered. Wondered about the day, wondered about the world. Her thoughts turned to the old year 2000 scare as she returned to the dining table. Bibi gave her a "magic" blanket to "protect" her from the evil happenings, which worked well for a six-year-old girl. At 27, she didn't fear the same bogeymen and no grandmother could negate the words of her visitors. With her first bite, her hands wandered toward the books, but she knew there wasn't much more to learn. For one thing, not even Mr. Tutti-Frutti said anything about Black fairies. Maybe she should have found an author of color. She laughed as she munched the organic turkey breast, soy cheese, and multigrain bread. Black fairies. That ain't political correctness; that's plain weird.

Thoughts turned to childhood. She remembered some of the stuff the old people believed, the old people in the neighborhood where she grew up. Lots of strange stuff, but no Black fairies. She paused midbite. Yemoja. Shida Matunda. The stories of her childhood made her smile, the stories told by her grandmother, her great-aunt. Stories she grew out of, like those cartoon movies—nice, but for children. There was nothing to them, she knew that. Yet something stirred inside her, something that pushed her on to keep learning. Surf the internet, search beliefs of her people, her ancestors. Surely there'd be some of that on the web. Maybe a lot. Hell, she didn't know nothing about her ancestors except some time long ago they were dragged over here from Africa. Could be that there are Black fairies. She laughed again and corrected her thinking. Not fairies. Faeries. To distinguish them from the little cartoon girls in miniskirts. She relished the crisp sweetness of the apple slice, licked the juice from her lips. In spite of the craziness of the day, she had learned a few things. Real faeries didn't have wings; they were taller than six inches; they didn't carry magic wands. Like what she saw. Black faeries—on the short side but mature, intelligent, and, she had to admit, powerful. Like the ones she read about in all these books. Just nobody mentioned them appearing in people's offices.

She finished her meal like a hungry statue, stiff arms moving food to her mouth and staring at the kitchen wall, wishing to know a lot more, wishing she could know a lot less. As she walked her plate to the kitchen sink, cleaning it under a trickle of water, she heard the call from the heaps spread about her office. She breathed deep as she wiped her hands on the dish towel, hung it from the handle of the seldom-used dishwasher, and turned toward her office. Back to work. She caught sight of a little box on her table, one final item calling for her attention. She had forgotten about the cards. The kind that the gypsies and witches used. She glanced toward her office, glanced toward the cards, glanced toward her office. Another couple minutes wouldn't matter. She'd take a look at the cards.

She edged her way into the dining chair, peeled the cellophane wrapping from the yellow box. The deck was thick, not like regular cards, but her large hands made shuffling easy. She discovered a little booklet, she'd check that out after she, after she…she stopped midshuffle, not sure what to do. A few more aimless shuffles and she sat the deck on the table, face up. As she reached for the booklet, the card on top caught her attention. The picture wasn't strange. It was totally bizarre. As she wondered what kind of game you would play with these things, she noticed writing at the bottom of the card. Tiny letters telling you something. She read, picked up the card, read it again, looked at the crazy picture. Old castle, lightning, two guys falling. The Blasted Tower. Crazy picture, silly title, and chills shaking her lanky stature like an oak tree in a gale.

For the second time, she popped off her left shoe, stretched the scrunches out of her sock, and with trembling hands stuffed her foot into the seldom-used walking shoe. The same hands then wrangled the shoelaces, a knot for each foot tied like a worm wiggling in a bird's beak. She clutched the arms of the chair, breathed deep, and pushed herself to her feet. Her knees wobbled as she grabbed her purse, sweat dampening neck and armpit. Deep breathing didn't calm her. Two valerian capsules didn't calm her. A cup of kava tea didn't calm her. Two tokes of that really good Hawaiian reefer that her coven sister gave her didn't calm her. Outside. She had to get outside. Feel sunshine on her body. Release the chaos of a mind spinning like a pinwheel on steroids. Maybe the spirits told her to go outside. The spirits she knew, not *them*. The spirits that she, well, she thought she knew the spirits. Rituals, tarot readings, meditations—she had contacted them a thousand times. Two thousand times. Those warm feelings, the voices that sounded like hers but couldn't be her voice, those were the spirits. The ones she knew. The ones she never saw because they lived in the spirit world, but she knew them. Then today. Today. They stood right there, right in front of her. In the flesh! Her body quaked, her thighs shaking like dangling gelatin, the scene replaying in her mind. She fought the urge to go back to her meditation space. *Those* spirits. The ones that came to her. In the flesh. She knew they were gone; maybe they weren't. As she reached for the door, a smile beamed across her face. They had come to her! The spirits had come to her! Out of all the people in the world, they had come to *her*. Selected. *Chosen*. She stepped into the hall and secured the lock. She convulsed in fear. Yep, they had come. And it weren't no social call.

A heat unaccustomed in winter's depths greeted her as she crossed the threshold of her building. Yet it wasn't heat that made her sense a difference about the street, the city. As she stood in the late afternoon lull, the shoppers and lunch crowds gone, the entertainment folk yet to appear, the allure of the city vanished as thoroughly as her two otherworldly visitors had. Fume belching automobiles, drab concrete, litter, dirt. The buildings loomed like tottering heaps of rubble, sterile, lifeless. Not a single tree grew on her block. A few potted plants in front of her building, some flowers in front of the real estate office, but not a single tree. She stepped from the curb, squeezed between two parked sports cars to scan the street to the right. There, two blocks, maybe three blocks, she spied naked branches reflecting winter's bareness. A tree. She shivered, adjusted her black knit cape about her shoulders. It wasn't cold, but she felt more secure with a wrap. She turned left, waited for a bright green cargo truck to clear the intersection. Green. Not the green of advertisement painted on the truck. Trees. Maybe two, huddling like embarrassed bumpkins amid the technical sophistication of the city.

The lingering smell of diesel assaulted her lungs, but on the next block the air seemed cleaner, clearer. She crossed another street, then slowed in front of an older building set back from the sidewalk, allowing space for greenery between its antique facade and the modern world. Two pines flanked neatly trimmed evergreen shrubs, patches of well-mulched dirt where flowers would bloom in the proper season. Nearer the building stood a gnarled trunk and tangled bare limbs, some tree whose age surpassed the building's. She wondered if the tree would flower in the spring, leaf out, live. She wondered why she had never noticed this spot before. She wondered why this tree struck her as strange. One thick, twisted limb on the right hung by the merest strands of wood. Two branches near the top dangled by ribbons of bark alone. A shiver rained from forehead to feet. Come spring, this tree would bear nothing. She could feel as much as see that this tree was not asleep for winter. This tree was dying. Echoes of the morning's visitors chilled her. She pulled her cape tighter.

As she walked on, pleasant and unpleasant melded into a chaos of sights and emotions. Two stately blue spruce graced the entrance to a mortuary, more alive than any of the clients inside. When she crossed the next intersection, two more conifers stood, drooping, gangly, unsightly brown. There were no dogs large enough to use these as their relief stations. These trees were dying. She continued on, aimless, taking a left after another block, wondering, wishing, reciting affirmations and entreaties to the ascended masters, to the archangels, to every spirit she could think of. She paused to determine her location; just a block to the right was the coffee shop with the incredible pastries. Perhaps a nice latte with a cheese danish. Not today. She continued, turned left after three more blocks, thinking a big circuit through the city blocks would relieve her angst. Yet everywhere she looked, she noticed signs of death and decay, exactly what her morning visitors had talked about. She felt like sitting down; she felt like throwing up; she felt like she had no idea how she felt. On their own her feet slithered to a stop. With a deep breath, she looked around and found a sight new to her.

Not one or two, but a whole plot of trees. A wrought iron fence, two brick columns, a gate open wide. A park. She shrugged, never realized such a place occupied such valuable city real estate. She would have to remember this place and oriented herself to find the straightest path between here and home. Once she noticed the landmarks, the street signs, she tried to pirouette back toward her apartment, but her feet decided otherwise. Maybe there was something to see within those wrought iron gates. Traffic was light; a quick look left and right and she crossed in the middle of the block. The trees seemed inviting, even though most had shed their leaves. She looked down the paved path past an old bike rack, past something wrapped in plastic atop a couple pipes sticking from the ground, wrapped for winter even though this winter was as warm as some of the springs she had experienced. The park called to her, invited her to traverse the paths, walk amid the trees, yet she paused. Maybe something would happen. Maybe someone would come along. A bench awaited her.

Tomorrow. Tomorrow, goddamn it! Nobody needed their damn tax returns on a weekend. Taxes could wait until tomorrow. Clients could wait until tomorrow. *She* needed something. She didn't know what; she just stared at her feet as they led her to the foyer closet. After a moment those feet nestled into their running shoes; a fanny pack was strapped to her waist. She extracted her wallet from the leather purse hanging in the closet, checked the contents, a couple twenties, debit card, ID. Into the fanny pack with it. She pulled out her green track jacket just in case a chill entered the air. When she reached the front of her building, she tied the sleeves around her waist. The air hung heavy above the pavement, temperature more appropriate to the coming spring, not the depth of winter. The first elements of the evening crowd strolled past her, heading two blocks away, where eight different ethnic restaurants lined the street. She turned right, toward the health food store. She didn't need anything but felt more comfortable with a destination in mind. Maybe she'd grab a veggie wrap for dinner. Her athletic legs soon had her in front of the establishment, peering through the windows at rows of vitamins and herbs, coolers and shelves of ingredients and prepared foods. The lady at the deli counter recognized her and waved. With a wave in return, she walked on. No appetite for food or conversation. Her mind wandered as aimlessly as her body. She had thought the books would answer her questions. Instead she had learned of underground kingdoms, eternal parties, stealing babies, pots of gold. No one could believe that crap. But, but…here they were. In her office. Talking to her. *Preaching* to her. Then those damn cards. *Divine destruction*. It had to be a coincidence that her little visitors said the same thing. Of course, if she was crazy, it made sense. All of her hallucinations would say the same thing.

Fourteen more blocks of feet slapping concrete, fourteen more blocks of rumination. Once again her morning replayed in her head. Once again her heartbeat intensified. Wake up, potty, shower, breakfast. Another potty, get dressed, ready to dive into her clients' financial worlds, sit in front of the computer, bring up the spreadsheets, check the manila folders. Then a little meditation before jumping in. Relax, close your eyes, moderate your breathing. Calm, clear. Open your eyes. Boom! Two Afro-elves or whatever they were in her office, speaking economics and ecology and entropy, taking a book off the shelf, opening it to the exact page, finding the exact quote to make their point. The book was still there, on the printer table. She *saw* it. Hallucinations don't move books. She stopped at the blinking orange crossing signal, eyes darting to the people around her, to the cars chugging by, hands clasping and releasing like clams trying to filter sanity from the air. She had the urge to walk up to a car and tap on the window and when the window rolled down, whisper, "Guess what I saw!" She could not head home, could not enter her apartment no matter how much she loved it, enter and pace back and forth like a like a compulsive animal in a too-small cage. The walk signal appeared; she crossed the street and turned right. Keep walking, just keep walking. Walk or go insane.

He laughed. He hid this bottle so his friends wouldn't find it in his liquor stash, hid it so well that he forgot about it. He laughed as the golden liquid spiraled across the bottom of the sink toward the drain in its inexorable quest to flow downhill. He remembered his college days when he would drink any cheap whisky that gave him a buzz. Now he was pouring out seventy-dollar-a-bottle scotch. He sat the empty bottle on the kitchen table to glimmer in the late afternoon sunlight that poured through his window. Three months ago he had gotten his second bonus of the year. A splurge on that bottle. A couple of hefty pours that night, then save it for the next special occasion. Three months ago. The day before he met Her. He broke his gaze from the shimmering bottle. Why was he so anxious? There was nothing in the news, nothing in his life that made him feel like a goldfish in a bowl surrounded by cats. No. He tried house cleaning; he

THE TREES ARE DYING

ended up with a tidy apartment and an empty scotch bottle and just as many jitters as when he had started. His skin felt as if covered by a colony of vindictive ants. He took a deep breath. As he had done so often these past three months when his skin crawled, he would head outside. And today his skin crawled. Crawled as if those ten thousand ants pricked every inch of his skin, each tiny leg a microscopic needle that threatened to inject insanity.

Scotch. Nightclubs. Marijuana. Poker. Sex. Video games. All the things that meant nothing anymore. He remembered the look on his friends' faces when he canceled the big ski trip. They thought he had lost his mind. Maybe he had. Lost his mind or left it somewhere? Somewhere, like a place that couldn't exist but was more real than the apartment he now stood in. A place that couldn't exist but did, where he spent a few minutes or a lifetime. Never the same. Everything changed, an earthquake tearing a fissure through his mind, through his soul. All those times he wished, he prayed that he had experienced one big hallucination. He had not had a hallucination. She wasn't a figment of his imagination. She didn't lie to him. What difference did all that "fun" he gave up make? Would the next chick he met at the bar make a difference? Make him feel any better? A few rounds of sex, a few dinners, then the boredom, then the just forgetting to call each other, and so on. And work. Hour upon hour in front of a computer, kissing the asses of some people and screwing others, making sure his name was known on the successes, blaming anyone when things went wrong. Accomplishing what? A bonus to blow on scotch or a trip to impress his friends. No matter how hard he worked, he couldn't stop the trees from dying. He walked the park—what, two, three times a week? He drove North one weekend. He drove West one weekend. Went where trees grew. Saw them lying like gnarled dominos tumbled one upon the other. Never seeing Her, but always feeling Her presence as he looked upon the desiccation. Fighting to keep his life the same but watching one thing after another in his life tumble upon the other, until he was left as—as what? Never feeling lost but never knowing what direction to take, sometimes surrendering, sometimes fighting against the inspirations, the messages in his head. He fought an urge for what—a couple weeks now, an urge to go to that airy-fairy store. So he went and what? A card. One card. One card and he literally shook. He had to get outside.

He walked through his living room, weaving through a couple months' worth of news magazines lying in various piles on the coffee table, on the end tables, on the floor. Why did he devour every story between the covers? He had no need to read magazines to know what was going on with the climate. With the economy. With the wars. With the diseases. With the lives of tens of millions, hundreds of millions, billions of people. He felt it. Deep within, almost subconscious but always popping out like one of those whack-a-mole games; for months he had tried to beat it back into hiding. Then today he went to that foo-foo shop and bought a stupid deck of cards. And the card confirmed it. Confirmed everything. And worse, pried open the tenuous lid he had put on his feelings, released the horde of emotions that had been seething within every article he read, every sight he saw. He wondered where he would be when the lightning struck, when the tower was blasted apart, when the occupants fell to their destruction. He wondered what the magazines would say, what the news channels would broadcast. If such things remained. Get outside. He was making himself sick. Go. Walk.

For no reason he grasped the casual leather lace-ups that

he had bought for standing at singles bars. As he slid his feet in, balancing against the door frame while he tied the laces, he peeked again toward the kitchen. The sunlight poured through the window, but he grabbed a jacket just in case. Pounding down the stairs, he thought of all the places these shoes had been, wondering if they would like to return for one last fling in the bars. Have a few drinks, make some time, get a phone number. It was early, but Roscoe's would be open. So would the Golden Fern. Who knows? Maybe he could find a chick that looked like Her. Yet at the bottom of the stairs, a different face flashed in his mind. A face from the morning, staring through a window. He shook his head. He could not tell why he liked that face, but he knew he would never see her again. He passed through the front door as if closing that face out of his mind. Once outside he did not hesitate. He directed his leather lace-ups to the iron gates of the park.

The Sun was behind his building, but he knew evening approached by the bustle taking hold of the street. So many people looking for ways to escape the boredom or anxiety or oppression of their lives. Men in their untucked shirts and soft leather loafers, women in their printed tops and matching pumps. Scurrying to and fro, a little shopping, an early dinner before the theater, anything, anything but look at themselves and the world around them. He felt judgment rise, breathed deep and let go. He used to be one of them. No, he was still one of them. No, there was no one of them. Not them and us, them or us. Just us. He rounded the last corner, walked the half block and stepped between the pillars. A soft smile came upon him like a comfortable sweater. Even in their winter hibernation, the calm energy of the trees was palpable to him. Except for some. He could sense the dying. Whether they were deciduous or coniferous, their pain rang out through the enclave, howled above the cacophony of city sounds to those who could hear. He stopped, absorbed the good and the bad, wishing he could affect the change, knowing that somehow he would learn to help yet realizing that everything was as it was, that it would not be preference, it would not be judgment on his part that would alter what unfolded. So, where should he go, what place in this bit of Nature within Man's madness would give him solace and inspiration? The goldfish pond? The carousel? He wished to see Her again, wished She would give him guidance, give him more than the bit of wisdom She had bestowed upon him yet knew that what She said could be enough, was enough. A gasp came to his lips. He felt a strange pull, a warmth in his heart. His breath quickened; his body tensed. Could it be Her? He looked around. Her flowing hair, her milky skin—nowhere to be seen. He stepped past the rusty old bike rack, stepped past the winterized water fountain, felt a calling from his right. He was like a puppet; his head was turned, his body followed. There, at one of the benches, a woman came to her feet. Dressed in black except for the bright white sneakers on her feet, a twenty-first century witch combining morbid fashion with healthy practicality. He stepped her way, an irrational flutter stirring within, connecting with her eyes, remembering something, somewhere, as she connected with his eyes, as they walked the few steps to where they stood face-to-face. They fell into each other's gaze, connecting, recalling, and then smiling. Self-conscious, grateful, platonic, lustful, understanding smiles crossed both faces, crossed the gap between them, crossed whole worlds and brought them together.

It was she who spoke first.

"I couldn't have wished for anything better…"

His arms extended, palms open, gliding toward her. Her hands met his, grasped in warmth and recognition. He nodded.

"I never would have believed how much I wanted this."

She nodded in return. "Where we are going?"

He gazed down the path. "Forward. Forward." They turned together, adjacent hands still entwined, looking into the depth of the park, looking beyond any aspect of physical reality. They had walked only a few places when footsteps slapped up behind them, running footsteps below an almost desperate panting breath. They turned, not knowing who approached yet not surprised when the saw her. Each extended a hand as she trotted to a stop, leaning, pulling breath into her lungs yet eager, desperate to speak.

"Okay, you might think I'm crazy," she gasped out, shivers warbling her words. "I, I mean I, I—"

He clasped her long black hand in his, a squeeze meant to empower, as his companion did the same. The couple gazed soft at their new companion, sharing their connection with the disheveled lady. She felt the breath return to her lungs. She felt her legs strengthen beneath her. A look of concern crossed her face, but when she met the eyes of the couple, a feeling of safety blossomed within her.

"I don't do stuff like this. I'm an accountant. But something really crazy is going on," she informed them, her conviction coming clear through her whisper.

The woman in black reached out, fluffed their new companion's hair from her face, then rested her hand calmly on the anxious woman's shoulder.

"I don't know why," their new companion continued, "but I have to go with you. I feel, I feel—"

"Connected?" he inquired, not hiding his grin. His new mate took up his smile as their companion continued.

"Something's wrong. Everything's wrong. I don't know…"

She sucked in a breath. "I have to find answers." She met his eyes, met her eyes. Their understanding provided strength, acceptance.

"Of course. Come with us. We want you to."

Her large brown eyes focused, taking both of them in, sensing the friendship that flowed from these strangers. She stepped toward them, had a brief wobble on her exhausted legs, accepted a supportive hug from the woman in black, who maintained complete composure as she questioned the new arrival.

"Did you see them too?"

The new companion gasped, eyes ogling toward this strange but knowing woman.

"You saw them? The little black, little black…" The woman dressed in black smiled, swung their hands to eye level.

"Mine were a bit lighter in color," she giggled out to her companion. The Black woman nodded, gave a squeeze of gratitude to the hand in front of her. The two companions turned toward the path, placing their new friend between them, hands clasped. They felt the quivers in the limbs of the new arrival.

"Did they talk? I mean, did they say something? Something that's gonna happen?"

The woman in black gazed at her male partner; he chose to answer.

"We don't know what's going on." The Black woman gave him an odd glance. "We don't know what we're supposed to do. We do know that something's happening."

"Maybe," his partner said, chiming in, "we're supposed to do it together."

"Maybe it's too late," he continued, without moroseness. "But we can always do something."

His partner gave the Black woman's hand a comforting squeeze.

"The smallest act of kindness might change the world."

The Black woman's gasp combined shock and joy.

"That's what they said to me!"

He smiled as he nudged the Black woman affectionately.

"Like she said, maybe we're supposed to do it together."

A full-throated laugh burst from their new Black friend. The couple felt her tension drain. They headed toward the path, then stopped. A Latino man stared intently their way. The Black woman turned back toward the gate. An older couple—Jewish, he still wore his yarmulke—approached hand in hand, smiling. The three paused to let them approach, feeling, knowing that still others were coming their way.

Chapter 4

SPRING

Minds boiling like tea kettles upon a roaring fire, hearts beating like leaves flapping against a gale—thought and feeling surged through each one of The Twelve. Their anticipation was topped only by their rapture, geysers of ecstasy that

Her presence always drew forth. She summoned them. Not laying some hoary task upon them, not dispensing platitudes as one would reward children. She summoned them, requested their presence, brought them together for what none of The Twelve could guess, but for what they could sense, what they could feel would be an event spectacular. Now they stood in Her radiance, radiance that enflamed heart and mind, radiance that brought hope and longing. Now each of The Twelve—Red, Brown, White, Black, Yellow, and Beyond Color—had the time to ponder Her announcement, to stir up images of what was to come, to stir their passions once more. The Twelve prided themselves on the completion of their task, on their connection with the Human race, on their blood-curdling warnings, yet gave no thought of reward. Once the seeds were sown, they spent their time in repose, alone and together, meditating for the good of all concerned, invoking Powers beyond themselves for assistance and inspiration. But never did they expect what She had announced. Never did they expect one of The Bright Ones to gather. Never did they expect to be invited to be part of the occurrence. Now as they sat cross-legged upon The Hill, twelve little bodies gritted their teeth, clenched fingers and toes as their imaginations conjured every conceivable outcome to the events that would unfold. Such was the anticipation coursing through their veins as they waited for Her to speak again, hoped for Her to speak again so they could drink in the soothing strains of Her voice and perhaps bring focus to their scattered awareness.

Silent She stood. Her eyes scanned the horizon as Her flaxen hair floated upon the wind, petals of primrose, sweet violet, and ivy fluttering in the wreath that encircled Her brow. Her flowing white dress rippled from the neckline to Her bare feet, Her trim midriff bound and buttoned within gold-threaded fabric. Her cape displayed all the flowers of spring as it billowed behind Her, and as the breeze enlivened Her garment, flower petals erupted from the cloth and floated in the air like sylvan confetti. Her slender staff stood taller than Her, grasped in Her left hand, the crystal tip flickering like a lively candle. The Twelve fought their urges to question Her, fought their urges to squirm, fought their urges to do something, anything as they sat in a semicircle about Her. They knew She would speak when appropriate and that She delayed not for selfish reasons. This made The Twelve only more anxious.

Each breath of The Twelve stretched like an entire day passing as they sat in silence upon The Hill. He of White leaned forward, caught the eyes of He of Red, who replied with a shrug. She of Black massaged the rocky ground with her feet. He and She of Yellow nudged each other, nudged their partners left and right. They hoped She would turn and address them, since the praise She laid upon them for their services showed more than gratitude. Her words acknowledged what they had always wished yet doubted in the farthest recesses of their hearts. The Twelve had served The Worlds. The Twelve *were* the potent beings of Love, Power, and Spirit they had always strived to be. Now they were summoned. More surely awaited them. Their role could not end here. This would not be The End.

She did not turn. She did not speak. She stood in stillness, a statue of pureness, yet the consuming anticipation of The Twelve was fulfilled. A shimmy through the fabric of Reality and some deep, satisfying feeling washed over He of Black, She Beyond Color, every one of them, shaking the thoughts from their heads, shaking the breath from their lungs. They rose as one, twelve pairs of eyes upon the horizon, traversing the land with their sight as She did, to see, to feel, to experience the approach. His white garment, His glowing countenance, the radiation of Love flowing from Him as He patiently stepped along the land. To His left a red robe billowing behind a women clad in red, raven-black hair billowing from Her beautiful, brooding head. To their right one armed as a warrior, lance in one hand, shield in the other, muscles ripping across the bare chest above the brilliant tartan kilt. One whose skin radiated a subtle sapphire blue. One clad in yellow robes. One of mahogany skin whose garments shimmered like the sea; one in flowing desert robes. Another, and another. The Bright Ones. The Bright Ones approached.

Their previous excitement proved minuscule. As The Twelve looked across the land, The Bright Ones approached, emerging from forest, from sky, from solid ground or gentle sea. Though the Sun neared the horizon, the landscape brightened before Them, illuminated by Their holy presence. The wave of luminosity glided across the land and brought its benevolent warmth to the twelve little beings who gasped in amazement. Gasped at the sheer power that the presence of The Bright Ones engendered. Gasped as that power flowed about and through Her, making Her radiance even more awe-inspiring. The Twelve quivered at the approach of the magnificent beings, shock atop anticipation. And then Peace poured over them like a cooling rain, enveloping them like a comforting blanket. One by one The Bright Ones mounted The Hill, greeting Her with affectionate grasp, acknowledging the twelve diminutive presences that stood there with teary eyes. Radiance covered The Hill, left, right, and above, while below the glorified Beings the ledge stood empty, waiting, before the blackness of The Cave.

THE TREES ARE DYING

Traffic, merriment, all the sounds of the city wafted through the air as resident and visitor alike enjoyed the summerlike atmosphere, the breeze carrying scents from the restaurants, from the perfumed ladies promenading down the sidewalk with friends or lovers at their sides. Even though the first spring buds had just popped upon the branches of the few trees and manicured shrubs, even though the first daffodils had just opened their blossoms, the mood was festive. Was it just the temperature? Or were there other vibrations in the air, bringing forth some cheer in the city? Two who walked down the street did not know but connected with the lighthearted mood. The crowd managed to avoid being snagged between the giddy couple's arms as they walked, fingers clasped, smiling and nodding pleasantly at the passersby. Though they avoided collision, many of the pedestrians gave more than one glance toward the happy lovers, thinking them lovestruck or intoxicated; the couple would have acknowledged the presence of a little of both. Dressed in her traditional black, a flowing ramie skirt slit on each side and sleek blouse with silver accoutrements, happy that the warmth allowed her to exchange boots for sandals, showing off her glowing red pedicure, which matched her fingernails and lipstick. A look she knew that he liked, a look he knew she displayed for him. Her clothing was as eclectic as his was drab—traditional khakis, polo shirt, athletic shoes. The contrast drew more stares from the pedestrians enjoying the night, nor were those on the sidewalk the only ones to notice. Their new circle of friends took great pleasure at teasing the couple over their differences: her fashions to his, her diminutive stature to his tall, her ample to his lanky, her demonstrativeness to his reserve. The couple took the teasing with enjoyment; all agreed that in the few months the couple had been together, a love had blossomed that few could fathom.

Just as the circle of friends had blossomed. Twelve people who lived scattered about the city—uptown, downtown, in the bedroom neighborhoods. Twelve people who had never known one another until one day last winter. Twelve people who drifted, scurried, or outright ran to a small park on the West Side, a park known for nothing notable. A park where all came and recognized one another without introduction, without analysis, without asking how or why. Now these twelve, once strangers, connected on so many levels, like a multidimensional spider's web, more intimate than lovers, except for the two walking toward their apartment, who were both kindred souls and lovers. Lovers who swung their arms and giggled through the knowledge that the glamorous, comfortable, predictable life of the city was the most fragile of illusions.

A mature man and woman, dressed to the requirements of the French restaurant a couple blocks away, huffed at the couple's antics as they pranced stiffly toward their rendezvous with truffles and champagne. The couple straightened, walked genteelly by the elder couple, then burst into laughter. They squeezed hands as she leaned against his arm.

"What a good night."

He kissed the top of her head. "A great night. *You* were great. That meditation you did, the way you led us, the connections you made for all of us, I felt, mmm, tingly, you know? I felt something there, like something was going to happen any second. I mean, it felt like those little people, like they might come—"

She nudged him with an elbow. "Who said they *didn't?*"

His step paused a moment. "Hmm…" He gave her hand an affectionate clasp. "Could be. But I don't think that's what I felt. I wouldn't call it that, like them coming. It was like energy, yeah, but I don't know, it seemed like something was coming. I mean something was going to happen, not some person show up. Or faery, or whatever they are. I mean, like some energy or force coming to me. To us."

The tip of her left eyebrow lifted. "Now that's funny. That's what I felt too. I'm not just saying that. I thought about them; I wanted them to be there with us. But now that you mention it, it was like something coming to me. Not them, but what did you call it? Something coming to me. No, not to me. Something coming for me. Like something was coming to take me somewhere." A little shiver jostled her flesh. "You know what I mean?"

He gave her hand a squeeze.

"Yep, I know what you mean. But you know what? I'm disappointed. I want to see them. I want to see what they look like, talk to them. But you know what I'm going to say."

She squeezed his arm with her free hand, a clutch of affection, connection, mutual longing.

"I know, I know. We are going to find out. I know that. They'll tell us." She gripped him tight in her resolve. "We have to get ready."

He stopped, placed his index finger to her chin, guided her lips to his.

"And you'll get us ready. You will."

She rubbed her check to his arm with a contented purr. They stepped forward. He placed his free hand over hers, which remained on his arm.

"Still, I'd like to see the little dudes."

She leaned into him, pushing him two steps to the right. "Remember what people say. 'Careful what you wish for; you might get it.'"

He laughed, kissing her head, pushing her to the left, almost running them into a gaggle of teenage girls. The girls giggled, blushed, longed for such affection themselves as he winked at them, then turned to her. "You know what I'm going to say now, don't you?"

She bumped him hard with her hip, then burst into laughter. "Yes I do!"

"Well then, I'll keep wishing for things and be happy when I get them."

She pulled him to a stop, pulled his head toward her, kissed him deeply on the lips. Through her passion he heard those girls indiscreetly whispering over the couple's antics. He didn't care; he wrapped his arms around her and completed the kiss.

"You want to see them," she said. "I know, I know, you keep saying that. But"—she pulled his arm so that he staggered against her—"you keep forgetting who *you* saw." Her grin enveloped her face, knowing that he would blush over his initial carnal longing for Her, the mysterious lady who had walked before him, whom he thought just another park patron. Blush he did.

"Why do you say I forget Her?" he whispered. His lover rubbed against him in acceptance.

"You don't talk about Her."

He let out a breath of surrender.

"I know. But it's not about Her, you know? You had little people. They scared you. I had Her, and what happened to me, well—"

She raised his hand to her lips.

"Whatever happened made you a new man. The man I love."

He rubbed the back of his hand against her cheek.

"All I could think of was how hot She looked, what a good f—" He stopped, crimson blush covering his face like a frantic sunburn.

THE TREES ARE DYING

She pulled him to a stop, pulled his lips toward hers.

"She's beautiful. But I'm the one who has you."

He smiled and completed the kiss. She wrapped her arm around his and led them toward their apartment. Cross one street, turn right, cross another, turn left, walk down three buildings. Home. He ascended the steps, following her, his hands caressing her hips to suggest his desire, she giggling at the attention. As he sighted their apartment door, a warmhearted thought popped into his head.

"You know what's funny?"

"The people on the sidewalk?" she quipped.

He grinned as he pulled the key from his pocket.

"Well, them, yeah. But you know what else is funny?" His right hand turned the key as his left hand swung open the door and flipped on the light in one graceful gesture. They entered a living room comprising an eclectic blend of furniture, accessories, and mementos of two lives blended together for happiness, not appearance. She kicked off her sandals and plopped onto the middle of the couch. He unlaced his shoes and sat to her right. She reclined, resting her head on the arm of the couch, her feet in his lap.

"So what's funny?"

"Well," he began as his hands wrapped firmly about her feet, kneading the evening walk from her tired soles, eliciting a contented sigh. "For one thing, we don't say, 'my apartment' anymore. We say, 'our apartment.' Like tonight, when you said we got rid of those old lamps from 'our apartment.' Did you notice that?"

She gave a languid smile, melting to the touch of his hands upon her ankles. "I'm glad you noticed."

"It's funny," he continued, "all these things that have

happened since we met. Move in together, get all these friends, and, and..." She couldn't tell whether he was struggling for the right words or struggling to admit all that had transpired.

"And connect with energies from beyond this world?" she offered, knowing that "energies" was a much more palatable word for him. He took a foot in each hand, firmly pressed on the instep, eliciting a purr.

"'Energies.' Yeah, I guess you could put it that way. But that's not exactly what I'm thinking. You know, look at everything that's happening right now. All the, well, all the shit happening in the world. And what happens to us? We meet each other. We—"

"Fall in love."

He commenced stretching her toes. "We start all this spiritual stuff—"

"You started. I've been doing it a long time."

"We connect to, well, they're not just energies."

"You mean Her."

He stared out the window into the dark sky, as if just the mention of Her had altered his state of consciousness. She watched him for a couple minutes, then wiggled her feet to call him back. He looked toward his lap, apparently having forgotten what he had been doing, and resumed the massage.

"Yeah. Her. And those little ones that you saw. That our friends saw. And how these meditations, well, charge us up when you lead them. And how I know things—"

"We know things."

"Before they happen. All this stuff. Something's up. And then I have to ask, why me? Why you? Why our friends? Why the twelve of us?"

She took a deep breath. He had asked these questions before, never in animosity or regret, as if each time he asked, he gained more acceptance, more understanding, even though he always answered when anyone else inquired with the same line.

"Someone I love very much always says this: 'We'll find out. We'll know.'"

He lifted a foot to his mouth and kissed her big toe. She giggled.

"What if," he pondered, "what if tonight is the night we find out?"

She raised her head to meet his eyes.

"Do you *know* something?"

He slipped his fingers between her toes, providing a stretch that pushed her near ecstasy. He kissed her other foot, then enfolded both feet between his hands.

"No, I don't. I'm just thinking…"

"Sometimes your thinking is a lot more than you think."

He shot her a sideways glance; she grinned at her twist on words. They sat silent for several moments.

"What could it be?" he finally asked, barely above a whisper.

"We will know," she replied equally as gently.

"And now?" he asked with no hidden agenda.

She bent her knee, positioning the ball of her foot upon his thigh, with grace gliding along his khaki pants. "And now, let's forget all of this stuff. Forget all of it and do something completely different." Her caresses triggered the desired effect. He pressed her feet to his cheek, stood, and helped her rise. They walked hand in hand to the bedroom.

The night was young; they took advantage of every minute, one peak of pleasure after another until they fell into each other's arms, exhausted, satiated, floating on a level of bliss that could only be called spiritual. A physical, emotional, mental nirvana that grew with each warm breath that flowed gently across each other's skin, with each heartbeat within the other's chest. Off they passed from their physical world, eyes closed, senses abated, off to what they called the dream world, the place where their minds could operate without inhibition; sometimes it seemed fanciful, sometimes meaningful, but never a place they considered real. Just fantasies of a mind releasing the tension of the day, embracing hidden desires and fears. Certainly not the gateway to another dimension.

One more minute in front of the computer screen, sagging eyes willing themselves open to finish this spreadsheet two days ahead of schedule. No, not ahead of schedule. This client wasn't salivating for his tax returns; he could have waited a month of Mondays since he would be sending in a hefty check. No. She had to keep her commitment to herself. Finish the spreadsheet today because *she* had committed to that. Integrity. Integrity had become a principle of life to her, ever since…she breathed into the tension that encrusted her shoulders after a mere ten minutes of calculations. She knew that was not the source of her fatigue. She focused on the screen, typed in expense entries for the last two days of the year, watched the formulas do their magic to produce a fat, four-digit sum in red numbers. She had done her part; the sum had been five digits when she had begun. She saved the file, rotated her shoulders, and again felt the droop in her eyes. Her tiredness was not the tension in her shoulders. Her tiredness was not the exhaustion she felt after the morning's ten-mile run. Her tiredness was not the mental fatigue she felt after a day of double-entry bookkeeping and

Generally Accepted Accounting Principles. The evening had been more than inspirational. Every time she gathered with her new friends, the energy poured through her, enlivening, uplifting. No. Something called her to her bed, summoned her to her pillow, a force that glided over her like a winged fairy spreading pixie dust. She laughed out loud as she approached her bathroom. Not fairy. Faery. The sight crossed her mind again as she performed her evening toilette, changed into her cool silken pajamas. They weren't watching. They weren't anywhere near her. Just like her friends had experienced—one appearance and they were gone. She grinned over the memory, over her attachment to her new friends. A young Black lesbian whose best friends were an elderly orthodox Jewish couple. They even referred to her as "their girl." And she loved it. She paused to observe herself in the mirror. All the craziness that had happened since… she would have chalked the entire incident up to overwork had she not found her new circle of friends. She turned down her thin cotton blanket, fluffed her pillow, but turned away from her bed. As she had been doing every evening, she sat in the corner of her room, her sacred space, meditating before a single candle flame, drinking in all the positives that had been flowing to her for the past several months. Then she prayed, prayed in a manner personal, prayed for the Earth, prayed for Earth's inhabitants, knowing that those inhabitants were in peril, from the smallest protozoa to the largest creatures of land, sea, and air. Including humans. Especially humans. She leaned toward the flame, blowing it forward with the commitment to return to this spot again the next night, and the next night after that. Her practices calmed her, yet as she pulled the soft sheets to her neck, she could not let go of a feeling of anticipation, a feeling that something—good or not—was going to happen. She lay on her back for a few minutes, wondering about life, about what was beyond the dimensions that she spent her days in, what lived in those dimensions besides Black faeries. Her musings did not last long; the tiredness took over like a cloud blotting out the Sun. She turned on her side, curled her knees toward her waist, and closed her eyes.

Like a humble tide encroaching from a calm sea, night spread over the city. A shop closed, a restaurant served its last pizza or chateaubriand of the day. People abandoned the sidewalks, taking refuge in their domiciles or departing for their dwellings in the suburbs. Sound diminished; if there were night creatures about, their voices would become obvious. And twelve who lived among the concrete and traffic and activity found sleep upon them, yet closed their eyes in joyous anticipation or doleful trepidation, anticipating, expecting, knowing that something awaited them this night. Twelve strangers who shared an undeniable experience, who found each other in a minuscule enclave of Nature among the artifacts of modern civilization, who bonded, chatted, visited, texted throughout the week, who spent every Saturday evening together in meditation, exploration, and camaraderie. Whether their bedtime ritual was passionate, holy, or mundane, each closed his or her eyes with the feeling that something awaited. Yet much more stirred in the diverse levels of Reality than human intuitions could reveal. They did not know that others, across the home they called Earth, others were responding to a call, answering a feeling, acknowledging that Something Greater had touched them and now commanded their attention, their presence metaphysical.

All of them, touched by some life event they could not explain yet could not deny. Time, distance had no effect; the rules of the physical had no role within these events. All were called. All responded.

No sound, no twitch, no sign at all that the twelve small bodies were animate. No amount of knowledge, no amount of wisdom, no amount of enlightenment prepared The Twelve for the drama unfolding about them. Afraid to move, afraid to speak, afraid to call notice to themselves, here they sat, not just among The Bright Ones but also in an honored place in front of the assembly, an assembly that had not occurred for a time that the humans would have counted as millennia. They might have thought they were being patronized, their stature making sight of the unfolding event difficult, nay, impossible. Then twelve of The Bright Ones escorted them to the front of the gathering where She bestowed upon them the accolades of the assembled. The work they did, crossing barriers of time, space, dimension to bring a message, a warning to a planet collapsing upon itself, to seed a pitiful few with tidings of demise and possibility of hope. Bridging the worlds was not without risk; The Bright Ones had determined that earthly fable and myth, attendant to creed and country, made their own appearance either threatening or infatuating. Thus The Bright Ones sent The Twelve, and The Twelve succeeded beyond expectation. For this they gained the cusp of the panorama unfolding below them, a sight nearly as magnificent, nearly as terrible as the gathering of The Bright Ones themselves.

And The Twelve knew that the spectacle below would

provide the remaining answers, enlighten and direct mortal and immortal alike Below; on that skinny ledge thought barely wide enough to hold them, humans sat in front of the mysterious opening. Had The Twelve blinked? Had they collectively looked aside? At one moment they gazed upon a skinny ledge. The next moment, humans, 144 of them, sat comfortable in a friendly gathering. Humans who understood not what they faced, humans with no conception of what lived in the inky blackness, if the term "live" applied to The Oracle. Yet wonder congealed with their anxious stoicism; each of The Twelve smiled, inward and outward. One hundred and thirty-two of those humans had met a pair of The Twelve, and now The Twelve relished the fact that all of those humans had responded, had found one way or another to assemble here in front of The Cave. Still puzzle remained, for of those humans gathered there were twelve that none of The Twelve could recognize. None of The Twelve had made appearance before those twelve humans, and The Twelve could find no explanation for the extraneous attendees. Finally She of Brown lifted her head, caught the eye of the Bright One closest to her, a male figure of radiant strength and wisdom. He smiled; she felt His enrichment through her heart and knew. She of Brown turned to He of Yellow, nudged him, whispered her question to him, pointed to one then another of the unforeseen humans, including one who stretched his arm to the ground so his black-clad companion could rest against his side, against his polo shirt and khakis. One by one The Twelve realized so much more had transpired, currents and undercurrents flowing to bring about some spectacular happening.

The excitement of The Twelve did not permeate the human gathering. One hundred forty-four sat calm, casual, chatting with their friends or coolly observing the wonders in front of them, as if the happening were a common occurrence. Not a one of the humans raised a voice in question or wonderment. Not a one frighted or rejoiced at the convocation before The Cave. A person here, a person there noticed attendees beside them, making casual introductions to persons from around the human planet, never registering that somehow conversations were understood upon The Hill that would never have been grasped upon the Earth. Each human reacted in his or her own peaceful way, as if some spell of harmony had enfolded them in gentle acceptance.

She smoothed her flowing ramie skirt upon her lap and leaned contentedly against his chest. Something tickled the edge of her consciousness, her skirt, his pants, walking, walking. But the thought could not emerge amid the other stimulations that confronted her. He chatted with their friends around them and even made acknowledgement to a tall slender man on their left, a short, stout couple on their right, people outside their friend group. Their friends…another thought tried to emerge, something about them being together, a quiet time followed by tea and conversation. Again the idea could not be pursued, for on the hillside a sight called her full attention. There was no doubt who She was, no need for him to point Her out. There She was, sitting in Her radiance, now dressed as a princess rather than a virago. There was no surprise at seeing the two small beings that had appeared one day in her meditation space, now sitting on the hillside above this strangely dark cave. They looked like children, grinning like ones who knew a secret to be revealed. Surprise came in seeing ten other little people assembled upon The Hill, ten others seated in front of a glowing congregation of Beings that were as radiant as She who had appeared to her partner, who had jostled his mundane life and propelled him to seek what awaited beyond.

She shifted her head against his side, his arm extended behind her, making a comfortable rest for her back. The feeling was warmth, wonder, the excitement of something to be revealed, almost like a child's Christmas, looking over a stack of brightly wrapped presents bound up in curly ribbons. He ceased his conversing and faced forward, as did others, finally opening to the prospects of what might unfold. The little groups buzzed with subdued excitement, soft laughter, soft words, feelings of contented expectancy. Yet what all looked upon with anticipating eyes offered no clue as to what would be unveiled—an inky void in the side of a hill, black, featureless, topped by some of the most remarkable Beings they had set eyes on.

As if someone had thrown a cosmic switch, conversation ceased. One hundred forty-four pairs of human eyes turned toward the depthless black upon the hillside. A shimmer, a fold in the darkness, barely perceptible, then another. Eyes widened, a gasp snuck out here and there as the ominous sounds and imperceptible sensations within The Cave continued. Twitches, shivers overtook the humans as some form took hold within the formlessness. A heave of iciness roiled across the ledge. Human huddled with human in an intimacy birthed in occult suspense. Theirs were the first human eyes that gazed upon The Cave; theirs were the first human eyes that gazed upon The Oracle. Forgotten were The Twelve; forgotten were The Bright Ones. Now 144 human bodies tasted the uncensored power of The Underworld. They were not alone. The emanating power fluttered the chests of The Bright Ones, an impact so deep, so awesome that glowing bodies dimmed and sturdy bodies swayed. The magnificent Beings responded, a wave of energy coursing through the air like an avalanche, pouring forward toward the summoned upon the ledge, pouring through The Twelve with such force that not even they could maintain composure. He of Black swallowed, hard. She of White quivered, as did both He and She of Brown. He of Red placed hand to stomach; She of Red placed hand to mouth. Anticipation and power reached a crescendo. The generous calming hands of The Bright Ones came to rest upon each of The Twelve's shoulders. Each small body rose as if lifted from the land. The humans positioned themselves for ultimate attention upon the that which rose from the abyss, bolstered by the benign energies of The Immortals. Pregnant twilight covered the land. And now all, regardless of position, felt the peering eyes of The Oracle upon them, peering through atmosphere and rock, piercing heart, mind, and soul. Sounds of uncertainty, fear grew from the human assemblage. A shared cringe overtook The Twelve. Even The Bright Ones wavered, feeling the dread power of The Underworld emanating from The Cave below.

Human eyes looked upon the foreboding apparition, dread pouring upon them like a tsunami of invisible hornets. Gone were the sounds of confusion and dismay; neither speech nor exclamation found escape from mortal awareness. The couple attained even tighter contact; their friends shimmied closer in ineffective defense against the power that stared at them. The two opalescent eyes shook every thought, every movement from their consciousness, demanding such attention as to allow no turning away. Nor could eyes be closed. Friend packed with friend; not even the radiance of The Bright Ones could now be felt. The consuming presence from The Underworld demanded all, received all. The faintest hopes arose in the assembled— hopes for question answered, for direction set forth—yet the overwhelming presence allowed none to voice such hopes as barely a thought could manifest. A quiver passed through all present. Whatever hopes emerged, whatever knowledge desired, now was when it would come forth.

> The Oracle spoke:
> "Where sea kisses seeming solid shore,
> Which one rocks the highest?
> Lamentations rise above the tremors,
> Through fire and ruin heads bow to Death."

The icy words broke the paralytic spell, piercing the assembled like steel through flesh, ripping pleasant expectation and simplistic hope from all present. Mortals scratched heads or rubbed chins in bewilderment. Inquisitive looks, hushed questions passed between those populating the ledge, now set free of entrancement. The Bright Ones stirred, maintaining their stoic empowerment yet unable to suppress their own signals of bafflement and apprehension. The Twelve simply winced, ducking their heads, averting their eyes. Dread quiet sat upon The Hill as all wondered what would come forth next. He of Brown, She Beyond Color, He of Red passed the slightest whisper between them at the aloof, ominous words. No acknowledgement of the those present, and no demand of respect from any present, The Oracle simply spewed forth a proclamation incomprehensible. To most. Yet below and above, an inkling of understanding blossomed, here in one human, there in one of The Ascended, tiny seeds sprouting in the darkness of The Oracle's obscurity. The couple broke their grip; she looked to her lover, seeking what she knew not. His eyes remained fixed upon The Cave. He felt his lover's hand upon his shoulder, acknowledged her gesture, turning toward her with a glance that brought a gasp. The beginnings of dread unfolded in her. He knew. He understood the obscure lines. He wrapped his fingers about her hand, gave a squeeze of support. She leaned against him, seeking comfort, assurance, realizing that like her, most present had no idea about what had been spoken. Yet some did, here and there among the gathered, and he was one of those who grasped within the proclamation something dark and terrible. She wished to ask him as she perceived the feelings from above, from The Twelve, from The Bright Ones, and shivered. The urge came upon her to turn away, to run from what had begun as a festival and now seemed to be a funeral. Yet she could not turn away, none could break the vice grip that The Oracle maintained on those assembled.

> The Oracle spoke:
> "Small, yet great its grasp,
> Unseen makes much undone.
> Flesh no match for whispers in the wind,
> No matter which direction, Oblivion."

Subtlety no longer reigned. Human emotions sprouted among the 144 humans upon the ledge. A moan, a curse, even a wretch, a gag emerged as the words of The Oracle erupted from The Cave. He maintained his eye lock upon the specter in the darkness, but gave a tight hug to his mate. Their Black friend quivered behind them as the realization of The Oracle's words sunk into her lanky frame. Their other friends—the couple from the suburbs, the undocumented gardener, the elderly Jewish couple, the devout Muslim, the Christian couple and their teenage son—they had yet to understand the words, yet they felt the force upon body and soul. Across the ledge human realization began to grasp what emanated from the denizen of The Underworld. She brushed back her hair, wrapped her arm around her loving partner, touching his cheek, guiding his head against hers in the most comforting gesture she could manage, aware that he fathomed The Oracle's meaning, feeling his breath heave like the bellows of a foundry. She sensed the desire of The Bright Ones to deliver aid in light of the severity, bring comfort against those disturbing utterances. She needed no communication to know The Bright Ones could no more lift a foot than could the humans, humans struggling to reach calm through whatever techniques they knew before the appearance of The Twelve, or whatever techniques they had learned after their lives were upended.

> The Oracle spoke:
> "Like dogs aroused,
> Pissing on what sustains them,
> All assert their greatness.
> Banners fly high before they fall."

Few there were who did not grasp the meaning. The humans felt the crush upon them—not physical in cause, yet malignantly physical in effect. Tears flowed. Shivers ran rampant. All desired the cessation of the moment, the end of such thought, the end of such feeling, escape from those ineffable eyes that glared at them, glared through them. If any could have raised a voice, he, she would have begged for an end.

> The Oracle spoke:
> "A sun upon the Earth,
> Its light a flower of destruction.
> Death rides forth like unkept wind.
> None recall the reason for its blossom."

THE TREES ARE DYING

The words scorched the assembled like a fiery tsunami. Stomachs turned; moans echoed from the rocky hillside. She buried her face in his chest; he kissed the top of her head, his tears plinking upon her raven-colored hair. The undocumented gardener vomited; the elderly woman lost her bladder. They were not the only ones to react thus. He looked across the crowd, though his feelings alone were enough to sense the terror of the gathered. In hope he raised his eyes above The Cave, to The Bright Ones assembled, found Her face, luminescence paled, breath apparent. The shiver of his spine rattled his teeth. Even They felt the impact; even They were frightened.

> The Oracle spoke:
> "Flowers where winter's snow should lay,
> Untimely beauty betrays what is hidden.
> Not seen, not sensed, despair blossoms.
> From the North, poison flows."

The humans assembled heaved a sigh as one, a disheartened chorus of lament. The Twelve huddled against each other, heads bowed, afraid to gaze upon the humans they had met in hope and love, frightening them only for motivation, wishing for them a future of happiness and peace. The couple embraced as if such a future would soon be extinguished. Their Black friend leaned against him, seeking solace in a way that somehow brought a warmth to both. Again his eyes rose above the specter of Darkness, rose above The Cave, focused on Her, and this time She sensed his glance. Their eyes linked, and in spite of the terrible utterances, in spite of the Darkness upon them, in spite of the terror seething around them, he heard in his mind Her gentle voice and the last words she had uttered on that crazy fateful day in the park. Warmth grew. Both his partner and his friend sensed the energy unfolding within him. They pressed him close, connecting, drawing a strength from him that rose from unknown depths, kindling a brightness in their own hearts, sensing the icy fear soften in the unfolding glow.

> The Oracle spoke:
> "Where once green thrived and creature roamed,
> Fever creeps upon land.
> Not for animal or human are bellies filled,
> None there are that can eat the dust."

Mortal and beyond mortal lost capacity to vocalize; not even a whimper escaped. Yet his silence was not of fear or overwhelm. That light within brightened; that warmth kindled into a subtle internal fire. He peered across the ledge, across the assembled humans, most of the heads bowed in terror. But not all. Over there, a Nordic-looking woman, the Valkyrie type, her blue eyes glowed in subtle power. There an Asiatic man, there a man of Africa, there a woman as plain as vanilla ice cream—each seemed to shine. As if it were a sound beneath perception, he felt a something begin to vibrate, to energize, a something rising from a few that rippled out to the many. His eyes shot toward The Bright Ones, toward Her. Her face radiated expectant pleasure.

> The Oracle spoke:
> "More and more, as if land endless,
> Till nowhere feet find to stand.
> Shoulder to shoulder, room not to breathe,
> What else would come but hate?"

His partner threw her arms around him, pressed her cheek to his chest, sharing her heart, her soul, her stability. Their Black friend leaned her head to his shoulder, declaring a bond, a oneness such as might be found among travelers having traversed a rough sea. His arms extended to both, enfolded them in a gesture that transcended togetherness. The Black woman straightened, breathed deep, her muscles flexing in empowerment. His partner knew that he grasped it all and in that awareness projected her power to him, finding in that gesture a power of her own. As did their gardener friend. As did their Christian friends. As did all of their circle, as did each cluster of companions assembled upon the ledge forming twelve circles of light like a burst of sunlight falling upon a sudden spring day. Strength blossomed upon the ledge, as if the darkness germinated seeds that now rose toward the illumination, seemingly fragile, the beginnings of a mighty forest. And so the forests responded, a metaphysical union between the denizens of the forest and those before The Cave. Oak, baobab, sycamore, banyan, sequoia, teak—the spirits of the great trees descended upon the gathering, inviting the 144 to rise with them and face the future. Within The Cave a shimmer, a ripple of light and then darkness. Infinite darkness. The Oracle returned from whence it came. Light returned to the land.

Across the ledge woman and man shook the heaviness from their brows, breathed the tension from their shoulders, rose with the power emanating from the land as if mighty roots nourished each of them. At first they were silent as the forest sentinels; none could put description to their experience. But being human they craved bonding, a chance to acknowledge one another, first by glance, then by touch, then by open affection, hugging each other in congratulations for weathering the deluge of somber utterances spoken by The Oracle, for finding the strength to stand tall. In spite of the fatal predictions, in spite of the enormous consequences, each human sensed a glimmer of hope always within reach no matter how occluded. This hope rose from the hearts of all assembled—accountant, engineer, farmer, homemaker, father, mother, peasant, princess—regardless of where they were domiciled across the planet they called Earth. Though the enormous power of The Underworld had quaked all pretense out of the humans present, each woman and man present felt the light rise within, a light born of a single, simple declaration that brought retort to the dread prophecies. Knowing that the humans had grasped both the dread and the aspiration, The Bright Ones, The Twelve descended from their perches above The Cave to mingle with the mortals.

The couple faced each other, connected in slow embrace and soulful kiss. In their circle of friends, hugs passed one to the other and back again, all of them realizing the significance of their weekly gatherings, of their communications, their favors to one another, their camaraderie, and how those encounters had prepared them for what had happened, what was yet to come. The friends laughed, recounted their experiences with the small beings they recognized on The Hill as each remembered his or her personal encounters with The Twelve, visitations overwhelming. Two of those diminutive beings approached. A woman dressed in black, once terrified of these two, flicked her hair aside and felt a warmth enter her bosom like a whirlpool of softness, blooming into a smile upon her face. Before, they scared her worse than inserting a bare foot into a shoe and finding a spider. Now as she looked upon these two, she welcomed them like a pair of comfortable slippers, warm, personal, succoring. Those two returned her smile, each taking a hand, squeezing an energy sublime into every aspect of her being. He stepped to his partner's side, curious to see these Otherworld beings she had so much talked of. Those two of The Twelve, one a subtle red and one subdued yellow, beamed at him, and as he placed his hand on his partner's shoulder, he felt the enormous loving power, power flowing into her, through her, into him, a blessing indescribable. Her two visitors moved on, reconnecting with the other mortals whose lives they had upended. The couple relaxed into a side-by-side hug, satiated by the harmonious energy, thinking never could they feel better, when a bliss encompassed them beyond their comprehension. Light bathed them as if a star had descended to hover over their heads. The couple melted in the radiance, would have flowed to the ground had not some equal power upheld them. Like a flower unfolding to the sun, their faces turned upward to that sublime power radiating above them, about them, through them. A blink of their eyes and the light faded, revealing an ivory-colored staff, a milk white hand holding the light-tipped rod. The chills that rippled through him were matched only by the chills that rippled through his partner. Both knew She had come. Eyes drifted shut as the couple embraced even more deeply, and when they looked again, She stood to face them. Yet it was not he that first received Her acknowledgement. She fluffed aside a lock of jet-black hair that fell about his partner's face and pressed Her cheek to hers, the two clasping in a deep hug, mortal and Bright One embracing as old friends do. Only then did She rise upon tiptoes and plant a kiss upon his cheek in a dainty yet poignant gesture. With Her staff She nudged him closer to his partner, then notched it in the crook of Her elbow so She could clasp a hand of each of the lovers, sealing the connection between the two, sealing the connection between Her and them. Both looked upon The Bright One through tears of contentment and thanksgiving. He grinned at Her, once the object of his lust, now something grandly beyond mortal pleasure. She sensed his desire to tap Her immortal wisdom.

"Your words I would love to hear." Her words lilted like kittens sleeping in a ball.

He took a breath, not of apprehension but of acceptance, of understanding, his eyes casting about the ledge, seeing Bright Ones conversing with humans, one here, one there, as it dawned upon him that in each human cluster, one member had been selected by one of The Bright Ones, he being the chosen one of his group, She being the one to make the connection. At the same time, those of The Twelve caught his eye as they mingled with other groups, with his own group, two by two, the black members embracing their Black friend, the one of red returning with a male of the same hue, visiting the Christian couple—and so on with all The Twelve, even the two whose color he could somehow not describe. The circles themselves then garnered his attention. Skin, clothing, voice brought forth the realization that the assembled came from different parts of his world, different peoples, different races, all joined together in this infatuating presence yet all present to hear the prophecies of unrelenting disaster. His friends gathered to absorb both the goodness and knowledge emanating from Her. The two diminutive ones, one skinned a ruddy red, one a golden yellow, the two who had appeared to his lover, returned. He looked at his friends and recognized their differences in color, in age, in gender, belief. The selection could not have been random, a question he wished to ask, a question among many rising in his thoughts. So much to be answered, so much to be asked, but the question of most importance was the first for him to ask.

"Why me?"

A subtle lift of Her left eyebrow, a gesture both challenging and inquisitive. His partner gave him an affectionate squeeze, which he returned unabashedly. His friends chuckled; those behind him patted his back. The gestures were not unnoticed, yet he wanted to hear Her words, Her thoughts, Her answer.

"Really. Why me instead of someone else? Like her. She did the spiritual stuff," he inquired with another hug for his partner. "What did I do? I hung around in bars, picked up chicks, played poker, drank a lot, swore a lot, especially at work. I—" He was silenced by the touch of Her fingers to his lips.

"Is too much being asked of you?" Her smile betrayed Her knowledge of him, reinforced by the stifled giggle of his partner, the conspicuous chuckles of his surrounding friends. A touch of crimson crossed his cheeks, not embarrassment about the question, nor the answer, but rather about the honor, the responsibility bestowed upon him. A realization bloomed within, a knowing that what unfolded here before The Cave was not mere histrionics; this event, the words spoken, the shape and color of future's unfoldment brought a responsibility almost insurmountable. Yet the simple realization that he was called brought empowerment beyond the mere human. Empowerment to the point where even humor was available.

"Is too much being asked of me?" He leaned toward Her, his smile betraying both amusement and challenge. "Can someone tell me what is being asked of me?"

His friends—even his lover—shivered at his ostensible insolence. She answered with perfect silence, poised stillness, complete composure within the glow of Her radiant staff. He sensed the embrace of his lover at his side, affection and affirmation, reflected in the presence of friends about them. He focused upon Her before him as the little female with the pale of red came to Her side, joined by the short male of yellow. His eyes looked to the darkness of The Cave as a chill vibration brought back the memory of the despondent utterances from below. His eyes surveyed the other groups, the other gatherings of friends who stood about grouped around Bright Ones and members of The Twelve. Within each circle one stood out, a human whom friends surrounded, just like him, yet each different, a man here, a woman there, different skin colors, different costumes. His recognized his own clothing, the standard khaki pants and polo shirt, the wardrobe he lived in, the wardrobe so typical of many males of his land. Once more his gaze swept the other groups. Different clothing, different skin, different voices, different genders, yet each one as common as him in their own way, in their own land. As each face appeared to him, as each person registered within his awareness, his breath fluttered at the immensity of the happenings before The Cave. An immensity that included him, incorporated him as one of the foci, one of the points around which what was happening revolved, what would happen would revolve. And he felt small. Not the small of withdrawal, not the small of fright, but the small of humility. For a moment he wondered if indeed too much was being asked of him. His answer came from the presence of those around him: his partner, his friends, She of Red, He of Yellow, Her. He blinked, blinked again, not because he thought his eyes deceived him but to clarify the vision that now appeared, strands of light glimmering, pulsing, throbbing among those gathered before The Cave. The strands connected him with all, human and beyond human, a scintillating web that not only joined those present but also stretched in every direction to infinity, a geodesic light show that brought tears flowing. A smile crept upon him as he breathed out the tension, breathed in the feelings surrounding him, flowing to him, a feeling he could only describe as Love. Eyes closed, a deep breath, and when he opened his eyes again, She stood there, they stood there. He knew that whatever transpired, all was well.

"You understand." Her face radiated below Her flaxen hair. A puff of wind fluttered Her cloak; the assembled humans fluttered as flower petals issued from Her garment and drifted through the air. He was distracted for but a second.

"I hope I can do my part." He kissed his partner on the head as She raised Her staff above him.

"Those chosen become those qualified." Sounds of contentment rose from the friends as he bowed before Her gesture, then straightened to grasp Her staff, a display of strength and courage to proceed. Tears flowed from the humans. The diminutive red being extended her hand to him, which he clasped as if holding hands with a child. She of Red took no offense, nodding in approval and squeezing her palm to his. He of Yellow likewise extended a hand, playfully squeezing his hand with a strength well beyond stature. The friends came close, surrounding the Immortals in a communal hug. From the tip of Her staff came an energy that poured through them like a gentle breath from The One Beyond All. The feeling, the light overpowered them, an overpowering that brought joy unspeakable as all felt themselves melting into unformed, unencumbered Bliss. Through the unimaginable sensations, Her voice lilted toward them.

"In all that you encounter, in all that you face, remember but one thing: the slightest act of kindness might change the world."

Then as gently as a baby falling off to sleep, each one let go of consciousness, let go of identity, let go of self and surrendered to the Greatness that enveloped them. All turned to silent, nurturing Darkness.

The smell of brewing coffee wafts passes his nostrils; the gurgling of the pot informs his ears that morning has come, an aromatic, harmonious call to awaken much more congenial than a blaring alarm. Though it is Sunday, he still wishes to rise at his selected time so that morning rituals sacred and profane are maintained. He rolls over to where morning light shines gently through the curtains, morning's illumination caressing his closed eyes with welcoming light. Against his back her body glows with its own appeal, soothing warmth against his flesh, bringing the thought of rolling over and wrapping his arms about her in delicious sleep. But coffee is calling, morning light is calling, his bladder is calling. A little stretch, a toss aside of the covers, he rises to address the necessities. He slips on a pair of flip-flops, his at-home footwear, and glances at the clock. Six-thirty, a few minutes past sunrise. His eyes gaze upon his mate, curled up fetus-style, breathing softly, oblivious to his movements. Good, he tells himself—he wants her to enjoy all the restful sleep she can consume. From the bathroom door hang two bathrobes; he dons his after addressing his bodily needs, then he drapes hers upon the bed as he passes by.

In the kitchen he pulls two cups from the cupboard, places them on the countertop. He fills one to the brim, again the aroma rising to his nostrils, triggering the first of coffee's arousing effects. Something sloshes around in his sleepy consciousness, some idea, some remembrance, some bits and pieces of a dream. An image here, an image there as he takes his first sip. He quietly slides a chair out, places his cup on the kitchen table, and sits. What was he dreaming? It was pretty intense; that's all he recalls as he takes another sip. Outside the window a sparrow zooms by in the morning light, then another. The coffee achieves its desired effect—he wakes up, begins to function, begins to think again. A smile accepts his next sip. Her. He dreamed of Her. He closes his eyes and recalls. Yes, Her face, Her voice. What was She doing? Who was at his side? Not Her; he could see Her face in front of him. In front of them. Them! A dream: him, his lover, and Her. Another sip of coffee, another. His cell phone is on the counter, charged, waiting. Read the news? Check email? No, not now. Something, something to remember…his cup approaches empty. Time to wake up his lover, his partner, his soul mate. With a cup of coffee? Or maybe slip back into bed beside her, massage her thighs, nibble the back of her neck, wrap a leg around her. His arousal captures his attention for a moment; this would be a perfect morning for making love. But…he takes the last sip of coffee, his eyes peering into the mug. A mute, black mug, one that she bought him when she moved in, now looking like some tunnel, some cave, some portal into the Darkness. He places the mug on the table with shaking hand. He remembers.

For one minute, for five, for thirty he sits at his kitchen table, eyes pointed outside, comprehending the sunlight, the tiny birds flitting by. His ears open to the sounds of the city below, a city emerging from its own slumber. All is the same. All goes on. Yet what awaits those cheeky little birds that alight on his windowsill? What awaits those motorists who travel past his apartment, on their way to whatever destination calls? What awaits them all? The words from The Cave undulate from one ear to another, silent yet louder than when he first heard them. The waves of angst, of fear that flowed from The Hill once more wash upon his person. Faces return to his memory: their friends, others, The Twelve, The Bright Ones, Her. His chest sinks under the magnitude of his memory. His feet tingle, itch. He kicks off his flip-flops and feels the cold linoleum on his soles. And then a warmth. A warmth rises from below, kindling an energy within his legs, his hips, his torso, his entire body. A pleasant, constant, strong energy. Images of trees permeate his awareness. Strong, reliant, steadfast yet flexible, pliant. Able to bend in the wind and return upright, unfazed, unshaken. The image of Her fills his mind. Something She said, something She said before, something important, vital, at the verge of his knowing. He breathes deep and relaxes. He will come to know.

His cup empty, he takes it to the sink for a rinse, then rinses his mouth with lukewarm faucet water. His eyes wander toward his phone; the urge comes upon him to view his electronic connection with the world. No. Not now. His desire returns to his partner, for reasons physical, mental, emotional, spiritual. He can't wait to tell her of his dream. He can't wait to make love to her. He can't wait to just be there with her, person to person, heart to heart, soul to soul. He grasps the coffeepot. Three-quarters of a cup. He goes to the refrigerator. One-quarter cup of vanilla almond milk. He reaches to the corner of the countertop, then to the drawer beneath him. One slight teaspoon of raw sugar. Her morning libation assembled, he carries it to the bedroom and places it on her nightstand.

He sits at the bottom of the bed, pausing to appreciate the king-sized futon they purchased the day they moved in together. His hands slip under the covers and find her feet, warm as bread fresh out of the oven. A hand wraps around each; a thumb presses firm into each insole, then again, again. Her body shifts; a welcoming hum sounds from her closed lips. He leans over and kisses her toes, continuing the massage down to the heel of each foot. Now she rolls to her back and stretches, a silent invitation for him to scoot up the bed and deposit light kisses upon her lips. Her eyes flutter, her mouth curves into a smile, her hand reaches for his shoulder, bringing him close where she can kiss him deeply, a kiss he more than appreciates, morning mouth and all. Her eyes open fully as they embrace.

"Your coffee is on the nightstand."

"I love you. I have to pee."

Another quick smooch and she swings her legs over the side of the bed, scurries to the bathroom. He waits; on her return she props her pillows against the headboard, sits with cup in hand, and wiggles her toes.

"Don't stop!"

He smirks in her direction, then hefts his legs upon the bed, feet toward the top, hands and arms where he can massage her feet. As she sips her coffee, she purrs to his touch yet looks blankly at the wall across the bedroom, as if thinking of something far away.

"Now I remember." She begins. "A funny dream last night. I'm going to write this one down." She rubs a foot against his wrist. "You know what? Your Goddess was there. In my dream. I remember that. Oh, and the two little ones—"

She stops at the pressure of his hands upon her ankles. Their eyes meet. Long, motionless silence. Finally she sips her coffee once more.

Each succumbs to a wave of chills, a wave of prickly energy, a wave of realization as remembrance happens, as scattered dream images become Reality. She places her half-empty cup on the nightstand as he shimmies up the bed toward her. They wrap each other in arms, aware of the implications, the destiny. Breath ragged, they press into each other for strength. Finally he relaxes, lies upon his back, guides her head to his shoulder. She cuddles against him, wanting closeness. From the kitchen they hear the electronic tones of the smartphones, indicating the arrival of an email, then another, then another. He takes her hand, kisses it, lays it upon his shoulder.

"I think that's our friends. Should we—"

Her shaking head cuts short his question.

"Think later. Hold me."

He responds with a hug, a kiss upon her forehead. For a minute, two minutes, three, they lie in silence.

"What do we do?"

Her fingers clutch at his body as if extracting hope, understanding from his flesh.

"What can we do?"

He breathes deep. "I remember asking that same question."

Her feet wrap around his leg. "Do we tell the world?"

He kisses the top of her head. "Imagine what the news channels would say." She giggles as he notes relaxation brush across her body.

"I know. You write a computer program." She tilts her head to kiss his chin. "A video game!" Her hand drifts down to his waist.

His hand drifts toward her chest. "Let me see. There's these twelve little people, these big shiny people, and the end of the world." He nuzzles her close. "Sounds like every other computer game to me."

"Hmm," she concludes, her fingers making seductive circles across his hips.

One of his hands finds her bosom, the other her thighs.

THE TREES ARE DYING

"Hey, don't you always say you want to write a book? Here's your chance."

"Nonfiction, of course," she responds, now bringing her fingers to deliver him pleasure. He greets her touch with a contented sigh.

"Maybe we can run for office," he proposes in a languid whisper. "You be president, and I'll be vice president." His hand reaches between her thighs, provoking a gasp of delight. They lie silent for a moment, letting their touch do the talking. She takes a deep breath, props upon her elbow, approaches his mouth for a kiss, and stops. Her eyes again gaze to an unseen distance. He does not mind the interruption.

"There was something."

He looks at his partner; she senses his gaze and meets his eyes.

He nods. "Something She said."

His lover looks away again. "Right at the end."

He lifts his head to kiss her cheek. "She said it to me before." A soft rush enlivens him. "I remember."

She pulls him to her breast. "The smallest act of kindness…"

He kisses her. "Might change the world."

Made in the USA
Monee, IL
10 February 2021

French Immersion: Myths and Reality
A Better Classroom Road to Bilingualism

Hector Hammerly

Detselig Enterprises Ltd.
Calgary, Alberta

© **1989 Hector Marcel Hammerly**
Simon Fraser University

Canadian Cataloguing in Publication Data

Hammerly, Hector, 1935-
  French immersion

  Includes index.
  ISBN 1-55059-004-9

  1. French language - Study and teaching as
a second language (Elementary) - Canada.*
I. Title.
PC2068.C2H43 1989   372.6'5'410971   C89-091199-1

Detselig Enterprises Limited
P.O. Box G 399
Calgary, Alberta T3A 2G3

All rights reserved. No part of this book may be reproduced in any form or by any means without permission in writing from the publisher.

Printed in Canada   SAN 115-0324   ISBN 1-55059-004-9

"Whatever is worth doing at all, is worth doing well."
                                                    Chesterfield

Contents

	Acknowledgments	1
1	Background of French Immersion	3
2	Effects and Results of French Immersion	9
3	The Assumptions on which French Immersion is Based	23
4	Various Attitudes Toward French Immersion	35
5	A Better Classroom Road to Bilingualism: General Principles	43
6	A Better Classroom Road to Bilingualism: Specific Pedagogical Principles	57
7	A Better Classroom Road to Bilingualism: More Pedagogical Principles and a Model	73
8	A Better Classroom Road to Bilingualism: Procedures and Techniques	89
9	Questions and Answers	109
10	Conclusions and Broader Implications	117
Appendix A:	Interview Transcripts	123
Appendix B:	Comments of an FI Graduate	147
Appendix C:	Results of Standardized Test	161

To Micheline, Mary, and M***** –
three courageous ladies from
whom I learned much of what I
know about French immersion

Acknowledgments

This book was born of the findings and concerns of many of my students, both graduate and undergraduate, at Simon Fraser University. I also owe much to French immersion parents, teachers, school administrators, and program graduates who have shared their experiences and impressions with me.

Specifically, I wish to express my gratitude to Micheline Pellerin of Simon Fraser University, who not only allowed me to use her interview transcripts but was willing to answer my numerous questions about them; to Vancouver writer Ellen Schwartz, who did a great job as preliminary editorial consultant; and to my wife Ethel, who read the manuscript and made many useful suggestions.

Of course, I assume responsibility for any shortcomings in the final product.

Hector Hammerly, Ph.D.

Detselig Enterprises Ltd. appreciates the financial
assistance for its 1989 publishing program from
Alberta Foundation for the Literary Arts
Canada Council
Department of Communications
Alberta Culture

1

Background of French Immersion

First of All

Any Canadian who wishes to become bilingual should be encouraged to do so. The well-being of our nation depends on it. The need for understanding between our two main cultures demands it. The desire of many Canadians for personal advancement and useful service requires it.

Nothing in this book, therefore, should be taken as an argument against second language study.

The Goal: To Produce Bilinguals

The goal of second language education is to produce bilinguals. What, then, is a bilingual?

In the past, bilingualism has been defined too loosely, even by certain scholars. Anyone with a smattering of a second language has been called a "bilingual." This won't do. A considerable *quantity* of second language knowledge must exist before we can call a person bilingual.

But quantity is not enough. A certain standard of *quality* should also be part of the definition of bilingualism. A person is not considered bilingual simply because they can put their ideas across in another language in any old way. Speech and writing that are full of errors can hardly be considered bilingual.

For example, suppose an immigrant, after many years in English-speaking Canada, were to say such things as:

Mary pack his own bags
I want buy book gift mother or

Yesterday I go fish.
Would you consider this speaker bilingual?

Clearly, being bilingual is not just a matter of being understood. The goal of bilingual education programs should be to produce graduates who can communicate *accurately* and *fluently*. People who speak a second language fluently but very incorrectly will at times be misunderstood because of their errors. Furthermore, such persons will frequently offend the sensibilities of native speakers, so they cannot function well professionally as bilinguals. Yet a very slow speaker, no matter how accurate, cannot communicate effectively.

French immersion [FI] programs have promised to deliver bilinguals. This means they should deliver graduates who can communicate accurately and fluently in French. That is what parents who place their children in FI programs expect.

A Brief Background

For most of the history of our country, languages were taught by what is now known as the **grammar-translation method.** This method is still used, with minor modifications, in parts of Canada and in much of the world.

In the grammar-translation method, the teacher explains rules, which the students memorize. For example, the teacher might present the rule "With a few exceptions, adjectives in French follow the noun." After memorizing each rule, the students memorize words, usually in two columns, one French, one English. Then they complete written exercises, mostly in translation, applying the rules. Gradually they do more and more reading, also with frequent translation. I was taught two languages by this method and after many years of study could not communicate well in either one.

A famous graduate of the grammar-translation method was the French author André Gide. He was also an excellent professional translator from English to French. Yet when he first visited England he found himself unable to exchange the simplest messages with anyone.

Many Canadians are familiar with this method, and the resulting inability to speak in the second language. If they can express themselves at all, the expression is either incorrect, or too slow, or both. Because the students spend most of their time learning rules and translating, they do not make the grammar of spoken French an unconscious set of habits, and thus they cannot produce many correct sentences. Nor can they communicate effortlessly in the language.

In the second half of the nineteenth century many Europeans became dissatisfied with the grammar-translation method, so they turned, by the late 1880s, to the **direct method**. This method won many supporters in Canada early in this century. The direct method is still in use today.

Proponents of the direct method believe that in order to teach French successfully in the classroom, no English should ever be used – not by the teacher – not by the students. Advocates of the direct method assume that, since very young children pick up their mother tongue "directly," without rules or translation, older second language learners should be able to do the same. This method emphasizes oral communication.

In the direct method, the teacher demonstrates everything by pointing and gesturing to aid understanding. The class is shown:

This is a table.
This is a book.
The book is red.
The book is on the table, and so on.

Given well-trained teachers with an excellent knowledge of French, and programs lasting many years, the results of instruction via the direct method seem to be fairly good. But there is a problem. Students already know the sounds, structure, and vocabulary of their native language, English, and this engrained knowledge is precisely what causes most of their difficulties in learning French – and many of their errors. In the direct method all this is intentionally ignored, as no word of English is supposed to be used in the classroom. As a result, the direct method is very inefficient, for it does not make use of what the students already know linguistically. The direct method takes many years to accomplish what could be done in far less time if English were used judiciously in conjunction with the second language.

In search of a more effective way of teaching languages, U.S. and British specialists in applied linguistics developed the **structural approach** during and after World War II. This approach uses both the native and the second language. In the beginning, students learn language samples in context (usually dialogues), practice structures via oral drills, and participate in graded conversation.

The structural approach takes into account the ways in which the native language can help second language learning, and can interfere with such learning. The teacher persistently corrects student errors to prevent the development of incorrect linguistic habits.

When used properly, the structural approach pays attention to both structure and communication. As structure and vocabulary are learned, they are used for increasingly freer communication. When thus applied, the structural approach yields very good results. Unfortunately, in the early 60s, when it was renamed the **audiolingual method,** this approach was distorted into a very mechanical way of teaching. Students memorized dialogues and participated in oral drills, but there was little or no communication in class.

It is this distortion of the structural approach that many Canadians know and reject – justifiedly so. For naturally, graduates of a mechanical audiolingual method, even if they could recite dialogues and respond to drill stimuli very well, could not speak the second language with any fluency.

Over the years there have been many other methods, but the grammar-translation method, the direct method, and the structural approach dominated second language education until the mid- to late 60s. None of these methods – either because they were unsound or because they were distorted – resulted in accurate and fluent speakers of French.

By the late 60s, Canadians realized that we needed more bilinguals and that the methods and approaches used in the past had not produced them. The time was ripe for the widespread adoption of a new approach to second language education, one that had been tried, on a very limited scale, early in the same decade.

The Beginnings of French Immersion

In the immersion approach, French is used to teach other subjects, rather than being itself the subject of instruction. In Canada this idea was first tried in the early 60s, originally in Toronto, then in Montreal.

FI is based on the belief that by engaging learners in communication in French, in the process of teaching them other subjects, much better results could be obtained than by teaching the language systematically. French would be picked up unconsciously, it was thought, and any errors would gradually disappear. Among the pioneers of this approach were the Toronto French School and a group of parents in St. Lambert, Quebec.

The latter consisted of 12 parents who in 1963 decided they wanted to implement such an approach. They wanted to have their English-speaking children learn French in separate FI classes within English schools rather than enroll them in French schools. After nearly 2 years of efforts and with the support of numerous parents and a few professors, they finally succeeded in convincing the South Shore Protestant School Board to set up an experimental Kindergarten class. The program began in September 1965.

This group secured the cooperation of McGill University psycholinguist Wallace Lambert. He and his colleagues provided an ongoing evaluation of the project, resulting in numerous reports and a book.[1]

Great success was repeatedly claimed, by all those involved, for these pioneering immersion programs. Because of their enthusiastic promotion of its achievements, the FI approach grew and continues to grow in popularity.

Types of French Immersion Programs

Total FI involves the entire school day in French; this is usually the way most FI programs begin.

Partial FI, whether early, middle or late, presents from the start half of the courses in French and the other half in English.

Early FI programs begin in Kindergarten or Grade 1 and the children usually receive the first 2 or 3 years of instruction in French only. In these "total" FI programs English is not introduced until Grade 2 or 3. Then the proportion of schooling in English gradually increases and the proportion in French gradually decreases, so that by the end of elementary school they are approximately balanced.

Late FI normally starts in Grade 7 and generally consists of 2 years of 100 percent immersion followed by several years during which up to half of the curriculum is taught in French.

Middle FI, used in some schools, begins in Grade 4 or 5. As with the other two starting points, it may be "total" or "partial," but it is usually total at the beginning.

Some of the Concepts Underlying French Immersion

Like any language teaching approach, FI is based on several assumptions about language learning, not all of them stated explicitly by its advocates. Among these assumptions are the following:

1. In second language learning, the younger the better. This is a widespread belief based on informal and questionable observations.

2. "Picking up" a second language naturally and unconsciously by using it to learn other subjects is better than learning it via systematic instruction.

3. It is possible to recreate, in the second language classroom, the conditions under which a language is acquired naturally in the nursery, the playground, the street, or the workplace.

4. If there is concentration on using a second language to communicate meaning, linguistic accuracy will take care of itself. Students will unconsciously learn the structure of the language, and errors will gradually disappear.

5. Immersion is the best way to develop bilinguals in the classroom.

In recent years, advocates of the immersion approach have often found support for their assumptions in the views of second language acquisition researchers like Stephen Krashen, of the University of Southern California. Since in his writings this psycholinguist has long promoted at least assumptions 2 to 4, it is not surprising that he should praise the immersion approach very highly. Krashen has said that immersion "may be the most successful programme ever recorded in the professional language-teaching literature...." He adds that "no other programme, to my knowledge, has done as well."[2]

But none of these five assumptions listed has been proven to be true and, as we shall see, there is much reason to think that they – and other related assumptions – are false.

What Really Counts

What really matters are the results of FI programs. Do English-speaking Canadians, after many years in immersion, understand French very well? Do they speak it and write it accurately and fluently? When a child is placed in a beginning FI class, can a bilingual be expected to come out at the end of the program?

The next chapter focuses on the effects and results of FI programs.

Notes

[1] Wallace E. Lambert and G. Richard Tucker, *Bilingual Education of Children: The St. Lambert Experiment* (Rowley, Mass.: Newbury House, 1972).

[2] Stephen D. Krashen, "Immersion: Why It Works and What It Has Taught Us," in H.H. Stern, ed., *The Immersion Phenomenon, Language and Society,* No. 12 (1984), pp. 61-64. Quotations are from page 61.

2

Effects and Results of French Immersion

Numerous reports, articles, and books on the advantages of FI programs have been published over the years. Faculty members at several universities, the staff of the Ontario Institute for Studies in Education (OISE), government officials, parents' groups, and many others have published and lectured extensively in support of FI.[1] At the same time, the major weaknesses of FI, which have been known since 1975, have not been sufficiently acknowledged. Only in 1986 did leaders state in print that immersion has "some weaknesses." And when in 1987 a major report (to be discussed briefly in this chapter) was published that acknowledges major problems with FI, the conclusions of the report – even its existence – did not become widely known.

In this chapter consideration will be given to the strengths and weaknesses of FI in light of both formal and informal evidence, as well as common-sense considerations. First to be considered, are the possible emotional effects of FI; second, its effects on English and other school subjects; and finally its linguistic outcome in terms of the ability to understand and produce French.

Emotional Effects

The emotional aspect is perhaps the least studied side of FI. The evidence for short-term effects is mostly anecdotal but compelling. It stands to reason that removing children from the company of their neighborhood friends and placing them in a socially and linguistically alien environment where they are unable to communicate even at the most basic level is bound to cause some emotional difficulties. FI teachers, parents and graduates tell stories of children coming home crying every afternoon for months. Being expected to communicate in a language they have no mastery of naturally causes anxiety in many children. While some children find it emotionally difficult to start school even in their native language, the FI situation makes the emotional disruption much more serious. Whether such emotional damage is only temporary is an important research question that, apparently, has not been looked into.

FI educators often assert that there is no pressure on pupils to speak French, and that they can speak in English until they feel ready to speak French. But the pressure, whether blunt or more indirect, is certainly there. There is teacher pressure and peer pressure for the child to speak French as soon as possible – thus the anxiety. And thus the decision, by immersion pupils, to speak French any way they can in order to relieve the communicative demands that cause the anxiety.

Another emotional difficulty for young FI pupils is that there is no one in the school they can discuss personal problems with, for FI teachers insist on speaking only French. Some people deny that this is a hardship, since FI pupils are free to speak to their FI teachers in English. But such a claim fails to admit that a conversation in two languages is very artificial, and that children should not be forced to engage in such strange, stilted talk when they have something especially important to say.

The pity is that such emotional difficulties – feeling isolated from neighborhood friends, feeling anxious, not having anyone in school to trust, and so forth – are all avoidable. Languages *can* be learned quite successfully without linguistic and psychological impositions. English-speaking learners can be *eased* into the French language.

Perhaps parents think that the emotional upheaval their children go through is worth it for the sake of bilingualism. It is therefore all the more important to determine how bilingual FI graduates are. Do the results justify the sacrifice made by parents and children? If not, an alternate road to bilingualism should be considered.

Effects on English

Numerous studies of the effects of FI on English language proficiency have been conducted. They show that after 2 or 3 years of instruction in English – which usually starts in Grade 3 in the case of early immersion – FI pupils seem to catch up in English proficiency with children in regular (English-stream) classes. These findings are based mostly on standardized tests and the writing of simple compositions.

But such tests do not measure either fluency or degree of sophisticated literary creativity in English. I am referring to unhindered fluency and richness of expression beyond the basics that standardized tests or simple compositions can quantify. I have known several bright FI graduates whose spoken English showed a higher-than-average incidence of false starts, hesitation pauses, "uhs," and even some definitely non-English use of words. While such observations are merely anecdotal, this may be a problem, and should be addressed in research.

In terms of writing, how many FI graduates will become novelists, journalists and poets in English? How will the proportion of creative writers among FI graduates compare to the proportion of creative writers among non-FI students? We do not know; but this too is a question worth thinking about.

Effects on Other School Subjects

Standardized tests have shown that immersion students can learn other subjects in French. But FI children's comprehension in French is far lower than regular students' comprehension in English, especially during the first several years of the FI program.

This means that, for years, most subjects have to be taught at a lower level of sophistication in FI classes than in classes taught in English. As a result, FI children who transfer to a regular program in the first few grades find themselves at a disadvantage in virtually all school subjects, including English.

French Listening and Reading Comprehension

It has been repeatedly pointed out that FI graduates score almost as high as native francophones on standardized tests of listening and reading comprehension. But these are multiple-choice tests which hardly explore all the linguistic nuances to which native French speakers are sensitive. Nor can such tests yield a reliable measure of the size of receptive vocabulary. Actually, when it comes to more sophisticated, wide-ranging listening, the comprehension of FI students may be well below that of francophones.

Lapkin et al. indirectly acknowledged this when they gave students with 7 to 10 years of FI the following advice about French-language television viewing: "try to select programs that are interesting and relatively easy to follow, such as hockey games, news reports, and weather forecasts."[2] If the students' comprehension were as good as claimed, the children would not need to limit their TV watching to such visually supported, linguistically undemanding programs.

Advocates of FI have often compared the good comprehension skill of FI graduates with the poorer comprehension skill of Core French graduates. But this is like comparing elephants and mice. By the time they graduate,

FI students have been exposed to French for about 7 000 hours; Core French students, from Grade 8 through 12, for as few as 400 hours. Comparing these two groups is not only pointless; it is misleading.

Naturally FI graduates have good listening and reading comprehension after so much exposure to the language. It would be unbelievable if they didn't! But it is possible to develop a high level of comprehension in a second language, if that is all we want, in far less than 7 000 hours – maybe in as few as 700 hours with the right approach. That's one tenth as long as early FI programs.

French Writing Ability

Learners can write in a second language a little better than they can speak it, for in writing more time can be taken to formulate thoughts and filter out grammatical errors. Still, without the frequent aid of a dictionary and a grammar book people cannot write much better than they can speak. After all, we write what we say to ourselves.

Several studies of the writing ability of FI students confirm that they write a little better than they speak. But their writing contains many errors and is far from matching that of native francophones. The writing difficulties of FI students have been known for a long time but are just beginning to be recognized by the second language establishment. As implied in the previous paragraph, however, efforts to improve students' writing skill will flounder as long as their speech remains poor.

The Tatto Study. The most direct data available to me about the writing skill of FI students is from a research project undertaken by Mabel Tatto, a student in the Master of Arts-Teaching of French (MA-TF) program at Simon Fraser University (SFU).[3] She found that Grade 11 early FI students (who had had about 5 300 hours of French) made, in writing, grammatical errors of the most basic kind. Their comprehension, which was measured through dictation, was naturally better than that of Core French students, who, in this study, had had less than 500 hours of instruction. But statistically there was no significant difference in the grammar scores of the two groups, either in a free composition or in written grammatical exercises.

French Speaking Ability

FI advocates have long emphasized that graduates of such programs can "function" in French. But they disregard or downplay much evidence that FI students make frequent errors of the most fundamental nature.

I became convinced in 1980, when I was writing a book on language teaching, that FI could not produce very competent speakers (or writers) of

French, for the immersion approach contradicted most principles of sound classroom second language learning theory.

The Gustafson Study. My first direct research exposure to FI came in 1982 when I was a member of the committee that supervised a project by one of our MA-TF students at SFU, Rosanna Gustafson.[4] After carefully selecting small groups of Grade 2, 4 and 6 FI pupils, she asked them questions and taped their answers on an individual basis. The results showed no apparent progress in the accuracy of spoken French through these three grade levels; there even seemed to be some deterioration.

This led me to take a special interest in FI. I found that all objective research reports that describe and analyze the speech of FI students in detail come to the same conclusion: Their speech is very faulty. (For examples, see the discussion of the Pellerin and Hammerly study which follows, or Appendix A in this book, from the same study.)

These are not "a few errors," as some leading second language educators have put it. It is rather a matter of frequent errors of the most basic kind, almost all of them errors that no native francophone would make.

In addition to small studies like Gustafson's, three larger research projects conducted, respectively, by Irène Spilka, Ellen Adiv, and Catherine Pawley, as well as a smaller study carried out by Micheline Pellerin and me, reveal how well FI students speak French, whether after a few years of instruction or near the end of their programs.

The Spilka Study. In 1976, Irène V. Spilka published a study of the speech of early FI pupils in Grades 5 and 6 (that is, after 6 and 7 years in FI, respectively).[5] These groups of 20 students each were part of the original and by-then well-known St. Lambert program. Spilka asked the children to retell stories, and then taped and analyzed their output. She compared the speech of these children with their own output in the first four grades, when they had undergone the same evaluation procedure. She also compared the scores of the FI classes with those of classes of francophone children the same age.

Spilka found that 52 percent of the sentences spoken by the Grade 6 FI pupils were incorrect, i.e., contained one or more errors in grammar or vocabulary. In marked contrast, only about 6 percent of the sentences produced by francophone sixth Graders were incorrect. Furthermore, the errors of the FI pupils were consistent with a faulty linguistic system (they had internalized a faulty grammar or had, in other words, poor linguistic habits), while the errors of their francophone counterparts seemed largely unsystematic, caused apparently by inattention.

Spilka also found that there was no evidence of progress in the accuracy of the speech of FI pupils from Grade 1 to Grade 6. The percentage of incorrect sentences of these children was as follows:

Grade	Percent Incorrect Sentences
1	42
2	48
3	50
4	43
5	54
6	52

In other words, the correctness of the French of immersion students did not improve over time. It should be noted that these children are from the original St. Lambert group on whose "very successful" program the FI movement has been based. It is important to note also that Spilka found the gap in correctness between FI pupils and francophones *increased* over the years.

Spilka analyzed the errors and included an error sample for Grade 4. She found that after nearly 7 years of FI, students avoided difficult constructions and that the common pronoun *en* was absent from their speech. Most of their errors involved verbs, prepositions, and gender.

One can conclude from this study that English was a very important factor in the FI children's errors. They seemed to be mixing French and English structures almost freely. (Note that the basic structural errors made by FI pupils are very different from the errors in style, orthography, and so on, characteristic of francophone school children.)

Since it was published in the best-known Canadian Journal in this field, Spilka's report should have had a greater impact than it did. Her data did not appear to affect the promotion of immersion nationwide. As to the FI advocates' expectation that there would be much improvement from Grade 6 to the end of secondary school, it did not appear to be justified by the facts. Besides, by 1976 the original St. Lambert classes were finishing secondary school, an appropriate time for further analysis.

The Adiv Study. The question that intrigued Ellen Adiv was whether the results of FI would differ from those of a program in which two languages – French and Hebrew – were being learned simultaneously via immersion. Both of the programs she studied were early immersion programs in Montreal.

Adiv studied a total of 114 children in Grades 1 to 3 using oral interviews supplemented by sets of pictures. All testing sessions were tape recorded and then transcribed.

Adiv published her study in 1980.[6] She found qualitative differences favoring the FI group over the French/Hebrew group. But her most interesting findings for us concern the immersion approach in general. She found that children transferred structures from the native language to the second language. For example, they said *il est faim* (from English "he is hungry") for French *il a faim*. Adiv also concluded that "there was little progress [from Grade 1 to Grade 3] towards mastery of the grammatical features. . . ." The reason, she inferred, was linguistic simplification. In immersion settings "the learner is under constant pressure to convey meaning in a great variety of contexts."[7] (In other words, when pressured to communicate beyond their knowledge of French, children in FI rely on what they know – the structure of English – and on simplification, that is, ignoring anything "redundant" to the message. The result is what I have called "Frenglish.")

The Pawley Study. In 1985 an article by Catherine Pawley appeared, entitled "How Bilingual Are French Immersion Students?"[8] This report summarizes 11 years of evaluation of the French of early and late FI students in Ottawa and Carleton, Ontario.

Pawley evaluated the four skills of listening comprehension, reading comprehension, writing ability, and speaking ability. As could be expected, the FI students did well in comprehension, poorly in writing, and worst in speaking. On the *Test de français,* a reading and writing grammar-based test, Grade 10 early FI students were outscored by 65-80 percent of Grade 10 francophones. An interesting finding is that by Grade 12 no appreciable difference could be noted between early and late FI students in listening or reading comprehension. Grade 12 and 13 early FI students felt most confident about their listening and reading comprehension, much less confident about their writing ability, and least confident about their speaking ability.

In what I think is the most significant part of her study, Pawley reported on Foreign Service Institute (FSI) oral proficiency interview (OPI) ratings given to 41 early FI and 56 late FI students in Grade 11. The early FI students had had about 6 600 hours of exposure to French, while the late FI students had had about 3 000 hours. The half-hour OPI rates the speaking skill from 0 to 5, with a plus (+) for intermediate ratings.[9] Someone with a zero rating cannot function in the second language at all and someone with a 5 rating is like a native.

Pawley found that the great majority of Grade 11 early FI students received an OPI rating of only 2 or 2+ and that late immersion students in the same Grade scored slightly lower. OPI level 2, according to the FSI, enables a speaker to "satisfy routine social and limited professional needs [the latter with assistance] . . . [to speak] with assurance but not without some difficulty. . . .; [the speaker has a] fluent vocabulary, sufficient for roundabout expression; an accent which though intelligible contains errors; [and] . . . lacks assurance in many aspects of grammar." In other words, a speaker with an OPI rating of 2 or 2+ is just able to cope in the language.

A 2/2+ OPI rating after nearly 7 000 hours of French seems especially low when we consider that, as long ago as the late 50s, most well-motivated young adults at the FSI reached the higher 2+/3 level in several languages, including French, in less than 700 hours of instruction. Moreover, they had the advantage of being actively discouraged from forming incorrect linguistic habits. Thus, they made continuous progress rather than settling, early, for a faulty classroom pidgin that would have enabled them to cope "functionally" but is extremely hard to get rid of later on.

The Ottawa-Carleton research Pawley reported on set out to "evaluate the communicative competence" of FI students, that is, how well they could put their ideas across. On the basis of interviews with twelfth graders I have listened to (see next study), I would estimate that the linguistic competence or "grammaticality" of FI near-graduates deserves an OPI rating no higher than 1+; I think it is the speed of their speech that is impressive and compensates impressionistically for their very low grammaticality, raising the overall average rating to 2/2+.

The speech of FI near-graduates is typical of what Higgs and Clifford have called the "terminal 2/2+"; a person who speaks rapidly but has little or no control of second language structure.[10] It is "terminal" because once this form of speech is perceived by the speaker as acceptable, it becomes extremely difficult to change. Such speech results from the learner being encouraged to communicate far beyond his or her knowledge of the language. Then, having found this knowledge sufficient to get by, the learner loses the motivation to speak accurately. Pierre Calvé of the University of Ottawa has noted that students are even *congratulated* in FI classes for "expressing themselves" in the second language, however ungrammatically.[11] This is how a young child, who does not have much motivation to speak accurately to begin with, settles for Frenglish.

The Pellerin and Hammerly Study. In the fall of 1984 Micheline Pellerin from Quebec, then a graduate student at Simon Fraser University, undertook an analysis of the French spoken by a small number of Grade 12 early FI students in two secondary schools in the Vancouver area. She tape-recorded and transcribed informal, unstructured interviews on very familiar topics. Then we both analyzed the errors. The results were published in a co-authored article in January 1986.[12]

In counting and analyzing errors, we did not include false starts, self-corrected errors, and stylistic "errors" natives normally make in speaking – such as *j'sais pas* for *je ne sais pas*. Only what native francophones would never say, that is, "non-French errors," were considered errors in our analysis.

Yet the average number of incorrect sentences among these twelfth grade early FI students was 53.8 percent when only grammar and vocabulary were counted and 55.3 percent when errors in the use of *liaison*[13] and major pronunciation errors were included. There were, of course, considerable individual differences: the strongest student had 40.3 percent incorrect sentences and the weakest 72.4 percent. This was after nearly 13 years – or about 7 000 hours in FI.

The students' "French" was repetitive, with frequent false starts, circumlocutions, omissions, and so forth. Most of their sentences were short, simple ones joined with connecting words such as *et, puis, pis, c'est, c'était,* etc. Such sentences are typical of the speech of linguistically immature young children in any language, not of 17-year-olds. For the few complex sentences they tried, they used, almost exclusively, structures common to both languages. When they strayed from very familiar topics, they made more errors.

There was a wide variety of errors. The most common errors involved verb tenses, conjugations, and auxiliaries (24.5 percent); vocabulary and idiomatic structures (17.3 percent); prepositions (17 percent); and noun gender (16.5 percent).

Verb errors included infinitives for conjugated verbs, as in **je aller** and **ils parler** (which is equivalent to saying "I to go" or "they to speak" in English); wrong tense, as in **nous écrivons** (present tense) for *nous écrivions* (a past tense); and wrong endings, as in **nous était** for *nous étions* (equivalent to saying "we was").

Often a preposition was omitted or the wrong one used, as in . . . **née** *dans* **New Westminster** (as incorrect as saying . . ."born at Toronto"). The influence of English was especially clear with prepositions: consider, for example, **Il écoute la radio** *pour* **quinze minutes,** instead of the correct . . . *pendant quinze minutes.*

Noun gender errors involved frequently occurring nouns which a regular student of French would know how to use after only a few weeks of instruction. These are everyday nouns the FI students must have been exposed to hundreds of times in 13 years, but continue to misuse them, as in **un classe, la cours, la mot, le chanson, la gouvernement, la examen, le communication, le science,** and **le grammaire.**

The common pronouns *en* and *y* were nowhere to be found, except for the fixed phrase *il y a* and its past form *il y avait.*

Syntactic and idiomatic errors included **Je parle deux différents langages** (similar in English to "I speak two languages different") and **Il est huit** for *Il a huit ans* (as incorrect as referring to age with "He has 8 years").

Clearly these FI near-graduates had not really separated French from English in their minds.

Although the students managed to communicate nearly all of their ideas, they did so in Frenglish, not French. Frenglish is not a language, nor a dialect, but an embarrassment. A 6-year-old may sound cute coping with communication needs in very faulty French, but would you say the same of a 30- or 40-year-old?

Micheline Pellerin, like many other francophones or bilinguals, expected to hear reasonably good French from FI students. Roy Lister, a graduate student at OISE, expected good French from his students when he started to teach in an immersion program. Instead, he found that after many years in immersion, children made numerous errors, a sample of which appears in his article, "Speaking Immersion."[14]

You can judge the output of FI near-graduates for yourself, since a transcript of the Pellerin interviews (with minor deletions to protect identities) appears in Appendix A.

Opinions Of FI

The leaders of the second language establishment in Canada have been very positive about FI, even though FI has shown poor results since the early 70s when reporting on FI began.

Throughout the oral tests referred to in Lambert and Tucker's book *Bilingual Education of Children*,[15] francophone pupils the same age made only one third to one seventh the number of grammatical errors of their FI peers. Even so, the authors say that by the end of Grade 1 the pilot classes were making "good progress" and "beginning to progress toward native-like command" (p. 40)! In this book, gradually less and less information is given about the grammaticality of FI pupils. At first, the authors supply percentages of grammatical errors. We are told that for the pilot classes at the end of Grade 1, 10.43 percent of words (and, of course, a much higher percentage of sentences) were grammatically incorrect (p. 39). For the follow-up classes at the end of Grade 1, we are only given the "number of grammatical errors" (pp. 60-61); we have to figure out the word percentages by ourselves (6.76 percent for story retelling, 12.1 percent for "story creation"). For the follow-up classes at the end of Grade 2, we are not told the number of grammatical errors in story retelling (p. 94). Later, the results table for the pilot class at the end of Grade 4 does not include any information at all about grammatical errors (p. 146). But throughout the book, we are given positive reports on FI by various "judges." As you might have guessed, these subjective evaluations compare FI pupils' speech favorably with that of Francophones.

Some major later publications were even less cautious regarding FI students' grammaticality. For example, a 1976 book that reports extensively on a story-telling test given in Ottawa and Carleton, and on other such FI studies, gives no information on the number and kinds of grammatical errors found.[16] Its only reference to that is in the statement that "informal learning through communication in an immersion program . . . may lead to a special 'interlanguage' – an immersion class dialect" (p. 101). The fact that this is not a dialect of French is not mentioned. The authors conclude that "the children learn French without undesirable consequences" and that "immersion is regarded by some as *the* answer to the second language problem of English-speaking Canadians" (p. 44).

In a 1984 article, Sharon Lapkin and Merrill Swain say that the productive skills of early FI students "do not reach native-like levels" and that "the way they express themselves is clearly different from the performance of native French-speaking peers." Yet they conclude that FI students become "highly proficient" in French.[17] In the same publication, Birgit Harley reports that by Grade 6 early immersion students "have made great strides in grammatical competence although they still make a number of grammatical errors in speaking French. . . ." This, however, is nothing the reader should worry about, for "native speakers of French consider such grammatical errors to be relatively unimportant. . . ." Besides, Harley sees as "refreshing" the "spontaneity with which young immersion children . . . express themselves" in contrast to the inhibited efforts of students in traditional programs.[18]

In 1986 Swain and Lapkin, while admitting that FI has "some weaknesses," failed again to indicate the extent of the incorrectness of FI students' output. Instead, they say that "the results do not show the immersion students to be equivalent to native speakers. . . ." Moreover, they imply that Grade 12 immersion students have accurate control of elementary constructions.[19] This, of course, is not the case.

Perhaps the clearest example of FI advocacy is the book, previously mentioned, *French Immersion: The Trial Balloon That Flew,* addressed to students. In it, Lapkin, Swain, and V. Argue claim that FI ". . . has proven to be a highly successful experiment" (p. 5). The authors give expression to their views through selected comments of FI children and parents. For example, a child is quoted as asking, "Why are some people still against it?" – as if anyone who criticized FI were an opponent of bilingualism. The book implies that "a true Canadian" (the title of the last section) would want to take advantage of the opportunities immersion programs offer.

In 1987 the OISE staff published a report, in three volumes, that acknowledges major weaknesses in FI.[20] It says for example, that FI students fail to master the distinction between *tu* and *vous* – an important distinction which, if not observed, can easily result in offending interlocutors. (This is one of many points of French structure and usage that can be taught systematically with ease but cannot be acquired well through immersion.)

While we should welcome this report and other such reports, it is nonetheless true that they come later than they should. Careful interpretation of data available since 1975, plus a touch of linguistic, psychological, and pedagogical common sense should have led to these "new" conclusions, and to others well beyond them, many years ago. If that had been allowed to be the case, the Canadian education system would now be producing speakers of French instead of continuing to produce fluent speakers of Frenglish.

Conclusions

As we have seen in this chapter, FI results in fairly good listening and reading comprehension (though quite inefficiently). But after 12 or 13 years of immersion, young people do not speak French but Frenglish, a very incorrect classroom pidgin – a hybrid between limited French vocabulary and mostly English structure – and seem to write only slightly better.

This is especially regrettable when one considers the great sacrifices that many highly motivated parents and children have made for the sake of a bilingualism that they are not getting, and that they cannot get through FI programs.

The next chapter explains why FI does not and cannot work. Appendix B is a FI graduate's account of her own experience.

Notes

[1] The title of a small book by S. Lapkin, M. Swain, and V. Argue is representative of this trend: *French Immersion: The Trial Balloon that Flew* (Toronto: OISE Press [co-sponsored by Canadian Parents for French], 1983).

[2] Lapkin, Swain, and Argue, *French Immersion: The Trial Balloon That Flew* (see Note 1 in this chapter), p. 22.

[3] Mabel A. Tatto, A Comparative Analysis of Grammatical Errors in the Written Code Between Grade Eleven Immersion French and Grade Eleven Core French, unpublished project, Master of Arts-Teaching of French, Simon Fraser University, 1983.

[4] Rosanna L. Gustafson, A Comparison of Errors in the Spoken French of Grades Two, Four and Six Pupils Enrolled in a French Immersion Program, unpublished project, Master of Arts-Teaching of French, Simon Fraser University,

1983.

[5] Irène V. Spilka, "Assessment of Second-Language Performance in Immersion Programs," *The Canadian Modern Language Review*, Vol. 32 (1976), pp. 543-61.

[6] Ellen Adiv, "An Analysis of Second Language Performance in Two Types of Immersion Programs," *Bulletin of the Canadian Association of Applied Linguistics*, Vol. 2, No. 2 (1980), pp. 139-52.

[7] Both quotations are from p. 150.

[8] Catherine Pawley, "How Bilingual Are French Immersion Students?" *The Canadian Modern Language Review*, Vol. 41 (1985), pp. 865-75.

[9] The FSI oral proficiency interview was developed in the 1950s at the Foreign Service Institute of the U. S. Department of State, where over 40 languages are taught to diplomats and other American government officials.

[10] Theodore V. Higgs and Ray Clifford, "The Push Toward Communication," in Theodore V. Higgs, ed., *Curriculum, Competence, and the Foreign Language Teacher*, ACTFL Foreign Language Education Series (Lincolnwood, Ill: National Textbook Company, 1982), pp. 57-79.

[11] Pierre Calvé, "L'immersion au secondaire: bilan et perspectives," *Contact*, Vol. 5 (1986), No. 3, pp. 21 and 23-28.

[12] Micheline Pellerin and Hector Hammerly, "L'expression orale après treize ans d'immersion française," *The Canadian Modern Language Review*, Vol. 42 (1986), pp. 592-606.

[13] A very simplified definition of *liaison* (and the related phenomenon of élision) is that it refers to sounds that are or are not pronounced depending on how the following word begins.

[14] Roy Lister, "Speaking Immersion," *The Canadian Modern Language Review*, Vol. 43 (1987), pp. 701-717.

[15] Wallace E. Lambert and G. Richard Tucker, *Bilingual Education of Children: The St. Lambert Experiment* (Rowley, Mass.: Newbury House, 1972).

[16] H.H. Stern, M. Swain, and L. D. McLean, *French Programs: Some Major Issues* (Toronto: OISE Press, 1976).

[17] S. Lapkin and M. Swain, "Research Update," in H.H. Stern, ed., "The Immersion Phenomenon," special issue of *Language and Society*, No. 12 (Winter 1984), pp. 48-54. Quotations from pp. 51 and 53.

[18] B. Harley, "How Good Is Their French?" in H.H. Stern, ed. "The Immersion Phenomenon, special issue of *Language and Society*, No. 12 (Winter 1984), pp. 55-60. Quotations from pp. 58 and 60.

[19] M. Swain and S. Lapkin, "Immersion French in Secondary Schools: 'The Goods' and 'The Bads'," *Contact*, Vol. 5, No. 3 (October 1986), pp. 2-9.

[20] B. Harley, P. Allen, J. Cummins, and M. Swain, *The Development of Bilingual Proficiency*, 3 vols. (Toronto: Modern Language Centre, OISE, 1987).

3

*The Assumptions
on which
French Immersion is Based*

As demonstrated in chapter 2 and illustrated with a transcript in Appendix A, FI programs result, not in linguistic competence, but in Frenglish. This chapter will attempt to answer such questions as: What assumptions about language learning is FI based on? Are they right? What is the relationship between these assumptions and the failure of FI to produce linguistically competent graduates? Can FI's problems be solved?

Much of our behavior is based on assumptions, many of them unconscious. We visit a doctor when we have a health problem because we assume he is qualified to help us. When we are driving, we stop for a red light because we assume it is safer to do so, whether out of fear of an accident or a traffic ticket. Whatever we do, we are bound to get poor results (or at least not the best results possible) if we follow incorrect assumptions. The consequences may range from the trivial to the tragic. I suppose the mislearning of a second language is far from trivial but falls short of being tragic, although students who have misused many years of their lives in a vain pursuit of bilingualism must feel cheated, as does Janice (see Appendix B).

Assumptions come from many sources – tradition, folk wisdom, expert opinion, and so on, but the origin of an assumption is much less important than whether the facts support it. In the case of FI, the facts show that the assumption that immersion would produce excellent linguistic results is incorrect. The FI approach itself is based on at least eight assumptions, which I shall discuss in turn.

1. *Children are better second language learners than adults, so the earlier second language learning starts the better.*

It is not difficult to imagine the origin of this assumption. Many of us know families whose children picked up another language quite well after a relatively short stay in a foreign country, while their parents never went beyond bare linguistic survival. It is only natural to conclude that children learn languages faster and better than adults.

But this assumption overlooks a crucial factor – the amount of time the children, as opposed to their parents, spend interacting with native speakers. Typically in such situations children (especially school-age children) interact linguistically many hours a day, while their parents do so only a fraction of that time. Thus comparing them linguistically at the end of their stay abroad is unjustified. I think that, given the same amount of time communicating with native speakers, adults should be able to acquire a second language as well as, and probably better than, children except, if not carefully instructed, in pronunciation.

As early as 1928, psychologists knew that adults were superior to children in almost every aspect of learning.[1] Adults are more sophisticated learners in general. They have developed more efficient learning strategies than children. They have greater ability than children to aim their efforts at specific short- and long-term goals. Adults do not make analogies on a hit-or-miss basis, as children tend to do, but guide the process through reasoning. Because of their wider experience they have a much larger mental framework with which to associate new items. Adults are better at restructuring information for storage in long-term memory, and their short-term memory can accommodate bigger "chunks." Their attention span is longer than that of children, and they are less subject to frequent distractions.

In the classroom, adults not only have better study skills but are more capable than younger learners of steady work of a routine nature, something that may be essential to success in second language learning. Furthermore, unlike young children they can focus for fairly long periods on language per se and can respond well to appropriate linguistic correction. Adults can use rational thinking and learning; children are weak in this area until about the age of 10 or 11. We see, therefore, that whether in the field or in the classroom, adult learners have major advantages over children.

Still, certain advantages have been claimed for children as second language learners. Stern, for example, noted that the younger child is believed to possess ". . . greater spontaneity and fewer inhibitions than the adolescent or the adult."[2] But in learning a second language in the classroom, a certain amount of inhibition is *desirable* – not to the extent that it will keep learners from speaking, but enough that they will not fall into the habit of blurting out the first faulty utterance that comes to their minds. A good rule of thumb in second language learning is, "Think (very quickly) how you are going to say something, then say it." Young children are too spontaneous and uninhibited to follow such a rule.

It is a truism that most children are more creative than most adults, and that they remain so until gradually forced into conventional ways of thinking by the adult world. However, creativity is not helpful in learning to control a complex tool that involves numerous rules. While a language can be used creatively to the extent it has been learned, learning must come first. Creativity beyond one's growing control of a tool can only lead to its misuse and to poor performance. Would you entrust your car to a novice mechanic who is not sure how to use his tools and enccurage him to be creative? Then why encourage English-speaking children with very little knowledge of French to be linguistically creative in the classroom?

Children, up to the age of about 12 or 13, do have one important advantage over older second language learners: if surrounded by native speakers of the language, they can develop, unaided, perfect (native-like) pronunciation and intonation.[3] This is not a matter of their being better imitators than adults; Politzer and Weiss found that the older the English-speaking school children, the better they could imitate French words and phrases.[4] It may be that younger children remember physical movements better, i.e. possess a better motor memory. Such an explanation would account for, among other things, the need of future concert musicians to start practicing at an early age and the difficulties of adults in learning to ride a bicycle or develop some other skill involving physical coordination.

Please note, however, that the pronunciation advantage of children seems to apply to a natural second language acquisition environment, that is, a situation in which they are surrounded by native speakers – contrast that with the fact that all of the Grade 12 FI volunteers Pellerin interviewed (as reported in chapter 2) had an English accent. Adulthood by itself does not prevent a classroom learner from developing near-perfect pronunciation and intonation; given motivation, expert guidance, and sufficient practice of the right kind and at the right time, young adults can succeed in this aspect of second language learning too.

Several studies have shown that, up to young adulthood, the older the classroom second language learners, the faster and better they learn. Even within immersion research, this has been the case in many respects. We see, then, that the assumption that children are better second language learners than adults is false. Consequently, its corollary – that the earlier they start to learn a second language in the classroom the better the results will be – is also false.

2. *Unconscious second language acquisition is better than conscious second language learning.*

Young children *have* to acquire a second language unconsciously, for they are too immature to learn primarily through the power of reasoning. However, such unconscious second language acquisition has proven to be unreliable unless the child interacts much of the time with native speakers of the language. In other words, unconscious second language acquisition may work well when pre-teens pick up Urdu in Pakistan, but it does not work well in learning French in classrooms in English-speaking communities like Halifax, London or Victoria.

Unconscious learning is a necessity with young children, but there is no reliable evidence for its supposed superiority with older children or adults, in languages or anything else. On the contrary, it makes sense that cognitive maturity (the power of reasoning) would facilitate any complex learning task.

Advocates of natural second language aquisition through classroom communication/interaction (SLACC/I), such as Krashen, have gone so far as to state that only language that is acquired unconsciously can be used to produce sentences, or, conversely, that language that is learned consciously cannot be used to generate sentences.[5] This contradicts the everyday experience of thousands of second language teachers, who know they can lead the older learner to master something consciously, intelligently, and then make that knowledge unconscious through systematic practice. The initially conscious knowledge can be used to generate a very large number of sentences, long before it becomes unconscious. Besides, the learning process is more interesting and challenging for the students when their minds are called upon to contribute to it.

But second language students in many classrooms – not only in FI – are expected to soak up the language unconsciously. Their attention is seldom drawn to learning problems. Their oral errors are rarely corrected, or are corrected in a superficial, ineffective way. What they soak up this way is faulty speech patterns.

We must conclude, therefore, that the belief that unconscious second language acquisition is superior to conscious second language learning is unjustified, and that any second language program based on that assumption (such as the immersion approach and other communicative approaches) lies on a shaky foundation. Second language learning is difficult enough without asking our students to leave their reasoning powers outside the classroom door.

3. *Classroom second language acquisition can/should imitate the process of first language acquisition.*

In the opinion of some, like Swain and Lapkin, bilingual and mother-tongue education should essentially be the same.[6] In FI, French is supposed to be picked up by using it, the way the very young child picks up the native

English at home. But there are two major differences that lead others to conclude that the two processes are quite different.

The first of these is that by the time children are 4 or 5 years old, they already know a language, and filter the new things they learn through what they already know. As a result, the concepts, syntax, and sounds of the new input (French) are seriously affected by unconscious, pre-existing knowledge (the conceptual and structural framework of English). And unless there are very strong reasons not to do so, the learner favors the established knowledge. This is demonstrated by the fact that many of the errors of beginning FI pupils and FI graduates show the influence of English.

It is thus foolhardy for the FI approach, or for any approach to second language learning, to ignore the native language – the source of many student errors – and treat English-speaking children as if they were learning French as their first language. It would be better to take English and its influence into account, by fostering the transfer of whatever English structures can be used in French and systematically countering all undesirable transfer or interference – both overtly.

The second major difference between first language acquisition and second language learning in the classroom is that, while in mother tongue learning the child is surrounded by more mature speakers of the language, in the FI classroom there is only one native speaker, if that, and each child is surrounded by, and frequently interacts with, 20 or 30 peers who also misuse French.

Peer pressure is a major influence on children. It reaches its strongest point in adolescence but is strong throughout childhood. In immersion, the negative linguistic influence of peers cannot be effectively counteracted, and in Canada the outcome is Frenglish (Spanglish in US immersion programs, and other classroom pidgins elsewhere).

With a systematic approach to language instruction, in which the language is *taught* step by step (not expected to be picked up naturally), peer pressure *can* be controlled, even turned into a positive linguistic force. But such an approach requires older learners, at least 10 years old; furthermore, adolescence, the period of greatest peer pressure, would be undesirable as the starting point of instruction. The immersion approach (early or late) is linguistically so unsystematic that control of linguistic peer pressure is impossible. And without such control, peer pressure pushes individual learners toward the lowest common linguistic denominator, Frenglish. Our linguistic standards are normally not better than those of the people with whom we interact.

First language acquisition is also unsystematic, but it usually produces perfect results because very young children start the learning process without previous knowledge of another language and because they are strongly motivated to communicate like those around them – Daddy, Mommy, and so on – that is, like more mature native speakers of the language. To expect a 5- or 6-year-old child to behave the same way in learning a second language (French) in a classroom full of monolingual (English-speaking) peers is naive.

All normal children develop into expert "linguistic swimmers" in their first language; but "sink or swim" is not the best approach to learn a second language. It is only the best way to ensure that children quickly develop an unsightly linguistic dog paddle that just allows them to survive.

First language acquisition is a natural development; however, being "natural" about second language learning is not a valid principle. There is nothing natural about learning a second language within four classroom walls. Rather than trying to do what is natural or "authentic" in the bilingual classroom, we should do what works.

Classroom second language learning cannot be like first language acquisition, so any attempt to make it so is bound to produce poor results. First language acquisition is what it is; classroom second language learning can be what we make it.

4. *Early second language learning should emphasize listening.*

In a natural linguistic environment – whether acquiring the mother tongue or a second language – children spend some time listening before they begin to speak. This may be the main reason why some people advocate a fairly lengthy period of listening at the beginning of classroom second language programs. The idea is that by providing students with increasingly complex listening activities (language slightly more difficult than what they already understand, called "comprehensible input" by Krashen), they will unconsciously process this material, and correct speech will develop as they are ready to use it.

There is only one problem with this reasoning. When we hear something strange, we first repeat it mentally, often incorrectly. If we do not say it out loud and get feedback, we may simplify it even further for memory storage, eliminating parts that we consider redundant. For example, if you hear the sentence "A Mr. Kajangroupfules called and would like you to call him back before five," you would first, with difficulty, try to say the new name to yourself and then try to reproduce it aloud, expecting to be corrected if it was mispronounced. As an English speaker, once sure of the name, you would probably simplify the message to be remembered as, "Call Kajangroupfules before five." If English were a new language for you, and if you just listened and received no feedback, your memory would probably record something like "Kajanofles cole an like I cole four fie." This garbled sentence would hardly help your goal of becoming proficient in English.

Listeners to a second language interpret what they hear on the basis of the language or languages they know, eliminating what seems redundant, such as certain endings, little unstressed words like articles and prepositions, and so forth, even though they are important in the second language. Of course, the listener *as listener* cannot be corrected by anyone, so without saying a word faulty second language structures are internalized.

I think that by the time FI pupils start to speak French, at the end of Grade 1 or in Grade 2, they have mentally stored so much incorrect and oversimplified material (mixed, in their minds, with English) that inevitably they will start speaking in a very faulty classroom pidgin. To avoid this, there must be controlled speaking from the start, so that it can be corrected and will not be stored in distorted form.

As already noted, young children acquiring their mother tongue face a very different situation, so for them the subvocal memory storage of incorrect language – which, in any case, turns out to be only temporary – is not a problem. For the older child or the adult, however, classroom learning conditions are such that the subvocal memory storage of faulty language very easily becomes permanent. And by then it is too late; extensive exposure to the language and intensive correction will result in some improvement, but much long-term harm is already done.

It is rewarding to see that in the last year or two certain advocates of FI have adopted the view that maybe "comprehensible input" (graded listening) is not enough and that perhaps we should insist on "more native-like output" (correct speaking). But this belated admission does not go far enough. If output is to be accurate, it must be *manageable*. To be manageable, it must be carefully *managed* by the teacher. Since the output of 6-year-olds cannot be carefully managed (young children being spontaneous and uninhibited), this brings us back to the earlier conclusion that the learning of a second language in the classroom should be systematic and should start at a later age, with older children or young adults.

5. *Early second language learning should emphasize vocabulary.*

Another widespread assumption is that learning another language is primarily a matter of learning words. Of course, vocabulary learning is an important part of developing the ability to communicate in a second language. But even if English speakers were to memorize an entire French dictionary, they would still be unable to produce anything but unconnected strings of words that make little sense to native speakers of French.

The fundamental problem in learning a second language is not learning its words but mastering its structure. This is where FI fails: the great majority of errors made by FI students, beginners or advanced, are structural ones, far more so than errors in vocabulary. If we teach structure first, with limited vocabulary, we can easily expand vocabulary later, without sacrificing control of structure.

The opposite, however, is not true: in the classroom, an early emphasis on vocabulary virtually guarantees linguistic incompetence at the end of the program. By emphasizing the learning of vocabulary early on, FI programs encourage children to use all the words they know, but they have not mastered enough structure to use them accurately. So they still use the words they know, making in the process far more errors than the teacher can even attempt to correct. Thus Frenglish gets started, soon becoming resistant to change.

In the classroom, vocabulary should never be allowed to develop faster than the knowledge of structure required to use it in accurate communication. Structure should be emphasized first.

6. *One learns to communicate in a second language by communicating in it.*

This is like saying that if parents want children to become excellent pianists, all they need to do is have them listen to good piano music for a year or so and then place them in front of a piano and ask them to play sonatas and concertos. Of course this will not happen; all that will occur is that the children will become poor piano players. Excellence in any complex skill demands commitment and years of intensive, systematic practice.

We "learn by doing"; but if the goal is mastering something complex, we must proceed step by step under careful guidance with continual feedback, ensuring that the prerequisite subskills are acquired before attempting to perform skillful, expert, advanced behavior. Beginners do not become experts by directly imitating the terminal behavior of experts; they must, instead, go through the long process of mastering basic subskills first. There is no shortcut.

Thus, second language students must be led through the steps that will enable them, eventually, to become bilinguals. FI pupils, however, are encouraged to do the most difficult thing – communicating freely in French – quite early. Naturally, they do it poorly, and after they have done it poorly for a while, their errors become resistant to correction.

If our educational goal in Canada is to have high school graduates just cope linguistically in Frenglish, as "functional bilinguals," then the assumption discussed in this section is valid and all they need to do is "frattle" on (rattle off French words with largely English structure).[7] But if our goal as a nation is that English-speaking Canadians should have the opportunity to learn to speak and write acceptable French, so that they become real, employable bilinguals, then the assumption just discussed is quite wrong.

7. *If you just use the second language for communication, linguistic accuracy will take care of itself.*

FI advocates state that immersion programs do not teach French but that a high level of proficiency in French results from teaching other subjects in French. Competence in French, they say, is a byproduct of teaching the regular curriculum in French; no special or specific effort to teach or learn French as such is necessary. Their only concession to the need to learn the structure of French is the one class in *français*, which usually begins in Grade 1, but FI students see this class as quite apart from the rest of their school day in French. To be effective and prevent the establishment of Frenglish, attention to structure must be part of everything students do in French.

FI and SLACC/I advocates in general argue that by communicating, learners will be forced to bring their structural control up to native-like standards in order to be understood ("negotiating meaning"). They seem to forget that learners can manage to be understood quite well with very faulty language, especially in a second language classroom, and that therefore classroom communication does not provide them with a strong incentive to bring their speech up to par.

Although incidental learning occurs in a variety of settings, we cannot expect it to account for a task as complex as mastering a second language. We cannot expect students to learn something difficult (the structure of French) by doing what should be its result (communicating in French); to do so would be like saying, in order to become competent in French, you must communicate in it, but in order to communicate in it, you need considerable competence in French.

If English-speaking Canadian students are to learn to control the structure of French, they will have to focus consciously on the structure of French early in the program. And this young children cannot do.

Learning another language well is not easy. It should be undertaken with the realization that it will require specific, considerable effort on the part of the teacher and the students. Becoming bilingual in the classroom is not the free byproduct it has been billed as.

Traditional language teaching produced graduates who knew the rules but could not communicate. But immersion produces graduates who communicate without rules – that is, put their ideas across in any way – and this is worse. At least with the former there was no permanent damage.

8. *Given the state of our knowledge, immersion is the best we can do to develop bilinguals.*

It has been known since 1975 that FI children mix French and English rather freely;[8] and it has been known since 1976 that FI children speak poorly in Grade 1 and speak just as poorly in Grade 6, without significant improvement being observed.[9] Furthermore, much data showing how deficiently FI students speak and write has become available since then. In view of that knowledge, it is hard to see how FI advocates could have insisted on saying, for so many years, that FI is "very successful." It is hard to see how, instead of admitting that FI students speak and write poorly, they say that FI students "may" use ungrammatical forms and that their speech and writing are "less native-like" than their comprehension.[10]

Students will generally do best in what their program emphasizes; this fact can be abstracted from many studies and should be no surprise. Thus, grammar-translation students learn to memorize rules and vocabulary, to read (more or less) and to translate a little. Similarly, FI students, exposed to much oral and written French, learn to understand the language quite well; at the same time, encouraged to express themselves freely without much concern for grammar, they soon learn to communicate in very deficient speech and writing.

One thing I can say with assurance: all my experience, research, and thinking lead me to conclude that *FI is not, nor can it be, the best way to develop bilinguals in the classroom.* But, you might ask, if FI is not working well, why not improve it by solving the problems?

The recent admission by leaders of the FI movement that there are problems with the immersion approach is encouraging. For years they avoided the real issue by saying that FI students are "not perfectly bilingual" (nobody is) or that what they speak is "not Parisian French" (any kind of native-like French would be welcome, but what they speak is not French at all). It is refreshing that now the leading FI advocates are using words such as "problems," "weaknesses," and "deficiencies." But while admitting that there are serious problems with FI, most FI advocates add that these difficulties can be "solved," "addressed," or "remedied." Apparently it is just a matter of "better teaching materials," or "better-trained teachers," or "better teaching procedures," or of applying more effective correction techniques, etc.[11] Some leading FI advocates are now saying that the problems of FI will be solved when the students have more communication in French. Since frequent interaction with native speakers of French cannot be arranged in English-Canadian classrooms, we are left with the "solution" of more communication among the FI students themselves – and can anyone honestly believe that more practice in Frenglish will lead to real French?

The reader who has followed my argument so far will know the conclusion: because it is based on numerous incorrect assumptions, the French Immersion approach to the classroom development of bilinguals is *fundamentally flawed* and no amount of patching can make it viable. Given the false philosophical foundation underlying FI, this approach could be improved in only minor ways. Furthermore, while FI never produced good linguistic results, as the popularity of FI programs has grown, less qualified teachers are being pressed into service to meet parental demand. So, if anything, we can expect the results of FI programs to be even poorer in the future.

In conclusion, for the classroom development of bilinguals to be improved significantly, it has to be based on very different assumptions from those underlying FI. Correct assumptions about successful language instruction will lead to teaching procedures very different from those of the FI approach, that is, if the desirable changes are made, FI will in effect cease to be FI and will be something else, with far better results.

Different assumptions call for a different approach. There is a better way to develop Canadian bilinguals in the classroom – and I am not referring to traditional grammar-translation teaching or to Core French. The better way, most of whose components have been tested at various times, is discussed in chapters 5 to 8. But let us first, in the next chapter, consider the attitudes of different groups of people toward FI.

Notes

[1] Edward L. Thorndike, Elsie O. Bregman, J. Warren Tilton, and Ella Woodyard, *Adult Learning* (New York: Macmillan, 1928).

[2] H. H. Stern, *Foreign Languages in Primary Education: The Teaching of Foreign or Second Languages to Younger Children* (London: Oxford University Press, 1967), p. 11.

[3] Anne Fathman, "The Relationship Between Age and Second Language Productive Ability," *Language Learning,* Vol. 25 (1975), pp. 245-53.

[4] Robert L. Politzer and Louis Weiss, "Developmental Aspects of Auditory Discrimination, Echo Response and Recall," *Modern Language Journal,* Vol. 53 (1979), pp. 75-85.

[5] Krashen, *Second Language Acquisition and Second Language Learning* (Oxford: Pergamon Press, 1981).

[6] Merrill Swain and Sharon Lapkin, *Evaluating Bilingual Education: A Canadian Case Study* (Avon, England: Multilingual Matters, n.d. [apparently 1983]), p. 4.

[7] Even if this questionable goal is considered acceptable by some, it could be attained in about one tenth the time an early FI program takes.

[8] Larry Selinker, Merrill Swain, and Guy Dumas, "The Interlanguage Hypothesis Extended to Children," *Language Learning,* Vol. 25 (1975), pp. 139-52.

[9] Irène Spilka, "Assessment of Second-Language Performance in Immersion Programs," *Canadian Modern Language Review,* Vol. 32 (1976), pp. 543-61 (already referred to in chapter 2).

[10] Merrill Swain and Sharon Lapkin, opus cit. (see Note 6 in this chapter), pp. 50 and 54.

[11] Please note that all of these proposed improvements contradict earlier claims that children can become bilingual by simply having the regular curriculum taught to them in the second language.

4

Various Attitudes Toward French Immersion

As part of my increasing involvement with the FI question over the last several years, I have interacted with people with a great variety of attitudes toward immersion programs. In this chapter I will discuss most of those attitudes.

Any discussion of attitudes is necessarily rather subjective, for attitudes do not easily lend themselves to evaluation and quantification (there is subjectivity even in designing and analyzing attitude questionnaires). So I will start by revealing my own attitudes about FI and how they have evolved.

I have approached the FI question with a strong belief in the importance of learning languages, a lifetime commitment to a career in that field, and the knowledge that excellent results can be (and have been) obtained in language classrooms.

But my many years of research on language teaching and learning did not prepare me for the strong claims of FI advocates. I assumed that if so many scholars said FI was successful then it must be successful.

Yet the idea of the immersion approach being successful puzzled me, for many of the assumptions on which it is based are the opposite of those on which successful classroom programs I knew had operated. When two graduate students who were directly involved with FI produced evidence contrary to the immersion approach, this prompted me to look further into the matter.

In approaching the study of FI, I had the advantage that my background was in applied linguistics and second language learning in general rather than primarily or exclusively in French. This was an advantage because it enabled me to see the whole forest.

When, after some research, I discovered considerable evidence that FI was not linguistically successful – that is, that it resulted in Frenglish – I naively assumed that others would accept this fact. I still find it hard to believe that a language learning approach that does not work well has become established and continues to be touted as "very successful."

The most widespread attitude I have found among those connected with FI is that they no longer question its effectiveness. FI is claimed to be effective in producing "functional bilinguals," and advocates argue that this is the best we can do in a classroom situation. At most we might need to make certain improvements on the basic immersion model.

Attitudes of Parents

English-speaking Canadian parents, like parents everywhere, want the best for their children. In a bilingual country like Canada, the best includes being bilingual, because it should open up opportunities in business, education, government, and so on that may be denied to monolingual speakers of English. Some are also motivated by the patriotic/egalitarian ideal of unity in a bilingual Canada.

As Canadian parents have been repeatedly assured that the best way for a child to become bilingual is through the immersion approach, they have a high stake in the idea that FI is successful. Indeed, it was parents, in reaction to the poor results of traditional French instruction, who started the whole immersion ball rolling.

After putting their children through many years in immersion, parents are unlikely to admit that maybe this is not, linguistically speaking, the best thing for their children. Instead they are inclined to accept that their children are bilingual when they emerge from the immersion program. Having failed to become fluent in French after years of traditional school French as a Second Language, English-speaking parents are naturally ready to accept the assurances of educators that children are bilingual as a result of immersion programs. Furthermore, since they do not know French themselves they mistakenly assume that what they hear their children speak fluently must be acceptable French.

A great many parents want their children to be in immersion programs. In recent years, for example, as many as two out of three parents in British Columbia have indicated this preference. Figures are similar in other provinces. One of the consequences of this parental pressure is that less qualified teachers, including non-native speakers of French, are teaching immersion classes. (If under favorable conditions FI does not produce good results, what is happening to children whose immersion teachers do not speak French well?)

The fact that educators who advocate immersion have been forced to modify the word "bilingual" with the adjective "functional" seems to have had little impact on parents. Bilingualism is what they want for their children, and as long as a "bilingual" label of some sort can be attached to them, they are satisfied. But, as we have seen, a "functional bilingual" is not necessarily able to speak French or write in it; there is a point where errors are so frequent and so serious that the output can no longer be considered French.

Many parents find themselves in a quandary. There are places in Canada, such as Ottawa, where FI has become so dominant that one can no longer speak of a "regular" English stream. In such places, parents who wish their children to spend their first few years of school in English are in the minority. Some parents may face hardship in doing what only a few years ago all parents could do with ease. The fact that a better alternative road to bilingualism is not available in later grades is a severe drawback.

Attitudes of Immersion Pupils/Students/Graduates

Young children usually do not choose what kind of school they will attend; nor would one expect their parents to ask them. But young children who are placed in FI programs find themselves lost, linguistically, at first. They soon yield to the pressure to communicate, however inaccurately, in the language of the classroom. When they are congratulated for whatever output they produce in the new language, they begin to view themselves as bilinguals.

Correction of their oral output does not make much of an impression on young children, as the emphasis of the FI program is almost exclusively on meaningful communication, and children in Kindergarten or the early grades cannot focus well on language structure anyway. When, later, the written work they do for their French language classes keeps coming back with the same red-mark corrections, they initially find this puzzling. But soon it stops bothering them, for they perceive the few French language classes as unrelated and largely irrelevant to their use of "French" the rest of the time.

Older FI beginners have had some say in whether or not to enroll in an immersion program, but they still go through a similar process of being so overwhelmed by communicative demands that they neglect grammaticality for the sake of expressing their ideas. After a while they too feel encouraged – by teachers, parents, and their own fluency – to think of themselves as bilinguals.

During the program, many immersion students seem unaware that they frequently misuse the French language. Furthermore, they are encouraged to believe that if teachers corrected them strictly they would become so inhibited that they would be unable to communicate. Many immersion students accept the view that the important thing is communication and that grammatical "details" are unimportant. As one student said in a letter: "Naturally, we make mistakes in grammar. Is that not to be expected?" And another one wrote: "What is so wrong with making a few mistakes, if we are understood and we can understand others? The idea is to communicate."

Most students in immersion programs like the programs and would recommend them to others. The few who are aware that their French is not very good still see whatever French they learn as a bonus to the rest of the curriculum.

Immersion students think they are bilingual. They continue to think so until reality – in the form of a French-speaking community they visit or a frank person they meet – outside the FI class opens their eyes. This may not happen until after graduation from the program.

FI graduates have a major investment of time and energy in immersion, so naturally they praise and defend such programs. They almost invariably say that they would go through an immersion program again. They think that the program has made them bilingual and culturally aware.

Interestingly, however, neither early nor late FI students or graduates often use their knowledge of French beyond the classroom. They rarely listen to French radio or watch French television programs. When they meet a French speaker, they prefer to converse in English if at all possible.

Nor do many FI graduates apply for jobs that require bilingual skills. Only a minority of graduates feel they can write or speak in French with confidence, and this is false confidence, uninformed by reality. At least unconsciously the majority of immersion graduates seem to be aware that they cannot function well in real French.

Attitudes of French Canadians

French Canadians find the Frenglish of immersion graduates, with its frequent errors of the most basic kind, peculiar to say the least. At the same time, a frequent comment they make is that they welcome the fact that French program graduates can now speak some French, while before they could not say anything.

Like all people, French Canadians appreciate the efforts of others to learn to communicate in their language. They do not seem to realize, however, that they are entitled to expect much greater linguistic accuracy from students who have gone through as many as 13 years (7 000 hours) of exposure to French.

French Canadians will say privately that FI graduates are not bilingual. Still, they will not criticize FI programs openly because they think that the existence of such programs strengthens French awareness in Canada.

Employment opportunities in English Canada are not a matter of concern to French Canadians. With a reasonable knowledge of English, they have no trouble finding middle- and high-level jobs that require use of the two languages, for they can rely on an English-speaking secretary to correct errors they might make in English.

Attitudes of English-Speaking Canadians

The attitudes of English-speaking Canadians cover a very wide range, from advocacy of bilingualism to rejection of anything French. The former are committed to turning Canada into a truly bilingual country; the latter see "the French fact" as an unwelcome imposition. Most English-speaking Canadians are somewhere between these two positions.

The great majority of English-speaking Canadians apparently see immersion programs as the best way to attain bilingualism. Not surprisingly, many misinterpret any criticism of FI programs as a negative attitude toward bilingualism.

Attitudes of School Officials

School officials in our system of education usually respond to political pressures. When parents, students, advocacy groups and government are pushing for more immersion programs and trumpeting their success, it would be rare for a school official to resist and to promote an alternative program.

But some school officials are aware of serious administrative problems with immersion. Demand for FI puts pressure on them to hire less qualified teachers. Teachers of French as a Second Language and of the rest of the English-stream curriculum feel resentful because students are taken away from them. Monolingual francophones joining the school to teach FI cannot communicate with the other teachers and may not make much of an effort to learn English in order to do so. The logistics of offering an immersion program can be daunting. If school officials were also aware that FI programs can only result in Frenglish, I doubt that many would want to embark their schools on immersion programs.

Attitudes of English-Speaking Teachers

English-speaking teachers naturally feel threatened as they see the demand for their services dwindling while that for francophone teachers increases. Those who have expertise in the teaching of English literacy feel especially vulnerable and frustrated, for they see untrained parents taking their place as early English reading instructors or resource persons.

Attitudes of French Immersion Teachers

Many FI teachers are unfamiliar with other approaches to the learning of French and have no experience in successful, systematic, language-focused oral instruction. Some, who see their pupils within the limited context of the first few grades of immersion, assume that their pupils' errors will gradually disappear and therefore tend to think that the immersion approach is effective. Immersion is "best" for such teachers because that is essentially all they know.

But I have communicated with several FI teachers who are of a different opinion. They report that their pupils, after many years in the immersion program, still make the same major errors they made in the first few grades of immersion. Some of them also express concern for the effects the linguistic and social isolation of immersion programs seem to have on some children's emotional balance and personality.

The FI teachers I know who have misgivings about immersion programs also share the view that they are powerless, that there is nothing they can do to change the established system or introduce a better alternative.

Attitudes of Educators in General

Of all the professions, education may be the one most subject to trends. As immersion programs fit very well with a major trend that started in the late 60s, most educators naturally expect them to be successful and are nearly blind to counterevidence.

The major trend I am referring to is the idea that learning proceeds best "top-down," that is, by focusing on context and meaning rather than on form and structure first. In this view, learning a language is a matter of "communication before language," the way a toddler develops linguistically. This top-down idea of meaning before form is prevalent not only in second language learning but in the teaching of literacy and other subjects as well.

It is only normal that people tend to look for confirmation of their ideas and fail to see whatever contradicts them. But when the matter at hand is the education of millions of children, we must use caution and open-mindedness.

Of course truth, as we may be able to ascertain it, does not lie in whether an idea conforms to current trends but in whether it conforms to the facts as they can be determined, assuming facts and ideas are allowed to be obtained and communicated freely.

Attitudes of Government Officials

Just like school officials, government officials are subject to political pressures – only more so. Many may wish to promote bilingualism in Canada on principle, not just in response to pressures. Since they are assured by leading educators that immersion programs succeed in producing bilinguals, they naturally view these programs favorably.

Attitudes of Employers

Business and industry want bilingual employees who not only understand the two languages but can use them skillfully and with reasonable accuracy. Graduates of FI programs cannot be reliable bilingual employees: they understand French well, but their speech and writing are so faulty that they cannot carry out simple employment functions in French (like answering the telephone or writing letters), much less give their company a desirable image vis-à-vis francophone customers. If employers in English Canada would have to hire native francophones to correct the frequent errors of FI graduates, they will prefer, of course, to put the francophones directly in those bilingual positions.

The career opportunities FI was expected to offer its graduates have therefore not materialized. It is French Canadians with a knowledge of English who are taking the bilingual positions in Canada. This is true in government as well as business. French Canadians hold considerably more jobs in the civil service and in higher echelons of government than would be expected from their percentage of the population.

Attitudes of Advocates of French Immersion

There are academic careers and a whole immersion industry that depend on the immersion approach being considered successful. This immersion industry encompasses publications, teaching materials, research, teacher training, and so forth – with considerable government support. People who have been promoting FI would naturally find it hard to turn around and accept the evidence that, linguistically, it is a failure. Academic advocates probably will not accept the failure of FI unless the objective research, proving its ineffectiveness is made widely known, and studies which show FI in a very positive light are carefully scrutinized. In the past, much of the research supporting FI lacked detail. It often failed to indicate such things as what percentage of the sentences produced by FI near-graduates interviewed over the years contained one or more grammatical or vocabulary errors. It has also failed to acknowledge that FI graduates speak and write with frequent errors including errors of basic grammatical structures and distinctions. If they want an accurate perception of immersion, academic advocates of FI must confront these issues.

There are also various immersion advocacy groups. The best known of these, Canadian Parents for French, is an organization whose name expresses a worthwhile goal. But unfortunately it has promoted mostly immersion as the best way for a child to become bilingual and has down played the poor linguistic results of immersion programs. I hope that this worthy organization will accept that there may be a better alternative – systematic instruction in oral French – and will support its development, testing and implementation. Otherwise, it may be necessary for this organization to rename themselves "Canadian Parents for Frenglish" and for concerned parents and others to organize a new group called "Canadians for Good French."

As a result of individual and group advocacy of immersion, few parents are aware of the problems involved. A consequence of this is that very little pressure for significant change is coming from the "grass roots." And without parental pressure, not much change can be expected.

As we have seen in this chapter, many different attitudes and emotions surround the immersion phenomenon. So we need to go back to the basic question, "Does it work?" The answer is that FI results (inefficiently) in a good level of listening and reading comprehension but also in probably permanent defective speaking and writing skills.

Some have suggested that immersion graduates will speak and write better in French if only they get to communicate more in the language in the later grades. But more of the same is not the solution. Under immersion conditions, greater exposure to French will only reinforce the poor linguistic habits developed earlier. An alternate route to bilingualism through classroom instruction is needed.

The next four chapters are somewhat technical discussions – designed for educators – of a better classroom road to bilingualism. Others may wish to go on to chapters 9 and 10.

5

A Better Classroom Road to Bilingualism: General Principles

Those who are not familiar with successful classroom second language programs – not many people are – naturally assume that the immersion approach represents an improvement over all earlier approaches. But as I have shown, we are not forced to choose between fluency without accuracy (via immersion) and somewhat greater accuracy without the ability to communicate (via traditional methods). There is a better road to bilingualism.

It is possible, via classroom instruction, to ensure that students will be accurate speakers and writers of a second language and to help them become fairly fluent as well. To do this, however, certain general and specific principles must be observed, and certain procedures and techniques must be practiced.

This chapter will deal with general principles and the rationale behind them. Chapters 6 and 7 will go into more specific principles. Chapter 8 will offer examples of certain procedures and techniques with French as the target language.

The principles, procedures, and techniques that I will discuss yielded, for many years, outstanding results in my courses in a linguistic cousin of French – Spanish. Excellent results have been obtained with similar procedures at places like the Foreign Service Institute, U.S. Department of State, where diplomats have been trained successfully in over 40 languages, including French. (For a summary of the results my students obtained on standardized tests, see Appendix C. These excellent results attest to the soundness of the principles, procedures, and techniques I propose in these chapters.)

1. General Objective

There is in essence one general, multifaceted objective for a sound French language program: *that its graduates understand French and speak and write it accurately, in a socially appropriate manner, and with reasonable fluency.* To restate it in terms of the three types of competence we must develop – linguistic, communicative, and cultural – this means graduates should be able to perform in a linguistically accurate manner so as to communicate effectively in culturally appropriate ways.

Accuracy involves the absence or near-absence of errors in pronunciation, spelling, intonation, morphology, syntax, and words and their meanings. Appropriateness means using the French language, gestures, etc. in contextually and socially acceptable ways; it includes matters of style and register (for example, the use of the informal *tu* vs. the formal *vous*). Moreover, French program graduates need to know how to behave in a francophone milieu; this comes under the rubric of cultural competence.

There is no easy way to attain this general objective. As French-born Columbia University educator Jacques Barzun said, "It will always be difficult to teach well, to learn accurately."[1] Attaining real bilingualism in the classroom is a long-term endeavor that requires careful teaching and conscious student effort based on high motivation.

If we value accuracy and appropriateness, then, a high degree of fluency in free communication should be a goal beyond the program, for under classroom conditions an emphasis on native-like fluency tends to cause the underdevelopment of accuracy. High fluency *with accuracy* would be the eventual outcome of vocabulary expansion and frequent interaction with francophones once a solid linguistic foundation has been built.

Of course, fluency *without accuracy* is fairly easy to attain – FI students soon develop it, and Core French students need little encouragement to do the same. But I do not think fluency without accuracy or social appropriateness is a valid objective for French programs – yet that is the outcome of the immersion approach and a common result in other approaches.

One of the major factors that contribute to unsuccessful classroom language learning is doing prematurely things that in themselves are right. For example, free communication is desirable, but if it is emphasized too soon it will hinder accuracy (as in the immersion, communicative, and natural approaches). Similarly, reading is desirable, but emphasizing it from the start has a negative effect on the development of audio-oral skills (as in the grammar-translation method).

Successful classroom language teaching results in student knowledge (the "right ideas and facts") and skill (the "right behavior"). As these grow, the ability of the students to be linguistically intuitive in French also develops; but one can hardly be intuitive in French without a knowledge of the language. Knowledge and skill also gradually lead to creativity, both linguistically (recombination) and conceptually (e.g. metaphor).

Skill in the use of language structure is primarily a set of linguistic habits, the formation of which is of course aided by knowledge. By "linguistic habits" I mean ways of decoding and encoding language that have become automatic through practice. I do not mean the mindless conditioning of specific responses to specific stimuli. It is possible to condition responses with the intelligent cooperation of the learner.

2. Specific Objectives

Some learners of French have limited, specific objectives in mind. They do not want to make the major commitment involved in learning the language but may only wish to "survive" as tourists and so forth.

We can determine the needs of such learners and limit the scope and duration of their French instruction accordingly. Of course, we should warn them that by plunging into free communication without an adequate foundation they will develop an error-ridden and probably terminal Frenglish.

Most "specific purposes" cannot be attained without a general knowledge of and skill in the language. Can an English speaker, for example, really understand what is going on at a professional conference in Quebec City without a high level of general proficiency in French? Except for the survival skills needed by tourists and other casual travellers, specific objectives must be built on top of general objectives. Basic language skills are needed even for limited meaningful uses of French.

In this book, I am discussing a long-term program aimed at the development of real bilinguals. Short-term tourist/survival-type language courses will not be considered any further.

3. Adaptation

Nevertheless, language teachers should take into account the learners' characteristics and any specific communication needs they have. Teachers would do well to determine, and adapt to, the background, strengths and weaknesses that each student brings to the program.

Ideally, the teacher should evaluate at least the following characteristics of the student: level of cognitive and emotional development, personality, motivation and other attitudes, language learning aptitude, and any relevant previous knowledge the student might bring to the classroom. Knowledge not only of French but of any language, especially the native language of the student, is of course "relevant previous knowledge."

4. The Artificiality of the Language Classroom

The French classroom is an artificial language learning environment. In it, learners are surrounded by other learners who know as little French as they do, not by native speakers of French as they would be in Quebec or France. The teacher may or may not be a native speaker of French. And, unlike mother tongue learning conditions, the students in the French classroom already know a language, in Canada usually English, in which they can communicate very well. It is not natural for English-speaking students to communicate with each other in any language other than English.

In most of Canada, French need not be used outside the classroom. Exposure to it may be available at the turn of a dial, but French is, in fact, a "remote" language to most Canadians. It is not as if they were learning it in, for example, Trois-Rivières, where they would need to be able to use what they learn to communicate outside the classroom.

It is therefore unreasonable to expect the French classroom in English Canada to function as a natural language acquisition environment. There is nothing natural about learning another language within four classroom walls.

Successful results can be attained only when real classroom conditions – not an ideal, imaginary natural language acquisition situation – are taken into account in all aspects of the French program. Native language learners are exposed to an enormous amount of input from, and interaction with, native speakers of the language, while classroom language learners are not. It is claimed that native language learners acquire their language by unconsciously "testing hypotheses;" for good results, the learning of French in the classroom cannot rely on this unconscious process. The order and manner of learning French in the classroom must be based on classroom learning conditions, not on a theoretical or even demonstrable order of natural – first or second – language acquisition.

5. Organization

Many studies have shown that structured, organized data are easier to learn than haphazard information. Thus, the learner can grasp, remember and recall data more easily when they are or can be grouped and labeled at progressively more encompassing levels. Through this process, attention can be shifted to higher levels while maintaining control over lower-level elements and rules. For example, learners can attend to the meaning of conversation while also being accurate in their output *if* they have first attained a high level of control over the necessary sounds, words, and phrases and the rules that govern their combination.

In teaching French, the careful organization of data facilitates learning. I am not referring merely to making early classroom French "easy" and gradually letting it get "a little more difficult." Instead, there needs to be a specific progression according to which the students would be helped to make a series of overt, definite "discoveries" about the French language, discoveries which they would then internalize through practice and put to use, systematically, in increasingly freer communication.

6. A Systematic, Step-by-Step Approach

The language teaching profession has swung like a pendulum from wholistic[2] to step-by-step approaches, with each swing attempting to correct weaknesses but ignoring strengths in the current methods. Thus the excesses of the grammar-translation method were replaced by the excesses of the direct method, which in turn gave way to the excesses of the mechanical versions of the structural approach. Today, we have the excesses of the communicative/acquisitionist/naturalistic theory, which is part of a general nativistic trend, and the excesses of the wholistic methods and approaches associated with that theory, e.g., the communicative, natural, and immersion approaches.

Wholistic approaches to language learning have of course a number of apparent advantages. Students feel encouraged to communicate from the start, which lowers their inhibition so that they overcome their fear of speaking. Their motivation remains high, at least until they discover that they have formed many faulty linguistic habits. Also, especially in immersion, there is little chance of boredom, for a great variety of subjects, and the vocabulary that goes with them, can be presented.

The problem with wholistic approaches to language learning is that they force the students to either "sink or swim." The result is an unsightly linguistic dog paddle. Good swimmers, especially champions, have not just jumped in the water; instead, they have had systematic practice at every step of the process of learning to swim well.

While inhibition so severe that it keeps a student from speaking is clearly undesirable, some inhibition is desirable – enough of it to make beginning and intermediate English-speaking students think about how they are going to say or write things in French. And while having to make a systematic effort to learn French is not as motivating as just communicating freely, it is preferable to the major loss in motivation students experience when they realize they have internalized Frenglish.

Step-by-step classroom French instruction would leave the teaching of other subjects in French until the advanced level. But it could still offer a great variety of interesting topics, with the attendant vocabulary.

Underlying the nativist trend is the idea that unconscious acquisition is better and more permanent than conscious learning, and that conscious learning cannot be the basis for the production of sentences in a second language. This belief is more a matter of philosophy than fact. Experienced language teachers know very well that they can lead students from the conscious learning and manipulation of examples and generalizations to the production of an indefinitely large number of novel sentences. They know this because they have done it thousands of times.

Of course, I do not mean that a second language can be learned well "linearly." As will become clearer in chapter 7, gradation must be accompanied by integration at every step.

Under linguistically artificial classroom conditions, the initially conscious, step-by-step, systematic learning of a second language produces far better long-term results than inviting our students to plunge into a global language acquisition situation and start splashing every which way.

In the classroom a second language is best *learned* bottom-up (from elements and rules to meaningful communication); it should only be *used* top-down (focusing on meaningful communication). But even this top-down use should not be global, if we desire accuracy in the end. Use should be limited to what has been learned – no more, no less. If the lower-level boulders of the language mountain range are not solidly in place, skipping cheerily from meaningful mountain peak to meaningful mountain peak is not going to put them in place.

Lower-level French skills involve developing control over most of the structure of the language, such as sounds, spellings, nearly all of the morphology, most of the syntactic structures of the language, and the forms and basic meanings of common words and phrases. All of these must come under control one by one if the students are to be able to operate at higher levels (that is, primarily paying attention to meaning in the context of discourse) without making frequent errors.

Whatever comes under control, however, must be used. This is where language-based, step-by-step methods of the past like the grammar-translation method and mechanical structural oral methods failed: they did not put what was learned, as it was learned, to communicative use.

To be successful, a French classroom program must incorporate such fundamental pedagogical principles as selection, gradation, imitation, manipulation, guided production, feedback, integration, control before use, etc., ending (not beginning!) with creative use. Some of these classroom teaching principles were enunciated as early as the 17th century. Unfortunately they have been largely ignored – in second language teaching and in other areas of the curriculum – for about two decades. Most of these principles will be considered in chapters 6 and 7.

7. Age

Much has been written about the "ideal" age to begin second language instruction. Most research on this question is based on what happens under natural acquisition rather than systematic instruction conditions. As we have seen, many believe that the younger the child, the better. While this is probably true when a child older than two or so is surrounded by native speakers of the second language, as for instance, a child from Toronto in Quebec City, this is not a typical second language learning situation.

As already noted, younger children learn largely unconsciously, without focus on language per se, but in doing so "soak up" not only French but non-French or Frenglish as well. By Grade 3, early FI pupils have already formed faulty linguistic habits that tend to remain in their speech.

The artificial environment of the classroom calls for initially conscious, language-focused learning which, through practice, enables students to increasingly use the language unconsciously. Older children and young adults can do this well.

Younger children want to communicate and many do not particularly care whether their speech or writing is linguistically accurate or not, for they have not developed as yet the concept of correct vs. incorrect speech. Of course, older beginning second language learners want to communicate in the language too – that is their main motivation, as several surveys have revealed. But while older children and young adults are willing and able to learn something systematically before using it, younger children seem largely unable to do so. Thus with younger children accuracy is sacrificed for the sake of communication.

Younger children have limited classroom-oriented skills. Older children and adults, on the other hand, have developed study skills and can be taught how to learn something new and different like a second language.

Due to their longer and more varied experience, older children and adults have more relevant pieces of knowledge to associate with any new item. This helps retention and recall. Older learners such as young adults can be helped consciously to distinguish between appropriate and inappropriate associations.

Younger children are largely unresponsive to linguistic correction, for they lack the linguistic awareness effective correction requires. Older learners can respond well to language-focused correction if it is done in the right way and at the right time. (Much second language teaching offers the students superficial correction, often inconsistently or too late.)

Perhaps the only advantage younger children have over people beyond the age of about 13 is that they can acquire, unaided, native-like pronunciation and intonation – *if they interact frequently with at least one native speaker of French.* Younger children are less inhibited about imitating new sounds, and also remember physical movements better. But older children and young adults can also develop excellent pronunciation and intonation with appropriate guidance.

In conclusion, cognitively developed older children and young adults, because of their conscious linguistic awareness, their ability to focus on accuracy, their study skills, their rich experience/memory, and their responsiveness to appropriate correction make better classroom language students than younger children. Children, however, have better motor memory than adults. The best age, then, to begin systematic classroom learning of a remote second language is 10-11, when cognitive development has reached an adequate level, peer pressure and inhibition are not excessive, and motor memory is still fairly strong.

The second-best age to begin the classroom study of French is young adulthood, about 18-25. The years of puberty are third-best as a starting point, as in those years peer pressure seems to be greater than the influence of the teacher. Many older adults, especially after about age 35, find it difficult to learn a second language, although most can still succeed if offered adequate guidance. Kindergarten and the early grades are the least desirable point of departure, as very little focus on language per se is possible, thus ensuring the internalization of Frenglish. (Frenglish, of course, results from starting with "immersion" rather than systematic instruction at any age.)

8. The Native Language

The native language of the learners (English in most of Canada) is a major factor in the French classroom; it represents the most relevant knowledge – i.e., linguistic knowledge – that the students bring to the program. Naturally, students will see an unfamiliar language through the filter of the familiar one.

The effect of English on the learning of French takes three forms: facilitative, intrusive, and inhibitive. Facilitation is evident in the fact that, because French is a close linguistic relative of English, it takes much less time for an English speaker to reach a given level of proficiency in French than in, say, Japanese or Chinese. This difference may be largely due to the magnitude of the lexical learning task; without any instruction, an educated English speaker already knows about 30 percent of French vocabulary.

The intrusive effect occurs with those structures in which the two languages differ in partial, often subtle, ways. When faced with such distinctions, the learner of French who is not made clearly aware of them will fall back on English and will substitute English sounds, rules, or word meanings for the correct French ones. Thus English intrudes on the learner's French. This was long emphasized in contrastive studies of "linguistic interference," only to be neglected in the nativist wave that started in the late 60s.

Crosslinguistic influence is inhibitive when French makes a distinction that does not exist in English. In this case, English tends to inhibit the learning of the French distinction. Whether consciously or unconsciously, the student thinks, "I've communicated all my life without making such a distinction, so I don't really need to make it in French." When the student is allowed – or even encouraged – to communicate without making the distinction in question, the inhibition of learning is further strengthened. Thus French features that are communicatively redundant, that is, that carry little or no meaning (for instance, the gender of most nouns, correct liaisons, the right choice of auxiliary) will be ignored when the communication of messages is what counts.

Student knowledge of English is very relevant to the teaching and learning of French in the classroom. Even in a naturalistic situation like the immersion approach, many errors are clearly due to the influence of English – this in programs that may have entirely avoided English in the classroom. Ignoring or forbidding English will not do, for learners inevitably engage in French-English associations and formulations in their minds. Since many of these subvocal associations are evidently incorrect, it is far better to deal with crosslinguistic influences overtly.

By referring to English openly, teachers of French can ensure that the correct associations are made. They can lead their students to make full use of the facilitative (positive transfer) effect of English and to beware of its intrusive (negative transfer) and inhibitive ("I don't need to learn this") effects.

Classroom instruction in French as a second language calls for approaches, methods, procedures, and techniques that not only take English into account but use it – as little as possible but as much as necessary – to facilitate the learning of accurate and fluent French and prevent the internalization of Frenglish.

Any explanations and clarifications should be done in a language that is understood by the students, otherwise they are worthless. For most beginning students of French in North America, this language is English. Gradually, as the students learn more and more French, it can be increasingly used for such purposes.

In summary, the development of bilinguals in the classroom calls for bilingual methods of instruction.

9. Oral Samples

When classroom learners try to use French, they need to be able to base their output on thoroughly learned French. If they do not know any French utterances well, they will fall back on what they do know well: English structures, sounds, and meanings. The mastery of oral samples, then, gives a foundation on which to build increasingly freer use of the language.

The mastery of oral samples does not mean the memorization of long dialogues, as in much oral instruction in the 50s and 60s. Most oral samples could be dialogues, but they would be very short and it would rarely be necessary to memorize the order of sentences in them. Furthermore, many things besides dialogues could be used as oral samples, such as proverbs and sayings, quotations, verse, ads, anecdotes, parts of monologues, and so on.

Oral samples offer the opportunity to reinforce sounds or intonation patterns that have already been taught systematically, to teach new vocabulary and expressions, and to illustrate grammatical structures that are to be taught systematically. They also provide the students with definite short-term goals and a sense of accomplishment.

The mastery of oral samples is of course not an end in itself but a point of departure for the lessons at the beginning level of the program. Once learned, the samples should be fully manipulated and exploited, in a variety of ways, over a period of several weeks. Traditionally, oral sample manipulation has been limited to structural exercises containing model sentences selected from the samples mastered. But far more can be done to exploit samples linguistically as well as communicatively and culturally. Linguistically, the idea is to lead beginning students from accurate sentence reproduction through sentence manipulation, variation, and combination to the semifree use of the structures and vocabulary involved.

Compare this carefully guided progress with the situation of beginning students of French who are encouraged to talk freely about anything. They have nothing to go by, so they freely and uninhibitedly produce Frenglish.

10. Practice

Probably the most damaging assumption of the wholistic, top-down educational trend that started in the late 60s is the belief that systematic practice is unnecessary, that if the students concentrate on the ideas, the details will take care of themselves. This view is especially harmful to subjects that involve skill development, such as literacy, languages, and mathematics. In skill subjects, minimizing practice results in the skills being only partially developed or not developed at all.

Practice does not mean mindless drilling. The kind of practice needed in learning French in the classroom is intelligent practice, the informed making of choices with appropriate and timely feedback on accuracy.

Of course a person who knows a language well rarely has to make conscious choices about structure; he has the system of correct choices "built in." This kind of system is built unconsciously by young children in their native language. But that is a once-in-a-lifetime experience for most people. In the classroom, older remote-language learners who already know their native language very well need to proceed consciously and to turn their awareness into unconscious behavior through practice.

If conscious awareness of structures, sounds, and forms is to become unconscious, practice cannot remain at the mechanical level but must gradually move to the meaningful use of the rules and elements. Thus, for each rule and element, practice should shift gradually through a series of steps from attention to form to attention to meaning.

Initial practice with focus on form is especially necessary with rules and elements that are communicatively redundant, whether partially or completely so. For example, even the most fervid advocates of the idea that grammatical distinctions are learned through the "negotiation of meaning" cannot attribute to such "negotiation" the learning of the gender of common French nouns like *table, classe* or *pomme*. Nor can they support the view that other grammatical features that are similarly redundant to the communication of meaning are learned through "negotiation."

11. Errors

In a natural acquisition situation certain errors may indicate that the learner is unconsciously testing the limits of rules. In such a situation, these "hypothesis testing" errors are not undesirable, provided the learner is given feedback. In a natural situation, communicative feedback results in the disappearance of many errors without linguistically focused correction.

The remote-language classroom situation is very different from the above. In it, communicative feedback from a native speaker (*if* the teacher is one) is insufficient to result in the disappearance of errors without their correction. As a result, linguistically deficient rules and elements are internalized if the errors are not dealt with promptly and appropriately.

Within a systematic second language program most errors are due to one or more of three causes: (1) the teacher or the program did not develop sufficient student awareness of, or provide enough practice on, a given point, so the student has not mastered it; (2) the teacher provided the student with sufficient and appropriate instruction but the student did not make the necessary effort to master the point; (3) the student, contrary to appropriate advice, has ventured communicatively well beyond what he or she has learned linguistically. So in this situation most errors represent a failure on someone's part.

Careful step-by-step instruction can prevent many errors from occurring and can keep the number of errors manageable so that they can be corrected efficiently and effectively. But there will be errors, for whenever students are learning something new or using something familiar in new ways they are bound to make errors. The important thing is to deal effectively with errors, not ignore them. This means addressing the causes of errors, rather than their surface manifestations. Effective correction will empower students to self-monitor and self-correct their errors, that is, to internalize the *criteria* by which they can avoid making such errors in the future. (More on errors and their correction in chapters 6 and 8.)

12. Cultural Competence

In Canada, a French language program should not only teach the French language but also the Quebec culture. While that includes Quebec history, geography, literature, the arts, etc., the emphasis needs to be primarily on cultural behavior. In order to communicate adequately with Quebecers, the anglophone Canadian student of French must know how Quebecers behave, why they behave so (to the extent that is possible), and how to behave when in their company.

This type of knowledge, and the ability to apply it, are not part of linguistic competence or performance but must nevertheless be imparted. This can be done using activities that are quite different from – though they can be integrated with – the teaching of French language rules and elements. Furthermore, much about Quebec cultural competence can be taught in English without fear of harm to the students' French.

13. The Ideal French Language Program

As already stated, the French language program would ideally start in Grade 5 or with young adults, that is, with students who have the necessary cognitive maturity to learn a second language well through systematic, step-by-step classroom instruction.

But before the French language program itself starts, there should be an "exploratory" course or courses. This course could be called "Languages and Peoples of the World" and would present interesting facts about various languages and customs, and information about what is involved in learning a language in the classroom. It would be the only language course required, for language students who are simply completing a language requirement generally lack the necessary motivation to do well. This course would be offered before any particular language is studied, for example, in the first semester in college or the first four grades in elementary school. Upon completing it, students may be able to decide which language they want to study in depth – high motivation is essential to such a long-term endeavor. In Canada, most students who complete the initial course will no doubt want to learn French, but they would be doing it with full awareness that learning French well is difficult and requires persistent effort.

Phase One of the French language program proper should be intensive or semi-intensive. Since intensive programs (4 hours per day or longer) may not be feasible in a school or college setting, this first phase would have to be semi-intensive (2 hours per day, preferably not consecutive). Two important advantages of intensiveness in second language learning are that (1) what is learned is remembered better, as less time elapses between successive exposures to any rule or element, and (2) students can see the results of their efforts, and can begin to use the language with some freedom, much faster, which of course helps enhance and maintain motivation.

This semi-intensive phase would last 4 years in school (e.g., Grades 5 through 8) and 1 year in college, making it, in the latter case, the equivalent of at least 2 regular years of French instruction. All of the basic structures of French can be mastered in that time.

In Phase Two (e.g., Grades 9 through 11 in school or second year of college), students would have 1 hour per day of systematic French instruction and take one or two subjects taught in French. The emphasis here is on expanding active vocabulary, including idioms.

Finally, in Phase Three (e.g., Grade 12 and beyond for school students, upper level and beyond in college) we need to surround students with a francophone environment. This can be done, partially, by teaching most subjects in French. To accomplish this fully, of course, students would be encouraged to spend at least a few months in a francophone community.

The first 15-20 hours of the ideal French language program would consist of an introductory minicourse, different in many respects from the rest of the program. This minicourse would gradually and systematically teach control over the sounds of French and then awareness of how they relate to orthography, in alternation with brief meaningful activities. The latter would include an orientation to the course and the program (how to study, basic terminology, nature of tests and grading, etc.), student background and motivation questionnaires, short graded oral samples, a very brief introduction to Quebec culture, and so on. Developing a good level of control over French sounds in the first few hours eliminates many long-term problems in this aspect of the language.

The ideal French language program would use a sound eclectic method of instruction, avoiding extreme trends. Haphazard eclecticism – putting things together from here and there with no system or principle – is of course not defensible and can hardly produce good results. But excellent results can be obtained with a Principled Eclectic Method (PEM) that combines demonstrably successful procedures from a variety of sources and integrates them or adapts them so that they harmonize and facilitate the attainment of the goals of the program.

The Principled Eclectic Method I have recommended incorporates the principles discussed in this and the next two chapters. Some of the procedures and techniques of PEM are illustrated and discussed in chapter 8.

Notes

[1] Jacques Barzun, *Teacher in America* (Indianapolis: Liberty, 1981), p. xix.

[2] Since the spelling "holistic" is associated with a philosophical movement unrelated to our purposes, I will use the alternate spelling "wholistic" in this book.

6

A Better Classroom Road to Bilingualism: Specific Pedagogical Principles

In addition to the general principles discussed in chapter 5, success in teaching French in the classroom depends upon certain pedagogically oriented principles which are discussed in this and the next chapter.

Teaching Makes a Difference

It is a fact that good teaching can inspire students to attain excellence, while poor teaching is demotivating. But, the question arises of what constitutes teaching in the French language field. Just exposing students to communication in the language, as in FI, is not teaching. Teaching is a much more systematic effort to induce learning, the kind of step-by-step pedagogical endeavor in which teachers have traditionally engaged.

Of course, teaching has to be adapted to the characteristics and goals of the learners; but that is not the same as saying that teaching must be subordinated to learning. Competent teachers should have a good idea of how, under given conditions, a second language is best learned, and should share that knowledge with their students rather than let them try to learn the language whichever way they want. Facts about learning and about learning a second language cannot be established democratically, nor are they matters of common public knowledge, so the knowledgeable French teacher should not be afraid to assume direction of the learning process.

To teach French well, teachers must have certain qualifications. An excellent command of the French language is essential. To be able to help English-speaking students learn French effectively and efficiently, French teachers should also know English well. They need to have a good knowledge of the structures of the two languages and the ability to transmit this knowledge to linguistically unsophisticated students. They should have a knowledge of psychology, methodology, testing, and technology as they apply to language teaching. They need to be able to present and explain the facts and behaviors relevant to the two cultures. Finally, they should have some skill in natural (rather than professional) oral and written translation, so they can implement bilingual instruction and correction as needed.

Methods Make a Difference

Some educators have been saying, for some time, that methods are not very important. People who say this form two major factions, those who assert that what matters is the personality, etc. of the teacher and those who affirm that what really matters is the motivation and behavior of the learner. The experimental methodological comparisons of the 60s and early 70s failed to keep methods distinct long enough, if at all, and so did not clarify the issue.

In a complex teaching/learning situation, however, all major factors and their interactions are bound to have some effect on the eventual outcome. To say that how French is taught is not a major factor in how well French is learned is untenable.

Even if less than 20 percent of result variance was directly attributable to the choice of method, the way the language is taught is bound to affect motivation. And very few question the importance of motivation, at least when students are allowed free choice.

A sound method is open to demonstrably better ideas but does not follow trends slavishly. It incorporates whatever works well as long as it harmonizes with the other successful components of the method so that the whole helps attain the general objective of the program efficiently and effectively. This is the basis on which I have attempted to organize the Principled Eclectic Method (PEM).

Teaching in Harmony with What Is to Be Taught

Teaching must be based on the nature of what is to be taught. It makes little sense to proceed otherwise.

Even a highly literate language like French is primarily an audio-oral means of communication. It therefore goes against the nature of the French language to follow a general program that offers mostly reading, as appropriate as that might be for a graduate reading course or for a program in Latin or classical Greek. To learn the French language as a whole, one needs to concentrate on the skills that are primary in using French, that is, listening and speaking. We should also be careful not to overemphasize writing in the French language program.

There are marked differences between spoken and written French. If the spoken forms are not attended to, early and separately from the written forms, many avoidable errors will result.

What needs to be taught is the ability to communicate *accurately* – an ability that any well-educated native speaker of French has, and not unreasonably, expects to find in those who have spent many years learning French. Teaching must therefore reflect this emphasis from the start.

Teaching materials must also be in harmony with what is to be taught. The presentations and exercises in textbooks should conform to the fact that French is primarily a means of audio-oral communication. Those who really agree with the primacy of speech in French will not have the students rely mostly on textbooks, workbooks, and computer screens for their out-of-class French input. Instead, they will ask their students to study mostly with audio and videocassettes and other such media. Audiocassettes, for example, are widely available but underused in language programs.

Selection

Consider three points: (1) The best educated and best read native speaker of French cannot come close to knowing all of the French language. (2) Even a comprehensive, excellent French language program can teach only part, perhaps no more than one third to one half, of what the average educated native knows of the language. (3) Within the French program, what is most basic needs to be taught and what is of little importance or too specialized need not be taught; this is to ensure that students learn what is linguistically, communicatively, and culturally fundamental in French.

All three of these considerations point to the need for principled selection. Decisions must be made about what to include in the French language program and what to leave out. For example, *manger* and *livre* would be selected for early inclusion in a French language program; *juguler* and *dossard* could safely be left out.

Decisions about what to include in the program and when to introduce it need to be made about all aspects of French. If teaching specialists do not make these decisions and leave the matter to the chance processes of natural language use, students may not learn much that is basic and may spend an inordinate amount of time on things that are not. It is therefore essential that French materials developers guide the learning process in this regard.

The principle of selection applies most strongly to the largest and most open language component, vocabulary, including idioms; less strongly to syntax, for only infrequent syntactic rules and patterns can be excluded; and least of all to morphology, as only certain technical, scientific, and otherwise specialized morphemes should be excluded from the program. All French sounds, useful phonological rules, intonation patterns, and orthographic rules should be included in the program.

The use of "authentic" language, that is, real communication between native speakers of French has been much emphasized in the last 10 years or so. This has gone hand in hand with the tendency to ignore that the classroom is not a natural or authentic second language acquisition environment. The problem with authentic language is that it includes rules and elements that are either premature (linguistically too advanced) or unimportant (communicatively not useful) for classroom learners. Often, authentic language is nonstandard and even idiosyncratic. Beginning students of French need to rely primarily on realistic but specially designed oral samples, although the use of carefully selected short segments of authentic language may be possible after about 100-150 hours of instruction.

Gradation

No one can master something very complex by trying to learn it all at once. Even young children who (successfully) acquire their mother tongue do so by gradually expanding the variety and sophistication of their messages. But for classroom students who already know a language and lack sufficient interaction with natives, it is impossible to learn a second language well by approaching it globally and concentrating on meaning from the start.

Mastery of any complex body of knowledge or set of habits (learning a second language is both) requires focusing on what is to be learned one point at a time. Gradation involves going from the simple to the complex, the regular to the irregular, the frequent to the infrequent, the concrete to the abstract, the important to the less important, the basic to the derived, the independent to the concomitant, the useful to the less useful, and so on.

For instance, students should learn French articles (at least definite ones), subject pronouns, and a few nouns and verbs before they can be taught the use of direct object pronouns. They need to learn *avoir* as an independent verb, common types of present tense verbs, and the formation of perfect verb forms before they can be taught *avoir* as a concomitant auxiliary in the *passé composé*. Study of the imperative and subjunctive moods should follow mastery of much of the indicative mood.

This is not to say, of course, that every example of later structures should be completely avoided in earlier parts of the program. Some examples can be used, for instance, in oral samples to be mastered and in frequent classroom directions, provided the teacher makes it clear to the students that the grammatical points involved will not be studied systematically for some time and that all they need to do before then is learn the utterances as unanalyzed wholes – with comprehension, of course.

Sometimes gradation criteria are in conflict. For example, the verb *être* is quite irregular but is very frequent. Cases of high frequency call for exceptions to other gradation criteria. Pedagogical principles are not meant to be applied rigidly but can be broken when the facilitation of learning requires it.

Gradation means *easing* students into the French language. This is especially clear in the use of French and English in the classroom. While from the start French should be produced most of the time, beginning students need to have structure rules, sounds, and sentence and word meanings clarified briefly in the language they understand, which is English. Gradually the use of English can be phased out, so that by the late intermediate and advanced levels very little is needed. This assumes, of course, teachers who keep their use of English to the minimum needed for effective and efficient teaching and who are assertive enough not to let their students get away with saying in English anything they should know how to say in French.

Gradation is essential in moving from control of form/structure to attention to meaning/communication. Top-down, wholistic learning advocates do not see the need for careful step-by-step gradation. The proficiency movement and several classroom approaches, including immersion, are based on the idea of communicative survival needs being met first; but this notion is invalid. First, in a remote-language learning situation there are no linguistic survival needs, so instruction can follow any course that leads to success, regardless of what the survival needs might be in a distant francophone environment. Second, students who want to learn French well do not just want to survive – they want to become successful (fluent and accurate) users of French. By urging them to interact beyond their linguistic competence we simply ensure their internalization of Frenglish.

In the classroom, students do not learn to speak (or write) a second language well by going ahead and speaking it poorly at first, in the expectation that it will gradually improve and become near-native. That is not what I mean by gradation. To develop fluency with accuracy, students should first master one small area of the language (including the mastery of samples), and then gradually expand, step by step, the areas under excellent control, mastering each one in turn and integrating each with what they learned previously. An error-laden interlanguage is avoidable in the classroom.

Gradation also applies within each new aspect of the language to be mastered. To achieve both fluent and accurate use, the study of any given point should shift from (1) attention to form only, to (2) primary attention to form with some attention to meaning, to (3) attention to form and meaning equally, to (4) primary attention to meaning with some attention to form. If students begin to make many errors at any point in this sequence, the teacher should go back to the preceding step. Attention to only meaning is satisfying, even exhilarating at times, but it is linguistically risky until a very advanced level is reached, beyond the French language program.

Throughout the program, the emphasis should be on mastering, additively and integratively, a long series of uses for a complex linguistic tool. To the extent that "creativity" means using French in ways not yet learned, it does not belong in the program. Creative use of what has been learned should of course be encouraged; but that means recombining what is known in novel ways, not recklessly experimenting with the language. Linguistic adventurism – communicating beyond one's knowledge of French – leads to the establishment of Frenglish. Why should we, who reject the spirit of adventure in an airline pilot, an automobile mechanic, or a surgeon, welcome it or even encourage it in students of French? Granted, in the latter the consequences do not involve life or death; but they are, nevertheless, very serious – linguistically.

In the classroom, excellent results with most students can be obtained by following a carefully graded, step-by-step, bottom-up process in learning French, and a top-down process in using it. Of course, as the language is learned, the top gets integrated at increasingly higher and more encompassing levels, until it includes all of the basic structures and vocabulary of the language, thus enabling students to communicate a great variety of meanings.

Guidance

Unlike young native language learners, older classroom learners need considerable guidance in order to learn French well. This guidance, in addition to providing selection and gradation of content, should show students how to study and focus their attention on specific learning problems or tasks.

For each point under study, students need guidance in perceiving (hearing and seeing) and understanding what is involved, in using it with increasing freedom, and in paying attention to corrections. They also need to be reminded, as often as necessary, not to venture far beyond what they know.

Teachers who relinquish control to the students cannot offer effective guidance. As the person in the classroom who knows French best and who has a good idea of how it can be learned well, the teacher should not be afraid to exert his or her authority. It is a matter of balance: neither overguidance nor underguidance is desirable.

Guidance on any one point should gradually become unnecessary as the students internalize the criteria for using an aspect of French accurately and take it into account when they speak. As the teacher guides the learning of more advanced points, guidance should become unnecessary for earlier points. The ideal teacher gradually becomes unnecessary – not because he or she ignores errors but because the students master those points when guidance is gradually phased out.

Attention and Variety

Beyond the largely unconscious learning associated with childhood, we cannot learn much without paying specific attention. Without focusing our attention on meaning, for example, we can hear a great deal of talk or read a considerable amount only to miss the content entirely or be jolted into asking ourselves, "What was that?"

The first requirement for the learning of French in the classroom is that students pay attention to what is going on. Within reason, anything should be done to ensure attention. If the teacher enthusiastically presents a variety of activities, the students will usually pay attention. Variety is very important in keeping a second language class interested and motivated. To maintain student attention, long learning activities should be broken into segments, with a variety of things to do during the breaks. But the emphasis on variety should not be such that important learning activities or segments are kept too short to be effective.

Bizarre teaching methods are not necessary to maintain adequate attention. (There are methods of language teaching, such as John Rassias' Dartmouth Method, that use bizarre behavior as an attention-getting and mnemonic aid.) It simply is not necessary for the teacher to come to class dressed as Napoleon or Joan of Arc to ensure attention, nor is there a need to throw a chair around or break an egg on a student's head for the class to learn the words *une chaise* or *un oeuf*. No doubt, such excentricities are memorable, but they are hardly necessary. Besides, bizarre behavior is impressive a few times, but beyond that it does not make much of a dent on memory – the teacher who exaggerates everything fails to highlight anything.

There should be variety both at the micro- and macro- levels. Macro-variety involves a class or series of classes, such as in teaching the usage and forms of a new tense. But micro-variety with the specific activities done in one class is also necessary, for some activities, such as certain drills and exercises, become tiring or boring if done for more than 5 or 10 minutes at a time.

Emphasis

If something has been learned from the experimental methodological comparisons of the 60s and early 70s, it is that students learn best whatever the program emphasizes. If the program stresses reading and vocabulary recognition, students will develop a fairly large receptive vocabulary but will not be able to speak in the language. If a program concentrates on the mechanics of speaking, the students will master them, although they may not be able to communicate. The results of FI programs show that when an approach emphasizes communicative fluency at the expense of linguistic accuracy, students learn to do precisely that: communicate with Frenglish habits.

But emphasis is not only a matter of what to stress, i.e., selection; it is primarily a matter of when to stress each aspect of French that must be learned, i.e., gradation. We will place emphasis on something, whether we admit it or not, so we might as well do so in a conscious, intentional, principled manner. Even if we were to give equal emphasis to everything at the same time, that would be an emphasis decision – and an unwise one.

A French program designed to produce graduates who can communicate accurately and with reasonable fluency should clearly emphasize throughout the two main skills that contribute to that goal: listening comprehension and speaking ability. This does not mean, of course, that there should not be considerable reading and writing – at the right time. The right time is not the beginning of the program, when basic audio-oral control needs to be established without distractions or interference. (English-filtered interpretations of written French, the only interpretations beginners can make, result in more pronunciation errors than can be effectively corrected.)

Of the components of the French language, the small, closed system of sounds obviously needs to be mastered first, since accurate sound perception and production facilitates comprehension of much that will be said, by both the teacher and the students. The morphosyntactic component of French, which is also a closed system but much larger than phonology, should be emphasized through the intermediate and even at the advanced level. Emphasis on expanding the (open) stock of vocabulary and idiomatic expressions should be placed at the advanced level and, in fact, for the rest of the learner's life – not early in the program, for this invites students to try to communicate beyond their limited knowledge of the structure of French. Discourse rules, which govern communication acts, do not need special emphasis at any point but should be learned as situations that call for their use are simulated or occur naturally in the classroom.

Class Participation

Learning a second language well is a good example of "learning by doing," but in order to do something well, students must understand what is involved.

We must be wary of both understanding without doing and doing without understanding. Having the teacher do almost all of the talking will not work, unless the program objective is simply an intellectual awareness of structure, as in the grammar-translation method, or the ability to understand French speech, as in certain comprehension methods. Both of these are instances of understanding (in the former, structure, in the latter, meaning) without doing. Having students converse without much guidance and with little or no correction will not work either, unless we are ready to accept fluency without accuracy, which is the result of communicative approaches such as immersion. This is doing (meaningfully but inaccurately) without understanding (structurally).

Ideally, all class participation should consist of individual student output; most school and college French classes are so large, however, that each student gets to say very little unless the teacher uses some choral responses. These can be used effectively only with highly mechanical responses such as imitation and simple oral drills, for a group response to any stimulus requiring mental processing and choice-making is bound to produce confusion as students generate different utterances at different speeds. Even with imitations, the first few guided attempts with any difficult utterances should be individual only, because a high standard of accuracy cannot be established in a jumble of responses. Once the students clearly know what constitutes a good response – by having the errors of a few students corrected effectively – some choral participation can be tried. One advantage of occasional choral responses is that they provide a chance for each student to participate more often; another (minor) advantage is that they help the teacher keep the class "on their toes," as students never know when they will be asked to join in a response. Choral responses do not have a great deal of value, but they do have some.

All meaningful, constructed output must necessarily be individual. It can take the form of responses to the teacher or supervised interaction in small groups of students. The problem with unsupervised verbal interaction between students is that the reward of communicating tends to make incorrect French habitual. The teacher must find some way to provide supervision and correction during small group activities. (A few suggestions are offered in the next chapter.)

Perception

Unless students can hear the important distinctions in French sounds and intonation patterns, they will not be able to understand spoken French well or to produce it with native-like pronunciation and intonation. Not only do students need to distinguish sounds within French, they also need to know how French sounds differ from their closest English equivalents, since unconscious anglophone habits play such a major role in this area.

Students should be helped to develop this phonetic and phonological awareness very early in the program. Learning things right the first time is much more efficient than mislearning them first in the hope that the damage will be undone later. Once students decide that a particular French distinction or French-English difference is unimportant, these incorrect perceptions may never be undone.

Auditory perception in French, which should not be divorced from sound production, can be developed in a relatively short time through careful, point-by-point guided exercises and other activities that lead from form to meaning. Unfortunately, most approaches to the learning of French as a second language ignore training in sound perception (and production), on the false assumption that communication will take care of it in time.

Visual perception should not present a problem to English-speaking learners of French, as the two languages use the same alphabet and the few additional symbols (accent marks, etc.) found in French are easy to differentiate. Learning how certain French sounds correlate with French orthography is not easy but that is not primarily a perceptual task.

Understanding

Understanding means a conscious grasp of what is involved in producing French, both spoken and written. Even sophisticated learners can have serious problems if they do not understand what they may and may not do in the target language. The understanding we are discussing is not, of course, an end in itself (except perhaps as part of training in linguistics). In the French language program, knowledge *about* French is useful insofar as it speeds up the development of knowledge *of* French, that is, practical ability to use the language well.

Much of the knowledge required to use French already exists in English and can be transferred to French, provided students are made aware, explicitly, of what they may and may not transfer. But the need to understand affects all aspects of French, not just those influenced by English.

Logically, there cannot be accurate production in French as a second language without high standards; and since students cannot observe high standards without clearly knowing what is expected of them, it follows that understanding exactly what is involved is a prerequisite to accurate production.

Of course, I do not mean that class time should be spent on lengthy or involved explanations. The teacher can help the students understand many points about French by presenting carefully chosen contextual examples that illustrate the nature of the point being introduced. By helping the students compare the examples to each other, within French and when necessary across languages, the teacher can lead them to identify what is the same or different. Examples to help them notice the distribution of forms can also be used.

If explanations are necessary to ensure clear understanding of a rule, or of the distribution of forms, they should be brief and explicit. They should deal with one point at a time. For both ease of understanding and practical mastery, complex rules should be broken into their components and taught one by one.

Production

As noted earlier, consistent accurate production requires clear perception (of sounds or letters) or clear understanding (of rules) or both. Perception/understanding and production help each other through reciprocal causation or mutual feedback; but normally a high level of receptive control of any particular point must be developed before a high level of productive control can exist.

This is not to say that the students should initially just listen to French for a long or even a short time. The well-attested phenomenon of subvocal speech (covert mimicry) probably extends to many other types of covert responses. Learners say to themselves what they think they heard or what they think they should say. Such "silent speech," which can be quite inaccurate, cannot be evaluated or corrected by the teacher. There is no such thing as just listening to a new language one is learning. Listening is an active process in which students subvocally (even with some muscular activity) echo what they hear, interpret it, and simplify it.

Naturally, beginners are often inaccurate in their subvocal echoings, interpretations, and simplifications. During an active listening period, the teacher can only be vaguely and indirectly aware of the students' covert inaccuracies. In such situations, the teacher cannot provide prompt, discriminative feedback.

In order to be able to evaluate individual responses and prevent the formation of faulty linguistic habits, we need to avoid an introductory "silent" period. From the beginning of the program, we should primarily rely on individual, overt responses. That is, there should be guided production from the start.

Rule Learning

The word "rule" has two different meanings that are often confused. In the traditional sense, rules are "statements about a language as found in a grammar book." Such statements are knowledge *about* the language and have been the object of much lecturing and memorization, as in the grammar-translation method. In the modern sense, a rule is the actual "linguistic behavior involved in using a language structure," that is, knowledge of an aspect *of* the language. It is in the latter sense that I use the word "rule" in this book.

Both inductive and deductive language rule learning have strengths and shortcomings. I would like to suggest a third option that combines the best of each in a new way.

Inductive rule learning – often called *discovery learning* – relies on the largely unconscious internalization of a rule from examples and practice. The rule is not stated explicitly. This type of teaching and learning is a necessity when the teacher cannot communicate with the learners in a cognitively mature manner, such as when the learners are young children or the teacher does not speak their language. But while under those conditions, only unconscious learning can take place, at least initially, there is no proof that unconscious learning is better than conscious learning.

When the students are cognitively mature and the teacher can speak their language, there is no need to rely on inductive learning. It is more efficient and effective to utilize the greater abilities of learners who can deal with language at a higher cognitive level.

Deductive rule learning progresses from the general to the particular. It starts with the teacher or the textbook providing a rule statement which the students are supposed to clearly understand and then to apply. This makes use of the higher cognitive abilities of older children and adults, so it is efficient. The problem with deduction is that teachers tend to move on as soon as something is understood and practiced a little. This accounts in part for the ineffectiveness of the grammar-translation method which produces graduates with a fair theoretical understanding of French rule statements but poor linguistic and communicative behavior in the language.

In the alternative I propose, the teacher starts by providing carefully selected examples, making sure the students understand the meaning of each; with questions the teacher then guides the students into stating, in their own words, the point the examples illustrate; and then makes the student-generated rule statement more precise. Unlike the usual unconscious discovery learning, this process of guided discovery is always overt and conscious. It combines the activity of testing hypotheses and discovering rules – something the students find quite interesting – with the teacher guidance needed to make sure that the rules are precisely stated and clearly understood. Finally, the teacher provides the students with all the practice they need, from mechanical to communicative, to make the corresponding linguistic behavior habitual through numerous associations.

Guided discovery is an active, cognitive process. Students are much more likely to remember a solution they helped discover than a statement by the teacher. They *own* the solution which they arrive at by *doing*, not by listening passively. This process also ensures understanding of which the teacher cannot be sure under inductive procedures.

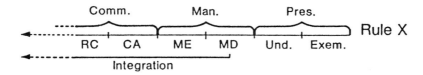

Figure 1

```
Pres. = Presentation
Exem. = Exemplification
Und.  = Understanding (guided discovery or
Man.  = Manipulation              explanation)
MD    = Mechanical Drills
ME    = Meaningful Exercises
Comm. = Communication
CA    = (Realistic) Communicative Activities
RC    = Real Communication
```

Although practice should initially focus on form rather than meaning, it should never be mindless and meaningless. What I recommend for the initial phase of practice is "intelligent conditioning" in which (1) the students know the meaning of every drill sentence or, if they seem uncertain, are asked to provide it (no new word is introduced initially); (2) they have a clear, conscious awareness of the choices they must make in order to respond; and (3) they are therefore in a good position to evaluate discriminative feedback and, soon, to self-monitor their production. This is an intelligent process of mini-problem solving – each drill and exercise frame constituting a mini-problem – that uses high-level cognitive abilities. It is therefore very different from the mindless conditioning of drills used in most audiolingual classes in the 60s and early 70s. Figure 1 is a representation of the steps involved in teaching a rule, from the recall and/or presentation of sample occurrences of the rule to its use in real communication.

Deep and Surface Correction

A carefully graded systematic program of French instruction should not result in frequent errors. If there are frequent errors, it means that someone has failed in some way. The teacher may not have presented a point clearly. Maybe insufficient practice was provided to lead the students to mastery of each point before going on to the next; as a result, errors are so frequent and entrenched that it is extremely difficult for the teacher to correct them and this can be done only sporadically. Maybe the students are not sufficiently motivated to try hard for excellence – something the teacher's attitudes and actions strongly affect. Maybe the students are venturing well beyond what they control linguistically, something the teacher can largely prevent.

But while in a good systematic French program errors would not be very frequent, even in an ideal program some errors would occur as students learn new rules and as they try to recombine what they have learned to construct their own meaningful messages. The teacher must therefore know how to deal with errors in an efficient and effective way.

The traditional way of correcting errors – asking the student to imitate the correct utterance or write the correct written words – is *surface* correction. It is cognitively very passive and rarely engages higher-level cognitive abilities. Because it fails to engage the student's mind, it remains ineffective. The proof is that many students continue to make the same errors throughout the program, regardless of how many times they have been corrected in this manner.

To be effective, correction must be *deep*. It must (1) focus on the likely cause of the error; (2) remind the student of the criteria for accurate output, (3) recall the criteria and thus make them part of the student's mental structure. Only then should the teacher ask to have the given output produced again. Deep correction does not tell the student, "Imitate this." Instead it says, "Make an effort to intelligently recall how this should be said or written, and why, and then say it." In the classroom, not much learning can take place without effort.

Correction is not punishment. It is essential information that students need on the accuracy and appropriateness of their output. Without this information – without an authoritative answer to the question, "Am I doing this right or not?" – the student will not know what is needed to improve the output. Of course, for correction not to be punishment, it must be given in a kind, matter-of-fact manner, never impatiently. And, although for the sake of effectiveness the teacher should correct errors promptly, the student should not be interrupted in mid-sentence, for this is disruptive, communicatively and sometimes even linguistically.

Initially, at least, older children and adults want to be corrected linguistically – even more than teachers want to correct them. This is because cognitively mature students approach a second language like French with the desire to speak it well, not just to survive in Frenglish.

Deconditioning

Some students, despite careful instruction and correction, may form a few faulty linguistic habits. Also students with a bad case of Frenglish frequently transfer into good programs. In either situation, remediation in the form of deconditioning is needed.

Deconditioning – unlearning an undesirable response – is a matter of learning a new response in the presence of the same stimuli. If the student's mangling of a French structure or word meaning results from transposing it from English to French, clearly the most direct and efficient way of dealing with the problem is to make sure that the difference between the two is understood and that the desired French structure or word is produced in response to the stimulus that is causing the difficulty – the English structure or word on which the faulty output is based. The same process of deconditioning can be used with overgeneralizations within French.

Memory

The power of memory should be used systematically in the French language program. While there is no need to memorize long dialogues, the memorization of individual sentences in oral samples provides a base to which to refer and on which to build.

To facilitate recall and to make knowledge of French rules and words permanent, the program should reintroduce them in several contexts first, and then cyclically, at increasingly longer intervals. (Research is needed to determine the most effective patterns of reintroduction.)

If the teacher wants the students to have active control of a given rule or word, they should be required to recall and use it. Just introducing a structure, word or phrase a few times may result in recognition without the ability to use it.

If the students do not use what they have learned, their knowledge turns from productive to receptive; in time what they are not exposed to is, for all practical purposes, forgotten. True, nothing seems to be completely forgotten – the proof is that it can be relearned faster than if learned from scratch – but when one cannot understand what once was familiar (I am not talking about a brief lapse), that knowledge is no longer functional.

Intensive or even semi-intensive language programs are helpful in that new items recur much closer together, thus facilitating both learning and recall. They also help prevent the process of "dememorization" described above.

7
A Better Classroom Road to Bilingualism:
More Pedagogical Principles and a Model

This chapter continues the discussion of PEM principles and concludes with a model that incorporates several crucial principles.

Out-of-Class Study

North America must be the only continent where the social aspect of education is considered as or more important than studying and learning. Parents of school children may complain to the principal if a teacher assigns more than minimal homework. Children who take studies seriously are shunned as "eggheads." Many people believe that conscientious study belongs, if anywhere at all, in universities and research centers. These attitudes affect the entire curriculum – from preschool to graduate school – and second language programs are among the subjects most severely hurt.

In a systematic French program that values accuracy, it takes considerable time for the students to reach the point where they can be trusted, linguistically speaking, with the freedom to say more or less what they want. When the program is slow – three hours a week or so – student motivation decreases as that point is long delayed. This is especially a problem in our culture, with its near-obsession with immediate gratification.

One way to shorten the time needed to reach a satisfying level of communication is to make the language program semi-intensive (two hours a day) or even intensive (four or more hours a day). Another – and they are not necessarily mutually exclusive – is to require the students to do some out-of-class study.

When the French language program emphasizes listening and speaking throughout, and even exclusively at first, out-of-class study should agree with this emphasis. It should primarily consist in the study of recordings. Graphic media such as books, workbooks, etc. should be secondary rather than dominant, particularly at the beginning level. At the late intermediate level and beyond, recordings can be supplemented with listening activities involving unedited, ungraded language, e.g. radio and television broadcasts.

Whether out-of-class study is done at home, in a laboratory, or elsewhere, students have to be guided so they know clearly what they are supposed to observe, do, and learn. In many cases, especially at the beginning of the program, this requires some training. There are ways, for example, of training students, step by step, in the discrimination of sounds and in awareness of what they have to listen to in the tapes they will study. Materials developers or teachers can intersperse self-tests for the students to check their own progress throughout the tape program.

Out-of-class study, through whatever medium, should be coordinated with classroom materials and presentations; not duplicated, as many materials do. The out-of-class material should consist in receptive and productive variations on the current "theme" – point of structure, situation, cultural topic, and so forth – as well as recombinatory material. When recordings for individual study, for example, merely duplicate textbook content and classroom activities, we cannot expect students to have any motivation to study them.

Communicative Use

An element or rule has not been fully learned until it can be used with attention primarily on meaning, that is, used in realistic or real communication. This is where several structurally oriented methods failed: they did not provide sufficient opportunity and encouragement for the students to use what they had been learning in personally meaningful ways. The result was that the students could understand rule statements and readings or function within the boundaries of memorized dialogues and mechanical drills but could not communicate in the language.

Communicative use of any particular rule should of course be built up to, not jumped into. Well-mastered samples can be manipulated fairly mechanically at first and gradually varied more freely. Then the students can progress from mastered samples and drills to semi-free personal communication by a variety of activities using everything learned up to that point. These activities are not limited to questions and answers but also include directed conversation, realistic situations and simulations, certain language games, etc. Finally, as each point approaches a good level of control, students can be given ample opportunity to use it to express personal meaning, together with everything they have learned so far in the program.

I refer to this as "semi-free personal communication" because it is still necessary to control it to prevent linguistic harm. The control is structural rather than lexical. If the class has not been taught the two past tenses of French, for example, and these tenses will not be taught systematically for several weeks, the students should be discouraged from speaking in the past, except perhaps by simple mechanical substitution of words in contextualized phrases they have mastered as part of thoroughly learned samples. By allowing and even encouraging students to freely use rules and forms they do not yet control, we are consenting to their misuse of the rules and forms. We are helping them to begin forming faulty habits before they even have a chance to learn them right.

Teachers can exert control of semi-free personal communication both explicitly and implicitly – explicitly by telling the students not to use certain tenses, constructions, etc. yet; implicitly by choosing activities and by guiding the selection of communication topics.

With unknown vocabulary, the situation is different. During semi-free personal communication students can obtain from the teacher essential lexical items they lack by saying, *Comment dit-on – X – ?* in a given context. Of course, they have to be trained not to ask for French "equivalents" of function words, which are often used very differently in the two languages. And, as noted, they need to be taught to ask for content words and phrases *in context*, for an English word or phrase in isolation may have two or more French equivalents and by learning it in isolation they will probably use it incorrectly.

The amount of semi-free personal communication can gradually increase throughout the program, from very little while a linguistic base is being established to about one-third or even one-half of class time at the advanced level. Some communication is essential from the beginning. But the gradation principle demands that, for best results, communicative output be subject to a certain degree of control. In this way, students will make few errors which, through effective correction, will largely disappear.

Mastery

In this book, the word "mastery" is not used in the sense of completely perfect and error-free control. The goal of teaching should be a high degree of mastery of each rule and element as it is taught. As already noted, this is not just a matter of mechanical practice, for mastery in language learning implies also the ability to use the rule or element in communication, albeit graded and controlled.

At each step in the presentation and practice of a rule, subrule or element, the teacher should insist on a level of mastery of about 90 percent.

This is of course with the understanding that the students are expected to develop fuller, if possible complete, mastery over the point in the weeks ahead.

We cannot realistically expect such a level of mastery of every point by every student in the usual program in which entire classes proceed together regardless of individual differences. Some students are not sufficiently motivated to do so. Furthermore, the time required for mastery of a rule through practice and use varies individually. Some students need much more time than others. It is for that reason that, ideally, French language programs should be individually paced – a very different program organization than the usual one.

Individualization of pace allows the best students to proceed faster than the rest and thus avoid boredom, and saves the slow ones from constantly having to catch up. In this way, students who are above and below average in their language learning aptitude can master French at their own speed without causing each other frustration. (Enrichment and remediation essentially apply band-aids to this pace problem. Besides, language-related enrichment actually increases the gap between the best students and all others.)

With individualized pace, each student will not be at a different point in the program, as many teachers and especially administrators fear. There would have to be a fastest group and a slowest group, for frequent small-group interaction is part of the approach. A more valid concern, perhaps, is that individualized pace may not work well with children who lack sufficient maturity to do the independent work necessary for this approach to succeed.

Whether the program is individualized or lockstep, mastery of each point is not just a matter of covering a given book chapter or some other material. Teachers must maintain high standards of performance through the correction of errors, evaluation, and so on, and of course all the principles discussed in these chapters are relevant to the attainment of mastery.

It is a serious mistake to move on to the next point in the program before students develop a high level of control over the one being taught. If the class has spent too much time on a point that is still just half-learned, it means that the point was not adequately subdivided into subpoints that could be mastered, one at a time, in a reasonably short time. Even so, with slow students it may be necessary to come back to a given point later, sometimes more than once. The principle of variety at the macro level applies here: even students who require more time to master a point need variety.

Passing a French course should be a matter of having mastered a given content, not of having occupied a chair for X number of months. If the principle of mastery is not followed, an otherwise well-conceived program will turn out speakers of Frenglish – just as immersion programs do.

Integration

The French language program recommended in this book is not a "linear" program. That is, the students do not learn and use point A this week, point B the next, point C the week after that, and so on. Learning a second language involves not only step-by-step learning and use of its rules and elements but also integration of what has been learned up to that point, all through the program.

Let us suppose that point A is learned and used the first week. When point B is learned the second week, then A and B should be used together. After C is learned the third week, graded communication should involve the use of all three – A, B, and C, and so on. People may joke about "students speaking only in the *passé composé* this Tuesday," but this does not happen when a systematic French language program carefully observes the principle of integration, not just that of gradation.

Evaluation

In addition to the ongoing correction of errors and informal evaluation of the students' comprehension and output on specific points being learned and in general, both students and teachers benefit from periodic formal evaluations. To be most useful to students, tests, interviews, etc. should provide them with fairly detailed diagnoses of the specific points where their output falls short of justified expectations. This means, of course, that students should be tested, with ample advance notice, only on what they have been taught and been given sufficient opportunity to learn.

Evaluation should be in harmony with the goals and emphases of the program. It is highly inconsistent, for example, for any program claiming to have an oral emphasis to rely mostly on paper-and-pencil tests. It is also counterproductive, as students will naturally want to spend most of their study time on "what counts" on tests and will therefore spend much less time developing audio-oral skills.

Teachers can test almost everything about the French language orally. For sound discrimination and listening comprehension there are several test question formats. Probably the most useful one for listening comprehension is a brief listening passage followed by intelligently designed, inferential multiple-choice items.

Teachers can also test the various components and elements of the speaking skill as well as more global functioning at any point in the program in several ways. If laboratory oral tests cannot be used (the usual reason being the lack or inadequacy of facilities), then occasional, specific progress interviews (not general proficiency interviews) can be administered – in fact, it is best to alternate between both types of test. Teachers who cannot conduct even brief interviews can at least keep a systematic, linguistically specific record of classroom oral output, periodically giving a summary to each student.

The results of carefully designed tests are useful to the teacher too. They show what the students have mastered and what they need to practice further; this enables the teacher to take timely appropriate action.

Continuity

All learning suffers when there is no continuity. This is especially true of subjects that involve practical skills, like French. When learning or use are interrupted for any significant length of time, some active control becomes passive and even the ability to recognize many words and certain structures fades. With languages as with physical fitness: either use it or lose it. Even a break of a few months can result in considerable loss, forcing the French teacher in the next course to spend an inordinate amount of time reviewing what the students used to know.

If we make beginning courses at least semi-intensive, we can ensure that students will reach, within their first school year or term of French, a linguistic level high enough to be able to have meaningful practice on their own during any long interruptions in the learning process. Well motivated students may be ready to do that. But we can hardly expect them to do it if it means that they will have to wait while the rest of the students review and catch up. (This is a further reason for establishing individualized-pace, continuous-progress programs.)

For continuity (that is, transfer and orderly progress) across schools, from schools to colleges, or from one university to another – what is usually called "articulation" – a detailed record indicating what each student has mastered would prove far more useful than a transcript that simply states the grades or courses completed and marks earned. Given the different goals and standards of different programs, marks can be meaningless.

Visual Aids

Visual aids can be used to advantage for many purposes. They can stimulate conversation in specific directions, motivate in general, provide cultural information, and offer general referential meaning to a situation or reading activity. I am in favor of visual aids being used for such purposes. But visual aids have two major minuses as well.

First, several studies have shown that visual aids are unreliable in conveying the specific meanings of new words and phrases. In one study, for example, I found that even with concrete words there was some misinterpretation and considerable uncertainty.[1] Contexualized phrases such as those in dialogues presented with the help of filmstrips are frequently misinterpreted, even by experienced teachers of French.[2] Students often end up asking each other, after class, "What did word or phrase X with picture such and such mean?" – a case of the incompetent enlightening the uninformed.

Beyond presentations, visual aids are also problematic in the area of listening or reading comprehension of specific vocabulary or structures. It is virtually the converse of the difficulty just discussed. The drawback here exists when visual aids *are* easily understood. To the extent that students understand anything thanks to a visual aid, they do not have to rely on the French language in order to understand it. So they do not have to make the effort needed to fully process and internalize the language itself. Therefore, visuals aids have to be used selectively and with a definite rationale.

Technology

Technological aids can be very helpful in a second language program. But they, too, perform certain functions well and others poorly or not at all.

The low-tech cassette machine can serve most types of listening activities as well as controllable oral output tasks. Making copies of tapes readily available to students can be of great help. Today many students have access to such machines, and schools can provide access for the rest without having to build an expensive laboratory.

For individual pronunciation and intonation practice and for oral tests, the recording function is essential. This is more expensive, of course, and rarely practicable other than in a laboratory of some kind.

High-tech equipment, namely computers and computer-controlled audio-visual devices, are excellent aids. We must not forget, however, several limitations they will continue to have even when their cost comes down drastically. First, the computer by itself is primarily a graphic medium; as such it is effective in presenting language in written form but it is not suited to a program that emphasizes audio-oral skills. Of course, computers can control audio-visual devices in very flexible ways and this makes their audio output useful in practicing listening comprehension. Second, the software produced so far is fragmentary rather than part of an integrated program. Third, no matter how sophisticated the design of computer language learning software, it will be able to interact with students only on the basis of what has been programmed into it in advance. Computers cannot evaluate free output well, whether oral or written, nor is interacting by typing messages on a computer keyboard real communication in any sense;

for good results students must have considerable personal interaction. Furthermore, artificial intelligence experts are beginning to say that a computer will never be able to function as the human mind.

In terms of the needs of learners of French, rather than those of the high-tech industry, beginning students need to work primarily with audio devices and tape recorders. It is mostly at the late intermediate level and beyond, when reading and vocabulary expansion become more important, that computers should have an important role in a French language program that adequately integrates human and technological resources.

Technological aids can greatly enhance a French language program, but we should not expect machines to do what they cannot do. Certain things will always have to be done by live teachers, warts and all. We should not let hardware or software manufacturers influence us to deviate from what we think is best in language teaching. Instead, we should tell them what we need; it is up to them to supply it if they can. Let us not allow "the tail to wag the dog" as we did with the language laboratories in the 60s.

Self-Instruction

With sufficient help from technological aids, students can learn much of a second language independently. But only another human being – preferably a trained teacher – can converse with students, evaluate their free speech and writing, and provide the necessary feedback. It follows that a French program should not be entirely self-instructional. I estimate that no more than 60 to 70 percent of the total contact between the student and the second language can be self-instructional if good results are to be obtained.

Staffing

French classes have traditionally been staffed by one teacher per class. Some programs employ teacher's aides in various capacities. I think we should make use of all the human resources the community, the program, and the class have to offer. We especially need to be flexible in finding human help for small-group interaction and individual tutoring.

Students need to use what they have learned for semi-free, personal communication more often than the few opportunities they have in class. This is why small-group activities are essential. But simply dividing the class into small groups and encouraging them to talk will do the students more harm than good linguistically. A person capable of directing the group, evaluating its members' output, and providing reasonably useful feedback must be in charge of each group. In order of pedagogical preference, French-speaking people with the following backgrounds could help (given a suitable personality and adequate knowledge of English):

(1) Francophones with some training in teaching. This is the background of many teacher's aides.
(2) Francophones from the community who lack teacher training. They should be offered some orientation and training. Some of them may be willing to help as volunteers or for limited compensation.
(3) Francophone students, whether from Quebec, France, or other parts of the French-speaking world. Often these students are in classes in English as a second language.
(4) More advanced students in the program. Ideally, these should be very advanced students. They should get some credit toward their own courses as reward for their help.
(5) The best students in the class. This is the last resort, but it can work reasonably well if the small-group leaders are carefully selected and supervised.

When using small-group leaders and tutoring, the teacher is of course in charge. When the students are doing small-group activities, they can leave one chair in each group empty for the teacher, who would unpredictably move from group to group.

At the advanced level – especially if a stay in a French-speaking area is not possible – each student could be paired with an individual francophone in the local community for a certain amount of conversation per week, initially in person, later possibly by a combination of telephone and face-to-face conversations. This pool of local francophone resource persons would consist primarily of people who do not work full-time and who would no doubt welcome some compensation for conversing in French.

Summary and Integration of Theory and Practice: The Two-Cone Model

The most important features of the Principled Eclectic Method (PEM) of classroom language teaching are represented by a model consisting of two cones, one for French, the other for English. This Two-Cone Model is a model of systematic classroom language learning induced by teaching, not of natural language acquisition through communication/interaction.

Each language is represented by a cone, like the one in Figure 2, with pronunciation (P) at the apex, grammar (G: morphology and syntax) at the core, and vocabulary (V) surrounding the core. This is a simple representation of the linguistic components of a language as it is learned systematically.

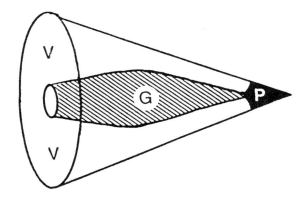

Figure 2

Initial contact between the two cones – that is, between the English that learners know and the French they are trying to learn – is at the apices (Figure 3). This contact represents the first thing to which students of audio-oral French are exposed, namely, the need to deal with pronunciation (P), to discriminate and produce the sounds of French, inevitably vis-à-vis those of English. For best results, the students should be taught to do this at this point in the program.

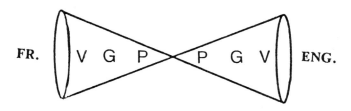

Figure 3

As students learn the French language, emphasis – not exclusive attention – should shift to grammatical (G) structure and then to the expansion of vocabulary. What they learn in terms of pronunciation, grammar and vocabulary emerges in reference to corresponding structures and elements in English (Figure 4).

A Better Classroom Road to Bilingualism 83

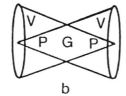

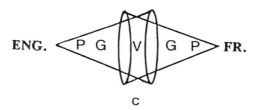

Figure 4

If the teacher does not overtly deal with this connection, does not take advantage of the positive influences from English and does not explicitly counteract the negative influences, the students will covertly refer to English, often inappropriately, without the teacher having control of the process.

Figure 5 shows that if students fail to attain mastery of any French linguistic behavior (rule), they will retain poor French linguistic habits (Frenglish). These are represented by dots in the white area emerging from the right, which is the area of French/Frenglish already learned.

84 *French Immersion: Myths and Reality*

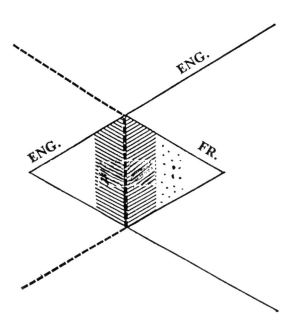

Figure 5

Poor habits come largely from not dealing adequately with English influence on each point as it is taught, that is, not properly or sufficiently addressing the French-English interaction represented by the shaded areas. Some poor habits also develop when inappropriate generalizations within French – extending something known in French to uses where it does not apply – are not dealt with adequately.

As the student masters each rule (cf. Figure 1) and the teacher ensures that it is used in conjunction with everything learned earlier, what results is a series of increasingly more encompassing transitional systems as shown in Figure 6.

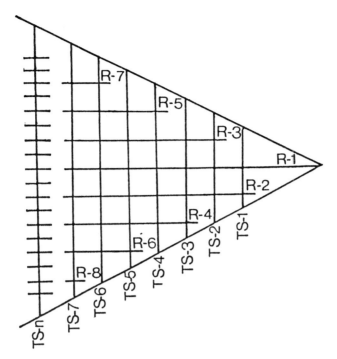

Figure 6

These systems add one rule (or subrule) at a time (TS-1, TS-2...), until the final system of the program (TS-n) is reached. Of course, even graduates of the most thorough language program will have to go on to acquire additional, infrequent rules and a large amount of vocabulary on their own. So TS-n does not represent the competence of a native speaker but *accurate* control of what should be known by someone with *transitional* FSI proficiency ratings of approximately (3 out of 5) in listening and speaking, about 3+ in reading, and 2 in writing.

When French as a second language is learned in a francophone community, as in Quebec, communication with French speakers will have a significant effect on the French/Frenglish that emerges from the French/English interaction that is an unavoidable part of the learning process. For beginners, this kind of communication seems to be more harmful than helpful because it forces them to use their limited linguistic means for global ends, thereby developing a tendency to see their own inaccurate output as acceptable.

86 *French Immersion: Myths and Reality*

Finally, the Two-Cone Model of classroom language teaching and learning is centrifugal (see Figure 7) because (1) its core of French *linguistic competence*, both structure and vocabulary, is used in cyclical communicative activities that foster the development of (2) *communicative competence*, within the framework of appropriate behavior being simulated so that students can also grow in (3) *cultural competence*.

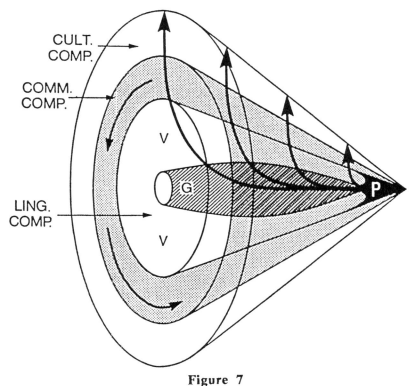

Figure 7

This direction of learning in the classroom is (and for good results has to be) the opposite of that in cribs and playpens. In the latter, the environment triggers the need to communicate and input-rich communication results, at a leisurely pace, in the linguistically unhindered internalization of rules.

In the French language classroom, there is no francophone environment, no strong need to communicate in French, and no rich interactive French input. Most French programs cannot afford the luxury of a leisurely pace, even if it were desirable. Too, classroom learners of French already have deep linguistic roots that affect any language learning.

The teaching and learning of French as a second language in our classrooms should be based on the foregoing considerations.

Notes

[1] Hector Hammerly, "Primary and Secondary Associations with Visual Aids as Semantic Conveyors," *International Review of Applied Linguistics,* Vol. XXII, No. 2 (May 1974), pp. 119-25.

[2] Hector Hammerly, "Contextualized Visual Aids (Filmstrips) as Conveyors of Sentence Meaning," *International Review of Applied Linguistics,* Vol. XXII, No. 2 (May 1984), pp. 87-94.

8

A Better Classroom Road to Bilingualism: Procedures and Techniques

In this chapter, I will discuss and give examples of a number of Principled Eclectic Method (PEM) procedures and techniques. The reader will recall that PEM is a step-by-step, oral-emphasis, bilingual method in which each point is dealt with consciously at first and then made unconscious through practice which moves gradually from single-point, structural/mechanical to cumulative, communicative/meaningful integration using everything learned to that point. This is a rough, "shorthand" reminder of important features of PEM.

Because PEM is primarily an audio-oral method, the examples given below focus on listening and speaking skill practice. Of course students of French need reading and writing activities as well, but ways of teaching reading comprehension and writing ability have been known for a long time and are widely available in the professional literature. Please note also that *the samples in this chapter are of bilingual, skill-building, audio-oral procedures and techniques with an overt cognitive orientation.* While I also discuss "bridging" activities briefly, I do not think I need to give examples of monolingual, communicative activities – these are widely used (too early and too much, in fact, for good results) and other authors have dealt with them at length in the last 15 years or so.

The teaching activities briefly illustrated below include a pronunciation problem, a morphological (conjugation) lesson, a short oral sample, a sociolinguistic usage point (*tu/vous*), and examples of bridging activities to cover the gap between fairly mechanical, controlled use of something in French and its use in semi-free communication.

The point where each sample activity would fit in a complete French program would depend on how the program is organized, but pronunciation activities should come at the very beginning of the program and the other samples early in it. The sample activities were written with young adults (18-25 years of age) in mind; the contents of these mini-lessons would have to be adapted if used with younger learners (10-years-old and up), to fit their interests. At several points in the samples, I will show "deep" correction techniques that make students aware of the criteria for accurate production.

In order to make the activity samples that follow clear and precise, I will use the following symbols and other ad-hoc conventions in this chapter:

C	Class or group is invited to produce and/or produces output
S	A Student, *specific* to our discussion if numbered (*any* otherwise), is invited to produce and/or produces output
Ss	Various Students
T	Teacher behavior
*	An asterisk immediately precedes linguistically incorrect student output
/.../	Slant lines enclose *phonemes* that need to be highlighted in our discussion
[...]	Square brackets enclose *phones* that need to be highlighted in our discussion
<...>	Angle brackets enclose what the students read
(...)	My comments to the reader, when introduced within a teaching activity, appear in parentheses

Cognitively mature learners should not have to do purely mechanical, mindless drills – in all practice, they should be made aware of the crucial points involved. But at the beginning of each point being taught, a few minutes spent on *intelligent* conditioning pay off in the long run. In all largely mechanical exercises, the pace should be brisk, although it is often necessary to ask individual students to pause and think briefly before responding, especially in exercises beyond the repetition/imitation type. The teacher should call on the students (and, when appropriate, the class) in unpredictable order – this will enhance attention. Largely mechanical exercises should be done for no more than 10 minutes at most, even if they are lively and varied. Otherwise, language students' attention and motivation will flag.

In a point-by-point approach to the teaching of French, the first significant task facing beginning students is not learning vocabulary or a dialogue or trying to understand fluent speech. It is not even getting to know the teacher and each other in French, for this can temporarily be done in English, as part of a multi-segment orientation to the program, approximately 10 minutes at a time. Their first significant learning task is developing skill in discriminating and producing French sounds accurately. If they are not explicitly taught how, they will find their own ways of doing so.

True, some general improvement in pronunciation and intonation takes place as a result of interaction, without focused phonological instruction at the beginning of the program or even without careful correction. But I have observed over the years that best long-term results are obtained when pronunciation is taught systematically at the start. This is not surprising, for everything the students hear or say in French mostly reinforces their earliest ideas of how the French language sounds and how they can pronounce it. Besides, an early emphasis on pronunciation and intonation saves teachers much time in the long run, as it spares them from frequently having to correct pronunciation remedially for the rest of the program.

So I will start the illustration of PEM procedures and techniques with an example of a pronunciation "mini-lesson." Such activities would be interspersed through the first 15 hours of the program, in alternation with more meaningful graded activities. Each class hour would have no more than two 5 to 10 minute pronunciation or intonation activities. Together with an orientation to the program, cultural overview, and so on, these phonological activities would form part of a 15-20 hour introductory mini-course easing beginners into the study of French.

Sample Pronunciation Activity: "Clear" [l]

The French [l] is always pronounced as a "clear" [l] with the tip of the tongue touching the back of the upper teeth and the body of the tongue in the [i] position, as in *sel*, never with the spoon-like, concave position used in the English "dark" [ɫ] as in *sell*. Before [iː], as in *leave,* many speakers of English have an [l] almost as clear as the French [l]. An English dark [ɫ] usually does not interfere with communication in French but is a major factor in an English accent.

A mini-lesson on this problem could be as follows:
T: "Raise your hands when the two words or syllables you hear are different:"
"sell – sel"
(Both utterances are pronounced with the same falling intonation. Whenever an exercise calls for such distinctions, the order in which various combinations appear in the cues should be unpredictable. To faciliate discrimination, the first few pairs may be articulated with slight exaggeration.)

C: (Most raise their hands).
T: (Raises hand to indicate they were different).
"sel – sel"
C: (Some raise their hands).
T: (Indicates they were the same. Repeats the previous pair and contrasts it with):
"sel – sell."
C: (Nearly all raise their hands).
T: (Raises hand, continues):
"bell – belle"
C: (Nearly all raise their hands).
T: (Raises hand, continues):
"bell – bell"
C: (No student raises hand).

This is followed by further rapid practice with monosyllabic words and word syllables that are identical across languages except for the [l]. In the discrimination phase of a pronunciation mini-lesson *there must be only one difference* between the utterances; otherwise the answer is given away and no discrimination takes place. The only sequences meeting this requirement are made up of the vowel [ɛ] followed by [l] or [ł] and possibly preceded by [s], [b], as above, or other consonant sounds that are perceptually identical in both languages, such as [š] as in *Mi(chelle)* – *shell* and [m] as in *ju(melles)* – *(Mel)vin*. The teacher helps individual students who are having discrimination problems, if necessary exaggerating articulations or providing brief articulatory pointers. After the class has had further practice, the teacher can give them a sound discrimination mini-test with, for example, the following format:

T: (Students listen and read) – "<Circle the letter corresponding to the word or syllable that is the same as the model. For example, you hear:> sel; <(A)> sell- <(B)> sel- <(C)> neither A nor B. So you circle (B) which is the French word for "salt" (the sound discrimination mini-test should contain 6-8 items).

Once the students learn to discriminate well auditorily between a French [l] and an English [ł] in this limited phonic context, they can be asked to *produce* the French [l] in the same context. The first step in the production phase is to make sure they know how the desired French sound is produced as opposed to the undesirable English sound. This is accomplished by providing the articulatory pointers mentioned at the beginning of this section. It will be helpful for the students if the teacher initially exaggerates articulations slightly (as noted earlier) and if he or she refers to diagrams of the two different tongue positions. Before proceeding to production, the teacher should make sure that the students have understood the explanation/demonstration. Then the teacher can go on, for example, as follows:

T: "Répétez: belle:"

S1: "belle"

T: "Bien!" – (to S2): "sel"

S2: "*se[ɫ]"

T: "Pas *se[ɫ] (exaggerating dark [ɫ]) – sel (exaggerating clear [l]):"

S2: "*se[ɫ]"

T: "Add an [iɪ̯] to it – [ˈseliɪ̯]." (Since most English speakers produce a clear [l] before [iɪ̯] they can usually imitate the clear [l] correctly in this context. Do not just ask students to "put the tongue in the [i] position," because they will end up saying *[sejl] or "sale," *[bejl] or "bale/bail," and so on.)

S2: "[ˈseliɪ̯]"

T: "Make the [iɪ̯] shorter – [ˈseli]:"

S2: "[ˈseli]"

T: "Without changing your tongue position, make the [i] still shorter, so short it almost disappears – [ˈseli̯] . . . [sel]:"

S2: "[ˈseli̯] . . . [sel]"

T: "Oui – sel! Magnifique!" (This technique is called "shaping.")

When the teacher helps individual students to overcome typical difficulties, the rest of the class can observe how to do so. After that, the teacher can occasionally call on the whole class to repeat [-ɛl] utterances. When almost all students can produce clear [l] in this context, the teacher can help them to master a short phrase such as *Quelle belle demoiselle!*, with aids and English equivalents as needed. They should memorize such a phrase for future reference, and the teacher should make sure they know what it means. The few who are still having problems can be helped individually. (All students should have access to recordings with which to practice, after class, audio-oral lessons covering the same points taught in class. These materials should not be the same used in class, or they will not be studied. Recorded out-of-class lessons should involve not only pronunciation but most of the contents of the entire program.)

This procedure looks long and complicated, but it can be done by a skillful teacher in a few minutes. Later, in about 5 minutes, the teacher can teach discrimination and production of clear [l] in other phonic contexts, i.e., (1) following other vowels, (2) in initial positions, (3) following other consonants, and (4) before other consonants – which is an approximate progression from next-harder (after [-ɛl]) to most difficult. Since in other phonic contexts there is more than one difference between French and English, the principle of the single difference during the essential discrimination phase can be observed only by asking students to differentiate between French words that are pronounced with a French [l] and the same words mispronounced with an English [ɫ] — but that must be the only English sound in them for there to be any meaningful discrimination. For example:

T: "Raise your hands if both words have the French [l] sound:"
"il – il" (both with French [l])
"balle – ba[ɫ]" (second one has English [ɫ])

(or)

T: "Raise your hands if the word has a French [l] sound:"
"lundi" (French [l])
"[ɫ]aisser" (no French [l])

(or, especially to test discrimination:)

T: <"Circle the letter corresponding to the French word whose [l] sound is correctly pronounced:" (an example or two should be given before the test itself)
"<(A)> avri[ɫ] – <(B)> [ɫ]apin – <(C)> louer"

At this point the students would accurately and thoroughly learn a very brief oral exchange — just a couple of phrases, along with their meanings — containing the French /l/ in a variety of contexts. These phrases can be used for future reference if students revert to the English [ɫ], as some probably will tend to do. (In correcting such errors, the teacher can remind the students of the phrase in which they had learned to produce an /l/ accurately in that particular phonic context.)

Similar procedures can be used for other pronunciation problems and to teach French intonation patterns. In the case of French phonemes that have no English counterparts (the /y/ of *du*, for example) an articulatory phonetic approach is not enough. In this example, students first need to learn how to produce the French [u] rather than the English [uŭ] and the French [i] rather than the English [iɪ̆]. Then they need practice discriminating /y/ as in *du* from the /u/ in *doux* and, to a lesser extent, the /i/ in *dit*. Only then should they go on to guided production.

Sample Morphological Activity: Conjugation of Present Tense of -er Verbs

The present tense of *-er* verbs like *parler* — as do other French conjugations, etc. — has fewer forms in speech than in writing. In speech there are only two endings attached to the stem *parl-*, namely, the /-[ɔ̃]/ that goes with *nous* and the /-ə/ that goes with *vous*. In order to avoid confusion we should observe the differences between the two sets of forms. Since the spoken set is smaller and more useable in the classroom, it should be taught first.

The traditional way of dealing with conjugations is to have the students memorize a series of forms almost like a little poem (except they do not quite rhyme). But memorizing forms in a particular sequence makes them less readily available to the students when they try to use them in normal oral production, because they must recite the little poem first. Learners of French should be able to access each verb form directly from the subject nouns or pronouns that condition it. For example, they should learn to produce, automatically, *parlez* after *vous,* not because it follows *parlons* on a list of forms.

When dealing with a set of forms involving more than two correlations – in this case, matching verb forms with subjects – students learn best when they practice only two forms first and then the others are added one at a time. If the morphological set allows it, as it does in this case, it simplifies learning if the teacher points out, "All the others use X."

More generally, in teaching a grammatical point, the point of departure should be a few examples from previously mastered oral samples, supplemented as needed by further examples. These examples (with their meanings) serve as a "linguistic beachhead" from which to "conquer" the grammatical structure involved.

After students learn each subpoint, they should have a certain amount of meaningful practice (*"Maintenant, la vérité."*) After they have learned all forms or operations involved, there should be substantial meaningful practice.

In PEM, this activity with *-er* verbs could proceed as follows:

T: "Remember what Janine asked Peter when they met?"
S: "Vous parlez français?"
T: (Signals approval) – "Vous parlez français?" – (Signals students and then class to repeat):
T: (Signals a student to provide natural equivalent):
S: "Do you speak French?"
T: (Same signal to another student)
S: "Vous parlez français?"
T: "What did Jacques say to Mr. Roberts at the office?"
S: "Les samedis nous dînons au Café de Paris."
T: (Signals approval) – "Nous dînons au Café de Paris."
  – (Signals student and class repetitions) – (Signals a student to provide the crosslinguistic equivalent):

S: "We have dinner at the Café de Paris."
T: (Signals French again):
Ss: and then C: "Nous dînons au Café de Paris."
T: "Répétez: – Nous parlons français." (Repetitions and student-produced or teacher-provided equivalent follow)
T: "Répétez: Vous dînez au Café de Paris." (Repetitions and equivalent)
T: "Répétez: – Vous cherchez le stylo?"
T: (Provides equivalent, as this is new) "Are you looking for the pen?"
T: (Signals repetition) "Nous cherchons le stylo."
T: (Tries to elicit equivalent from a student)
S: "We are looking for the pen."
T: (To students) "What verb forms go with *vous*?"
Ss: "Parlez, dînez, cherchez. . ."
T: "Très bien." – "What is the ending?"
S: "/-e/."
T: "Magnifique." (To students) "What verb forms go with *nous*?"
Ss: "Dînons, parlons, cherchons. . ."
T: (Signals approval) – "What is the ending?"
S: "/-[ɔ̃]/"
T: "Très bien."
T: (To class) "Now change the sentences according to the cues I'll give you:" (a nonverbal signal can be taught and used for this) – "Vous parlez français" – "**Nous**. . .:" (To a student:)
S1: "Nous parlons français."
T: "Monique et vous, **vous**. . .:"
S2: "Monique et vous, vous parlez français."
T: "Jacques et moi, **nous**. . .:"
S3: "Jacques et moi, nous parlons français."
T: "**Vous**. . .:"
S4: "Vous *parlons français."
T: "*Nous* parlons français, mais **Vous**. . .:" (Correction uses contrast and tries to elicit form directly.)
S4: "Vous. . . vous. . ."
T: "Répétez: Vous parlez français."
S4: "Vous parlez français."

(The teacher will later come back to S4 to make sure this student can produce, not just repeat, the correlation *vous. . .-ez*. If a student is not paying attention, a mild form of "shock treatment" is to ask another student to respond.)

The class should then have similar *vous* vs. *nous* practice with phrases using several other familiar verbs beginning with a consonant. Then the teacher guides the class through similar procedures to discover the longer /vuz/ and /nuz/ forms used before verbs beginning with a vowel, such as *arriver* and *écouter*.

T: "See if you can tell me what spoken endings if any go with the other subjects with this type of French verb. Répétez:"

The class repeats phrases containing subject pronouns *je, il, ils, tu, elle, elles,* and *on,* and nouns and noun phrases with subject function, initially with verbs beginning with a consonant. Occasionally they are given or asked to produce the English equivalents. The teacher helps the students discover the generalization, such as:

S: "They all use the same (oral) form: /parl/, /din/, /ʃɛrʃ/. . .; there is no ending."

At this point the teacher helps the students to discover the shorter form of *je* (/ʒ/) and the longer forms of *ils, elles* and *on* (respectively /ilz/, /ɛlz/, and /ɔ̃n/) before verbs that begin with a vowel.

The class should then have substantial practice with *all* forms and after that spend considerable time on meaningful activities using the present tense of -*er* verbs. These activities could include directed dialogue, sentence generation, and semi-free personal communication. (See "Bridging Activities" below.)

The above presentation and practice would require at least two or three 10-minute periods.

To the reader who may wonder "Why not have *just* meaningful communicative activities from the start?" my response is: Some meaning-conscious mechanical practice makes the communicatively meaningful output that follows far more accurate. When attention is on meaningful messages from the beginning, control of form suffers because very few students can focus on form at the same time as message meaning.

Sample Dialogue Presentation: Four Sentences

At the beginning level it is useful to teach and fully exploit a good number of short oral samples, usually dialogues. But at that level the students do not know enough French to have the meanings of new words and phrases explained to them in that language. Visuals seem helpful, but they are unreliable for the initial conveyance of meanings. So for the sake of conveying meanings clearly, obtaining feedback on what is going on in the students' minds, and teaching efficiently, meanings have to be conveyed bilingually. The sample below shows therefore bilingual techniques for teaching sentences. Techniques for the correction of pronunciation and intonation errors apply here as well, of course.

The four sample sentences would be part of a dialogue of no more than about eight sentences in all. This dialogue would belong somewhere early in the program. The sentences contain several new lexical items (*penser, élections, discuter,* and *rester* plus examples of two structures to be taught systematically after the sentences are thoroughly learned: *aller* + *infinitive* (especially in the negative) and the pronoun *en.*

This activity could go as follows:

T: "Ecoutez:" (Plays once or twice an audio or audiovisual recording of the dialogue)
(Philippe:) "Qu'est-ce que tu penses des élections?"
(Lucien:) "Je ne vais pas parler de ça!"
(Philippe:) "Mais pourquoi pas?"
(Lucien:) "Si nous en discutons, nous n'allons pas rester de bons amis."

T: "Maintenant répétez:" (To a few individual students first, and occasionally to the class)
"une élection" (French nouns should be introduced whenever possible with the singular indefinite article so that their gender is clear; in the case of, e.g., **élection,** if the students hear /lelɛksjɔ̃/ they cannot be sure whether they are hearing **la** + **élection** or **les** + a nonexistent **lections.**)

T: "En anglais?" (Students should be able to guess the meanings of cognate words.)

T: "Répétez: les élections"

T: "...des élections"

T: "penser" (Before a verb is taught in one of its conjugated forms, it is a good idea to teach its infinitive, both because the two need to be related in the students' minds and because infinitives enter into several frequent constructions.)

T: "to think" (When there is no reason to think the students can guess the meaning of a word or phrase, the teacher should provide the equivalent. In this case, expecting them to figure the meaning of the French **penser** from the English **pensive** is unrealistic.)

T: "Répétez: penser de (quelque chose ou quelqu'un)" – "to think of/about (something or someone)"

T: "Répétez: penser des élections" – "to think of the elections"

T: "Répétez: Qu'est-ce que tu penses..."

S1:"Qu'est-ce que *t[u] penses..."
T: "Pas *t[u], t[y]."
S1:"*t[u]"
T: "Say [ti::::]."
S1:"[ti::::]."
T: "Now while saying [ti::::], without changing the position of your tongue, round your lips like this:" (Shows how)
S1:"[ti::::y:::]"
T: "Now alternate as I do: [ti::::], [ty::::], [ti::::], [ty::::]:"
S1:"[ti::], [ty::]..."
T: "[ty::], c'est bien ça. Now make it shorter – [ty]:"
S1:"[ty]."
T: "[ty]. Formidable. Répétez:...tu penses..."
S1:"...tu penses..."
T: "Qu'est-ce que tu penses..."
T: "...des élections?"
T: "Qu'est-ce que tu penses des élections?"
S2:(*Voice goes up in pitch at the end of "élections?")
T: "Regardez:....des élections?" (Uses hand signal to show intonation pattern and the fact that the voice goes **down** at the end of "... élections?") "When a question begins with a question word or phrase, the voice normally goes down at the end."
T: "Encore une fois: Qu'est-ce que tu penses des élections?"
S2:(Repeats with correct intonation this time.)
T: "En anglais?" (Once the students have learned the new words and have produced the sentence accurately several times, they should be able to produce its English equivalent. If they do not do this, the teacher cannot be sure that they have understood the sentence.)
T: "Répétez: Je vais parler..." (While teaching sentence segments, the teacher should pronounce them with the same intonation that they have in the complete sentence. It is confusing to at least some students when the intonation of the parts changes as they are placed in the complete sentence.)
T: "En anglais?" (Although this construction is new, the students should be able to guess the English equivalent.)
S: "I'm going to talk..."
T: "Répétez: Je ne vais pas parler..." (Signals negation.) (Students repeat.)

T: "En anglais?"
S: "I'm not going to talk..."
T: "Répétez: Je ne vais pas parler de ça!"
(Students repeat and then translate.)
T: "Répétez: Qu'est-ce que tu penses des élections?"
T: (Signals repetition) "Je ne vais pas parler de ça!"
T: "Mais pourquoi pas?"
S3: "Mais *pou[ɹ]quoi pas?"
T: "Pas *pou[ɹ]..., pou [R]..."
S3: *pou[ɹ]..."
T: "Tongue back high, close to uvula; tongue front flat, tip against lower teeth:" (Demonstrates [R:::], using hand signal) (This is just a "telegraphic" reminder of the initial teaching of the [R].)
S3: "[R:::]"
T: "...pou[R:]..."
S3: "...pou[R]..."
T: "...pou[R:]...quoi..."
S3: "...pou[R:]...quoi..."
T: "...pou[R:]quoi..."
S3: "...pou[R]quoi..."
T: "Mais pourquoi pas?" (S3, other students, and class repeat.)
T: "En anglais?" (Guessable: No new words or construction.)
S: "Why *not?*" (The teacher does not accept *"But why not?"* – which is not normal in English in this context. The teacher points out that the *Mais* here is used for emphasis and that in English this is done by simply stressing the word *not*.)
T: "Répétez: ...Rester de bons amis."
T: "To remain or stay good friends; in another context, *rester* means 'to be left'; it does *not* mean 'to rest.'" (In addition to providing the two common equivalents of this verb, the teacher warns the class about the apparent equation they should *not* make. The teacher will remind them of this warning if it is ignored. Not warning the students about this virtually invites them to make the false equation in their minds, something that may not show up in their output until much later.)
T: "Répétez: ...Rester de bons amis."
T: "En anglais?" (Students repeat and translate.)
T: "Répétez: discuter"

T: "En anglais?"
S: "Discuss?"
T: (Shows assent) "Discuss or argue about something."
T: "Répétez: Si nous en discutons..."
T: "If we discuss it... *or* If we argue about it..." (The teacher provides the English equivalent because the construction with *en* is new to the class and there is no reason to think they can guess it. This, as with most new words and phrases, is followed by "*alternation*," in which individual students and the class say it several times in French with occasional, unpredictably elicited oral translation. Alternation is a key bilingual teaching technique that helps fixate the connection between a correctly pronounced, *contextualized* French word or phrase and its correct English equivalent in that context.)
T: "Répétez: Si nous en discutons, nous n'allons pas rester de bons amis." (Students and class repeat.)
T: "En anglais?" (The class is now familiar with everything in this sentence and one or more students should therefore be able to guess its equivalent.)

At this point all four sentences in the first half of the dialogue go through some alternation. Then the teacher tells the students to learn them thoroughly, with the help of cassettes, for the next class.

In the following class or classes, the students would manipulate the dialogue by playing the roles, etc., preferably with the help of a performance script offering cues, since memorizing particular *sequences* of sentences is neither useful nor worth the effort. In exploiting the dialogue, the teacher also varies its sentences lexically and uses some of them – in our sample, sentences 2 and 4 – as preliminary examples in teaching new grammatical points. Maintaining active control of at least some basic dialogues is desirable for such long-term purposes as reference when errors are made and practice in reporting speech (recounting a dialogue in the third person), both in the present and the past. Reporting familiar dialogues in the past is especially useful in learning to tell stories while paying close attention to the difference between the *passé composé* and the *imparfait*. Of course, whatever is introduced in dialogues, other oral samples or, later, readings should be reintroduced cyclically from then on.

Sample Sociolinguistic Usage (*Tu/Vous*) Lesson

The distinction between (familiar) *tu* and (formal) *vous* is very important because its misuse often offends people. OISE scholars have acknowledged that FI students do not master this distinction even after many years in immersion programs. But students can easily learn the distinction in an early bilingual lesson if it is taught explicitly and reinforced through meaning-conscious practice.

Before there are enough examples to teach a lesson on *tu* and *vous*, the teacher could give brief situational pointers (e.g., "a conversation between classmates," "the Roberts meet the Joubert family"). After about 20 hours of instruction, a lesson on *tu* vs. *vous* could proceed as follows:

T: "French speakers have two ways of talking to people, *tu* and *vous*, depending on the relationship between the two persons. Let's repeat some examples and see if you can tell me when *tu* is used and when *vous* is used instead."

T: "What did Philippe ask his classmate Jean-Louis after class?"

S: "Tu vas a la bibliothèque?" (Students and class repeat, etc.)

T: "How did Marie ask her teacher for a pencil?"

S: "Vous avez un crayon, Madame?" (Students and class repeat, etc.)

T: "If Charles wanted change from an adult stranger in the street he would ask: Vous avez la monnaie de cinq dollars, Monsieur?" (Repetition, etc.)

T: "Because you are adult students, when I talk to each one of you or to all of you, I say: Donnez, écoutez, répètez... If you were children, I would still use those forms to talk to all of you, but I would address you individually with: Donne, écoute, répète... These verb forms go with *tu*, the others go with *vous*."

T: (Further examples, with repetition and alternation as needed)

T: "In your own words, when would you use *tu* and when would you use *vous*?"

A brief guided discussion follows: with the teacher asking a short series of questions and correcting the students' "discovery statements" as needed. This process of guided discovery, while not very long, is the heart of lessons involving rules, whether grammatical or of usage. It is followed by cognitively oriented practice such as what follows.

T: "Would you use *tu* or *vous* in talking to:
 ... a stranger at the Post Office?
 ... a close friend?
 ... a young classmate?
 ... your teacher?
 ... your mother?
 ... a bank clerk?"

T: "Complétez la phrase:
 Vous avez un moment, M. Lebrun?
 ... Marianne (votre amie)

... Papa?
... Mlle Lemieux?
... Charles? (un camarade)
... M. Paquin?"

Throughout the rest of the program, the teacher would reinforce the proper usage of *tu/vous* by correcting any errors deeply, with overt, "telegraphic" cognitive reference to the usage rules that were "discovered" earlier.

(The fact that *vous* is used for both singular formal and any plural deserves some separate practice. There should also be a considerable amount of integrated practice with *tu* – and the other pronouns. This is not reflected in the foregoing activities.)

Bridging activities, especially with this point of usage, include situations and simulations where the students play the roles of persons of various ages and relationships.

Sample Bridging Activities

For each point being taught, it is important that after some largely mechanical activities the class should also do a good number of bridging activities – which pay attention to both form and meaning – before moving on to freer activities with primary attention on meaning. Otherwise, output during communicative activities with primary attention on meaning tend to become linguistically very inaccurate – unless control of form is already built in, it suffers when attention shifts to the meaning of messages. In programs like FI where attention is never or hardly ever on form while the students are using the language, accuracy does not even have a chance to develop. (Of course, focus on form is not even possible in the early grades.)

The following are examples of some of the possible types of bridging activities, discussed approximately in order of lesser to greater freedom:

Dialogue (Oral Sample) Variations

After the students have mastered a dialogue or some other oral sample, they can use its morphosyntactic structures to express somewhat different ideas by substituting words of their own choice. For example, starting from *"Qu'est-ce que tu penses des élections?"* students can ask (and answer) many questions, including: *"Qu'est-ce que vous pensez des Jeux Olympiques?,"* *"Qu'est-ce que M. Morin pense de la télévision?,"* *"Qu'est-ce qu'ils pensent du livre X?"* The degree of freedom increases as the students distance themselves from the original wording of the dialogue.

Focused Sentence Generation

Students are each asked to produce one or more sentences containing a form, construction, or lexical item that they have just studied. Perhaps a more interesting variation of this, requiring a little imagination and effort, would be to join the sentences into a continuous discourse.

Directed Conversation

The teacher tells each of several students what to say or ask in a guided conversation. But if such directions are given in French, the students just change subjects and verb forms and occasionally reorganize sentences a little; so this would not be of much value beyond the first 50 hours or so of the program.

The problem with French-cued directed conversations is that the teacher furnishes the students with all the necessary French vocabulary and almost all of the sentence structure, so the students do not really have to generate French sentences. By cueing the conversation in English, however, the students have to come up with French words and constructions themselves. (The students should know already the words and structures they are asked to use; nothing should be completely new).

Of course, from the first day of the program the students should be told about and given memorable examples of the linguistic monstrosities that can result from relying on word-by-word "translation." These warnings should be reiterated whenever a student falls into that trap. But with English directions, the students are not being asked to "translate" into French, especially not word by word (which is not translation at all). They are simply given an idea of what they should express in French. In fact, with most such directions, they could not translate word by word even if they wanted to do so. (To produce accurate French in response to a cue, the students must rely on internalized *French* samples and structures.) An example follows:

T: (Introduction describing the situation) "Jim, vouz allez acheter des chaussures. Michelle, vous pouvez être la vendeuse:"
T: "Jim, ask a store clerk (teacher points to Paul) where the shoe department is."
Jim: "Pardon, où est le rayon des chaussures?"
T: "Paul, tell him it's on the left, near the elevator."
Paul: "A gauche, près de l'ascenseur."
T: "Jim, tell the saleslady you would like to buy black shoes."
Jim: "Je voudrais acheter des chaussures noires."

T: "Michelle, ask the customer what his shoe size is."
Michelle: "Quelle est votre pointure, Monsieur?"

Once a directed conversation has been done about twice by different students, closely following the directions, it can be done by other students with variations and without the need for directions. The teacher should make it clear, however, that except for a few new lexical items that may be provided on an ad-hoc basis, the variations must not go beyond what the students have learned.

In addition to serving a bridging function to freer output in class, directed conversation can provide much useful practice outside the classroom. By requiring the students to recall vocabulary and construct sentences, directed conversation can help them maintain active control over what they have learned. Cassettes for extended take-home or laboratory practice with graded, English-cued directed conversation (with built-in pauses each followed by the most likely response, of course) should be a standard and significant part of the French language program.

Crosslinguistic equivalence usually requires some context. Early in the program students need to learn how to ask for French equivalents when they *must* say something they have not yet learned (*"Comment dit-on X?"*) as well as how to ask for English equivalents when there is a key French word they do not understand (*"Que veut dire X?"*). In either case, the teacher should make sure that enough context is taken into account, for "equivalences" without context are often partial and misleading. The students should understand that the equivalences apply to the contexts given unless otherwise indicated. Still, sometimes it is important to point the limitations of an equivalence or that an equivalence may be multiple (e.g., one word in French, two in English, or vice versa). Otherwise the students may make incorrect mental equivalences. PEM makes careful use of contextualized interlingual equivalences and makes students aware of multiple equivalences and of the limitations of equivalences.

Descriptions

The students can describe things, people, places and actions, whether physically present, brought into the classroom via visuals (a little harder) or through imaginative visualizing (freest and hardest to handle). While most descriptions will naturally be in the present, descriptions in the past, contrary to fact, etc. are also possible.

Focused Story-Telling

The use of wordless cartoons – carefully selected for the grammatical and lexical content needed to tell the story – is a good bridging activity. The teacher or the students can tell the story portrayed in the cartoon and can ask and answer questions about the story.

Depending on the grammatical point being emphasized, students can also be asked to tell various things about themselves; for example, for meaning-oriented practice with the *passé composé* and the *imparfait,* students can be asked to relate what they did that morning or the day before, or to describe a typical day when they were 8-years-old, and so forth.

Situations and Simulations

In a situation, students briefly play themselves in an imaginary French-speaking locale, closely following directions by the teacher, at least initially. In a simulation, which may extend over several classes or even over an entire course, students play the roles of typical French-speaking characters with detailed backgrounds, problems, and so on. Obviously the latter allows considerable freedom and so requires a good foundation in French.

Games

Many different games can be used in the French program. The important thing to remember is that a game should not be just a break to relieve boredom but should also enhance the students' French. For example, Twenty Questions is useful in giving practice in the construction of questions, but it loses much of its linguistic usefulness after the students have already had enough practice posing questions and know how to do it.

Another example: The basic idea of the old TV game Keep Talking can be adapted to the French classroom by having students complete sentences in a stream of speech and keep on talking until they are unpredictably interrupted, at which point another student must complete that sentence without delay and go on talking. This helps students listen closely and can already be used by the intermediate level. At the other extreme, time limits, team competition, and secret sentences are added, as in the TV game. At this level, fluency becomes important, so this full version of the game would belong to the very advanced level of the French program, and even then it would be very challenging (it is challenging for native speakers).

An Ongoing Story

As the students learn the language and master its structures, they can collectively tell an ongoing story or stories using what they have learned to describe imaginary characters. They can tell what the characters are doing or do, did, will or would do, would have done, should do or should have done, and so on – progressively adding tenses, words, idioms, etc. as they are studied.

Conclusion

The foregoing teaching activity samples should suffice to give an idea of the practical orientation of PEM. Throughout, the learner is treated as someone who knows much that is relevant to the learning of French, someone whose intelligence and conscious awareness can be directed to contribute in major ways to the learning process. It does not seem that the teaching of French could be very efficient or very effective any other way.

Throughout the PEM program, its long-term goal and that of most cognitively mature learners – to communicate accurately in French – is kept in mind. All activities are directed at the attainment of that goal, and the desire to communicate freely is regulated and subordinated to it. No doubt most students of French would rather succeed in learning French well in the end than learn to survive right away and in the process ruin their chances of long-term success.

9

Questions and Answers

In this chapter I will try to answer a variety of questions about FI and about the Intensive Systematic French (ISF) approach and the Principled Eclectic Method (PEM) I have proposed. Most of these are questions I have been asked, some frequently. Other than the fact that certain related questions are contiguous, the questions appear in no particular order.

At least they can speak now, can't they?

Yes, but do they speak French? If I were to say, "Mary is out walk his [Mary's] dog" or "I sorry you is catch cold," would that be English? Would you offer me a position in which a knowledge of English was important?

Is there no easy way to learn French well?

Yes, there is: To be surrounded by native francophones a good many of one's waking hours from about age 2 to age 4 or 5. This process is unconscious and seems to be painless, but it cannot be reproduced in the classroom.

Learning a second language *well* in the classroom is not easy, nor can it be done unconsciously. If we do not want poor results in our classroom French programs, we should stop looking for easy ways and start looking for ways that work, even if they require some effort.

If there are problems with immersion, why aren't they widely known?

Articles showing that there are serious problems with immersion have occasionally appeared in professional journals, especially *The Canadian Modern Language Review*, since 1975. Unfortunately, researchers who advocate FI have not paid sufficient attention to this evidence. The media have at times focused briefly on the question but do not seem to see it as a significant issue. Once a perception – such as "FI is wonderful" – is firmly lodged in the public mind, it is very hard to change.

Can't the immersion approach be improved and made linguistically successful by solving its problems?

It is always possible to make certain improvements on an approach; but when the approach is based on fundamentally incorrect assumptions, improvements can only be minor. Thus, a little more focus on structure, a little more correction, and other changes will not help an approach based on the false assumption that the French language can be acquired well in the classroom by communicating, the way young children acquire their native language.

What we need is not band-aids but another approach based on sounder assumptions.

Why can't children in Kindergarten and the early grades acquire French naturally the way they learned English in early childhood?

Because they already know a language (English). They are therefore different learners, with a different cognitive organization than they had as pre-lingual young children. In the classroom, not only the learners are different but the environment, the learning conditions, motivation, and many other factors are also different. By equating two very different situations, all we can get is poor results.

FI graduates can communicate. Isn't that what matters?

It does matter, very much, but it is not *all* that matters. When communication is plagued with errors, not only is it harder to follow but it creates a poor impression. Furthermore, a Frenglish outcome negates the objective of most parents for their children – that they qualify for bilingual positions. FI graduates are not confident that they can fill such positions, for they are aware that they do not measure up linguistically.

We can have both grammaticality *and* communication if we make sure that our students master rules and elements *before* they use them freely with a focus on messages.

You refer frequently to errors. Aren't errors to be expected?

In systematic instruction errors occur too, sometimes frequently in the early phases of teaching a new point. But by making sure that previous material has been mastered and by correcting errors intelligently on the new material, we can drastically reduce the variety and the number of errors.

There will unavoidably be some errors. There is nothing wrong with that if they are handled properly so that they do not turn into linguistic habits. But when entire classes make frequent errors of the most basic kind, retain them for years, and still have them at graduation time, the teaching approach must be at fault. Even excellent teachers cannot get good results if they must follow a fundamentally flawed approach.

Don't many speakers of English make errors too?

Native speakers of English make a few errors, of course. So do native speakers of French. But FI graduates make more than 7 *times* as many errors as native francophones.

But in addition to quantity, the errors of FI graduates differ almost completely in quality from the errors that native speakers of French (or English) make. Those of native speakers are usually stylistic and orthographic, and to be expected given social factors and spelling inconsistencies; those of FI graduates involve the basic structure of French and are quite foreign to the French language. The latter are not even part of any variety of non-standard French.

Native speakers' errors are difficult to avoid by those who grew up speaking a non-standard dialect but can be compensated for by a solid education. In a good French language program, Frenglish errors would be reduced to a minimum.

FI students do fairly well on *rendement de français* tests designed for francophones. This is precisely because FI students, not being native speakers of French, do not often make the types of errors francophones make, the types of errors these tests are designed to spot. Their frequent errors, as already noted, are of a different kind – they are "non-French" errors.

Communicating from the beginning of the program is what learners both need and want to do, isn't it?

No doubt learners want to communicate freely from the start, but in a remote-language learning situation they do not need to, as their survival needs are perfectly provided for even if they do not speak French. For the sake of attaining the long-term goal of fluency *with* accuracy, they should *not* communicate freely from the beginning. Instead, communication should be stressed within the limits of what they know, and those limits gradually expanded as a result of systematic instruction.

By all means, there should be communication from day one, and not only for its motivational value. But it should be controlled, graded communication until all the basic structures of French have been learned. The dam must hold back a flood of Frenglish and ensure that *French* comes through in a controlled fashion; first as a trickle and then as a river.

In regard to your Intensive Systematic French, doesn't the linguistic failure of FI show that intensive programs are not the answer?

What I have proposed is intensive or semi-intensive *systematic* instruction, which is very different from FI. FI is not linguistically systematic because it does not ensure the orderly mastery of the important structures of French.

One reason linguistically structured French instruction has not worked in the past is that it has been so slow. Students get discouraged as the time to express their ideas, to speak in the past or the future, etc. is long delayed. By making the first 2 or 3 years of French at least semi-intensive (2 hours a day) we bring the goal of self-expression much closer. This helps the students motivationally and also cuts at least in half the time between recurrences of grammatical and lexical items. In college or university, students would be much more ready after 2 years for courses taught in French, including literature. (Ideally, the 2 hours of instruction would not be consecutive, but one in the morning and one in the afternoon.)

Isn't 4 or 5 the optimal age to start to learn a second language, as opposed to the age of 10 or 11 that you recommend?

After the age of 4 or 5, when children already know their native language quite well, second language learning cannot be the same as native language acquisition. Under the fundamentally different conditions prevailing in the classroom learning situation, the more second language learning tries to be like native language acquisition, the more likely it is to fail linguistically.

The best French classroom program will take full advantage of the learners' minds. Even H.H. Stern, a leading language teaching scholar who in his later years joined the overwhelming FI movement, wrote in bold letters, in 1970: ". . . **remember that your students, young and old, have heads.**[1] FI treats students as if they did not have heads that could contribute to the learning of French.

Of course, cognitive ability is limited in children in the early grades and grows only gradually, reaching the point where children can deal with more abstract material by age 10-12, as Piaget noted. Theodore Andersson of the University of Texas observed that the declining line of unconscious learning intersects with the rising line of conscious learning at age 10.[2] Since unconscious second language learning has not been found to work well in the classroom, the ideal starting age should be 10 at the youngest and preferably 11, when there is greater cognitive ability but motor memory is still strong.

It is a myth that younger children are generally better classroom second language learners than older children and adults. Their only advantage seems to be in the ability to remember movements (motor memory), which helps them develop very good pronunciation without focused instruction, especially if they are surrounded by francophones. But with careful instruction, older children and young adults can develop excellent pronunciation.

And the ability to remember and internalize rules and vocabulary increases with age. Even the capacity to imitate and produce sentences increases with age up to the age of 18.[3] Furthermore, the older the students start to study a second language, the fewer the errors in pronunciation and comprehension.[4]

Wouldn't a conscious approach be too intellectual, too abstract?

In PEM, whatever is complex is simplified by breaking it into its parts, to be mastered orally one by one, and whatever is abstract is made more concrete by illustrating it profusely with examples, many of them mastered verbatim in advance. And of course PEM has to be slower and simpler with 10-year-olds than with university students.

Our approach should challenge students. As Genesee pointed out, when IQ makes little or no difference, the teaching approach is not challenging students of average and above-average intelligence, which gives such students an easy ride.[5] This is unfortunately the case with FI.

PEM makes use of the students' minds but does not advocate going back to traditional language teaching in which the emphasis was on abstractions and no systematic effort was made to turn those abstractions into the ability to communicate in French.

Should pupils be specifically motivated to learn French?

Since learning French well in the classroom requires determination and effort, it follows that students of French should *want* to learn French. This is not the case with young children who are enrolled by their parents in early FI; they are not there by choice. They are more or less coerced to communicate in a language they do not know, a fact that has serious sociopsychological implications and leads, as we have seen, to poor linguistic results.

A lack of dedication to the goal of learning the French language has a variety of negative effects, especially on the motivation of pupils to excel and their willingness to do homework.

Don't FI students do a lot of homework?

Yes, in some FI programs pupils do a great deal of homework. But while all this homework is in French, it seldom focuses on the French language itself, and even less on its structure – it largely deals with other subjects in the curriculum. Moreover, the homework that specifically addresses the French language is not the kind of homework most needed to learn French well.

What kind of homework do French language students need?

Beginners in particular need to concentrate on basic spoken French structures and vocabulary (in context, of course) with the help of audio or audiovisual recordings. Today most school children have access to cassette machines; arrangements can be made for those who do not.

As early emphasis should be on developing an audio-oral foundation, it would be better to delay the introduction of written French for a while and wait even longer to introduce writing exercises as homework. Homework (or initial study) with computer software showing written French should, for the same reason, be delayed until the intermediate level. Of course, computers can be used to advantage from the start to control audio as well as video output that does not include written French.

By making use of English, doesn't the ISF/PEM encourage translation errors?

We should not ignore the native language of the learners. As Stern put it in 1970, again in bold letters: **"You must not and cannot ignore the student's mother tongue."**[6] FI does; ISF/PEM does not.

Translation errors would result if students were encouraged to "translate" word by word (this is not real translation). In PEM, they are actively discouraged from doing this. Anything transposed orally from one language to the other is in context, so what the students have to deal with is an idea, not a word-to-word "equivalence" (which is not a true equivalence). With PEM, English is never the basis for generating original French sentences. Furthermore, PEM students are clearly warned and reminded of the limitations of equivalences. Without such warnings, even students in completely monolingual French classes make errors due to incorrect French-English mental "equivalences."

English should be taken into account in designing all French teaching materials, to ease beginners into the French language and to make clear to them anything that cannot be made perfectly clear in French. But except for the first few hours of instruction, the teacher should make sure that English is not the dominant language in the French classroom. Anything the students can be helped to understand clearly in French and anything they can be expected to know how to say in French should be done in French.

Doesn't the strict correction of errors inhibit students to the point that they are scared to talk?

It depends on how it is done. If the students understand that correction is for their long-term benefit and if the correction itself is done in a kind, matter-of-fact manner, without interrupting them in mid-phrase, they will not be afraid to talk and will in the long run appreciate conscientious correction.

As for inhibition, which is preferable – enough inhibition so that beginning and intermediate students think twice before they speak or write in class or permanent inhibition leading to the avoidance of French outside the classroom by advanced students or program graduates because they know that their French is very faulty? The former is merely an uncomfortable but necessary prelude to fluency with accuracy. For the latter type of inhibition, which FI students and graduates certainly have, there is no easy cure.

Wouldn't a FI graduate speak French very well after a few months in Quebec or France? So why worry about it?

That's the crux of the matter. After a student has formed poor linguistic habits and further reinforced them by misusing French for many years, they are so deeply embedded that it would take years of systematic instruction to undo the damage. I estimate that it takes 5 times as long to unlearn a faulty skill and relearn it well than to learn it well the first time. FI graduates can expand their vocabulary significantly in a few months in a francophone environment, but, as speakers of a "terminal 2/2+" interlanguage, they find the structural damage very hard to correct.

Would a good university program help FI graduates?

The universities are in a quandary over what to do with FI graduates. These students are more fluent than graduating majors but less accurate than first-semester students. They do not fit anywhere in a regular sequence that follows a progression through the French language. If placed in third- or fourth-semester courses that emphasize accuracy, they do not do well. What FI students who decide to study French in university need is special, intensive remedial work on linguistic structure. Instead, they are getting "sheltered" courses taught in simplified French!

Is it reasonable to claim that what FI students learn in 13 years could be taught systematically in 6 months?

In 6 months of 4 to 6 hours a day of systematic French instruction it is possible for many, perhaps the majority, of well-motivated young adult learners to reach FSI/ILR oral proficiency level 2+/3 – without significant faulty habits. Early FI graduates rarely reach higher than 2/2+ on these proficiency interviews – with many faulty linguistic habits.

ISF/PEM graduates might not be as "fluent" (if by that we mean speed of oral output) as FI graduates, but they would have a solid foundation on which to become very fluent and, given time and motivation, become native-like in their use of French. FI graduates end up with terminal Frenglish and never come close to reaching native-like French – except in "fluency."

Would you say, then, that FI graduates are not bilingual?

Yes. They do not speak (or write in) two languages. They speak English plus Frenglish. Frenglish is not a language nor can it pass for one.

Is there nothing good you can say about French immersion?

FI has several good points. The main one is that it has made English Canadians more aware of French language and culture and has encouraged the idea of bilingualism.

Another strong point is that FI graduates have good listening and reading comprehension. The same result, however, could be obtained in about 700 hours of systematic instruction that includes comprehension practice.

The idea of teaching content courses in French is a third strength of FI. But it would be far better to do this after a solid foundation in the language has been established. Furthermore, this idea is not an innovation of the immersion approach, as it goes back a long way in the second language field.

Anything else?

Nothing beyond conclusions and broader implications discussed in the next chapter. I think it is time for the advocates of FI to respond to the evidence that immersion has linguistically harmed millions of children, in Canada and in other countries. Wherever immersion has been tried, the result has been the same: Frenglish, Spanglish, Japglish, and so forth. Other than for brief, casual travel purposes, it is hard to see any valid use for such classroom pidgins.

Notes

[1] H.H. Stern, *Perspectives on Second Language Teaching* (Toronto: OISE, 1970), p. 54.

[2] Theodore Andersson, "The Optimum Age for Beginning the Study of Modern Languages," *International Review of Education,* Vol. 6, No. 3 (1960), pp. 298-306.

[3] J. Dodson, 1966, referred to by H. H. Stern, ed., *Languages and the Young School Child* (London: Oxford University Press, 1969), pp. 33-35.

[4] L.H.Ekstrand, 1964, referred to by Stern (1969), p. 33.

[5] F. Genesee, "The Role of Intelligence in Second Language Learning," *Language Learning,* Vol. 26 (1976), pp. 267-80.

[6] Stern, *Perspectives,* p. 54.

10
Conclusions and Broader Implications

The main conclusion the evidence points to is that students in FI programs *do not* learn to speak or write well in French. Another important conclusion is that, given its fundamentally flawed philosophy that puts use before control, the immersion approach *cannot* yield a high level of proficiency in French, regardless of how much it may be patched up and repackaged. The process whereby young children acquire their native language cannot be reproduced in the classroom, for the learners and the conditions of learning in the two situations are radically and permanently different.

Therefore, FI should be replaced by a better, more effective approach suited to remote-language learning conditions in the classroom. In this book I have proposed such an approach in the form of (Semi-)Intensive Systematic French (ISF) via the Principled Eclectic Method (PEM).

Trends and Dogmas in Education

The rise and institutionalization of FI is a good example of how a trend starts, gathers momentum, and becomes established in education. Except for the fact that immersion programs were started by parents, this trend followed the usual path of educational trends:

(1) A few academics/educators promoted FI, backing their claims with much partial – though superficially impressive – data giving a one-sided interpretation.

(2) These exaggerated claims were precisely what concerned parents, certain educators and many politicians wanted to hear. They accepted the claims and thus strengthened the case of FI advocates.

(3) Many individuals made major commitments of time and effort to FI; once such commitments are made, there is a tendency to defend them.

(4) Advocates of FI promoted it nationally and even internationally without sufficiently considering the validity of the ideas or the effectiveness of the approach. FI was tied to national identity as something that a "real Canadian" would favor.

(5) FI became an institution, hailed as our country's contribution to world bilingualism.

Even when an educational idea is based on sound premises, it may be distorted into an extreme trend that is then replaced, as a reaction, by another trend that is not much better. Education will continue to be an unstable field until it gets away from trends and establishes a sound foundation of knowledge based on careful research on the comparative results of teaching.

A Major Trend from the 60s

The 60s saw the start of a major educational trend that affected much of the curriculum and especially hurt skill-intensive subjects. I am referring to the idea that learning should be wholistic, top-down, and immediately "meaningful," which of course rules out lower-level mechanical practice. This approach has largely displaced systematic (step-by-step), bottom-up instruction, particularly if it requires practice that is not immediately rewarding, useful, or gratifying. Even the idea of students using what they learn *as* they learn it – and not before – is largely rejected by this wholistic trend.

While wholism had been advocated earlier, in the 60s it became a strong trend, beginning in the field of English literacy. Beginning readers were expected to rely on meaningful context to guess, not just whole words, but whole phrases and even sentences. Reading test scores plummeted. While wholism is not, of course, the only factor in reading-skill decline, it is hard to see how encouraging beginning readers to guess their way through texts can do anything but harm the development of early reading skill. (Of course, *advanced* readers, by guessing intelligently, can increase their speed with certain texts without significant loss in comprehension.) I think that the teaching of early reading calls for a systematic approach – more systematic, in fact, than "phonics" – that helps preliterate and illiterate learners internalize all the relationships between sounds and spellings that are governed by "rules," i.e., that follow predictable, consistent patterns. English spelling has many inconsistencies but it is not chaotic; with all its imperfections, there *is* a system, so the initial phases of learning to read should not rely on wholistic guessing.

Wholism, with its stress on immediate meaning, has also affected the teaching of mathematics by shifting emphasis almost completely toward "understanding concepts" and away from the development of basic skills. The result of this (and, again, there are other factors) is that many high school graduates find it difficult to perform simple arithmetic operations. Naturally, the development of mathematical skills requires much practice, in class and as homework – and "practice" is the taboo word of the wholistic movement.

In second language learning, wholism is represented not only by the immersion approach but also by other meaning-based, communication-first approaches such as the communicative approach and the natural approach. They all share the same philosophy of developing linguistic proficiency through meaningful communication and assume that errors will disappear naturally without much correction. *Since the non-immersion wholistic approaches are of much shorter duration than FI, they can be expected to result in lesser comprehension without any better grammaticality.*

The emphasis on *immediate* meaning and usefulness seems to be largely responsible for the curricular decline of the arts and humanities. What need is there, for example, for any detailed knowledge of history, geography, or civics when they can all be blended under "social studies"? What immediate gratification is there in literary masterpieces or in philosophy? According to this viewpoint, whatever does not meet the criterion of immediacy is not worth teaching or learning.

The wholistic movement, with its emphasis on the immediately meaningful, useful, and pleasurable, is contrary not only to the idea of classroom practice but also, of course, to that of practice-oriented homework. North American students spend only a few hours a week on homework – Americans average 3 hours – while Japanese students devote some 30 hours per week to it. It is no wonder that Japanese secondary school graduates are academically superior to their North American counterparts in almost every respect.

What wholism and immediate relevance mean to second language teaching is that today's beginning language students need to be persuaded by their teachers of the relevance and long-term benefits of practice, controlled communication, correction, and so on. An orientation in English at the beginning of the French language program can help persuade today's students that step-by-step learning of structures and graded conversation are in their long-term interests.

What Can Be Done

What can people do who are concerned about the poor results of FI? What can they do about the development, testing, and implementation of a better classroom road to bilingualism?

Generally, they can demand that high standards be observed, insist on excellence in education, and refuse to accept poor performance as "the best we can do." They can also hold educators – from new teachers to Ministers of Education – responsible for the outcome of teaching, and pupils responsible for their learning. Actions should not be freed from consequences. Of course, if people are to be held accountable for the results of their actions, they must have the power of choice and a clear awareness of the likely results of their choices.

Specifically, concerned people can share their knowledge that FI does not work, that because of its faulty philosophical foundation it cannot work linguistically. Concerned people can share this knowledge with their friends and with parents of school-age children, as well as with school officials, politicians, and the media.

Those concerned about the results of FI can put pressure on FI advocates to acknowledge that the immersion approach has major weaknesses that cannot be remedied without abandoning its original premises. They can insist that the extent of the problems with FI be made public. They can challenge still-repeated claims that FI is "highly successful." Concerned people can ask that research be conducted comparing various approaches to the learning of French and that the results of this research be made widely known.

Those who want Canadians to learn French, not Frenglish, can urge school officials to make other, more balanced approaches, available. In particular, Intensive (or Semi-intensive) Systematic French via a Principled Eclectic Method should be an option.

I conclude with a few words to parents:

If you have a child of school age, you should consider the evidence that if you enroll him or her in a FI program, your child will become a fluent speaker of Frenglish, not French. (While there is much data showing this, no objective data that I know of show FI graduates speaking or writing French well.)

There is no reason to rush children into learning French. Enrollment in a good non-immersion French program later – in secondary school or college – will be better for children in the long run than immersion. They will probably not emerge speaking fluently, but at least they will not have formed deeply embedded incorrect linguistic habits.

There is no major advantage, and there are serious disadvantages, in starting the classroom learning of French early. Starting with immersion, at any age, is linguistically harmful.

Appendix A
Transcript of Interviews with Students Who Had Nearly 13 Years of French Immersion

This is a transcript of interviews with six Grade 12 FI students from two secondary schools in British Columbia. The students had spent nearly 13 years in immersion programs considered very good in quality. They were interviewed informally by Micheline Pellerin, then a graduate student at Simon Fraser University who is a francophone from Quebec.

A description of the procedures used in these interviews and a summary of the results appeared in *The Canadian Modern Language Review.** The six students volunteered for the interviews, so it is safe to assume that they felt competent and confident in French – and that they probably were among the best in the class. They were all successfully completing Grade 12.

On average, 54 percent of the sentences produced by these students contained one or more significant errors in grammar or vocabulary. There were individual differences, of course: the strongest had errors in 40.3 percent of her sentences, the weakest had errors in 72.4 percent of hers.

Details that would reveal the identity of the individual students or of the schools have been left out. The students are only identified as "M" for male and "F" for female. The interviewer's questions and comments are identified by "I". The errors appear in bold type. If the student omitted something required in French, this is shown in parentheses (x). Omissions of required *liaison* are shown with a vertical line (|); liaison-type intrusions are shown phonetically. Major errors in pronunciation are shown in square brackets [x]. When it is not clear what the student meant to say, question marks in square brackets are used. My own occasional comments also appear in square brackets.

As can be seen, the first few questions in each group interview yielded essentially correct and linguistically sophisticated responses. Obviously these students must have been asked these and most of the other general questions in these interviews several times before. With less-predictable questions, even on familiar topics, the students expressed themselves in very simple sentences – almost childishly simple – and made frequent false starts as well as many errors with very basic structures.

School A:

I: Dites-moi d'abord où est-ce que vous êtes nées?
F1: Ici, à [name of town].
I: Toutes les deux?
F2: Non, j'**étais** née **dans**... [name of city].
I: Et vos parents sont anglophones...
F1: Ouais, très anglophones...
I: Qu'est-ce que ça veut dire, ça, très anglophones...
F1: Ils parlent aucun mot de français.
I: Vraiment?
F1: Vraiment, rien du tout.
I: Et toi?
F2: Même chose.
I: Alors pourquoi est-ce qu'ils vous ont mis à le'école d'immersion?
F1: Parce que c'était une... oppror... une opportunité, euh, que mes frères pis mes...mes soeurs n'ont pas eu, alors ils m'on... ben mis là-d'dans.
I: Est-c'qu'i avait une raison spéciale – non, pas vraiment...
F1: Euh, c'**est** just' une opportunité...
I: Toi [name]?
F2: Moi, j'ai pensé, je l'aimais quand j'**étais introducée** dans, dans la classe et puis euh, je l'aimais plus que je l'aimais l'anglais... c'était.... quelque chose (**de**) différent...
I: Vraiment, même quand tu étais toute petite, hein...
F1: Le français était plus facile que l'anglais...
I: Expliquez-moi le programme, comment vous avez vu ça... d'abord comment ça s'passe quand vous commencez?
F1: C'est presque la même chose; à (**la**) maternelle vous apprenez les couleurs puis les nombres, puis tout ça... puis nous avons appris en français. C'était la même chose qu'en anglais mais c'était en français.
F2: ça c'était la seule différence.
I: Si j'ai bien compris, le professeur ou la maîtresse, ne parle jamais anglais.

F2: Non.
F1: C'est vrai.
I: Comment est-ce que... est-ce que c'est difficile?
F1: Je n'ai pas trouvé difficile.
F2: Non.
I: Mais comment est-ce que vous arrivez à comprendre?
F1: Euh... En maternelle vous avez des pancartes avec les photos et puis les messages en-d'sous, alors vous regardez la pancarte puis la, la **peinture** ou la... photo puis associez **la mot** avec la photo.
I: Mais à la maternelle vous savez pas lire encore?
F1: Non mais, elle disait, OK. C'est un chat pis nous voyons un chat qui –
F2: Elle **avait toujours répété** des choses et puis quand...
I: Et vous finissez par bien comprendre hein...
Oui.
I: Sans que ça vous rende mal-à-l'aise ou...
F1: Quand vous êtes jeunes c'est pas, c'est pas grand chose... je peux le voir en français tardif, mais... en maternelle c'est pas grand chose, c'est juste apprendre et...
I: Alors là, ça se fait tout en français pendant la maternelle...
F2: Oui, jusqu'en **Grade Five** on n'avait pas l'anglais.
F1: Oh non! On [z'] avait le fr... l'anglais en première année avec [teacher's name] –
F2: [Corrects name.]
F1: [Name], ou quelque chose comme ça... on avait 20 minutes par jour, c'est pas grand chose... mais en cinquième année on avait une heure, en sixième, on avait deux heures, puis...
I: De première année a cinquième année, seulement 20 minutes... pour lire, pour écrire...
F1: Juste apprendre les verbes, les sujets...
F2: La même chose en français.
I: Vous aviez des cours comme ça de grammaire en français aussi...
F1: [Misunderstands imparfait] **Ici, c'est** le français... juste une classe –
F2: [Same misunderstanding] –français 12, français 12 immersion.
I: Ah oui, mais, quand vous étiez petites là, au tout début, est-ce que vous aviez des cours...

F2: Oui, on avait le français puis on avait **le grammaire tous les choses** euh... **différents**, la musique...

F1: C'était presque **la même cours** que les anglophones avaient mais c'était en français... C'était la seule différence, oui.

I: Vous étiez nombreuses, en maternelle?

F1: En maternelle, **c'était** nombreuses mais, euh...

F2: – en **Grade Two** ç'a commencé à descendre...

I: Et après ça, qu'est-ce que vous m'avez dit tout à l'heure, en sixièmes...

F1: En sixième, on était dans **un classe** de... y avait trois classes, les cinquièmes, les sixième et les septièmes, y avait, je crois qu'y avait huit septièmes puis **nous étaient**, je pense qu'il y avait dix.

F2: Oui, dix...

F1: Dix sixièmes puis y avait à peu près ben cinq cinquièmes, alors ils étaient **un petite classe.**

I: Vous étiez ensemble, la cinquième et la sixième?

F1: Oui, la cinquième, la sixième et la septième aussi.

I: C'était difficile ça?

F1: Non, pas trop. Les cinquièmes étaient pas là, avec nous; quand les sixièmes et les septièmes avaient le français, les cinquièmes avaient l'anglais, pis quand les cinquièmes avaient le français, **nous avaient** l'anglais.

I: Alors vous étiez pas toujours ensemble?

F1: Non, pas toujours ensemble mais on était **un classe.**

F2: Il y avait un jour par semaine qu'on avait, qu'on était avec les cinquièmes, **on avait chanté** et **(fait)** le théatre, et tout ça...

F1: La même chose qu'**on faite** ici.

I: Pourquoi "ici"? Qu'est-ce que vous faites?

F1: C'est **(le) French Eleven**, le français 12 pis le **French Eleven, ils** vont ensemble vendredi, le matin pis **on** chante et...

I: Ç'a pas l'air de te plaire beaucoup... T'aimes pas ça, chanter?

F1: [Unintelligible response.]

F2: Ils sont bêtes, c'est tout; et puis y a pas **de** enthousiasme avec le **French Eleven** avec **le chanson** tout ça.

I: Non? Mais ça c'est seulement l'vendredi. Les autres jours, ça va mieux?

F1: Les autres jours on fait la grammaire et pis... on fait...

F2: "Savoir écouter."

I: Qu'est-ce que c'est ça?

F1: Nous écoutons un texte et puis nous devons répondre à des questions. Des fois les questions sont si faciles pis si bêtes que nous essayons pas.

F2: Il y a des... **temps** qu'ils sont difficiles...

F1: Qu'**ils** sont très difficiles... mais quand **ils** sont difficiles c'est –

F2: Oui, mais c'est pas le contexte, c'est **le personne** qui parle. Ils parlent si vite...

I: Ce sont des choses enregistrées?

F2: Oui, parce que nous avons... mois, j'avais **les professeur[z]** qui (**sont**) venus de la France, puis du Québec, **il y a** tout différent.

F1: Les dialectes sont différents –

F2: – et puis quand **il[z] parler** c'est comme deux différents langages.

I: Mais ce sont vos professeurs qui parlent sur les cassettes?

F1: Non. Des fois **c'est** pas... c'est... des fois on a des personnes comme National Film Board, ils sont là...

I: Alors on les prend et on les fait parler?

F1: Je crois des fois que c'est des... euh... des textes pour les **French Twelve** ou les **French Eleven**; moi je trouve que **la cours** est **trop simple que** je n'essaye pas, pis mes **marques** sont pas très bonnes parce que je n'essaye pas... et c'est difficile quand c'est comme ça, parce que **tu** sais que **tu**... que vous pouvez faire beaucoup mieux, mais quand c'est trop facile...

F2: Ça c'est le problème maint'nant parce **que** on **utiliser** les textes qui sont pour **French Twelve** et puis c'est si facile que (**on?**) **ne** essaye pas et puis nos notes sont **basées.**

I: C'est à dire "French Twelve," pas d'immersion...

F1: French Twelve, il y a un **curriculum**... pour French 12 **c'est** donné par **la gouvernement** mais pour français 12, c'est quelque chose (**de**) très nouveau. Nous sommes la deuxième classe de... de French Twelve?

F2: Oh, oui...

F1: Alors ils n'ont pas [?] pis quand nous **écrivons** le, le... l'examen **de gouvernement** à la fin d'un semestre c'est **la même examen** que les French Twelve **écrivent.**

F2: Mais on doit (**en**) faire un autre aussi...

F1: Si, si... On écrit la même que **celle** du gouvernement si nous **écrivons la bourse**, mais si non, nous **écrivons** pas, nous **écrivons un examen** fait par [teacher's name].

F2: C'est plus difficile...
F1: Oh oui, tout le monde **écrit la bourse**...
F2: Oui, parce que l'année passée, y avait **(des)** personnes qui [z']ont, avaient raté l'autre test de [teacher's name] et puis ils ont... tout le monde **(a)** passé le test du gouvernement, et puis...
F1: La bourse. Parce que [teacher's name] fait **la test** pour l'immersion **mais si nous avons**, nous apprenons pas l'immersion. [?]
F2: Ça veut dire qu'on va avoir des problèmes –
F1: – des problèmes avec l'examen d'immersion. Alors quand le gouvernement nous donne un **curriculum** pour le français 12 (?).
I: Vous faites combien d'français là, maint'nant, présent'ment?
F2: Un heure vingt minutes... oui, par jour.
I: C'est tout, le reste c'est d'l'anglais, hein...
F1: L'année passée, c'était quoi... deux heures quarante.
I: Et ça, depuis qu'vous êtes à l'école secondaire, c'est comme ça?
F2: Non, on avait **le communication pour** un an.
F1: En huitième année on avait le francais, **le science humain**, puis... Neuvième année on avait communication, puis –
F2: – et **dix** aussi.
F1: Oui, et **dix** aussi. Alors il y avait trois heures heu, **huit, neuf** et **dix**.
F2: Oui mais, chaque année ils coupent.
I: Oui, maintenant une heure c'est pas beaucoup. Vous aimeriez qu'il y en ait plus?
F2: Maintenant, j'ai des problèmes en anglais parce que j'avais pas beaucoup de... anglais quand j'étais jeune.
F1: Oui, les termes sont différents, alors quand quelqu'un vous enseigne quelque chose **vous dire**, ah! je... (?) le moment... d'apprendre ça mais qu'est-ce que c'est et tout le monde dit: c'est ci, c'est ça... et moi j'dis...
F2: Oui, c'est si facile, non... [?]
F1: En neuvième année, c'était la première fois que j'avais les mathématiques en anglais, puis **la première trimestre** que j'ai... presque raté, parce que j'avais jamais eu les mathématiques en anglais; les termes c',étaient bien différents. C'est pas que je ne savais pas les choses, mais c'était les termes qui c'étaient différents. Alors il y a des avantages et des désavantages.
I: Dites-moi: les autres étudiants qui ne font pas l'immersion dans votre école, comment est-ce qu'ils sont à votre égard?
F1: A l'élémentaire c'était les "French Frogs" pis tout ça, ils nous –

F2: – (on) **fait** beaucoup de sarcasmes [**sarkazəm**].

F1: Oui, ils faisaient les plaisanteries...

I: Ça d'vait être difficile ça...

F2: Oh un peu, mais, on avait notre petit groupe et c'était pas, c'était pas mal...

F1: Pas si pire mais il y avait toujours la plaisanterie entre nous deux mais en se[k]ondaire ce n'était pas si pire, ils, ils nous acceptaient puis maintenant je trouve que tout le monde est... jaloux. Pourquoi vous avez cette chance pis moi je n'(l')avais pas?

I: Est-ce que vous avez fait partie des échanges qui ont eu lieu?

F2: Non.

I: Aurais-tu aimé ça?

F2: Oui, mais mes parents voulaient pas que j'**apporte** quelqu'un ici et puis je (?) pas **faire** juste aller là et puis, mais... j'**allais** au Québec avec [name of F1] quand j'étais si jeune...

F1: Troisième année.

I: Alors tu es allée quand même une fois.

F2: Oui, mais on n'**avait** pas –

F1: – on n'**avait** pas parlé français; c'était comme un... **un vacance** d'été où nous sommes allées.

I: Toi, où est-ce que tu es allée?

F1: En, hem, dixième année je suis allée avec... avec la classe à [name of place] et c'était, c'était pas pire. Hem... j'ai trouvé que, eh, je parlais plus que... plus d'français et... ma... ma jumelle elle parlait pas l'anglais quand (**elle**) a été ici. Euh... elle (**a**) dit: Oh! mais vous parlez français, alors parle... parle-moi français. C'était pas pire quand j'ai rev'nue je pouvais pas bien parler l'anglais...

I: Combien d'temps est-ce que tu es restée?

F1: Juste... seul'ment dix jours, mais j'étais **dans un famille** qui parlait pas l'anglais, alors...

I: Et toi, si on te donnait la chance d'aller au Québec est-ce que t'aimerais ça?

F2: Maint'nant je fais beaucoup de commerce en anglais.

I: De commerce?

F2: Oui, comme la **ditographie** et puis tout ça, et puis je **pouvais** pas prendre le temps de l'école pour aller **au échange**, mais si c'était **dans** l'été ou quelque chose je v... je vou... je **voulais** prendre si j'avais la chance encore.

I: Tu pourrais peut-être t'informer parce que'il y a des bourses pour les étudiants pour aller quelques semaines pendant l'été.

F1: C'est **qu'est**-ce que [name] a fait **dans** l'été passé. (**Elle**) est allée à Québec pour quelques semaines pour **faire des enseignes.** [?]

F2: Je **l'aimais** aller à la France plutôt que je **l'aimais** aller au Québec.

I: C'est peut-être possible?

F2: Je ne sais pas, mais lang... (le) langage des français **au** France **c'est** plus –

F1: – (?) **parisienne** c'est bien différent que... la Fr...

F2: Oui, et je pense que c'est **plus meilleur** que le... (?) le Québec. Ils **utiliser** beaucoup de **slang** là-bas... au Québec, **I mean**, en France c'est **plus bon.**

F1: C'est bien difficile pour un... un québecois **pour** comprendre un... hem... un parisien. Ma soeur habite en France maint'nant pis elle me téléphone pis elle me parle en français, mais je ne peut pas la comprendre et elle ne peut p... elle ne peut pas me comprendre.

I: Vraiment? Parce qu'elle parle...

F1: Ouais, français français.

F2: Le vrai français...

I: Est-ce que vous avez l'occasion d'employer l'français en dehors de l'école?

Non.

I: Jamais?

F2: **J'avais** de fois qu'on avait parlé français, mais c'était quand je **suis** jeune et mes parents **on avait apporté** quelque part **qu'**ils parlaient français pis on devait parler français, mais...

I: Est-ce que ça vous arrive quelquefois d'aller voir des films en français?

Non.

F1: Les films en français ici sont pas très bons. Ils sont pas très bons. C'est la même chose avec la... heu... **télévision français.**

F2: C'est ennuyant [ãɲʊã], c'est vraiment ennuyant [ãɲʊã].

I: Pourquoi?

F2: Les choses... **ils** sont stupides.

F1: Tous les films qu'ils ont **sur le français c'est** des films, heu, qu'on a déjà vus **qui sont le français** qui était mis au-d'sus d'(l') anglais. [?]

F2: C'est pas très bien oui.

F1: Un fois j'ai vu un film **sur** la "Super-Channel" et c'était pas pire.

C'était... hem... un film un peu –

F2: – comme la Cage aux Follies ou des choses comme ça...

I: Vous avez vu ça?

F2: Non, j'ai juste entendu (**parler**).

I: Et puis les lectures, est-ce que vous lisez en français?

F1: Oui.

I: A l'école ou...

F2: Oui, maint'nant on lit "La Seigneuresse."

F1: C't'un roman, heu, **québécoise**.

I: [Name of F2] a pas l'air très heureuse avec le français?

F2: Non, je l'aime le français mais je pense que... (**la**) lecture et **le télévision** c'est... je pense que c'est très ennuyant [ãɲv̥ã] et il y a pas **de** action, rien, et comme ces livres ils...

F1: Il y a des **romances** dans "La Seigneuresse."

F2: Oui, il y a **un romance** mais c'est très **boring**. C'est juste... il y a rien de faire et je perds **le concentration** et je ne fais pas et... mais **je l'aime** quand **j'avoir les** livres en français qui sont excitants et il y a beaucoup de mystères ou que'q' chose comme ça.

I: Quels sont vos projets pour après la graduation?

F2: Je (vais?) aller au [name of college] pour deux années, puis après ça j'(vais?) aller au [name of university] pour faire le français si je peux pas faire parce que il y a beaucoup de... problèmes parce que je suis pas... très... vite dans la **ditographie** et quelque chose comme ça pour être **un secrétaire** ou quelque chose comme ça... et puis **je l'aimer** faire le français parce que mon amie prend le français **au** [name of university] pour être un professeur et puis elle m'a dit que c'est un cours très intéressant et puis j'pense que je **voulais** essayer encore parce que tout ce (que) j'ai fait **pour** treize ans – pourquoi arrêter main'nant.

I: Oui, faudrait utiliser ça.

F2: Parce que tu vas perdre ton accent pis comment **parle** et pis –

F1: Les parents sont des anglophones...

I: Alors tu aimerais faire un cours pour être professeur?

F2: Oui, j'ai pas les notes pour aller **au** [name of university] maint'nant. C'est très difficile d'entrer dans les universités maint'nant. C'est pourquoi **j'aller** au co – collège en premier.

I: Et toi?

F1: Je veux aller à... [name of institution] pour faire un cours de "**Hospitality** et **Tourism**" et puis après ça...

F2: Tu peux utiliser ton français là...

F1: Après ça je veux être... heu... **un hotesse d'(l')air** pour utiliser mon français pis mon allemand pis mon espagnol.

I: Parce que tu parles d'autres langues toi. Et toi?

F2: **J'essayer** de parler l'espagnol mais **j'arrêter. J'(l') avais pris pour** six semaines ou quelque chose comme ça.

I: Et ç'a pas marché?

F2: Je l'aime (le) langage mais j'avais pas le temps pour **apprener**, et maintenant quand je –

F1: C'est très facile...

F2: Oui, le français, l'anglais et pis tout ça...

I: T'en a fait combien d'temps d'l'espagnol?

F1: Hem... **un et demi semestre**, parce que j'ai... je **fais** l'espagnol en dehors de l'école, par correspondance pis maint'nant je l'apprends à l'école pis je **fais** l'allemand **pour un année.** [?]

I: Alors tu peux parler assez bien?

F1: Pour communiquer.

I: Tu penses poursuivre l'étude de ces langues?

F1: Oui, heu... si je n'peux pas être une hotesse **d'(l')air** je veux avoir mon... heu... **"bachelor of arts"**? de langage.

I: Tu ferais ça où?

F1: En Suisse. Oui, c't'un programme d'université. J'ai juste entendu **(parler)** un peu alors c'est... Il faut que **j'aille**!

I: Il faut que tu partes? Vite, vite, avant de partir: est-ce que vous avez de commentaires à faire sur le programme d'immersion?

F1: Il faut **que il**... le gouvern'ment ou bien quelqu'un regarde **à la programme** pis heu... dis...

F2: L'améliorer.

F1: Oui, l'améliorer. N'**utilise pas la programme** de **French Twelve.**

F2: Oui, mais je pense **que on** doit avoir beaucoup d'autres cours en français que juste **un classe** parce que c'est pas beaucoup.

F1: C'est pas assez! Je sais que **ma français c'est basé,** oui, c'est **plus pire**, il n'y a pas assez parce que je n'parle pas français à la maison alors... alors qu'est-ce que je peux parler en français.

F2: Et puis dans les classes de français on parle anglais, **you know**, des fois. Oui, on n'utilise pas (le) français beaucoup. Je pense que le français, le système, il y a les avantages et puis les désavantages.

I: Qu'est-ce qu'elle s'en va faire?

F2: **Elle prendre** son —

F1: Je vais (à) **un leçon** de... conduire.

I: Toi tu sais conduire?

F2: Non.

I: T'aimerais pas ça?

F2: J'étais dans un (|) accident, l'année... heu... passée et je pense que je ne veux pas conduire maintenant.

I: Un accident grave?

F2: Oui, c'était grave. Nous avons... heu... c'était terrible. **J'avais juste allée**... heu... j'ai reçu mon **court settlement deux jours passés** et c'était pour $4 500, quelque chose comme ça, parce que j'avais... **j'avais cassé** ici et ici dans mon **cheekbone** et puis j'avais **un dent** qui **avait manqué** puis j'avais quelque chose **(de)** mal avec **mon tête**. Ils ont pensé que **fracture** le **skull** et puis j'étais dans l'**hospital pour** beaucoup de temps et avec un... **plastic surgeon** et **neuro-surgeon** et tout ça. [Unintelligible to monolingual francophones.]

I: Vraiment! On a du te faire de la chirurgie plastique?

F2: Non parce que ça... parce que tout **partir** maintenant. **J'avais parlé différent** quand j'avais l'accident, c'était difficile **(de)** parler français parce que mon... je parlais et je **peux** pas faire les accents et puis... (?) était **tout frozen** et puis je ne **peux** pas parler. [?]

I: Cet accident... c'était avec tes parents?

F2: Non, avec mes amis. **C'était** très noir et puis on, ils ont... **qu'est-ce que arriver**, je ne sais pas **qu'est-ce que arriver** mais ils ont dit après que... elle avait conduit et puis il y avait **loose gravel** et puis ça c'est **qu'est-ce que arriver**.

I: C'etait ici, à [name of town]?

F2: Oui, c'était près de ma maison. Je peux marcher, c'était juste euh... c'était quoi euh... c'était pas un kilomètre, c'était... mais j'ai pas l'argent pour conduire, mais je l'aime. Je voudrais faire ça. Mais j'ai pas... mes parents ne **conduit** pas et puis si je **reçu** mon "license" [English] c'est pas bien parce que j'ai pas une auto. C'est ça. **J'attends pour un auto**, quelque chose comme ça. Tous mes amis **(en)** ont et puis **je voudrais que j'aille**...

I: Dis-moi, qu'est-ce que tu fais pour tes loisirs, pour te divertir?

F2: Maintenant **j'aider** une amie [see below] qui **est un handicap mental**. Mon ami, **il est huit**, et il y a **un bonne** chance qu'il **venir** peut-être normal et puis, c'est excitant, mais... je l'aime mais...

I: C'est quelqu'un que tu connaissais?

F2: Oui, **ils aller à le même église** que **j'alle** et puis ils m'ont demandé, puis j'ai dit oui, c'était comme ça...

I: Il y a longtemps que tu fais ça?

F2: Heu... avec le programme... heu... c'était deux mois et puis peut-être **à société, associé** avec lui c'était un an, quelque chose comme ça.

I: Et maintenant c'est un programme spécial?

F2: Oui, le **Ministry of Health** avait donné (?), et puis il y a des choses comme **d'être pour marcher** comme ça, avec... c'est très différent, je ne savais pas qu'on prend beaucoup de choses pour **granted** parce que je ne savais pas que c'est différent si on ne sait pas marcher, on sait... on sait maint'nant mais **you know** et puis c'est quelque chose (**d'**) intéressant. J'était dans... je l'amais la natation et puis tout ça mais maintenant je ne (**en**) fait pas, mais je pense que [|] après que **je graduer je recommencer** de faire tous les sports que je l'aime parce que j'étais... j'(**en**) ai fait beaucoup avec l'église et puis je n'avais pas le temps parce que je l'amais jouer **les** quilles et puis j'avais fait **la quille pour** dix ans et puis je devais arrêter parce que c'était **sur** le samedi et je n'avais pas le temps, mais je pense que **je vas** recommencer. [?]

I: Tu vas avoir plus de temps pendant les vacances?

F2: Oui. Les vacances je fais beaucoup de natation.

[Pause.]

F2: Est-ce que **tu as des** autres questions?

School B:

I: Vous êtes tous de milieux non-francophones? Même [name of M1] qui a un nom français?

M1: Non, mon père est français, mais on parle pas français à la maison.

I: Du tout?

M1: Non. On parlait avant quand ma grand-mère vivait avec nous mais maintenant on parle plus.

I: Mais quand tu étais petit?

M1: Je n'sais pas. Un peu, peut-être...

I: Est-ce que vous êtes tous nés à [name of town]?

F3: Non, je suis née à... au [name of non-Anglophone country].

I: Pourquoi l'immersion?

F4: Moi c'était mon père, il voulait... il pensait que c'était, je sais pas... pas necessaire mais ça serait... **une bén[i]fice**, oui, si j'avais une autre langue.

M2: Pour moi, l'école était proche puis et aussi ils pensaient que c'était une bonne idée. Ils ont entendu parler du programme. Ils ont decidé de m'envoyer... à l'école bilingue.

I: Et toi, [F3's name].

F3: Euh, je suis arrivée ici quand j'avais trois ans et mon frère et moi nous avons perdu notre langue, euh, notre première langue. J'ai commencé un p'tit peu a parler le [name of first language] mais j'l'avais perdu alors mes parents ont decidé que... qu'il serait utile d'apprendre une deuxième langue même si ce n'était pas le [name of first language], alors ils m'ont envoyée là.

I: Et [M1's name], lui?

M1: Je pense puisque mon père est français il voulait que son fils apprenne le français.

I: Vous avez commencé tous ensemble, à la même école?

Oui.

I: Alors vous vous connaissez depuis longtemps?

F4: C'est la famille.

I: Dites-moi un peu... [M1's name], toi c'est un peu différent parce que quand tu est arrivé tu pouvais comprendre le français, n'est-ce pas?

M1: Non. Je me souviens pas exactement, mais je pense pas. Peut-être quelques mots mais...

I: Comment est-ce que vous vous sentiez à la maternelle... je crois que les professeurs n'utilisent que l'français, n'est-ce pas?

F4: Oui. Moi, je l'ai détesté **pour** je pense la première année. Je... t... je voulais partir, je... mais **j'ai resté** et puis la deuxième année ç'**a devenu** plus facile... Mais c'était... j'n'avais pas peur mais c'était juste très différent et très difficile... fallait travailler... fallait travailler plu[∅].

F3: Je me souviens pas bien (**de**) ce qui s'est passé mais je sais que je n'avais pas eu (**de**) difficulté, ce n'était pas un obstacle de devoir parler, de **commencer encore** une deuxième langue, je ne trouvais pas **la** difficulté... je pense que c'est... c'est à cause de c'la que je ne me souviens pas très bien... des premières années...

I: Toi, ç'a été dur?

M2: Non, à peu près la même chose, parce que encore, je me souviens pas de ces années-là... c'était naturel je pense... parce que c'était le début et... j'étais si jeune que c'était assez facile (**à**) apprendre.

M1: Je suis du même avis et je n'(me) souviens de rien. . . J'ai difficulté de (**me**) souvenir de. . . de c'que j'ai fait hier, alors. . .

I: Comment est-ce que ça s'passe à la maternelle, comment est-ce qu'i font?

F4: Les couleurs, les jours, les semaines. . .

F3: On chantait beaucoup de chansons. . .

M1: Qu'il avait des petites cartes avec, heu, des maisons et puis on devait décrire les parties **du maison** et. . . visuel. . .

F3: On écoutait pultôt que parler aussi. . .

I: Vous n'êtes pas obligés de parler tout d'suite?

F4: Oh. . . répéter peut-être. . .

F3: Pas la première semaine peut-être. . . C'n'est pas le fait que c'était l'immersion ou apprendre le français mais c'est que l'école toujours est nouvelle, alors. . .

F4: Oui, je pense que ça c'est vrai. . . C'est **une nouveau expérience,** même si s'était (**en**) anglais, ça s'rait. . .

I: Les autres étudiants dans l'école, qui faisaient pas l'immersion, est-ce qu'ils étaient gentils avec vous?

F4: Il n'ya avait pas **des** autres (|) étudiants. . . c'est juste depuis (**la**) huitième année quand on est venu ici à. . .

M1: Oui, mais, un peu en cinquième, peut-être que **c'est** une vingtaine, il y avait **un école,** on a changé d'école parce qu'y avait trop d'élèves alors on est allé à [name of school] qui est juste, euh, c'est. . .

F4: [Address of school.]

M1: . . . il y avait des étudiants de cette école, ils ont changé d'école et puis il y avait une vingtaine d'étudiants qui **ont resté.** Mais a part d'ça on était tout seul. . .

F4: Mais nous étions la majorité, alors. . .

F3: Mais j'n'sais pas pour la plupart **de** temps il n'y avait pas d'autres étudiants. . . [?]

I: Mais j'comprends pas. Vous étiez nombreux?

M2: Trente.

I: Et il y avait une école pour trente?

F4: Non, mais, c'était une petite école, la première école était, euh. . . [name of school], alors **c'**était assez petite et il y avait deux classes de première année et une classe de –

F3: – jardin d'enfants –

F4: – je pense, oui, et puis et les classes, le nombre des classes (**se**) **sont**

agrandies avec le temps, alors...

I: En dehors des classes est-ce que vous parliez français?
Non... Non, jamais.

I: Est-ce que vous avez fait des programmes d'échange?
Oui, deux.

I: Deux! Vous allez m'raconter ça...

F3: Je ne me souviens pas de la septième année... ah oui, **la première échange** était en septième année.

I: Vous êtes partis ensemble?

(?): Oui, **tout la classe.**

M2: C'était de l'école bilingue et c'était avec une école à [name of town], Québec.

I: Vous étiez dans des familles?

M2: Oui, pour une semaine et demie.

I: Parlez-moi d'vos familles...

F4: C'était au temps du **referendum** alors c'était... Oui ou Non, ta famille oui, ma famille non... on avait les enfants de l'ouest qui disaient: Ah non, c'est ridicule ça. **Tous les familles**... ma famille etait **au** côté de oui, alors j'**étais** toujours Non, je n'comprends pas ça... et on... on parlait beaucoup d'ça.

F3: Ma famille, leur père travaillait pour le gouvernement, alors il... évidemment il ne voulait pas le séparatisme, et je me souviens pas trop de cet échange, c'était amusant.

F4: C'est difficile parce qu'on devait parler le français tout l'temps, ah ça c'était nouveau... c'était l'immersion...

I: Les gens où vous étiez ne parlaient pas l'anglais?

F3: Chez moi on parlait l'anglais mais la plupart du temps on parlait français parce que (on) savait que j'étais là pour apprendre le français ou **de** (me) perfectionner...

F4: Mais c'est comme apprendre... c'est... j'ai appris beaucoup quand j'étais à Québec mais j'ai perdu beaucoup quand j'**ai retourné** alors c'est... on peut toujours apprendre plu[∅].

F3: Oui, on sent beaucoup la différence d'être ici, (d') apprendre dans une classe et puis, (d') aller à trois heures prendre l'autobus, (d') aller à la maison jouer avec nos amies qui étaient anglophones puis d'aller à Québec et aussi **tous le...** expérience... satisfaisante. C'était pas facile mais à la fin, on sentait qu'on **a** appris beaucoup...

M2: Puis je m'**ai** fait un ami de **cette première d'échange**... J'ai encore son nom, c'est [name], pis c'était mon premier correspondant pis j'l'ai revu l'été passé...

I: Il est venu ici ou...

M2: Non. J'était là, j'était à [name of town], Québec, plus au nord pour un programme de bourse pour l'été, pis on a passé une fin d'semaine à Québec alors j'... j'(l')ai revu...

I: Et vous avez continué à correspondre tout c'temps-là...

M2: Pas souvent, non. Peut-être (à) Noël et... mais chaque fois que je vais là, je donne un coup de téléphone...

I: Et toi [name of M1]?

M1: Heu... j'me rappelle plutôt de... on a passé une semaine à Québec puis on est allé à Montréal pour visiter, passer un jour et c'est Montréal... je me souviens plutôt de... de... (?) industrielle et je pense qu'est-ce qui a... on **avait allé à**... **une**... parc d'amusement, la Ronde, c'est à Montréal et y avait d'autres qui **est** allés à – [**Unclear**]

M2: – I sont allés au –

F3: – au match de baseball.

M1: Au match de baseball, oui... et c'était plutôt l'atmosphère de Montréal qui... qui m'a (**plu**) plutôt que Québec. J'aime Québec mais c'est... c'est Montréal **que** je me souviens le plus.

F3: Tous les différents quartiers et toutes les différentes cultures qui étaient là... J'pense que ce qui était intéressant à voir c'était que les familles québecoises **est** si... heu... si proches et si... c'était une vraie famille et c'était... en particulier le deuxième échange, parce qu'on est allé –

F4: – en dixième année... c'était une petite ville de 20 000 personnes ou queq' chose, [name of town], alors c'était... et c'était en hiver... au carnaval –

F3: – alors on était dans les familles es **ils** étaient si chaleureuses, je pensais que les familles étaient si chaleureuses...

F4: Oui, et c'était si différent parce que comme moi, mes parents sont (**tous**) les deux professionnels et ils sont toujours (**au**) travail tout ça mais là tout était si... oh... leur tante cétait dans la maison **comme qui était à** l'autre côte **du rue**, l'école où ils ont... où ils **ont**... **allés** quand **il** était **petit** était là et puis le père travaillait **jusque à la**... **bout du rue** et pis tout le monde était toujours ensemble, toujours, toujours... c'était très différent.

F3: Et puis, la plupart des mères de **la** famille restaient à la maison, et n'allaient pas travailler et puis il n'y avait pas **des** parents divorcés... **well**, je ne me souviens pas... mais je sais que la plupart des familles étaient ensemble.

M2: Y avait toujours des tantes ou des (|) oncles qui passaient dans (**la**)

maison, toujours beaucoup de personnes. . . qui **rentrent** pis qui **sortent.**
F4: Ils voyagent pas (à) de longues distances de leur. . . pays natal. Ce sont. . . comme elle. . . c'était la première fois qu'elle allait dans un avion, parce qu'on a voyagé juste. . . [Reference unclear.]
F3: Ils étaient **toutes** très excités quand ils (|) **arrivent** dans **une avion** ou dans une partie du Canada et. . . ils voyagent jamais. . .

I: Et quelle a été leur réaction quand ils sont venus ici?
M2: C'était beau, les montagnes –
F3: – "Ben" beau –
M2: – la mer. . .

I: Est-ce vous aviez d'la difficulté à comprendre leur français?
F3: Un peu, la première journée, "ben" oui. . .
F4: Au commencement y avait queq' chose qui nous séparait et il fallait penser beaucoup et aller très **lent**. . . mais à la fin c'était très facile et **nous étaient les** amis et c'était. . .

I: Donc, y avait une différence d'accent mais on s'habitue vite?
M2: Oui, très vite. Ça prend seul'ment un p'tit bout d'temps pis ça. . . ça marche.
F4: Y avait beaucoup d'différence, pas juste (**d'**) accent et de langue mais. . . beaucoup beaucoup (**de**) différence.
F3: La culture était si différente. . .
F4: C'était dans **la même pays** mais. . . **ça semblait comme** (**si**) on était dans une. . .
F3: Oui, c'est choquant car le **contrat** était si. . . euh, euh, je n'sais pas. . . c'est comme. . .
M1: Hum. . . je pense que cette atmosphère qui diffère de **la nôtre c'est pas rien que juste que c'est de Québec** mais aussi que c'est une atmosphère **d'un petit ville**. J'pense que vous. . . si vous allez **à**, hum, Ontario et **que** vous allez à **un petit ville** qui est surtout, hum. . . agricole, vous trouvez la même chose et juste **cette** changement à vie à Vancouver qui est. . . heu. . . une gr. . . grande ville, et puis on va (**au**) Québec **dans un petit ville** industrielle et c'est différent. . .
M2: Mais quand même j'pense qu'y a des aspects qui s. . . **diffèrent** comme pour **le culture québecois** j'pense qu'y a. . . quelques aspects qui sont **différents que** notre culture et j'pense **que avec** [name], j'pense que, je suis d'avis que c'était si **petit** comme ville, peut-être si on avait **une échange** avec **un école** à Montréal ça serait. . . il y **aura** plus de similarités, j'sais pas. [Repetitious.]

I: Si vous aviez l'occasion d'y retourner, est-ce que vous le feriez volontiers?

F3: Ah oui. C'était incroyable, c'était merveilleux.
F4: Si on **aurait** le temps. . .
F3: On voulait pas rev'nir quand on était là, on voulait rester.
M2: Ah oui, tout l'monde pleurait à l'[aro]port. . .
F3: On te **verrai** dans trois semaines. . .

I: Et. . . comment est-ce qu'ils parlaient anglais, vos jumeaux?
F3: Pas très bien. . . I parlaient pas. . .
M2: Y en avait quelques-uns qui parlaient anglais mais la majorité c'était assez pire. . . ils savaient quelque mots mais pas. . . grand chose.
M1: J'pense (**que**) depuis (**la**) sixième année, ou quelque chose comme ça (?) l'anglais. . . mais à part ça c'est le français seulement.

I: Est-ce que vous utilisez l'français quelquefois en dehors de l'école?
F3: Pas très souvent, rarement. Je. . . heu. . . heu. . . l'ai utilisé quand je travaillais à [name of shopping district], parfois **il y a les** touristes puis ils ne **comprennent** pas l'anglais alors je. . . je **donne** le service en français.

I: Tu travailles à [name of shopping district]?
F3: Heu. . . pas maintenant, mais il y a quelque. . . un mois je travaillais là et puis surtout en été il y a beaucoup de touristes qui viennent **de** Québec et de la France.
F4: Ça me gêne de parler français en dehors de l'école. Je ne pense pas que. . . comme je travaille dans un magasin et même quand les **personnes français** viennent je ne leur parle pas français parce que. . .
F3: Oui, seul'ment quand je vois qu'ils ont vraiment de la difficulté. . .
F4: S'ils, s'ils ne **peuvent** pas parler anglais je le **ferai** mais s'ils peuvent parler anglais, je suis trop gênée. . .
F3: C'est comme. . . oh! ils vont nous **ridiculer** parce que notre français est pas. . . Les professeurs ont toujours essayé de nous forcer **de** parler **le** français en classe pis nous avons. . . ils nous ont donné des. . . des croix et des "**X**" quand on avait parlé **certaines** fois et puis **on** donnait les petites(|)étoiles d'or quand on était bons. . . ça n'marche pas. . .
F4: C'est pas possible quand **notre langue premier** est (**l'**) anglais de parler en français si, c'est comme c'est la prétence, c'est comme c'est pas vrai. . . je peux pas parler à [F3's name] en français et essayer d'être s –
F3: – une conversation serieuse –
F4: – sincère. . . Impossible.
F3: Mais quand on était à Québec pis on devait. . . si on faisait du magasinage. . . c'était pas gênant là-bas parce que tout le monde parlait **le**

français... Et puis j'étais bien déçue quand heu... j'allais dans **un rue**... **un rue** pis y avait de... un marchand qui voulait vendre ses... je me souviens pas du nom de la rue mais... une rue où, dans le vieux Québec, ils vendent tout le temps **les** peintures –

M2: – rue du Trésor –

F3: – puis je n'sais pas, ils savaient que nous étions **les** anglophones alors juste comme ça ils nous ont parlé en anglais et puis c'était... oh... oh...

M2: Mais quand j'était au Québec cet été, c'était plus facile, le plus je restais là, le plus c'était **plus** facile de m'exprimer, j'avais plus de confiance, alors j'pense que c'est **un**... **difficulté qui** peut être surmontée.

M1: Oui, quand on a le choix, quand on a le choix, naturellement on va **prendre** l'anglais parce que c'est bien plus facile que **(le)** français, mais quand **c'est le choix** et puis on l'a plus alors on va parler **le** français.

I: Et des activités comme aller voir des films...

M1: Je regarde **la télévision français**, mon père, il aime les films français, alors je regarde les films avec lui de temps en temps; **(à)** part de ça je vais pas aux films français.

F4: Mon père est (|) anglophone mais il pense qu'il peut apprendre le français s'il écoute la Radio Canada, **la radio français** CBC **pour** quinze minutes... le matin alors on écoute ça dans la voiture, oui... Il a l'espoir. Je pense qu'on apprécie pas ce qu'on a, d'avoir une autre langue... c'est pas possible pour nous de savoir, vouloir parler une autre langue comme **(le)** français, c'est difficile de voir pourquoi il veut apprendre le français.

F3: Oh, mais, nos amis qui n'sont pas en immersion parfois ils disent, oh, ah oui, j'aimerais avoir une deuxième langue aussi et puis vous êtes très chanceux, vous êtes tous très chanceux d'avoir l'... d'avoir eu... eu cet avantage... et les autres qui **dit**, "Oh, big deal!"

I: Après la graduation, qu'est-ce que vous avez comme projet pour l'avenir?

F3: Voyager... à Paris, (?) la Comédie de France, la Grèce, l'Italie... Mon amie et moi, nous avons un projet précis d'aller **à** Grèce hum... **en** deux étés; pas cet été mais le prochain, on ira en Grèce... ça c'est(|)un projet...

I: Et en attendant...

F3: Ah, heu... [M2's name] et moi nous allons heu **faire des applications** pour le programme-page... pour le **House of Commons**...

I: Qu'est-ce c'est?

F3: On serait employé par le gouvernement pour être des pages **dans** le House of Commons.

I: Des pages... Qu'est-ce que ça fait ça, des pages?
M2: Comme... ils apportent des verres de **l'eau** pour les –
F3: – des messages –
M2: – représentants...
F3: Est-ce que vous avez jamais **assisté** à la télévision quand ils font un... une –
F4: – débat –
F3: – oui, un débat ou queq' chose, puis y a des gens ou des filles qui sont là **dans** l'uniforme, qui passent les messages et... c'est ça les pages.
I: Vous aimeriez faire ça.
M2: Oui, j'pense (**qu'**) on gagne 7 000 dollars ou queq' chose et pis on a not... on peut heu... on a le choix entre l'université **de** Ottawa et **à** l'université de Carleton, comme y a deux universités à Ottawa...
F3: Il faut rester à Ottawa **pour** une année...
M2: On travaille comme page pis on... suit des cours à l'université...
I: Ah! ça vous permet de suivre des cours en même temps?
F3: Oui, je pense que c'est 14 heures par semaine ou queq' chose comme ça. Et puis l'université d'Ottawa est une université bilingue alors on peut prendre les cours en français.
I: Est-ce que vous avez l'intention de continuer avec le français?
F4: Pas comme carrière pour moi.
F3: Pas serieusement. Comme je n'veux pas le perdre **mais**, je n'vais pas **gagner un major** en français, queq' chose comme ça. [**?**]
F4: Je n'pense pas que je vais étudier le français en salle de classe après que je... Je veux voyager, je veux aller en France et tout ça, mais je n'pense pas que je veux suivre **une cours** très serieux... J'ai une base maintenant et je pense que je... peux utiliser ça mais je pense pas que je veux plus.
I: C'est précis ton projet d'aller en France ou...
F4: Oui, je sais que je vais (**le**) faire mais je sais pas quand... je sais ça, je veux que... je sais que je vais aller voyager partout en Europe mais je n'sais pas quand.
M2: Moi j'aimerais habiter en France pendant une année... travailler, voyager...
F3: Peut-être le programme au-pair.
F4: [Name], mon frère, a fait ça.
I: Ton frère?
F4: Non, il n'a pas fait le programme au-pair mais il voulait apprendre le français aussi alors il est allé à [French city] vivre pour six mois, il est allé

au... à l'Institut [name] à [French city], apprendre le français et il l'a fait, alors... je pense que j'ai le droit aussi...

I: Et il a bien appris?

F4: Il est parfaitement bilingue maintenant.

I: Quand il est parti, il parlait français?

F4: Un peu, mais pas beaucoup. Il a **fait** une bourse, comme [M2's name], à Québec, **pour** six semaines, mais c'était tout.

I: Et il travaillait à l'Institut [name]?

F4: Non, ça c'était l'école.

I: Et est-ce qu'il avait trouvé du travail en même temps?

F4: Non, il vivait très, très... il avait une existence très, très... il était dans **un petit, petit, petit salle** avec un lit et c'était tout et...

I: Alors tu penserais faire le programme au-pair?

F4: Je n'sais pas. J'ai entendu des histoires des amis qui ont fait ça, qui étaient pas très... ils n'avaient pas **un bon expérience** avec leur famille, alors je n'sais pas. Faut être... choisir **un famille** très... c'est difficile de choisir... Oui, c'est la chance pis je ne sais pas si... j'aimerais faire ça.

I: Et toi, [M1's name], qui ne dit rien...

M1: J'attends... Je pense cet été d'aller en Europe parce que, puisque mon père a **du famille** en France et ma mère sa famille est en... à l'Angleterre... alors j'espère faire ça et quand je **retourne** je veux aller à l'est et peut-être prendre quelques cours en français juste pour am[i]liorer mon français; puisque je suis venu aussi loin que ça je veux pas le laisser **partir**, je veux continuer un peu, puis le laisser **partir**...

I: Peut-être que là, il partira pas?

M1: Peut-être. Parce que... hem... on entend beaucoup **(dire), avec** beaucoup d'gens qui **dit**: Oh, je parlais bien le français, mais maintenant je l'ai perdu et [t]ils sont très déçus qu'ils (|) ont perdu leur français, ou leur italien ou quelconque langue... j'aimerais la garder. J'aimerais aussi **(en)** avoir une troisième, l'espagnol... peut-être **(que)** je prendrai des cours en espagnol aussi.

F4: Moi je veux apprendre l'italien.

I: Parlez-moi donc un peu de vos loisirs. Qu'est-ce que vous aimez faire?

F4: On n'a pas le temps...

I: Vous faites des sports...

F3: Oui, on joue **le** basketball maintenant, [F4's name] et moi.

M2: Je n'ai plus d'temps pour les sports. Avant j'était très actif mais maintenant j'ai que (**un**) p'tit équipe d'hockey les vendredis soirs à part de ça, les sports, non... mais la musique, je joue **au** piano alors le temps... j'pratique quelques heures par...

F3: Il est notre vedette...

F4: Quand on était à l'école élémentaire, quand la maîtresse disait qu'est-ce que vous voulez (**faire**) maintenant, on disait: on veut que [M2's name] joue **au** piano!

F3: Pis [M1's name] court les marathons.

M1: Hem... [name of town], l'année dernière en mai. Alors je veux le faire encore je pense... juste pour m'assurer que c'était pas un rêve...

    I: Tu l'as fini?

M1: Oui... trois heures cinquante-trois minutes...

F3: Et c'était **avec seul'ment faire**, quoi, **training** pour seul'ment deux mois avant...

F4: Mais il fait les courses de bicyclettes aussi.

M1: Oui, avant —

F4: — alors il était —

M1: — et puis avant ça je nageais aussi, j'étais dans un club de natation, mais c'est vrai, on n'a pas beaucoup de temps **à** faire (?)... d'abord si on, vraiment **on** veut le faire, y a du temps, mais si **tu** veux regarder la télévision ou queq' chose alors... et puis je travaille aussi alors...

    I: Oh, tout l'monde travaille... Que'est-ce que tu fais?

M1: Je suis un "gas-jockey" — ça ce traduit en français "je pompe le gaz..." C'est pas bien excitant mais c'est (**de**) l'argent.

    I: Oui, tu fais ça le soir...

M1: Oui, et les week-ends.

    I: Est-ce que tu peux étudier pendant que tu es au travail?

M1: Non... quand on travaille on est au travail alors...

    I: J'pensais, quelques fois dans les stations-services —

M1: — "self-serve" oui, mais non, c'est "full service."

    I: Alors tu n'dois pas avoir beaucoup d'temps, vraiment.

M2: Oui et non.

F3: Oui, ça depend de nos priorités... L'école, ah... on a toujours le temps **à** (**se**) plaindre et puis, ah, je n'veux pas faire ça, et **téléphone** (**à**) quelqu'un et... oh, non... et puis on parle **pour** deux heures, alors...

    I: Et [F4's name], où est-ce que tu travailles?

F4: Je travaille dans un magasin de vêtements, à [name of shopping center].

I: Les fins d'semaine...

F4: Oui, les jeudis, vendredis, samedis.

I: Toi tu travailles à [name of city area]?

F3: Oui, je travaillais **pour une an** et puis juste récemment j'ai quitté parce que j'n'avais pas assez de temps pour heu... quand j'ai **des** autres activités à part d'(l')école, comme le basketball et puis quelques autres choses alors je trouvais que je n'avais pas le temps... heu... **(de)** respirer... **c'est comme**... puis j'ai besoin de l'argent mais j'ai decidé que maintenant j'ai besoin plus de temps que de l'argent. Je travaillerai cet été.

I: Tu travailles toi [M2's name]?

M2: Non, je travaille pas. Ma famille voyage pendant l'été presque toujours alors c'est queq' chose que je dois faire... je sais que je dois trouver **d'emploi** bientôt, mais, maintenant je suis assez... mon temps est assez rempli.

Note

*Micheline Pellerin and Hector Hammerly, "L'expression orale après treize ans d'immersion française." *The Canadian Modern Language Review*, Vol. 42, No. 3 (January 1986), pp. 592-606.

Appendix B
Comments of a FI Graduate

What follows is a series of excerpts from a recorded interview with Janice (not her real name), a young woman who was exposed to 14 years of FI. She comes from an educationally oriented upper-middle class background; her father owned a construction company and her brothers are professionals. Since neither parent spoke any French at all, theirs was a completely Anglo-Canadian home. She is the youngest of six brothers and sisters, none of whom went through FI.

I came to know Janice fairly well when she was a student in one of my courses on theories of language teaching/learning. She was one of only two students in a large class to receive a grade of A+ in the course. To prevent a "pleasing-the-teacher" effect, this interview was conducted long after the course was over.

Only minor changes in the wording of some excerpts have been made, to protect Janice's identity. There has been some reordering of the interview material to make for a smoother topical flow. Material that didn't seem relevant or was repetitious has been omitted. My questions to Janice appear in italics. Also in italics, but within square brackets, are my occasional clarifications for the reader. Except for a few corrections, Janice's speech is reported as she produced it, including errors (for the light they might throw on the influence of French on her English); but many false starts, "uhs," etc. have been edited out in order to make the transcript more readable. (For a person of her intelligence, she had an unusually large number of such dysfunctional speech phenomena.)

* * * *

What kind of attitudes did your parents have toward French Canadians and FI?

Very positive. I don't know that their attitude was particularly directed towards French Canadians; it was towards the French language more than anything else. They looked at FI as a good opportunity to learn French. It was very fashionable at that time to send your kid to FI; it was during – just prior to Trudeaumania. They were more concerned about job opportunities for me later. They thought they would be enhanced.

Do you remember your first impressions of FI?

I had 2 years of French Kindergarten prior to going into Grade 1, and I remember it as being very festive. There were lots of games being played. . . .but I really didn't know what was going on. Actually I was physically ill for the first two grades, Grade 1 and 2. Physically ill because I was so worried about – I was convinced that my parents had sent me to the wrong school. For one thing, I came home saying, "They speak funny there." Other remembrances [sic] would be – I remember in Kindergarten we were told to put our heads on our desks and sleep for 15 minutes, and the teacher would say something like *Janice dort* (meaning "Janice is sleeping") and I would think I'd done something wrong, because I thought that she was chastising me and I didn't understand what she was saying.

Do you remember being sick?

Oh, I was physically ill every day for Grade 1 and 2, until my father took me to a doctor who said, "You must take the Green Pill every morning and you will not be sick." And I began to take the Green Pill, and years later my father said they were sugar. "We knew that you were upset being in Grade 1 – and it was way on the other side of town, which was very difficult." There were severe social problems with FI.

Were you sick mostly because of "linguistic shock"?

The linguistic shock and, too, most kids who go to FI – there aren't that many FI schools – so oftentimes kids are bussed way from the other side of town into a new environment – so I think both, unfamiliar setting and unfamiliar language – it's quite difficult. . . . I remember being very upset . . ., because I had no friends from my own neighborhood to play after school – this went on through elementary and secondary.

Were you aware that this was another language?

I did know; I was told that this was the French language and I was aware that it was going to be a different setting for me, although I didn't really understand why I was there, what the importance of French was until much later. And then I was quite proud of the fact by the time I hit Grade 2 and 3 because of the parental support and my brothers and sisters saying, "Well, she is going to French Immersion," so I began to feel a lot better about it by that time.

Was Grade 1 completely in French?

I believe so, although I am not positive. Remembrances [sic] of Grade 1 were a lot of French speaking. I remember a girl in an older grade saying, "You have to speak French or you will be sent to the Principal's office." Mind you, that could have been conditions for older grades and not for little Grade Ones. I do remember a lot of sentences on the blackboard. *René joue avec son ballon* – I'm never going to forget that one. Lots of sentences that we worked with in French.

[I remember now: We had] some English instruction in areas like Social Studies and Science, but the rest was in French, all the instruction, all the playtime, Music, Phys Ed, everything else.

After Grade 6, I don't remember taking Math in French. Math was taught in English, but everything else . . .

How good a student were you in general?

Not the best in the class, but I would say the top 10 percent. In Grade 9 they did, I remember – they did a reading comprehension test. All year, once a week, we would have to read some literature and then answer questions. At the end of the year I came out with the highest score for the Grade Nines, which I thought it was good because I beat all the French kids too. [Please note: Unlike today's FI classes, Janice's had the advantage of including a good number of francophone children].

How would you say you were placed in French?

Very high.

What were your marks in high school?

Well, it depended on the subject. I remember I was strong in English, Math, French, Drama. Social Sciences I didn't care about, and Sciences were bad.

I made a career decision in about Grade 10 or 11 that I was going to go Arts route [sic], so Sciences became less important. Plus I couldn't deal with [sic]; I thought – well, coming out of FI school I thought that I wouldn't do well in Sciences because there was so much switching back from French to English to French to English. As far as the terminology was concerned I was quite scared that I wouldn't be able to cope.

Did you find vocabulary a problem when you first started to study various other subjects in English?

Not at all. Mind you, my family really took quite an interest as far as my English was concerned because they were really concerned that it would suffer. I have three English teachers in my family, brothers and sisters, so they would really make sure that my English did not suffer. But the problem I found with the French [sic] is, I was thinking that I could walk over water after I graduated from Grade 12 because I had done well in my French classes and I went in and took French in my undergraduate degree at the University of X.

And [then] there were a lot of comments as to my accent. And I thought: What are you talking about? This accent is perfect, I know it's perfect. I have been doing well. Lots of comments as to accent and stupid mistakes.

Like what?

I remember in Grade 12. I'll never forget this: Going to the head of the French Department and asking her to give me a list of very common French words because I still wasn't sure whether they were masculine or feminine – and that's pathetic, really. Very, very simple words. And [when] I went on to the University of Y to do my Teaching Certificate – I wanted to teach French – I found that just in teaching French 8 and 9 I started to learn all the French grammar I didn't know.

You hadn't realized until you went to university that your French was very faulty?

No, I hadn't thought about it at all. Because – I don't know what it was. I always took my marks as being gospel; I always had done exceedingly well in French so I thought, "No problem."

Did you have French-speaking friends while at the university?

Very few. We would not speak French if we were socializing – it was predominantly English.

How well did you do in your undergraduate French courses?

I did well within the confines of the university setting. If I had to write a paper and had the time to do it, yes, but whether that – I don't think that I would do as well in a natural, in an ordinary, everyday situation.

What do you mean "if you had the time to do it?" When you had to write a paper, what did you do?

Oh, I would sit down with the dictionary, the grammar book, Bescherelle [a reference grammar], all those, certainly – and I could – but I would still make mistakes. It would still come back with mistakes.

The reason why I got [only] "A" minuses, in looking back, is that my grammar was so poor. . . . My reading was fine, my oral ability was fine.

You didn't make errors when you spoke?

Oh, of course, but much less than anybody else in the class, because they didn't have the background that I did – so they would forgive me a lot. They would think: "Oh, she is just excited." I don't think they realized that this was ingrained in my speech pattern.

[After I completed a B.A. in French,] I went to the University of Y to do my Teaching Certificate in French and English. And again it was further reinforced that my French was great, because given the people there in my French class who went on to teach French – it was scary how bad they were. I don't think I am qualified to teach French.

At what point did you reach that conclusion?

After going into the classroom and realizing how poor my grammar is. If I were to give a grammar lesson the next day – say I would have to give them sentences, and I would have to conjugate a verb – I would do every one of the exercises [in advance] and write them in my book because I did not trust my instincts to write – I didn't know that I would be passing on perfectly correct information. So I would have to labor over it myself before I went in. . . . I would stay one step ahead of [the students] . . . You see, I am fine to teach English, because I did well in English and I think I speak English better than most people who do speak English, but as far as the French [sic] is concerned my grammar is so weak.

I am so angry that I was led to believe that after 12 years of French I would be bilingual and there would be no problem. It hasn't – I can't even apply for jobs that require French-speaking persons, and here I was told all these years that you are learning French and that FI is going to help you as far as jobs are concerned. I don't think so. I do not feel qualified to act as the French-speaking person within a department.

You don't think that's putting yourself down?

No, definitely not.

At what point did you become concerned about your grammar in French?

I would say in about Grade 11 or 12, when I'd made the conscious decision that yes, maybe I want to be a French teacher, that I started to analyze what my French was really like and I thought, "Well, my goodness."

How did you get feedback to find out what your French was really like?

I would – we would have to do a lot of composition writing, and it would always come back with the red marks [sic] but it didn't affect my mark, this is what I can't understand. Lots of red marks of accents missed, or just more verb conjugations. I mean, it's easy to look up in the dictionary whether or not something is masculine or feminine, that was not a problem. But lots of little problems, like whether or not to use *de* or *du*, *à* or *au* – all those little subtleties that should have been mastered.

I remember teaching French and going through the Grade 8 and 9 textbook and saying, "Oh, that's how that works! I never knew that!" because it was never explained that *ce* is used with masculine . . . It may have been explained, but I don't think it was reinforced orally and there was so much oral work done that mistakes were made left, right and centre, and I was not corrected, nobody was corrected. . . . [Teachers] were more concerned with content.

It was funny, when we'd be doing a grammar class in French – fine, no problem. Grammar exams were – they'd give us a list of verbs to conjugate or auxiliary verbs – no problem. But when it came to using it in the sentences in my writing or using it orally I didn't do it. I took that as a separate exercise.

You mean it's like the rules are here and conversation and writing are over there, eh?

I think so, it's not habitual. There seems to be no transfer between the rules that we would learn and whether it's done in speaking and – these rules are not made habitual. . . . I know [the teachers] wanted it to be done properly but I think by Grade 11 or 12 they kind of thought, "Well, let's just deal with content, let's not correct them all the time."

Did they correct you in earlier grades?

I remember up to Grade 4 or 5 there being a lot of corrections. I think that there were just so many mistakes made in the class every day that they couldn't keep on top of all of them.

If I spoke now I'm sure you could pick out 20 mistakes in five or six sentences, and that is very unfortunate. And the thing that I found that is quite interesting is in first and second year university I was in the same class with kids who had not gone through FI, but had taken French classes at the junior high and high school level. Their vocabulary wasn't as good as mine – vocabulary was poor – but they knew their structure. It was just a matter of time. University for them was getting all the vocabulary and getting all the frills, and these are the people who started to do really well . . . after a while, because their grammar was good. . . . Their vocabulary was limited, but when they said something it was perfect. Mind you, their accent wasn't great, but they were very careful. The fluency would come and the vocabulary would come. As far as tests, composition tests and oral tests were fine – not oral tests – as far as their accent, that was coming, but their written ability was far better than mine. Here they'd had 5 or 6 years of French, 4 or 5 times a week, and I had all this French for 12 years and I would say that they were stronger.

And now I've got a friend who took French at the University of Z after doing it in high school and she just went off to Quebec, and I would say that she – my vocabulary again is better, but of the two of us, I would rather have her to teach [sic] [French].

Do you think that if you spent X number of months or whatever, a year or so in Quebec, your French would become native-like?

I don't. I'd like to think it would, but I'm just wondering if the damage might [not] be too extensive by this point.

But I think after a lot of time, yes, maybe I could be native-like, but my idea of native-like and someone else's idea of native-like are two different things. [I am told,] "You speak like a native speaker." and I am making all these mistakes and my accent isn't perfect – how can you say that I sound like a native speaker? The general public would say that I spoke like a native speaker, but I would know I didn't speak like [one]. The native speakers would realize that there was a big problem.

Do you feel culturally close to French Canadians?

Very close. Of the three groups – Anglo Canadians, French Canadians, and European French – if there were a racial comment made towards any of the three, I'd defend French Canadians first. I am not a French Canadian, and it would make sense for me to defend the Anglo Canadian first, but I would defend the French Canadian.

I get very upset when people say: "Oh, but you speak French Canadian, that's not real French!" That just drives me nuts, because my point of view is the difference between French-Canadian and Parisian French is the difference between [how] we Canadians speak English and what – Oxford English. . . . I get very upset when people make comments – get very ethnocentric about their language. I am culturally very close to the French Canadian. I am glad, very glad that I went to school in that way, it was very much promoted. We would have French-Canadian singers come to sing. The people I went to school with were – a lot of them were from French-Canadian backgrounds. So I am glad – that's one thing that I feel very fortunate for. I do feel I am very happy I went through FI. . . [because] . . . it did foster a very positive attitude towards French Canada. But . . . I make the same mistakes now that I made when I was in Grade 3 and there is no way that they can say I don't.

Now, I think that should have been caught. I get very angry about that. . . . If there were some way they could have a happy medium between fostering a positive attitude towards French Canada and other languages as well as a high level of proficiency in the language, that would be great.

Did you learn a great deal about English Canada?

English Canada – I never thought of it in terms of English Canada or French Canada actually. We learned a lot about Quebec, but we – it was taught that there were French-speaking people all over Canada, so it wasn't English Canada or French Canada – it was just Canada.

They did speak a lot about Quebec. I think my knowledge of Canadian history is very poor. . . . I think that they just assumed we were learning Canadian history through [FI activities] and I know absolutely nothing about Canadian history, really. I think they thought that through the literature they were giving us that we would absorb it. [For example,] they gave us a French-Canadian play that dealt with the separatist issue in Quebec and I think that they assumed from that that we would learn our history; but it was literature, so you didn't know... if it was factual. So nobody could learn history that way, unless it was told to us, "This is a historical novel" [or] "This is true."

From Grade 7 to 12, we would do Social Studies [in French].... I think the Social Studies Department was so concerned about the French [sic] and about us speaking the language and about us debating issues in French that they never, ever, taught us anything of much value. The only thing I can remember in terms of Canadiana was we had to memorize who the premiers of the provinces were, and capitals, and things like that which I think that should have belonged to Grade 4 or 5. If you were to ask me to draw a map of Canada – no, Geography, that was the other thing – I couldn't even tell you.

We had great vocabulary, our content as far as our French literature was fine – all the peripheral things of the circle were fine, but the nucleus was really weak. And so that's why I did well in university – they were so dazzled by the outside things, but then the core is weak.

What did your relatives and friends think about your French when you were going through the FI program?

Oh, they thought I was marvelous.

What do they think about it now?

Still [sic]. I have made the comment that my French isn't that good. I don't think my French is as good as it should be. [They say,] "Oh, sure it is. Don't worry." It's [sic] very hostile to any comments made against French, but they say better keep it up because you are going to lose it, and that's true.

I haven't studied French for a couple of years now. And I – a good example is, a couple years ago I saw an ad in the newspaper for something to do with the CN and I had to sit down and write a letter in French and it was the most frustrating experience in my life. I didn't know how to end the letter, I didn't know how to say "Yours truly." I didn't know how to say "Dear Sir." I thought, well, what do I say? Do I say "Cher Monsieur?" Doesn't that sound funny? I had no idea. And this is after 17 years of French – I didn't even know how to write a letter, and that's pathetic.

There was also a job at the University of M that said someone was needed to work, doing office work in the Department of French and "superior knowledge of French required,"... and I thought, well I can't apply for this. And that is bad, after that much time – that I don't feel confident...

And everybody else says, "Of course, you are just too hard on yourself." No, I don't think I am being hard on myself. I think [of] the mistakes that I would make, and my inability to do everyday tasks. Phoning someone up is another one – what do you say? I think it's *"Allo, puis-je parler avec . . . ?"* But I'm not sure. All those things, everyday . . .

Would it be wise for employers who need bilingual people to hire FI graduates?

I think they should hire someone from a French-speaking family before they hire someone who is from an anglophone family. . . If I were an employer and I needed someone to work the phones I would probably choose someone whose first language was French.

I don't know that I would trust [FI graduates] written command of the language to be error-free. . . . The translation [sic] would really scare me – if something had to be translated, because I would think I'd get into a lot of trouble because the nuances might not be the same. The spoken command of the language – it would depend on the student. I mean, I remember being quite bold upon graduating from FI and not being afraid to speak French at all, and then, after a while I realized, "Oh, gee" – it was almost an embarrassment to be making so many mistakes. . . . But, put it this way: When someone tells me they have graduated from FI, I know that means nothing, and [yet] you should be able to think that if they have had all this time with FI that their French is really good.

Have you noticed any short- or long-term difficulties with your English as a result of FI?

No, not at all. It is because of – we are a family that reads a lot. My brothers and sisters are quite articulate people, so the level was quite high. . . . I came from a family that stressed [education]. I had a lot of help in high school, I remember, writing compositions, from my brothers and sisters, but I don't think that many of the people I graduated with did very well in their first-year English course at university.

Do you find that learning French has improved your knowledge of English in any respect?

Yes; although my control and command of grammar I would say is not good in French, it gave me a sense of grammar. I think in terms of – I knew that I took all these verb tenses in French so I think in terms of auxiliary verb, noun, and that type of thing in English, so it did give me a firmer grasp of what language consists of.

Anything else? What about vocabulary?

Vocabulary, yes. If words have a French origin – the etymology – it helps. If someone says *vis-à-vis,* I will know what that means, or a word like "fortitude," or something like that, I say to myself, "fort" = "strength,"

OK. If I don't know what the word is in English I will see if there is a French root in it that perhaps I can understand.

What can you tell me about the attitudes of other FI graduates you know?

It would be interesting if you talk to them 3 or 4 years after they graduate from FI. When they graduate, they have been told that here they are, bilingual; and then they are going to get out into the real world and run across native speakers of French and realize in the workplace that their French isn't up to snuff. I really believe that.

Have you discussed FI with some of your former classmates?

Yes, and I think they are being totally unrealistic. A friend who did graduate from the same high school as myself in X – she was in town a couple of weeks ago. Well, I said – I really started to question FI . . . – it was very upsetting. [She said,] "Of course we speak like native speakers. We speak French better than most people." I said, "Well, yes, but speaking French better than most people is not the same as being native-like, and I think that the standard should be higher." It's all a question of standards through this whole thing. The standards weren't high enough. It was good enough – I think that they wanted to graduate people who – I am sure the teachers believed that we could speak French. . . . They graduated people who could speak French, yes, we could speak French, but to what standard? I don't ever remember any discussion of standards.

Did these former classmates have to face the fact, as you did, that they make a lot of errors?

They would never go into - they defend the FI system vehemently, but they would never apply for a job where French was required.

They know what their limitations are. They are saying that they speak like native speakers, but they don't think they are qualified to work in positions that require French.

Have they spent any time in a French-speaking community?

No – very few of them. Getting back to using French on the work site, I think I would apply for jobs that said that you should be able to speak French – I can speak French – but when they start putting any criteria down for – well, you have to have excellent grammatical – no, no way. I would even be embarrassed to be the person – if you phone a hotel to make a reservation and they have an English person and a French person, I don't think I would be qualified to be the French person.

Are your former FI classmates doing anything involving French?

Out of about 80 graduates in Grade 12, I would say only ten of them went on to university. I was the only one who went on to French courses. The only one – one person out of a whole FI class – the only one who took

French. That's pretty bad.
Could you get a job teaching French?

I know I can – no problem – because they would say, "Oh, she is from French Immersion, she must be able to speak French well," and I would get the job. No, I haven't – I don't think I could do it. I don't have confidence in my ability to speak French. I wouldn't want to do that to an employer – or to the children.

Can you think of anything else you would like to tell me about FI?

Just basically, I am glad I did it because it fostered a very positive attitude toward people of different ethnic groups. Maybe [FI programs] are much better now, but it would be interesting to see how [FI graduates] are in jobs that require them to be correct, as working doing office work and typing and sending out letters. It would be interesting to see if all the letters they send out are error-free, because I don't think they could be. I mean, I have to be corrected to this day. I don't remember ever writing a French composition that didn't come back with some red mark on it, and that's after having significant – a lot of time to do it, to sit down.

In the work setting they don't have that much time. When you are asked: "Please write to so-and-so about this," it would take me 3 days to make sure it was perfect, and this just doesn't work in the offices. I am glad I did it, I'd do it again, but I'd do it again because it was interesting and it was fun to learn about the culture. I think that's why I would do it again.

What do your friends and relatives think of your views about FI?

I'd say it's awfully controversial. Anybody I talk to now and say that I'm really debating about (sic) FI is the right thing to do – it's very, very upsetting. I think there are better ways. It's interesting – all of my sisters have pulled their kids out of FI. They put their children in FI because I had gone. One of them – they did Grade 1 to 3 in FI in Y – pulled them out and they were so behind when they got back to regular school. Their teacher could not believe – their reading, everything. My other sister had her kids in FI, pulled them out, found out that her Grade 4 could not read in English – so they have all pulled their children out of FI and their attitude now after listening to me and seeing for themselves what it did for their children is: "Well, let's encourage them in the French classes they take in regular school. It's more important to have all your bases covered, to do well in all your subjects, than concentrate so much on the French [sic]."

You are told, "Oh, but you will be able to apply for jobs where French is required," but my French is not good enough. So I think [FI] is the biggest scam ever to hit the educational system. It's a political thing; parents are caught up with the fact that is (sic) fashionable; it's an elitist thing, and that's why the kids are going; and I think that probably FI is going to be around for a long time – because people are basically pretentious.

Pretentious?

– pretentious, and they like to say: "My kid goes to French Immersion ..." They may not be learning [much], but their kid goes to FI. It's one-sided, you graduate with, yes, a better knowledge of French than most people, but your English may suffer, your Social Studies may be in big trouble, your other subjects may suffer, because French, in FI [programs], is considered the most important subject – and I think that's wrong. No subject should be more important than the other.

Would you send your children to FI?

Maybe it would be better to just encourage them in the regular schools, like the people I went to university with who'd done so well, just by going to regular school and who had parents who encouraged them – all these girls too had gone to Laval for a summer, and it was. . . . Maybe I wouldn't send my child[ren] to FI. I would make sure that they knew about French Canada, I would introduce them to French-Canadian authors, make sure they knew about the language, send them to Laval, and make sure that they were in a good French program at an English-speaking school, because I don't think that going into FI guarantees that you will be bilingual when you graduate.

If there were a program out there that stressed the structure, the core, involved French-Canadian readings, taught a bit about French-Canadian customs, definitely, I would take that over FI any day of the week.

It's the one reason why I am glad I did it – it's because of all the culture I learned, but if you could put that in a regular French program, there would be really no need for FI. I think it could become obsolete. That's a terrible thing to say, but it's true, I really believe that.

The following additional comments were written by Janice and mailed to me a few days after the above interview.

"Looking back on my experience with FI, I am filled with mixed emotions . . . I enjoyed learning of the culture and history of French Canada and believe that this enriched my education . . . My schooling in FI contributed a great deal to my desire to teach English to new Canadians and my sympathy in general towards the difficulties facing those from different ethnic groups; [it also gave me] a great deal of empathy towards those struggling with the learning of a second language.

"My teachers appeared to be more concerned about students using the language than how it was used . . . Lack of attention towards structure and infrequent feedback and correction graduated students who could write, speak and comprehend the language, but do so with much error . . . The word "standard" appears to be missing from the curriculum of FI.

"[FI] students are considered as [sic] an elite group. In fact, our group has been told many times that we were the *crême de la crême*. These students are coddled and pampered. It is frequently assumed that these students are brighter than others or else they would not be in such a demanding program. I find this absurd. These programs are not as demanding as they have been reputed to be. In fact, I would consider my past experience to have been a rather lax one. The French language takes precident [sic] over all other areas of study so as a consequence, I believe that standards for other core subjects to be quite relaxed. This pampering of students all in the name of learning the French language defeats the purpose of studying French in order to become more well rounded.

"Unfortunately it is exceeding [sic] difficult not to be cynical [about] a program that promotes the learning of French at the expense of all other subjects and then can't even do that right. "

Appendix C
Results of Standardized Tests

For a period of eight years, from Fall 1969 through Summer 1977, whenever I had the time to do so, I administered standardized tests to my classes as they completed the second and third semester courses at Simon Fraser University. The tests I used, which are available in parallel form for several languages, including French, measure the ability of students to understand and use the language they have been studying.

These tests are called the Modern Language Association-Cooperative Foreign Language Tests, and they are available from the Educational Testing Service of Princeton, New Jersey. They measure four skills: listening comprehension, speaking ability, reading comprehension, and writing ability. These tests are designed so that "functional competence" (putting messages across "any old way") is not rewarded: while all items appear in some sort of context, many require examinees to attend to linguistic detail. In the listening and reading comprehension sections, in particular, attention to overall contextual meaning is necessary as the students answer questions about conversations they hear or various passages they read.

The classes whose results are reported in Figure 8 were taught according to most of the principles, procedures, and techniques of the Principled Eclectic Method discussed in chapters 5-8 of this book. While these classes were taught Spanish, equally excellent results can be obtained in French.

While the test norms report the distribution of *individual* examinee scores, the results reported in Figure 8 are the *average* scores for the entire group of SFU examinees. For example, only 5 percent of all examinees (with two semesters of instruction) from many colleges and universities outscored the *average* score on listening comprehension of SFU students. Only 1 percent of all examinees with *four* semesters of instruction outscored the *average* listening comprehension score of SFU students with *three* semesters of study.

A variety of "tricks" can of course be used to obtain impressive results on standardized tests. For example, a teacher or teachers can teach to the test, preparing the students for the test both in general and in terms of specific items. Or a university teacher can be extremely demanding, with the consequence that, through high attrition, only the very best students remain at the end of the course or program to take the tests. It is also possible to administer a standardized test to the best classes only and conveniently ignore weaker classes.

I wish to assure the reader that no "trick" of any sort was played to get these results. These were regular classes in every sense and they received no special help.

The teacher factor must also be discounted, for while the language assistants who did most of the instruction were good, conscientious teachers, they lacked advanced academic qualifications and did not have much teaching experience. In any event, even what the best possible teacher might be able to do can be described and demonstrated for other teachers to emulate.

These outstanding results can be obtained in French too. It is a matter of applying the principles, procedures, and techniques that are highly successful in the classroom instead of trying to turn the classroom into a natural second language acquisition environment – which it cannot be.

Appendix C 163

Figure 8

**Results of Standardized Modern Language Association
Tests for Spanish Classes Taught under My Supervision
(Fall 1969 to Summer 1977; test not given every semester)
Expressed in mean scores and percentiles**

1. Form LA of the MLA/Cooperative Spanish test, administered after two short semesters (104-130 hours of instruction) at SFU, compared to two long semesters (96-160 hours of instruction) for the norm population:

Listening	Speaking	Reading	Writing
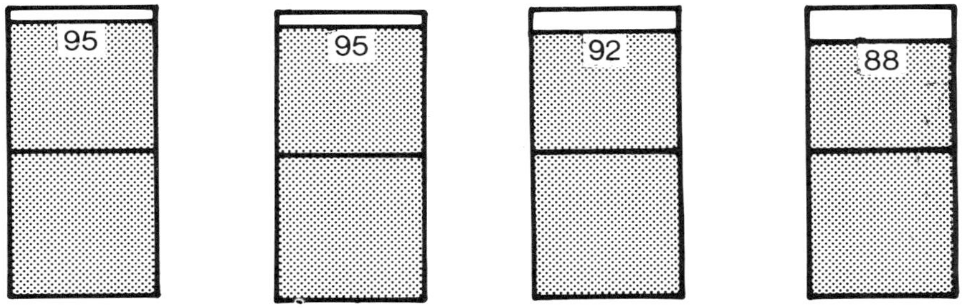 95	95	92	88
SFU N = 100	SFU N = 68	SFU N = 101	SFU N = 70
Pts. possible = 45	Pts. possible = 82	Pts. possible = 50	Pts. possible = 100
SFU $\bar{X}$ = 37.74	SFU $\bar{X}$ = 56.19	SFU $\bar{X}$ = 39.36	SFU $\bar{X}$ = 78.3
Norm $\bar{X}$ = 21	Norm $\bar{X}$ = 36	Norm $\bar{X}$ = 25	Norm $\bar{X}$ = 55
SFU %ile = 95	SFU %ile = 95	SFU %ile = 92	SFU %ile = 88

164 *French Immersion: Myths and Reality*

2. Form MA of the MLA/Cooperative Spanish test, administered after three short semesters (156-182 hours of instruction) at SFU, compared to four long semesters (192-256 hours of instruction) for the norm population:

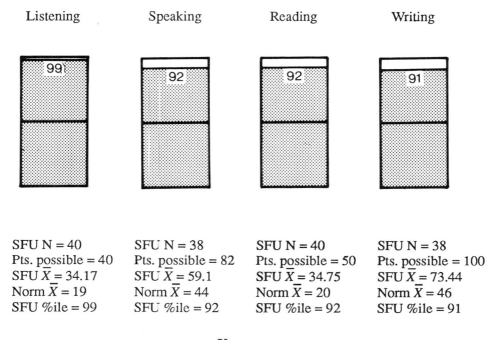

Listening	Speaking	Reading	Writing
SFU N = 40	SFU N = 38	SFU N = 40	SFU N = 38
Pts. possible = 40	Pts. possible = 82	Pts. possible = 50	Pts. possible = 100
SFU $\bar{X}$ = 34.17	SFU $\bar{X}$ = 59.1	SFU $\bar{X}$ = 34.75	SFU $\bar{X}$ = 73.44
Norm $\bar{X}$ = 19	Norm $\bar{X}$ = 44	Norm $\bar{X}$ = 20	Norm $\bar{X}$ = 46
SFU %ile = 99	SFU %ile = 92	SFU %ile = 92	SFU %ile = 91

Key

N = Number of students
$\bar{X}$ = Mean (average) score
%ile = Percentile, i.e., percent of individual norm - population scores matched or surpassed by the SFU average score